SF

SIL   Silverberg, Robert.

         The face of the
         waters.

$20.00

SIL   Silverberg, Robert

      The Face of the waters

FEB 13   Z 5556
JAN 12   Z 9393
APR 29   Z 7192
JUL 14   Z 8364
NOV 5   Z 2506
SEP 16   KNG1211

© THE BAKER & TAYLOR CO.

The
FACE
of the
WATERS

The
FACE
of the
WATERS

Robert Silverberg

BANTAM BOOKS

New York   Toronto   London   Sydney   Auckland

THE FACE OF THE WATERS
A Bantam Book
Bantam hardcover edition / November 1991
Bantam limited edition / November 1991

Copyright © 1991 by Agberg, Ltd.

BOOK DESIGN BY JAYA DAYAL

Library of Congress Cataloging-in-Publication Data

Silverberg, Robert.
The face of the waters / Robert Silverberg.
p.   cm.
ISBN 0-553-07592-6
ISBN 0-553-07598-5 (Limited Edition)
I. Title.
PS3569.I472F33   1991
813'.54—dc20   91-13530
CIP

Published simultaneously in the United States and Canada

Bantam Books are published by Bantam Books, a division of
Bantam Doubleday Dell Publishing Group, Inc. Its trademark,
consisting of the words "Bantam Books" and the portrayal of a
rooster, is Registered in U.S. Patent and Trademark Office and in
other countries. Marca Registrada. Bantam Books, 666 Fifth
Avenue, New York, New York 10103.

Printed in the United States of America

BVG   0   9   8   7   6   5   4   3   2   1

To Charlie Brown,

the focus of the LOCUS

—and probably about time, too.

And the earth was without form, and void; and darkness was upon the face of the deep. And the spirit of God moved upon the face of the waters.

—GENESIS I:2

The ocean has no compassion, no faith, no law, no memory. Its fickleness is to be held true to man's purposes only by an undaunted resolution and by sleepless, armed, jealous vigilance in which, perhaps, there has always been more hate than love.

—JOSEPH CONRAD
The Mirror of the Sea

The
FACE
of the
WATERS

*T*HERE WAS BLUE ABOVE AND A DIFFERENT BLUE BELOW, TWO immense inaccessible voids, and the ship appeared almost to be hovering suspended between one blue void and the other, touching neither, motionless, perfectly becalmed. But in fact it was in the water, right where it belonged, not above it, and it was moving all the time. Night and day for four days now it had headed steadily outward, traveling away from Sorve, sailing ever farther into the trackless sea.

WHEN VALBEN LAWLER CAME UP ON THE DECK OF THE FLAGSHIP EARLY on the morning of the fifth day there were hundreds of long silvery snouts jutting out of the water on all sides. That was new. The weather had changed, too: the wind had dropped, the sea was listless, not merely calm now but quiet in a peculiarly electric, potentially explosive way. The sails were slack. Limp ropes dangled. A thin sharp line of gray haze cut across the sky like an invader from some other part of the world. Lawler, a tall, slender man of middle years with an athlete's build and grace, grinned down at the creatures in the water. They were so ugly that they were almost charming. Sinister brutes, he thought.

Wrong. Sinister, yes; brutes, no. There was a chilly glint of intelligence in their disagreeable scarlet eyes. One more intelligent species, on this world that had so many. They were sinister precisely because they *weren't* brutes. And very nasty-looking: those narrow heads, those extended tubular necks. They seemed like huge metallic worms sticking up out of the water. Those obviously capable jaws; those small sawblade-keen teeth, scores of them, gleaming in the sunlight. They looked so totally and unequivocally malevolent that you really had to admire them.

Lawler played for a moment with the idea of jumping over the side and splashing around among them.

He wondered how long he'd last if he did. Five seconds, most likely. And then peace, peace forever. A nicely perverse idea, a quick little suicidal fantasy. But of course he wasn't serious. Lawler wasn't the suicidal type, or he'd have done it long ago, and in any case he was chemically insulated at the moment against depression and anxiety and other such disagreeable things. That little nip of numbweed tincture that he'd given himself upon arising: how grateful he was for that. The drug provided him, at least for a few hours, with a little impervious jacket of calmness that allowed him to look a bunch of toothy monsters like these in the eye and grin. Being a doctor—being *the* doctor, the only one in the community—did have certain advantages.

Lawler caught sight of Sundira Thane up by the foremast, leaning out over the rail. Unlike Lawler, the lanky dark-haired woman was an experienced ocean traveler who had made many interisland journeys, sometimes crossing great distances. She knew the sea. He was out of his element here.

"You ever see things like those before?" he asked her.

She glanced up. "They're drakkens. Ugly buggers, aren't they? And smart and quick. Swallow you whole, they would, if you gave them half a chance. Or a quarter of a chance. Lucky thing for us that we're up here and they're down there."

"Drakkens," Lawler repeated. "I never heard of them."

"They're northern. Not often seen in tropical waters, or in this particular sea. I guess they wanted a summer holiday."

The narrow toothy snouts, half as long as a man's arm, rose like a forest of swords from the surface of the water. Lawler glimpsed hints of slender ribbony bodies below, shining like polished metal, dangling into the depths. Occasionally a drakken's fluked tail came into view, or a powerful webbed claw. Bright flame-red eyes looked back at him with disturbing intensity. The creatures were talking to each other in high, vociferous tones, a hard-edged clangorous yipping, a sound like hatchets striking against anvils.

Gabe Kinverson appeared from somewhere and moved to the rail, taking up a position between Lawler and Thane. Kinverson, brawny and immense, with a blunt windburned face, had the tools of his trade with him, a bundle of hooks and line and a long wood-kelp fishing rod. "Drakkens," he muttered. "What bastards they are. I was coming back once with a ten-meter sea leopard tied to my boat and five drakkens ate it right out from under me. Not a goddamned thing I could do." Kinverson scooped up a broken belaying pin and hurled it into the water. The drakkens went to it as though it were bait, converging, rising shoulder-high from the water, snapping at it, yipping furiously. They let it sink past them and vanish.

"They can't come up on board, can they?" Lawler asked.

Kinverson laughed. "No, doc. They can't come up on board. Lucky thing for us, too."

The drakkens—there might have been three hundred of them—swam alongside the ships for a couple of hours, keeping pace easily, jabbing the air with their evil snouts, carrying on their ominous running line of comments. But by midmorning they were gone, abruptly slipping down out of sight all at once and not surfacing again.

The wind picked up a short while later. The crew of the day watch moved about busily in the rigging. Far off to the north a little black rainstorm congealed into being just below a layer of dirty-looking overcast and dropped a dark webwork of precipitation that seemed not quite to be reaching the water. In the vicinity of the ships the air remained clear and dry, and still had a crackling edge to it.

Lawler went belowdecks. There was work waiting for him there, nothing very taxing. Neyana Golghoz had a blister on her knee; Leo Martello was troubled by sunburned shoulders; Father Quillan had bruised his elbow falling out of his bunk. When he was done with all that, Lawler made his regular radio calls to the other ships to see if any medical problems had cropped up on them. Around noon he headed up to the deck to get some air. Nid Delagard, the owner of the fleet and the leader of the expedition, was conferring with his flagship captain, Gospo Struvin, just outside the wheel box. Their laughter carried readily the length of the ship. Two of a kind, they were, stocky thick-necked men, stubborn and profane, full of raucous energy.

"Hey, you see the drakkens this morning, doc?" Struvin called. "Sweet, weren't they?"

"Very pretty, yes. What did they want with us?"

"Checking us out, I guess. You can't go very far in this ocean without something or other coming around to snoop. There'll be lots more wildlife visiting us as we go. Look there, doc. To starboard."

Lawler followed the captain's pointing hand. The bloated and vaguely spherical shape of some immense creature was visible just below the surface. It was like a moon that had fallen from the sky, greenish and enormous and pockmarked all over. Lawler saw after a moment that the pockmarks were actually round mouthlike apertures, set close together over the entire surface area of the sphere, which were tirelessly opening and closing. A hundred gulping mouths, constantly at work. A thousand, maybe. A myriad long bluish tongues busily flicked in, out, in, out, like whips flailing the water. The thing was nothing but mouths, a gigantic floating eating machine.

Lawler stared at it with distaste. "What is it?"

But Struvin was unable to put a name to it. Neither could Delagard. It was just an anonymous denizen of the sea, hideous, monstrous, your basic floating king-sized horror wandering by to see if the little convoy offered anything worth ingesting. It drifted slowly past, its mouths chomping steadily away. After it, some twenty minutes later, the ships entered a zone thick with big orange-and-green-striped jellyfish, soft graceful shining umbrellas as big as a man's head from which cascades of coiling red fleshy strands, finger-thick and apparently several meters long, were hanging. The jellyfish looked vaguely benign, even clownish, but the surface of the sea in their vicinity bubbled and steamed as though they were giving off a powerful acid. They were so tightly packed in the water that they came right up against the ship's hull, jamming into it, bumping against the sea-finger plants that were growing on it, bouncing off with little sighing protests.

Delagard yawned and disappeared down the stern hatch. Lawler, standing by the rail, looked down in wonder at the massed jellyfish just below. They were quivering like a horde of plump breasts. He could almost reach over and scoop one out, they were so close. Gospo Struvin, heading past him down the deck along the port rail, said suddenly, "Hey, who left this net here? Neyana, was it you?"

"Not me," Neyana Golghoz said, without bothering to look up. She was busy swabbing down the deck, farther toward the bow. "Talk to Kinverson. He's the one with the nets."

The net was an intricate tangle of moist yellow fibers lying in a sloppy crumpled mass by the rail. Struvin kicked at it as though it were so much trash. Then he muttered a curse and kicked again. Lawler glanced across the way and saw that the net had become tangled somehow around one of Struvin's booted legs. The captain stood with his leg in the air and was kicking repeatedly as if trying to free himself of something sticky and very persistent. "Hey," Struvin said. "Hey!"

One part of the net was halfway up his thigh, suddenly, and wrapped tightly around it. The rest of it had slithered up the side of the rail and was beginning to crawl over the far side toward the water.

"*Doc!*" Struvin bellowed.

Lawler ran toward him, with Neyana just behind. But the net moved with unbelievable swiftness. No longer a messy jumble of fibrous cords, it had straightened itself out to reveal itself as some kind of openwork life-form about three meters long, and it was rapidly pulling Struvin over the side of the ship. The captain, kicking and yelling and struggling, hung suspended over the rail. One leg was in the grip of the net and he was trying to brace himself against the gunwale with the other to keep from going into the water; but the creature seemed quite willing to pull him apart at the crotch if he continued to resist its tug. Struvin's eyes were practically popping. They glazed with astonishment, horror, disbelief.

In the course of almost a quarter of a century of medical practice Lawler had seen people in extremity before, many times, too many times. But he had never seen an expression like that in anyone's eyes.

"Get this thing off me!" Struvin yelled. "Jesus! Doc—please, doc—"

Lawler lunged and clutched at the part of the net that was nearest to him. His hand closed on it and instantly he felt a fierce burning sensation, as though some stinging acid had cut through his flesh to the bone. He tried to let go, but it was impossible. His skin was sticking to it. Struvin was already hanging well over the side now. Just his head and shoulders were still in view, and his desperate clutching hands. He called out once again for help, a hoarse, horrifying cry. Lawler, forcing himself to ignore the pain, slung one end of the net over his shoulder and tugged it back toward the middle of the deck, hoping to bring Struvin up with it. The effort required was tremendous, but he was fueled by mysterious energies, rising under stress from he knew not where. The thing was searing the skin of his hands and he could feel its cauterizing touch on his back and neck and shoulder, right through his shirt. Son of a bitch, he thought. Son of a bitch. He bit down hard on his lip and took a step, another one, another, tugging against

Struvin's weight and the resistance of the net-creature, which had slithered well down the outside of the hull by this time and was heading purposefully for the water.

Something was starting to go *sproing* in the middle of Lawler's back, where overstrained muscles were jigging and leaping around. But he seemed actually to be succeeding in dragging the net up on board again. Struvin was almost to the top of the rail.

And then the net broke—or, more likely, divided of its own accord. Lawler heard one final terrible wail and looked back to see Struvin drop back over the side and fall into the bubbling, steaming sea. The water immediately began to thresh around him. Lawler saw movement just below the surface, soft quivering things coming in from all sides like darts. The jellyfish didn't look benign and clownish any more.

The other half of the net remained on the deck, snarling itself around Lawler's wrists and hands. He found himself contending with some fiery mesh-like creature that squirmed and wriggled and adhered to him wherever he touched it. He knelt and smashed the net-thing against the deck again and again and again. The stuff was tough and resilient, like cartilage. It seemed to weaken a little but he couldn't get rid of it. The burning was becoming intolerable.

Kinverson came running up and brought the heel of his boot down on one corner of the net-thing, pinning it; Neyana jammed her mop into its middle; and then Pilya Braun, emerging suddenly from somewhere, crouched over Lawler and pulled a bone blade from a scabbard at her hip. Furiously she set about cutting through the quivering rubbery meshes. Shining metallic-looking blood, deep blue in color, spurted from the net, and the strands of the creature coiled back crisply from the blade. In a moment Pilya had hacked away the section that was stuck to Lawler's hands, and he was able to rise. Evidently the piece was too small to sustain life; it shriveled and shrank away from his fingers and he managed to toss it aside. Kinverson was still stomping the other section of the net, the remainder of the piece that had stayed on board after Struvin had been carried over the side.

In a dazed way Lawler lurched toward the rail with some blurry intention of going into the sea to rescue Struvin. Kinverson seemed to understand what was in his mind. He reached one long arm toward him, catching him by the shoulder and pulling him back.

"Don't be crazy," he said. "There's God knows what swimming around down there waiting for you."

Lawler nodded uncertainly. He stepped away from the rail and stared at his blazing fingers. A bright imprinted network of red lines stood out brilliantly on his skin. The pain was phenomenal. He thought his hands were going to explode.

The whole incident had taken perhaps a minute and a half.

Delagard emerged now from the hatch. He came running toward them, looking annoyed and perturbed.

"What the hell's going on? Why all the yelling and screaming?" He paused and gawked. "Where's Gospo?"

Lawler, breathing hard, his throat parched, his heart pounding, could barely speak. He gestured toward the rail with a toss of his head.

"Overboard?" Delagard said incredulously. "He fell in?"

He rushed to the side and looked over. Lawler came up beside him. All was quiet down there. The jostling hordes of jiggling jellyfish were gone. The water was dark, smooth, silent. There was no sign at all of Struvin or of the net-creature that had taken him.

"He didn't fall," Kinverson said. "He got pulled in. This thing's other half got him." He indicated the broken, ragged remains of the part of the net that he had stomped. It was nothing more now than a greenish smear on the yellow wood of the deck floor.

Hoarsely Lawler said, "Just like an old fishnet, is what it looked like. Lying here on the deck, all crumpled up. Those jellyfish may have sent it up here to hunt for them. Struvin kicked at it and it caught him by the leg, and—"

"What? What kind of bullshit is this?" Delagard glanced over the side again, then at Lawler's hands, then at the smear on the deck. "You're serious? Something that looked like a net came up out of the sea and caught hold of Gospo?"

Lawler nodded.

"It can't be. Someone must have pushed him over the side. Who was it? You, Lawler? Kinverson?" Delagard blinked, as if the implausibility of what he had just said was obvious even to him. Then he looked closely at Lawler and Kinverson and said, "A *net*? A live net that crawled up out of the sea and caught hold of Gospo?"

Lawler nodded again, just the merest motion of his head. Slowly he opened and closed his hands. The stinging was very gradually abating, but he knew he'd feel it for hours. He was numb all over, stunned, shaken. The whole nightmarish scene was playing itself over and over in his head, Struvin noticing the net, kicking at it, becoming entangled in it, the net beginning to ooze its way up over the railing carrying Struvin with it—

"No," Delagard muttered. "Jesus, I can't fucking believe it." He shook his head and peered down into the quiet waters. "Gospo!" he yelled. "*Gospo.*" No reply came from below. "Fuck! Five days out to sea, and somebody gone already? Can you imagine it?" He turned away from the rail just as the rest of the ship's complement began to appear, Leo Martello in the lead, then Father Quillan and Onyos Felk, and the others close behind. Delagard clamped his lips together. His cheeks ballooned. His face was red with amazement and fury and shock. Lawler was surprised by the power of Delagard's grief. Struvin had died in an ugly way, but there were few good ways to die. And Lawler had never thought Delagard gave a damn for anyone or anything but himself.

The ship-owner turned toward Kinverson and said, "You ever hear of any such thing before?"

"Never. Never ever."

"A thing that looked like an ordinary net," Delagard said again. "A dirty old net that jumps up and grabs you. God, what a place this is! What a place!" He kept shaking his head, again and again, as if he could shake Struvin back up out of the water if only he shook it long and hard enough.

Then he swung around toward the priest. "Father Quillan! Give us a prayer, will you?"

The priest looked baffled. "What? What?"

"Haven't you heard? We've had a casualty. Struvin's gone. Something crawled up on board and hauled him over the side."

Quillan was silent. He held his palms outward as though indicating that things that crawled up out of the ocean were beyond his level of ecclesiastical responsibility.

"My God, say some words, won't you? Say something!"

Still Quillan hesitated. A voice from the back of the group whispered uncertainly, "Our Father, which art in heaven—hallowed be Thy name—"

"No," the priest said. He might almost have been awakening slowly from sleep. "Not that one." He moistened his lips and said, looking very self-conscious, "Yea, though I walk through the valley of the shadow of death, I will fear no evil: for Thou art with me." Quillan hesitated, moistening his lips, apparently searching for words. "Thou preparest a table before me in the presence of mine enemies. . . . Surely goodness and mercy shall follow me all the days of my life."

Pilya Braun came up to Lawler and took him by the elbows, turning his hands up so that she could see the fiery marks on them. "Come," she said quietly. "Let's go below, and you show me which salve to put on them."

IN HIS LITTLE CABIN, AMONG HIS POWDERS AND POTIONS, LAWLER said, "That's it. That flask there."

"This?" Pilya said. She looked suspicious. "This isn't a salve."

"I know. Put a few drops of it in a little water and hand it to me, first. Then the salve."

"What is it? A painkiller?"

"A painkiller, yes."

Pilya busied herself mixing the drug for him. She was about twenty-five, golden-haired, brown-eyed, broad-shouldered, thick-featured, deep-chested, with lustrous olive skin—a good-looking, strong-bodied woman, a hard worker, according to Delagard. Certainly she knew her way around the rigging of a ship. Lawler had never had much to do with her on Sorve, but he had slept with her mother Anya a couple of times twenty years ago, when he had been about as old as Pilya was now and her mother was a sleek thirty-five. It had been a stupid thing to do. Lawler doubted that Pilya knew anything about it. Pilya's mother was dead now, carried away by a fever from some bad oysters three winters before. Lawler had been a big man with the ladies at the time he was involved with her—it had been soon after the collapse of his one brief ill-starred marriage—but he hadn't been one for some time now, and he wished Pilya would stop staring at him in that eager, hopeful way, as though he were everything she might need in a man. He wasn't. But he was too courteous, or too indifferent, to tell her that, he wasn't sure which.

She offered him the glass, brimming with pink liquid. Lawler's hands felt like clubs. His fingers were as stiff as wooden rods. She had to help him as he drank. But the numbweed tincture went to work instantly, easing his spirit in its usual comforting way, nibbling away the shock of the sudden monstrous event on deck. Pilya took the empty glass from him and set it down on the shelf opposite his bunk.

Lawler kept his artifacts from Earth on that shelf, his six little fragments of the world that once had been. Pilya paused and peered at them, the coin, the bronze statuette, the potsherd, the map, the gun, the chunk of stone. She touched the statuette delicately with the tip of her finger, as if she expected it to burn her.

"What's this?"

"A little figure of a god, from a place called Egypt. That was on Earth."

"Earth? You have things from Earth?"

"Family treasures. That one is four thousand years old."

"Four thousand years. And this?" She picked up the coin. "What do these words say, on this little piece of white metal?"

" 'In God We Trust,' is what it says, on the side that has the woman's face. And on the other side, where the bird is, it says, 'United States of America' up here, and 'Quarter Dollar' down below."

"What does that mean, 'Quarter Dollar'?" Pilya asked.

"It was a kind of money, on Earth."

"And 'United States of America'?"

"A place."

"An island, you mean?"

"I don't know," he said. "I don't think so. Earth didn't have islands of the kind we have."

"And this animal, the one with these wings? There isn't any such animal."

"There was on Earth," Lawler said. "It was called an eagle. A kind of bird."

"What is a bird?"

He hesitated. "Something that flies in the air."

"Like an air-skimmer," she said.

"Something like that. I don't really know."

Pilya poked thoughtfully at the other artifacts. "Earth," she said, very quietly. "So there truly was such a place."

"Of course there was!"

"I have never been sure. Maybe it was only just a story." She turned to him, grinning coquettishly, and held out the coin. "Will you give this to me, doctor? I like it. I want to have an Earth thing to keep."

"I can't do that, Pilya."

"Please? Would you, please? It's so beautiful!"

"But it's been in my family for hundreds of years. I can't give it away."

"I'll let you see it whenever you like."

"No," he said. He wondered whom he was saving it for. "I'm sorry. I wish I could let you have it, but I can't. Not those things."

She nodded, making no attempt to hide her disappointment. "Earth," she said again, savoring the mysterious name. "Earth!" She put the coin back on the shelf and said, "You will tell me what the other Earth things are, another time. But we have work to do on you and we are forgetting. The salve for your hands. Where is the salve?"

He pointed it out to her. She found it and squeezed a little from the tube. Then, turning his hands palms upward as she had on deck, she shook her head sadly. "Look at them. You'll have scars."

"Probably not."

"That thing could have pulled you over the side too."

"No," Lawler said. "It couldn't. It didn't. Gospo was close to the side to begin with, and it got him before he knew what was happening to him. I was in a better position to resist."

He saw the fear in her lovely gold-flecked eyes.

"If not this time, it'll get us the next. We'll all die before we reach wherever it is we're going," she said.

"No. No, we'll be all right."

Pilya laughed. "You always see a good side to things. This is going to be a sorrowful deadly trip all the same. If we could turn around and go back to Sorve, doctor, wouldn't you want to do that?"

"But we can't go back, Pilya. You know that. You might just as well talk about turning around and going back to Earth. There's no way we're ever going to see Sorve again."

Part One

SORVE
ISLAND

1

*I*N THE NIGHT HAD COME THE PURE, SIMPLE CONVICTION THAT HE
was the man of destiny, the one who could turn the trick that would
make everything ever so much simpler and better for the seventy-
eight humans who lived on the artificial island of Sorve on the watery world
called Hydros.

It was a cockeyed idea and Lawler knew it. But it had wrecked his sleep,
and none of his usual methods seemed to work to fix that, not meditation,
not multiplication tables, not even a few pink drops of the algae-derived
tranquilizer on which he was perhaps becoming a little too dependent.
From a little after midnight until somewhere close to dawn he lay awake,
possessed by his brilliant, heroic, cockeyed idea. And then at last, in the
small hours of the morning when the sky was still dark, before any patients
could show up to complicate his day and ruin the purity of his sudden new
vision, Lawler left the vaargh near the middle of the island where he lived by
himself and went down to the sea-wall to see whether the Gillies really had
managed to start up their new power plant during the night.

He would congratulate them profusely if they had. He would call forth
his whole vocabulary of sign-language gestures to tell them how impressed
he was with their awesome technological prowess. He would praise them for
having transformed the entire quality of life on Hydros—not just on Sorve,
but on the whole planet—in a single masterly stroke.

And then he would say, "My father, the great Dr. Bernat Lawler whom you all remember so well, saw this moment coming. 'One day,' he would often remark to me when I was a boy, 'our friends the Dwellers will achieve the dependable production of a steady supply of electricity. And then a new age will dawn here, when Dweller and human will work side by side in heartfelt cooperation—' "

And so on and so on and so on. Subtly intertwining his congratulations with an expression of the need for harmony between the two races. Eventually working his way around to the explicit proposition that Hydran and human should put aside all past coolness and at last begin to toil together in the name of further technological progress. Evoking the sacred name of the late beloved Dr. Bernat Lawler as often as he could, reminding them how in his day he had labored to the full extent of his formidable medical skills on behalf of Dweller and human alike, performing many a miracle of healing, devoting himself unselfishly to the needs of both island communities— laying it on thicker and thicker, making the air throb with emotion, until the Gillies, teary-eyed with newfound interspecies affection, yielded gladly to his casual suggestion that a good way to start the new era off would be to allow the humans to adapt the power plant so that it could produce a supply of fresh water as well as electricity. And then his underlying proposal: the humans would design and build the desalinization unit by themselves, the condenser, the conveyer pipes, the complete item, and hand it over to the Gillies. Here: just plug it in. It costs you nothing and we won't be dependent on rain catch for our freshwater supply any longer. And we will all be the best of friends forever, you Dwellers and we humans.

That was the fantasy that had pulled Lawler from his sleep. He wasn't usually given to entangling himself in such farfetched enterprises as this one. His years as a doctor—not the medical genius that his father had been, but a hardworking and reasonably effective physician, who did a pretty good job, considering the difficulties—had led him to be realistic and practical about most things. But somehow he had convinced himself this night that he was the only person on the island who might actually be able to talk the Gillies into letting water-desalinization equipment be tacked onto their power plant. Yes. He would succeed where all others had failed.

A fat chance, Lawler knew. But in the small hours of the night chances sometimes tend to look fatter than they do in the clear light of morning.

Such electricity as the island had now came from clumsy, inefficient chemical batteries, piles of zinc and copper disks separated by strips of crawlweed paper soaked in brine. The Gillies—the Hydrans, the Dwellers, the dominant beings of the island and of the world where Lawler had spent his entire life—had been working on a better means of electrical generation as long as Lawler could remember, and by now, so the scuttlebutt in town had it, the new power plant was almost ready to go on-line—today, tomorrow, next week for sure. If the Gillies actually could manage to achieve that, it would be a tremendous thing for both species. They had already agreed, not very graciously, to let the humans make use of some of the new electricity, which everyone admitted was altogether terrific of them. But it would be even more terrific for the seventy-eight humans who scratched out narrow little subsistence-level lives on the hard narrow little place that was Sorve if the Gillies would relent and let the plant be used for water desalinization also, so that the humans wouldn't have to depend on the random and infrequent mercies of Sorve rainfall patterns for their fresh water. It must have been obvious even to the Gillies that life would become ever so much easier for their human neighbors if they could count on a reliable and unlimited supply of water.

But of course the Gillies had given no indication so far that they cared about that. They had never shown any particular interest in making anything easier for the handful of humans who lived in their midst. Fresh water might be vital to human needs, but it didn't matter a damn to the Gillies. What the humans might need, or want, or hope to have, was no concern of the Gillies. And it was the vision of changing all that by single-handed persuasion that had cost Lawler his sleep this night.

What the hell: nothing ventured, nothing gained.

ON THIS TROPICAL NIGHT LAWLER WAS BAREFOOT AND WORE ONLY A twist of yellow cloth made from water-lettuce fronds around his waist. The air was warm and heavy and the sea was calm. The island, that webwork of living and semi-living and formerly living tissue drifting on the breast of the vast world-spanning ocean, swayed almost imperceptibly beneath his feet. Like all the inhabited islands of Hydros, Sorve was rootless, a free-floating wanderer, moving wherever the currents and winds and the occasional tidal surge cared to carry it. Lawler was able to feel the tightly woven withes of the flooring giving and spreading as he walked, and he heard the sea lapping at them just a couple of meters below. But he moved easily, lightly, his long lean body attuning itself automatically to the rhythms of the island's movements. They were the most natural things in the world to him.

The softness of the night was deceptive. Most times of the year Sorve was something other than a soft place to live. Its climate alternated between periods of hot-and-dry and cold-and-wet, with only the sweet little summer interlude when Sorve was drifting in mild, humid equatorial latitudes to provide a brief illusion of comfort and ease. This was the good time of the year, now. Food was abundant and the air was sweet. The islanders rejoiced in it. The rest of the year life was much more of a struggle.

Unhurriedly Lawler made his way around the reservoir and down the ramp to the lower terrace. It was a gentle slope from here to the island's rim. He went past the scattered buildings of the shipyard from which Nid Delagard ran his maritime empire and the indistinct domed shapes that were the waterfront factories, in which metals—nickel, iron, cobalt, vanadium, tin—were extracted from the tissues of low-phylum sea-creatures by slow, inefficient processes. It was hard to make out anything clearly, but after some forty years of living on this one small island Lawler had no trouble getting around any part of the place in the dark.

The big two-story shed that housed the power plant was just to his right and a little way ahead, down at the water's edge. He headed toward it.

There was no hint of morning yet. The sky was a deep black. Some nights Sunrise, the sister planet of Hydros, gleamed in the heavens like a great blue-green eye, but tonight Sunrise was absent on the other side of the world, casting its bright glow on the mysterious waters of the unexplored far hemisphere. One of the three moons was visible, though, a tiny point of hard white light off to the east, close to the horizon. And stars shimmered everywhere, cascades of glittering silver powder scattered across the blackness, a ubiquitous dusting of brightnesses. That infinite horde of distant suns formed a dazzling backdrop for the one mighty foreground constellation, the brilliant Hydros Cross—two blazing rows of stars that arched across the sky at right angles to each other like a double cincture, one spanning the world from pole to pole, the other marching steadfastly along above the equator.

For Lawler these were the stars of home, the only stars he had ever seen. He was Hydros-born, fifth generation. He had never been to any other world and never would. Sorve Island was as familiar to him as his own skin. And yet he sometimes tumbled without warning into frightening moments of confusion when all sense of familiarity dissolved and he felt like a stranger here: times when it seemed to him that he had just arrived on Hydros that very day, flung down out of space like a falling star, a castaway from his true native place far away. Sometimes he saw the lost mother world of Earth shining in his mind, bright as any star, its great blue seas divided by the enormous golden-green land-masses that were called continents, and he thought, This is my home, this is my true home. Lawler wondered if any of the other humans on Hydros ever experienced something like that now and again. Probably so, though no one ever spoke of it. They were all strangers here, after all. This world belonged to the Gillies. He and everyone like him here lived on it as uninvited guests.

HE HAD REACHED THE BRINK OF THE SEA NOW. THE FAMILIAR RAILING, rough, woody-textured like everything else on this artificial island that had neither soil nor vegetation, came up to meet his grasp as he clambered to the top of the sea-wall.

Here at the wall the slope in the island's topography, which ran gradually downhill from the built-up high ground in the interior and the ocean bulwark beyond it, reversed itself sharply and the flooring turned upward to form a meniscus, a crescent rim, that shielded the inner streets against all but the most severe of tidal surges. Grasping the rail, leaning forward over the dark lapping water, Lawler stood staring outward for a moment, as though offering himself to the all-surrounding ocean.

Even in the darkness he had a complete sense of the comma-shaped island's form and his exact place along its shore. The island was eight kilometers long from tip to tip, and about a kilometer across at its widest point, measuring from the bayfront to the summit of the rear bulwark that held back the open sea. He was near the center, the innermost gulf. To his right and left the island's two curving arms stretched outward before him, the rounded one where the Gillies lived, and the narrow tapering one where the island's little handful of human settlers clustered close together.

Right in front of him, enclosed by that pair of unequal arms, was the bay that was the living heart of the island. The Gillie builders of the island had created an artificial bottom there, an underwater shelf of interlaced wood-kelp timbers attached to the mainland from arm to arm so that the island always would have a shallow, fertile lagoon adjacent to it, a captive pond. The wild menacing predators that haunted the open sea never entered the bay: perhaps the Gillies had made some treaty with them long ago. A lacing of spongy bottom-dwelling night-algae, needing no light, bound the underside of the bay floor together, ever protecting and renewing it with their steady stubborn growth. Above that was sand, washed in by storms from the great unknown ocean floor farther out. And above that a thicket of useful aquatic plants of a hundred different species or more, in which all manner of sea-creatures swarmed. Shellfish of many sorts inhabited its lower reaches, filtering seawater through their soft tissues and concentrating valuable minerals within themselves for the use of the islanders. Sea-worms and serpents moved among them. Plump and tender fish grazed there. Just now Lawler could see a pod of huge phosphorescent creatures moving about out there, emanating pulsating waves of blue-violet light: the great beasts known as mouths, perhaps, or perhaps they were platforms, but it was still too dark to tell. And beyond the bright green water of the bay was the great ocean sea, rolling to the horizon and past it, holding the entire world in its grasp, a gloved hand gripping a ball. Lawler, staring toward it, felt for the millionth time the weight of its immensity, its thrust and power.

He looked now toward the power plant, solitary and massive on its little snubnosed promontory sticking out into the bay.

They hadn't finished it after all. The ungainly building, shrouded in festoons of woven straw matting to shield it from the rain, still was silent and dark. A few shadowy figures were shuffling about in front of it. They had the unmistakable slope-shouldered shape of Gillies.

The concept of the power plant was that it would generate electricity by taking advantage of temperature differentials in the sea. Dann Henders, who was as close to an engineer as anyone was on Sorve, had explained it to Lawler after extracting a sketchy description of the project from one of the Gillies. Warm seawater from the surface level was pulled in through vanes and entered a vacuum chamber, where its boiling point would be greatly reduced. The water, boiling violently, was supposed to yield low-density steam that would drive the turbines of the generator. Cold seawater, pumped up from the deeper levels beyond the bay, was going to be used then to condense the steam into water again, and it would be returned to the sea through discharge outlets halfway around the island from here.

The Gillies had constructed practically the whole thing—pipes, pumps, vanes, turbines, condensers, the vacuum chamber itself—out of the various organic plastics they produced from algae and other water plants. Apparently they had used scarcely any metal in the design at all, not surprising in view of the difficulty of obtaining metals on Hydros. It was all very ingenious, especially considering that the Gillies weren't notably technological-minded, as intelligent galactic species went. Some exceptional genius among them must have come up with the idea. Genius or not, though, they were said to be having an ungodly time making the operation work, and it was yet to produce its first watt. Most of the humans wondered if it ever would. It might have been a whole lot faster and simpler for the Gillies, Lawler thought, if they had let Dann Henders or one of the other engineering-oriented humans sit in on the design of it. But of course the Gillies weren't in the habit of seeking advice from the unwanted strangers with whom they grudgingly shared their island, even when it might be to their advantage. They had made an exception only when an outbreak of fin-rot was decimating their young, and Lawler's saintly father had come to them with a vaccine. Which had been many years ago, though, and whatever good will the former Dr. Lawler's services had engendered among the Gillies had long since evaporated, leaving no apparent residue behind.

That the plant still didn't seem to be working yet was something of a setback for the grand plan that had come to Lawler in the night.

What now? Go and talk to them anyway? Make your florid little speech, grease the Gillies up with some noble rhetoric, follow through with tonight's visionary impulse before daybreak robs it of whatever plausibility it might have had?

"On behalf of the entire human community of Sorve Island, I, who as you know am the son of the late beloved Dr. Bernat Lawler who served you so well in the time of the fin-rot epidemic, wish to congratulate you on the imminent accomplishment of your ingenious and magnificently beneficial—"

"Even though the fulfillment of this splendid dream may perhaps be still some days away, I have come on behalf of the entire human community of Sorve Island to extend to you our profoundest joy at the deep implications we see for the transformation of the quality of life on the island that we share, once you have at last succeeded in—"

"At this time of rejoicing in our community over the historic achievement that is soon to be—"

Enough, he thought. He began to make his way out onto the power-plant promontory.

• • •

As he drew near the plant he took care to make plenty of noise, coughing, slapping his hands together, whistling a little tuneless tune. Gillies didn't like humans to come upon them unexpectedly.

He was still about fifteen meters from the power plant when he saw two Gillies shuffling out to meet him.

In the darkness they looked titanic. They loomed high above him, formless in the dark, their little yellow eyes glowing bright as lanterns in their tiny heads.

Lawler made the greeting-sign, elaborately over-gesturing so that there could be no doubt of his friendly intentions.

One of the Gillies replied with a prolonged snorting *vrooom* that didn't sound friendly at all.

They were big upright bipedal creatures, two and a half meters high, covered with deep layers of rubbery black bristles that hung in dense shaggy cascades. Their heads were absurdly small, little dome-shaped structures that sat atop huge shoulders, and from there almost down to the ground their torsos sloped outward to form massive, bulky, ungainly bodies. It was generally assumed by humans that their immense cavernous chests must contain their brains as well as their hearts and lungs. Certainly those little heads had no room for them.

Very likely the Gillies had been aquatic mammals once. You could see that in the gracelessness with which they moved on land and the ease with which they swam. They spent nearly as much time in the water as on land. Once Lawler had watched a Gillie swim from one side of the bay to the other without breaking the surface for breath; the journey must have taken twenty minutes. Their legs, short and stumpy, were obviously adapted from flippers. Their arms too were flipper-like—thick, powerful little limbs that they held very close to their sides. Their hands, equipped with three long fingers and an opposable thumb, were extraordinarily broad and fell naturally into deep cups well suited for pushing great volumes of water. In some unlikely and astounding act of self-redefinition these beings' ancestors had climbed up out of the sea, millions of years ago, fashioning island homes for themselves woven out of sea-born materials and buffered by elaborate barricades against the ceaseless tidal surges that circled their planet. But they still were creatures of the ocean.

Lawler stepped up as close to the two Gillies as he dared and signaled *I-am-Lawler-the-doctor.*

When Gillies spoke it was by squeezing their arms inward against their sides, compressing air through deep gill-shaped slits in their chests to produce booming organ-like tones. Humans had never found a way to imitate Gillie sounds in a way that Gillies understood, nor did the Gillies show any interest in learning how to speak the human language. Perhaps its sounds were as impossible for them as Gillie sounds were for humans. But some communication between the races was necessary. Over the years a sign language had developed. The Gillies spoke to humans in Gillie; the humans replied in signs.

The Gillie who had spoken before made the snort again, and added a peculiarly hostile snuffling whistling sound. It held up its flippers in what Lawler recognized as a posture of anger. No, not anger: rage. Extreme rage.

Hey, Lawler thought. What's up? What have *I* done?

There wasn't any doubt about the Gillie's fury. Now it was making little brushing movements with its flippers that seemed plainly to say, *Get away, clear out, get your ass out of here fast.*

Perplexed, Lawler signaled *I-mean-no-intrusion. I-come-to-parley.*

The snort again, louder, deeper. It reverberated through the flooring of the path and Lawler felt the vibration in the soles of his feet.

Gillies had been known to kill human beings who had annoyed them, and even some who hadn't: a troublesome occasional propensity for inexplicable violence. It didn't seem deliberate—just an irritated backhand swipe of a flipper, a quick contemptuous kick, a little thoughtless trampling. They were very large and very strong and they didn't seem to understand, or care, how fragile human bodies could be.

The other Gillie, the bigger of the two, took a step or two in Lawler's direction. Its breath came with heavy, wheezing, unsociable intensity. It gave Lawler a look that he interpreted as one of aloof, absentminded hostility.

Lawler signaled surprise and dismay. He signaled friendliness again. He signaled continued eagerness to talk.

The first Gillie's fiery eyes were blazing with unmistakable wrath.

Out. Away. Go.

No ambiguities there. Useless to attempt any further pacifying palaver. Clearly they didn't want him anywhere near their power plant.

All right, he thought. Have it your own way.

He had never been brushed off like this by Gillies before; but to take time now to remind them that he was their old friend the island doctor, or that his father had once made himself very useful to them, would be dangerous idiocy. One slap of that flipper could knock him into the bay with a broken spine.

He backed away, keeping a close eye on them, intending to leap backward into the water if they made a threatening move toward him.

But the Gillies stayed where they were, glowering at him as he executed his slinking retreat. When he had reached the main path again they turned and went back inside their building.

So much for that, Lawler thought.

THE WEIRD REBUFF STUNG HIM DEEPLY. HE STOOD FOR A TIME BY THE bayfront railing, letting the tension of the strange encounter ebb from him. His great scheme of negotiating a human-Hydran treaty this night, he saw all too clearly now, had been mere romantic nonsense. It went whistling out of Lawler's mind like the vapor it was, and a quick flash of embarrassment sent waves of heat running through his skin for a moment.

Well, then. Back to the vaargh to wait for morning, he supposed.

A grating bass voice behind him said, "Lawler?"

CAUGHT BY SURPRISE, LAWLER WHIRLED ABRUPTLY, HIS HEART THUN-dering. He squinted into the graying darkness. He could just barely make out the figure of a short, stocky man with a heavy shock of long, greasy-looking hair standing in the shadows ten or twelve meters to the inland side of him.

"Delagard? That you?"

The stocky man stepped forward. Delagard, yes. The self-appointed top dog of the island, the chief mover and shaker. What the hell was he doing skulking around here at this hour?

Delagard always seemed to be up to something tricky, even when he wasn't. He was short but not small, a powerful figure built low to the ground, thick-necked, heavy-shouldered, paunchy. He wore an ankle-length sarong that left his broad shaggy chest bare. Even in the darkness the garment glowed in luminous ripples of scarlet and turquoise and hot pink. Delagard was the richest man in the settlement, whatever that meant on a world where money itself had no meaning, where there was hardly anything you could spend it on. He was Hydros-born, like Lawler, but he owned businesses on several islands and moved around a lot. Delagard was a few years older than Lawler, perhaps forty-eight or fifty.

"You're out and about pretty early this morning, doc," Delagard said.

"I generally am. You know that." Lawler's voice was tighter than usual. "It's a good time of day."

"If you like to be alone, yes." Delagard nodded toward the power plant. "Checking it out, are you?"

Lawler shrugged. He would sooner throttle himself with his own hands than let Delagard have any inkling of the grandiose heroic fatuity that he had spent this long night engendering.

Delagard said, "They tell me it'll be on-line tomorrow."

"I've been hearing that for a week."

"No. No, tomorrow they'll really have it working. After all this time. They've generated power already, low level, and today they'll be bringing it up to capacity."

"How do you know?"

"I know," Delagard said. "The Gillies don't like me, but they tell me things, anyway. In the course of business, you understand." He came up alongside Lawler and clapped his hand down on the sea-wall railing in a confident, hearty way, as if this island were his kingdom and the railing his scepter. "You haven't asked me yet why I'm up this early."

"No. I haven't."

"Looking for you, is why. First I went over to your vaargh, but you weren't there. Then I looked down to the lower terrace and I caught sight of somebody moving around on the path heading down here and figured it might be you, and I came down here to find out if I was right."

Lawler smiled sourly. Nothing in Delagard's tone indicated that he had seen what had taken place out on the power-plant promontory.

"Very early to be paying a call on me, if it's a professional thing," Lawler said. "Or a social call, for that matter. Not that you would." He pointed to the horizon. The moon was still gleaming there. No sign of the first light of morning was visible yet. The Cross, even more brilliant than usual with Sunrise not in the sky, seemed to throb and pulse against the intense blackness. "I generally don't start my office hours before daybreak. You know that, Nid."

"A special problem," said Delagard. "Couldn't wait. Best taken care of while it's still dark."

"Medical problem, is it?"

"Medical problem, yes."

"Yours?"

"Yes. But I'm not the patient."

"I don't understand you."

"You will. Just come with me."

"Where?" Lawler said.

"Shipyard."

What the hell. Delagard seemed very strange this morning. It was probably something important. "All right," said Lawler. "Let's get going, then."

WITHOUT ANOTHER WORD DELAGARD TURNED AND STARTED ALONG the path that ran just inside the sea-wall, heading toward the shipyard. Lawler followed him in silence. The path here followed another little promontory parallel to the one on which the power-plant structure stood, and as they moved out on it they had a clear view of the plant. Gillies were going in and out, carrying armloads of equipment.

"Those slippery fuckers," Delagard muttered. "I hope their plant blows up in their faces when they start it up. If they ever get it started up at all."

They rounded the far side of the promontory and entered the little inlet where Delagard's shipyard stood. It was the biggest human enterprise on Sorve by far, employing more than a dozen people. Delagard's ships constantly went back and forth between the various islands where he did business, carrying trade goods from place to place, the modest merchandise turned out by the various cottage industries that humans operated: fishhooks and chisels and mallets, bottles and jars, articles of clothing, paper and ink, hand-copied books, packaged foods, and such. The Delagard fleet also was the chief distributor of metals and plastics and chemicals and other such essential commodities that the various islands so painstakingly produced. Every few years Delagard added another island to his chain of commerce. From the very beginning of human occupation of Hydros, Delagards had been running entrepreneurial businesses here, but Nid Delagard had expanded the family operation far beyond its earlier levels.

"This way," Delagard said.

A strand of pearly dawnlight broke suddenly across the eastern sky. The stars dimmed and the little moon on the horizon began to fade from sight as the day started to come on. The bay was taking on its emerald morning color. Lawler, following Delagard down the path into the shipyard, glanced out into it and had his first clear view of the giant phosphorescent creatures that had been cruising around out there all night. He saw now that they were mouths: immense flattened baglike creatures, close to a hundred meters in length, that traveled through the sea with their colossal jaws agape, swallowing everything that lay before them. Once a month or so, a pod of ten or twelve of them turned up in Sorve harbor and disgorged the contents of their stomachs, still alive, into huge wickerwork nets kept there for that purpose by the Gillies, who harvested them at leisure over the weeks that followed. It was a good deal for the Gillies, Lawler thought— tons and tons of free food. But it was hard to see what was in the deal for the mouths.

Delagard said, chuckling, "There's my competition. If I could only kill off the fucking mouths, I could be hauling in all sorts of stuff myself to sell to the Gillies."

"And what would they pay you for it with?"

"The same things they use to pay me now for the things I sell them," said Delagard scornfully. "Useful elements. Cadmium, cobalt, copper, tin, arsenic, iodine, all the stuff this goddamn ocean is made of. But in very much bigger quantities than the dribs and drabs they dole out now, or that we're capable of extracting ourselves. We get the mouths out of the picture somehow, and then I supply the Gillies with their meat, and they load me up with all kinds of valuable commodities in return. A very nice deal, let me tell you. Within five years I'd make them dependent on me for their entire food supply. There'd be a fortune in it."

"I thought you were worth a fortune already. How much more do you need?"

"You just don't understand, do you?"

"I guess not," Lawler said. "I'm only a doctor, not a businessman. Where's this patient of yours?"

"Easy, easy. I'm taking you as fast as I can, doc." Delagard gestured seaward with a quick brushing movement of his hand. "You see down there, by Jolly's Pier? Where that little fishing boat is? That's where we're going."

Jolly's Pier was a finger of rotting kelp-timber sticking out thirty meters or so beyond the sea-wall, at the far end of the shipyard. Though it was faded and warped, battered by tides and nibbled by drillworms and raspers, the pier was still more or less intact, a venerable artifact of a vanished era. A crazy old sailor had constructed it, long dead now, a grizzled weird relic of a man whose claim it had been to have journeyed solo completely around the world—even into the Empty Sea, where no one in his right mind would go, even to the borders of the Face of the Waters itself, that immense forbidden island far away, the great planetary mystery that apparently not even the Gillies dared to approach. Lawler could remember sitting out here at the end of Jolly's Pier when he was a boy, listening to the old man spinning his wild, flamboyant tales of implausible, miraculous adventure. That was before Delagard had built his shipyard here. But for some reason Delagard had preserved the bedraggled pier. He must have liked to listen to the old man's yarns too, once upon a time.

One of Delagard's fishing coracles was tied up alongside it, bobbing on the bay swells. On the pier near the place where the coracle was moored was a shed that looked old enough to have been Jolly's house, though it wasn't. Delagard, pausing outside it, looked up fiercely into Lawler's eyes and said in a soft husky growl, "You understand, doc, whatever you see inside here is absolutely confidential."

"Spare me the melodrama, Nid."

"I mean it. You've got to promise you won't talk. It won't just be my ass if this gets out. It could screw us all."

"If you don't trust me, get some other doctor. But you might have some trouble finding one around here."

Delagard gave him a surly look. Then he produced a chilly smile. "All right. Whatever you say. Just come on in."

He pushed open the door of the shed. It was utterly dark inside, and unusually humid. Lawler smelled the tart salty aroma of the sea, strong and concentrated as though Delagard had been bottling it in here, and something else, sour and pungent and disagreeable, that he didn't recognize at all. He heard faint grunting noises, slow and rasping, like the sighs of the damned. Delagard fumbled with something just within the door that made a rough, bristly sound. After a moment he struck a match, and Lawler saw that the other man was holding a bundle of dried seaweed that had been tied at one end to form a torch, which he had ignited. A dim, smoky light spread like an orange stain through the shed.

"There they are," Delagard said.

The middle of the shed was taken up by a crude rectangular storage tank of pitch-caulked wickerwork, perhaps three meters long and two wide, filled almost to the brim with seawater. Lawler went over to it and looked in. Three of the sleek aquatic mammals known as divers were lying in it, side by side, jammed close together like fish in a tin. Their powerful fins were contorted at impossible angles and their heads, rising stiffly above the surface of the water, were thrown back in an awkward, agonized way. The strange acrid smell Lawler had picked up at the doorway was theirs. It no longer seemed so unpleasant now. The terrible grunting noises were coming from the diver on the left. They were grunts of purest pain.

"Oh, shit," Lawler said quietly. He thought he understood the Gillies' rage now. Their blazing eyes, that menacing snort. A quick hot burst of anger went rippling through him, setting up a brief twitching in his cheek. "Shit!" He looked back toward the other man in disgust, revulsion, and something close to hatred. "Delagard, what have you done now?"

"Listen, if you think I brought you here just so you could chew me out—"

Lawler shook his head slowly. "What have you done, man?" he said again, staring straight into Delagard's suddenly flickering eyes. "What the fuck have you done?"

2

I T WAS NITROGEN ABSORPTION: LAWLER DIDN'T HAVE MUCH DOUBT of that. The frightful way in which the three divers were twisted up was a clear signal. Delagard must have had them working at some job deep down in the open sea, keeping them there long enough for their joints, muscles, and fatty tissues to absorb immense quantities of nitrogen; and then, unlikely as that seemed, they evidently had come to the surface without taking the proper time to decompress. The nitrogen, expanding as the pressure dropped, had escaped into their bloodstream and joints in the form of deadly bubbles.

"We brought them here as soon as we realized there was trouble," Delagard said. "Figuring maybe you could do something for them. And I thought, keep them in water, they need to stay underwater, so we filled this tank and—"

"Shut up," Lawler said.

"I want you to know, we made every effort—"

"Shut up. Please. Just shut up."

Lawler stripped off the water-lettuce wrap he was wearing and clambered into the tank. Water went splashing over the side as he crowded himself in next to the divers. But there wasn't much that he could do for them. The one in the middle was dead already: Lawler put his hands to the creature's muscular shoulders and felt the rigor starting to take hold. The other two were more or less alive—so much the worse for them; they must be in hideous pain, if they were conscious at all. The divers' usually smooth torpedo-shaped bodies, longer than a man's, were bizarrely knotted, each muscle straining against its neighbor, and their glistening golden skins, normally slick and satiny, felt rough, full of little lumps. Their amber eyes were dull. Their jutting underslung jaws hung slack. A gray spittle covered their snouts. The one on the left was still groaning steadily, every thirty seconds or so, wrenching the sound up from the depths of its guts in a horrifying way.

"Can you fix them somehow?" Delagard asked. "Is there anything you can do at all? I know you can do it, doc. I know you can." There was an urgent wheedling tone in Delagard's voice now that Lawler couldn't remember ever hearing in it before. Lawler was accustomed to the way sick people would cede godlike power to a doctor and beg for miracles. But why did Delagard care so much about these divers? What was going on here, really? Surely Delagard didn't feel *guilty*. Not Delagard.

Coldly Lawler said, "I'm no diver doctor. Doctoring humans is all I know how to do. And I could stand to be a whole lot better even at that than I am."

"Try. Do something. Please."

"One of them's dead already, Delagard. I was never trained to raise the dead. You want a miracle, go get your friend Quillan the priest in here."

"Christ," Delagard muttered.

"Exactly. Miracles are his specialty, not mine."

"Christ. Christ."

Lawler felt carefully for pulses along the divers' throats. Yes, still beating after a fashion, slow, uneven. Did that mean they were moribund? He couldn't say. What the hell was a normal pulse for a diver? How was he supposed to know stuff like that? The only thing to do, he thought, was to put the two that were still alive back in the sea, get them down to the depths where they had been, and bring them up again, slowly enough this time so they could rid themselves of the excess nitrogen. But there was no way to manage that. And it was probably too late anyway.

In anguish he made futile, almost mystical passes over the twisted bodies with his hands, as though he could drive the nitrogen bubbles out by gesture alone. "How deep were they?" Lawler asked, without looking up.

"We aren't sure. Four hundred meters, maybe. Maybe four fifty. The bottom was irregular there and the sea was moving around so we couldn't keep close track of how much line we'd paid out."

Clear to the bottom of the sea. It was lunacy.

"What were you looking for?"

"Manganese nuggets," Delagard said. "And there was supposed to be molybdenum down there too, and maybe some antimony. We trawled up a whole goddamned menagerie of mineral samples with the scoop."

"Then you should have used the scoop to bring your manganese up," said Lawler angrily. "Not these."

He felt the right-hand diver ripple and convulse and die as he held it. The other was still writhing, still moaning.

A cold bitter fury took hold of him, fueled as much by contempt as by wrath. This was murder, and stupid unthinking murder at that. Divers were intelligent animals—not as intelligent as the Gillies, but intelligent enough, surely smarter than dogs, smarter than horses, smarter than any of the animals of old Earth that Lawler had heard about in his storybook days. The seas of Hydros were full of creatures that could be regarded as intelligent; that was one of the bewildering things about this world, that it had evolved not just a single intelligent species, but, apparently, dozens of them. The divers had a language, they had names, they had some kind of tribal structure. Unlike nearly all the other intelligent life-forms on Hydros, though, they had a fatal flaw: they were docile and even friendly around human beings, gentle frolicking companions in the water. They could be induced to do favors. They could be put to work, even.

They could be worked right to death, it seemed.

Desperately Lawler massaged the one that hadn't yet died, still hoping in a hopeless way that he could work the nitrogen out of its tissues. For a moment its eyes brightened and it uttered five or six words in the barking, guttural diver language. Lawler didn't speak diver; but the creature's words were easy enough to guess at: *pain, grief, sorrow, loss, despair, pain.* Then the amber eyes glazed over again and the diver lapsed into silence.

Lawler said, as he worked on it, "Divers are adapted for life in the deep ocean. Left to their own devices, they're smart enough to know not to rise from one pressure zone to another too fast to handle the gases. Any sea creature knows that, no matter how dumb it is. A sponge would know that, let alone a diver. How did it happen that these three came up so fast?"

"They got caught in the hoist," Delagard said miserably. "They were in the net and we didn't know it until it surfaced. Is there anything, anything at all that you can do to save them, doc?"

"The other one on the end is dead too. This one has maybe five minutes left. The only thing I can do is break its neck and put it out of its misery."

"Jesus."

"Yeah. Jesus. What a shitty business."

It took only an instant, one quick snap. Lawler paused for a moment afterward, shoulders hunched forward, exhaling, feeling a release himself as the diver died. Then he climbed out of the tank, shook himself off, and wrapped the water-lettuce garment around his middle again. What he wanted now, and he wanted it very badly, was a good shot of his numbweed tincture, the pink drops that gave him peace of a sort. And a bath, after having been in the tank with those dying beasts. But his bath quota for the week was used up. A swim would have to do, a little later on in the day. Though he suspected it would take more than that to make him feel clean again after what he had seen in here this morning.

He looked sharply at Delagard.

"These aren't the first divers you've done this to, are they?"

The stocky man didn't meet his gaze.

"No."

"Don't you have any sense? I know you don't have any conscience, but you might at least have sense. What happened to the other ones?"

"They died."

"I assume that they did. What did you do with the bodies?"

"Made feed out of them."

"Wonderful. How many?"

"It was a while ago. Four, five—I'm not sure."

"That probably means ten. Did the Gillies find out about it?"

Delagard's "yes" was the smallest possible audible sound a man could have made.

"Yes," Lawler mimicked. "Of course they found out. The Gillies always know it, when we fuck around with the local fauna. So what did they say, when they found out?"

"They warned me." A little louder, not much, a sullen under-the-breath naughty-schoolboy tone.

Here it comes, Lawler thought. We're at the heart of it at last.

"Warned you what?" he asked.

"Not to use divers in my operations any more."

"But you did, is how it looks. Why the hell did you do it again, if they warned you?"

"We changed the method. We didn't think there'd be any harm." Some energy returned to Delagard's voice. "Listen, Lawler, do you know how valuable those mineral nuggets could be? They could revolutionize our entire existence on this fucking watery hole of a planet! How was I to know the divers would swim right into the goddamned hoist net? How could I figure that they would let themselves stay in it after we signaled that we were lifting?"

"They didn't *let* themselves stay in it. They must have been tangled up in it. Intelligent diving animals just don't let themselves stay in a net that's rising quickly from four hundred meters."

Delagard glared defiantly. "Well, they did. For whatever reason, I don't know." Then the glare faded, and he offered Lawler the miracle-worker look again, eyes rolling upward imploringly. Still hoping, even now? "There was nothing whatever that you could do to save them, Lawler? Nothing at all?"

"Sure there was. There were all sorts of things I could have done. I just wasn't in the mood, I guess."

"Sorry. That was dumb." Delagard actually looked almost abashed. Huskily he said, "I know you did the best you could. Look, if there's anything I can send over to your vaargh by way of payment, a case of grapeweed brandy, maybe, or some good baskets, or a week's supply of banger steaks—"

"The brandy," Lawler said. "That's the best idea. So I can get myself good and drunk and try to forget all about what I saw here this morning." He closed his eyes a moment. "The Gillies are aware that you've had three dying divers in here all night."

"They are? How can you possibly know that?"

"Because I ran into a few while I was wandering around down by the bayshore, and they practically bit my head off. They were frothing mad. You didn't see them chase me away?" Delagard, suddenly ashen-faced, shook his head. "Well, they did. And I hadn't done anything wrong, except maybe come a little too close to their power plant. But they never indicated before that the plant was off bounds. So it must have been these divers."

"You think so?"

"What else could it be?"

"Sit down, then. We've got to talk, doc."

"Not now."

"Listen to me!"

"I don't want to listen, okay? I can't stick around here any longer. I've got other things to do. People are probably waiting for me up at the vaargh. Hell, I haven't even had breakfast yet."

"Doc, wait a second. Please."

Delagard reached out to him, but Lawler shook him off. Suddenly the hot moist air of the shed, tinged now with the sweet odor of bodily decomposition, was sickening to him. His head began to swirl. Even a doctor had his limits. He stepped around the gaping Delagard and went outside. Pausing just by the door, Lawler rocked back and forth for a few moments, closing his eyes, breathing deeply, listening to the grumbling of his empty stomach and the creaking of the pier beneath his feet, until the sudden nausea had left him.

He spat. Something dry and greenish came up. He scowled at it.

Jesus. Some start to the morning.

DAYBREAK HAD COME BY THIS TIME, THE FULL SHOW. WITH SORVE THIS close to the equator, the sun rose swiftly above the horizon in the morning and plummeted just as abruptly at nightfall. It was an unusually magnificent sky this morning, too. Bright pink streaks, interleaved with tinges of orange and turquoise, were splashed across the vault of the heavens. It looked almost like Delagard's sarong up there, Lawler thought. He had calmed quickly once he was outside the shack in the fresh sea air, but now he felt a new wave of rage churning within him, setting up bad resonances in his gut, and he looked away, down toward his feet, taking deep breaths again. What he needed to do, he told himself, was to get himself home. Home, and breakfast, and perhaps a drop or two of numbweed tincture. And then on to the day's rounds.

He began to head upslope.

Farther inland on the island, people were up, people were moving around.

Nobody slept much past dawn here. The night was for sleeping, the day for working. In the course of making his way back toward his vaargh to wait for the morning batch of genuine sufferers and chronic complainers to start showing up, Lawler encountered and greeted a significant percentage of the island's entire human population. Here at the narrow end where the humans lived, everyone was on top of everyone else all the time.

Most of those to whom he nodded as he walked up the easy slope of the hard, bright yellow wickerwork path were people he had known for decades. Practically all the population of Sorve was Hydros-born, and more than half of those had been born and raised right here on this island, like Lawler himself. And so most of them were people who had never specifically chosen to spend their entire lives on this alien ball of water, but were doing it anyway, because they hadn't been given any choice. The lottery of life had simply handed them a ticket to Hydros at birth; and once you found yourself on Hydros you couldn't ever get off, because there were no spaceports here, there was no way of leaving the planet except by dying. It was a life sentence, being born here. That was strange, in a galaxy full of habitable and inhabited worlds, not to have had any choice about where you would live. But then there were the others, the ones who had come plummeting in from outside via drop-capsule, who *had* had a choice, who could have gone anywhere in the universe and had chosen to come here, knowing that there was no going away again. That was even stranger.

Dag Tharp, who ran the radio unit and did dental work on the side and sometimes served as Lawler's anesthesiologist, was the first to go by, a tiny angular man, red-faced and fragile-looking, with a scraggy neck and a big, sharply hooked nose emerging between little eyes and practically fleshless lips. Behind him down the path came Sweyner, the toolmaker and glassblower, a little old fellow, knotted and gnarled, and his knotted, gnarled wife, who looked like his twin sister. Some of the newer settlers suspected that she was, but Lawler knew better. Sweyner's wife was Lawler's second cousin, and Sweyner was no kin to him—or her—at all. The Sweyners, like Tharp, were both Hydros-born, and native to Sorve. It was a little irregular to marry a woman from your own island, as Sweyner had done, and that— along with their physical resemblance—accounted for the rumors.

Lawler was near the high spine of the island now, the main terrace. A wide wooden ramp led to it. There were no staircases on Sorve: the stubby inefficient legs of the Gillies weren't well designed for using stairs. Lawler took the ramp at a quick pace and stepped out onto the terrace, a flat stretch of stiff, hard, tightly bound yellow sea-bamboo fibers fifty meters wide, varnished and laminated with seppeltane sap and supported by a trellis of heavy black kelp-timber beams. The island's long, narrow central road cut across it. A left turn took you to the part of the island where the Gillies lived, a right turn led into the shantytown of the humans. He turned right.

"Good morning, doctor-sir," Natim Gharkid murmured, twenty paces or so down the road, moving aside to let Lawler go by.

Gharkid had come to Sorve four or five years ago from some other island: a soft-eyed soft-faced man with dark smooth skin, who had not yet managed to fit himself into the life of the community in any very significant way. He was an algae-farmer, who was going down to spend his day harvesting seaweeds in the shallows. That was all that he did. Most of the humans on Hydros followed a variety of occupations: in such a small population, it was necessary for people to attempt to master several skills. But Gharkid didn't seem concerned about that. Lawler was not only the island's doctor but also the pharmacist, the meteorologist, the undertaker, and—so Delagard apparently thought—the veterinarian. Gharkid, though, was an algae-farmer and nothing else. Lawler thought he was probably Hydros-born, but he wasn't certain of it, so rarely did the man reveal anything at all about himself. Gharkid was the most self-effacing person Lawler had ever known, quiet and patient and diligent, amiable but unfathomable, a vague silent presence and not much more.

They exchanged automatic smiles as they passed each other now.

Then came three women in a row, all of them in loose green robes: Sisters Halla, Mariam, and Thecla, who a couple of years ago had formed some sort of convent down at the tip of the island, past the ashmasters' yard, where bone of all sorts was stored to be processed into lime and then into soap, ink, paint, and chemicals of a hundred uses. No one but ashmasters went there, ordinarily; the Sisters, living beyond the boneyard, were safe from all disturbance. It was an odd place to choose to live, all the same. Since setting up their convent the Sisters had had as little to do with men as they could manage. There were eleven of them altogether by now, nearly a third of all the human women on Sorve: a curious development, unique in the island's short history. Delagard was full of lewd speculations about what went on down there. Very likely he was right.

"Sister Halla," Lawler said, saluting. "Sister Mariam. Sister Thecla."

They looked at him the way they might have done if he had said something filthy. Lawler shrugged and went on.

The main reservoir was just up ahead, a covered circular tank three meters high and fifty meters across, constructed of varnished poles of sea-bamboo bound together with bright orange hoops of algae fronds and caulked within with the red pitch that was made from water-cucumbers. A berserk maze of wooden pipes emerged from it and fanned out toward the vaarghs that began just beyond it. The reservoir was probably the most important structure in the settlement. The first humans to get here had built it, five generations ago in the early twenty-fourth century when Hydros was still being used as a penal colony, and it required constant maintenance, endless patching and caulking and rehooping. There had been talk for at least ten years of replacing it with something more elegantly made, but nothing had ever been done about it, and Lawler doubted that anything ever would. It served its purpose well enough.

As Lawler approached the great wooden tank he saw the priest who had lately come to live on Hydros, Father Quillan of the Church of All Worlds, edging slowly around it from the far side, doing something extremely strange. Every ten paces or thereabouts Quillan would halt, face the reservoir wall, and stretch his arms out against it in a sort of hug, pressing his fingertips thoughtfully against the wall here and there as though probing for leaks.

"Afraid that the wall's going to pop?" Lawler called to him. The priest was an offworlder, a newcomer. He had been on Hydros less than a year and had arrived on Sorve Island only a few weeks before. "You don't need to worry about that."

Quillan looked quickly around, visibly embarrassed. He took his hands away from the side of the reservoir.

"Hello, Lawler."

The priest was a compact, austere-looking man, balding and clean-shaven, who might have been any age at all between forty-five and sixty. He was thin, as if all the flesh had been sweated off him, with a long oval face and a strong, bony nose. His eyes, set deep in their sockets, were a chilly light blue and his skin was very pale, almost bleached-looking, though a steady diet of the maritime-derived things that people ate on Hydros was starting to give him the dusky sea-tinged complexion that the old-time settlers had: the algae cropping out in the skin, so to speak.

Lawler said, "The reservoir's extremely sturdy. Believe me, Father. I've lived here all my life and that reservoir hasn't burst its walls even once. We couldn't afford to let that happen."

Quillan laughed self-consciously. "That isn't what I was doing, actually. I was embracing its strength, as a matter of fact."

"I see."

"Feeling all that contained power. Experiencing a sense of great force under restraint—tons of water held back by nothing more than human will and determination."

"And a lot of sea-bamboo and hooping, Father. Not to mention God's grace."

"That too," Quillan said.

Very peculiar, hugging the reservoir because you wanted to experience its strength. But Quillan was always doing curious things like that. There seemed to be some kind of desperate hunger in the man: for grace, for mercy, for surrender to something larger than himself. For faith itself, perhaps. It seemed odd to Lawler that a man who claimed to be a priest would be so needy of spirit.

He said, "My great-great-grandfather designed it, you know. Harry Lawler, one of the Founders. He could do anything he put his mind to, my grandfather used to say. Take out your appendix, sail a ship from one island to another, design a reservoir." Lawler paused. "He was sent here for murder, old Harry was. Manslaughter, I should say."

"I didn't know. So your family has always lived on Sorve?"

"Since the beginning. I was born here. Just about a hundred eighty meters from where we're standing, actually." Lawler slapped the side of the reservoir affectionately. "Good old Harry. We'd be in real trouble here without this. You see how dry our climate is."

"I'm starting to find out," said the priest. "Doesn't it ever rain here at all?"

"Certain times of the year," Lawler said. "This isn't one of the times. You won't see any rain around here for another nine, ten months. That's why we took care to build our reservoirs so that they wouldn't spring any leaks."

Water was scarce on Sorve: the kind of water that humans could use, at any rate. The island traveled through arid territory most of the year. That was the work of the inexorable currents. The floating islands of Hydros, though they drifted more or less freely in the sea, were nevertheless penned for decades at a time within clearly defined longitudinal belts by powerful ocean currents, strong as great rivers. Every year each island carried out a rigidly defined migration from one pole to the other and back again; each pole was surrounded by a vortex of swift water that seized the incoming islands, swung them around, and sent them off toward the opposite end of the planet. But though the islands passed through every latitudinal belt in their annual north-south migrations, east-west fluctuations were minimal because of the force of the prevailing currents. Sorve, in its endless traveling up and down the world, had stayed between the fortieth and sixtieth degrees of west longitude as long as Lawler could remember. That seemed basically to be an arid belt in most latitudes. Rain was infrequent except when the island was moving through the polar zones, where heavy downfalls were the rule.

The almost perpetual droughts were no problem for the Gillies, who were constructed for drinking seawater anyway. But they made existence complicated for the humans. Water rationing was a routine fact of life on Sorve. There had been two years—when Lawler was twelve, and again when he was twenty, the dark year of his father's death—when freakish rainfall had pelted the island for weeks without ceasing, so that the reservoirs had overflowed and the rationing had been abandoned. That had been an interesting novelty for the first week or so, each time, and then the unending downpours, the gray days and the rank smell of mildew, had become a bore. On the whole Lawler preferred drought: he was accustomed to it, at least.

Quillan said, "This place fascinates me. It's the strangest world I've ever known."

"I could say the same thing, I suppose."

"Have you traveled much? Around Hydros, I mean."

"I was on Thibeire Island once," Lawler said. "It came very close, floated up right out there in the harbor, and a bunch of us took a coracle over to it and spent the whole day there. I was fifteen, then. That's the only time I've been anywhere else." He gave Quillan a wary glance. "But you're a real traveler, I understand. They tell me you've seen quite a chunk of the galaxy in your day."

"Some," Quillan said. "Not all that much. I've been to seven worlds altogether. Eight, counting this one."

"That's seven more than I'll ever see."

"But now I've reached the end of the line."

"Yes," Lawler said. "That you certainly have."

Offworlders who came to live on Hydros were beyond Lawler's comprehension. Why did they do it? To let yourself be stuffed into a drop-capsule on Sunrise, next door in the sky just a dozen or so million kilometers away, and be flipped out into a landing orbit that would dump you down in the sea near one of the floating islands—knowing that you could never leave Hydros again? Since the Gillies refused to countenance the building of a spaceport anywhere on Hydros, coming here was strictly a one-way journey, and everyone out there understood that. But still they came—not many, but a steady trickle of them, choosing to live forever after as castaways on a shoreless shore, on a world without trees or flowers, birds or insects or green fields of grass, without furry animals or hooved ones—without ease, without comfort, without any of the benefits of modern technology, awash on the ceaseless tides, drifting from pole to pole and back again aboard islands made of wickerwork on a world fit only for creatures with fins or flippers.

Lawler had no idea why Quillan had wanted to come to Hydros, but it wasn't the thing you asked someone. A kind of penance, perhaps. An act of self-abnegation. Certainly it wasn't to perform church functions. The Church of All Worlds was a schismatic post-Papal Catholic sect without any adherents, so far as Lawler knew, anywhere on the planet. Nor did the priest seem to be here as a missionary. He had made no attempts to make converts since his arrival on Sorve, which was just as well, for religion had never been a matter of much interest among the islanders. "God is very far away from us on Sorve Island," Lawler's father had liked to say.

Quillan looked somber for a moment, as though contemplating the realities of his having stranded himself on Hydros for the rest of his days. Then he said, "You don't mind always staying in the same place? You don't ever get restless? Curious about the other islands?"

"Not really," Lawler said. "Thibeire was pretty much like Sorve, I thought. The same general layout, the same general feel. Only there was nobody there that I knew. If one place is just like another, why not stay in the place you know, among the people you've always lived with?" His eyes narrowed. "It's the other *worlds* I wonder about. The dry-land ones. Actual solid planets. I wonder what it's like to go and go for days and never see open water even once, to be on a hard surface all the time, not just an island but a whole huge continent where you can't see right across from one end of the place where you live to the other, an enormous land mass that has cities and mountains and rivers on it. Those are just empty words to me. Cities. Mountains. I'd like to know what trees are like, and birds, and plants that have flowers. I wonder about Earth, you know? I dream sometimes that it still exists, that I'm actually on it, breathing its air, feeling its soil under my feet. Getting it under my fingernails. There's no soil anywhere on Hydros, do you realize that? Only the sand of the sea bottom."

Lawler glanced quickly at the priest's hands, at his fingernails, as though they might still have the black dirt of Sunrise under them. Quillan's eyes followed Lawler's, and he smiled but said nothing.

Lawler said, "I overheard you talking last week with Delagard at the community center, about the planet you lived on before you came here, and

I still remember every word of what you said. How the land there seems to go on forever, first grassland and then a forest and then mountains and a desert on the far side of the mountains. And the whole time I sat there trying to imagine what all those things really looked like. But of course I'll never know. We can't get to other worlds from here, eh? For us they might just as well not exist. And since every place on Hydros is the same as every other place, I'm not inclined to go roaming."

"Indeed," said Quillan gravely. After a moment he added, "That isn't typical, is it, though?"

"Typical of whom?"

"The people who live on Hydros. Never traveling anywhere, I mean."

"A few of us are wanderers. They like to change islands every five or six years. Some aren't like that. Most aren't, I'd say. At any rate I'm one of the ones who isn't."

Quillan considered that.

"Indeed," he said again, as though processing some intricate datum. He appeared to have exhausted his run of questions for the moment. Some weighty conclusion seemed about to come forth.

Lawler watched him without great interest, politely waiting to hear what else Quillan might have to say.

But a long moment passed and Quillan still was silent. Evidently he had nothing further to say after all.

"Well," Lawler said, "time to open the shop, I guess."

He began to walk up the path toward the vaarghs.

"Wait," said Quillan.

Lawler turned and looked back at him. "Yes?"

"Are you all right, doctor?"

"Why? Do I look sick to you?"

"You look upset about something," Quillan said. "You don't often look that way. When I first met you, you struck me as a man who just lives his life, day by day, hour by hour, taking whatever comes in his stride. But somehow you look different this morning. That outburst of yours about other worlds—I don't know. It didn't seem like you. Of course I can't say that I actually know you."

Lawler gave the priest a guarded stare. He didn't feel like telling him about the three dead divers in the shed on Jolly's Pier.

"There were a few things on my mind last night. I didn't get much sleep. But I didn't realize it was so obvious."

"I'm good at seeing such things," said Quillan, smiling. His pale blue eyes, usually remote and even veiled, seemed unusually penetrating just then. "It doesn't take much. Listen, Lawler, if you'd like to talk to me about anything—anything at all, any time, just get things off your chest—"

Lawler grinned and indicated his chest, which was bare.

"Plainly there's nothing on it, is there?"

"You know what I mean," Quillan said.

For a moment something seemed to be passing between them, a crackling sort of tension, a linkage that Lawler neither desired nor enjoyed. Then the priest smiled again, genially, too genially, a deliberately bland, vague, benign smile obviously intended to create distance between them. He held up one hand in what might have been a blessing or perhaps a dismissal, and nodded, and turned and walked away.

3

AS HE DREW NEAR HIS VAARGH LAWLER SAW THAT A WOMAN with long, straight dark hair was waiting for him outside. A patient, he supposed. She was facing away from him and he wasn't sure who she was. At least four women on Sorve had hair like that.

There were thirty vaarghs in the group where Lawler lived, and another sixty or so, not all of them inhabited, down near the tip of the island. They were irregular gray structures, asymmetrical but roughly pyramidal in shape, hollow within, twice the height of a tall man and tapering to a blunt drooping point. Near their summits they were pierced with window-like openings, angled outward so that rain would enter only in the most driving of storms, and then with difficulty. Some kind of thick, rugged cellulose, puckered and coarse—something drawn from the sea; where else but from the sea?—was what they had been made from, evidently very long ago. The stuff was remarkably solid and durable. If you struck a vaargh with a stick, it rang like a metal bell. The first settlers had found them already here when they arrived and had put them to use as temporary housing; but that had been more than a hundred years before, and the islanders were still living in them. Nobody knew why they were here. There were clusters of vaarghs on nearly every island: the abandoned nests, perhaps, of some extinct creature that once had shared the islands with the Gillies. The Gillies lived in dwellings of an entirely different nature, casual seaweed shelters that they discarded and replaced every few weeks, whereas these things seemed as close to imperishable as anything was on this watery world. "What are they?" the early settlers had asked, and the Gillies had replied, simply, "They are vaarghs." What "vaarghs" meant was anybody's guess. Communicating with the Gillies, even now, was a haphazard business.

When Lawler came closer he saw that the woman waiting for him was Sundira Thane. Like the priest, she too was a newcomer to Sorve, a tall, serious young woman who had arrived from Kentrup Island a few months before as a passenger aboard one of Delagard's ships. Her profession was maintenance and repair—boats, nets, equipment, anything—but her real field of interest seemed to be the Hydrans. Lawler had heard she was an expert on their culture, their biology, all aspects of their life.

"Am I too early?" she asked.

"Not if you don't think you are. Come in." The entrance to Lawler's vaargh was a low triangular gash in the wall, like a doorway for gnomes. He crouched and shuffled through it. She came crouching and shuffling after him. She was nearly as tall as he was. She seemed tense, withdrawn, preoccupied.

Pale morning light came slanting into the vaargh. At ground level thin partitions made of the same material as the exterior divided it into three rooms, each small and sharp-angled—his medical office, his bedchamber, and an antechamber that he used as a sitting-room.

It was still only about seven in the morning. Lawler was getting hungry. Breakfast would have to wait a while longer, he realized. But he casually shook a few drops of numbweed tincture into a mug, added a little water, and sipped it as though it were nothing but some medicine he prescribed for his own use every morning. In a way it was. Lawler gave her a quick guilty look. She wasn't paying any attention at all to what he was doing, though. She was looking at his little collection of artifacts from Earth. Everyone who came here did. Gingerly she ran her finger along the jagged edge of the little orange-and-black potsherd, then looked back questioningly over her shoulder at Lawler. He smiled. "It came from a place called Greece," he said. "A very famous place on Earth very long ago."

The drug's powerful alkaloids had completed their swift circuit of his bloodstream almost at once and entered his brain. He felt the tensions of the dawn encounters ebbing from his spirit.

"I've been coughing," Thane said. "It won't stop."

And virtually on cue she broke into a volley of rough, hacking rasps. On

Hydros a cough might be as trivial a thing as it was anywhere else; but it might also be something serious. All the islanders knew that.

There was a parasitic waterborne fungus, usually found in northern temperate waters, which reproduced by infesting various forms of marine life with the spores that it released into the atmosphere in dense black clouds. A spore, when inhaled by some aquatic mammal as it came to the surface to breathe, lodged in its host's warm gullet and sprouted immediately, sending forth a dense tangle of bright red hyphae that had no difficulty penetrating lungs, intestines, stomach, even brain tissue. The host's interior became a tightly packed mass of vivid scarlet wires. The wires were looking for the copper-based respiratory pigment, hemocyanin. Most of the sea creatures of Hydros had hemocyanin in their blood, which gave it a bluish color. The fungus seemed to have some use for hemocyanin, too.

Death by fungus infestation was slow and horrible. The host, bloated with gases excreted by the invader and floating helplessly, would eventually succumb, and soon after that the fungus would extrude its mature fruiting structure through an opening it had carved in the host's abdomen. This was a globular woody mass that shortly would split apart to release the new generation of adult fungi, which in the course of time would produce fresh clouds of spores, and so the cycle went.

Killer-fungus spores were capable of taking root in human lungs, a situation of no value to either party: humans were unable to provide the fungus with the hemocyanin it desired and the fungus found it necessary to invade and consume every region of the host's body during the course of its search, a useless expenditure of energy.

The first symptom of fungus infestation in a human was a cough that refused to go away.

"Let's get a little information about you," Lawler said. "And then we'll check this thing out."

He took a fresh records folder from a drawer and scrawled Sundira Thane's name on it.

"Your age?" he asked.

"Thirty-one."

"Birthplace?"

"Khamsilaine Island."

He glanced up. "That's on Hydros?"

"Yes," she said, a little too irritably. "Of course." Another siege of coughing took her. "You've never heard of Khamsilaine?" she asked, when she could speak again.

"There are a lot of islands. I don't get around much. I've never heard of it, no. What sea does it move in?"

"The Azure."

"The Azure," Lawler said, marveling. He had only the haziest idea where the Azure Sea might be. "Imagine that. You've really covered some territory, haven't you?" She offered no reply. He said, after a moment, "You came here from Kentrup a little while back, is that right?"

"Yes." More coughing.

"How long did you live there?"

"Three years."

"And before that?"

"Eighteen months on Velmise. Two years on Shaktan. About a year on Simbalimak." She looked at him coldly and said, "Simbalimak's in the Azure Sea also."

"I've heard of Simbalimak," he said.

"Before that, Khamsilaine. So this is my sixth island."

Lawler made a note of that.

"Ever married?"

"No."

He noted that down too. The general distaste for marrying within one's own island's population had led to a custom of unofficial exogamy on Hydros. Single people looking to get married usually moved to some other island to find a mate. When a woman as attractive as Sundira Thane had done as much moving around as she had without ever marrying anyone, it meant either that she was very particular or else that she wasn't looking at all.

Lawler suspected that she simply wasn't looking. The only man he had noticed her spending time with, in her few months on Sorve, was Gabe Kinverson, the fisherman. The moody, untalkative, crag-faced Kinverson was strong and rugged and, Lawler supposed, interesting in an animal sort of way, but he wasn't the kind of man that Lawler imagined a woman like Sundira Thane would want to marry, assuming that marriage was what she was after. And in any case Kinverson had never been the marrying sort himself.

"When did this coughing start?" he asked.

"Eight, ten days ago. Around the time of the last Night of Three Moons, I'd say."

"You ever experience anything like it before?"

"No, never."

"Fever, pains in the chest, chilly sensations?"

"No."

"Does any sputum come up when you cough? Or blood?"

"Sputum? Fluid, do you mean? No, there hasn't been any sort of—"

She went into yet another coughing fit, the worst one yet. Her eyes grew watery, her cheeks reddened, her whole body seemed to shake. Afterward she sat with her head bowed forward between her shoulders, looking weary and miserable.

Lawler waited for her to catch her breath.

She said finally, "We haven't been in the latitudes where killer fungus grows. I keep telling myself that."

"That doesn't signify, you know. The spores travel thousands of kilometers on the wind."

"Thanks a lot."

"You don't seriously think you've got killer fungus, do you?"

She looked up, almost glaring at him. "Do I know? I might be full of red wires from my chest to my toes, and how would I be able to tell? All I know is that I can't stop coughing. You're the one who can tell me why."

"Maybe," Lawler said. "Maybe not. But let's have a look. Get your shirt off."

He drew his stethoscope from a drawer.

It was a preposterously crude instrument, nothing more than a cylinder of sea-bamboo twenty centimeters long to which a pair of plastic earpieces at the ends of two flexible tubes had been affixed. Lawler had next to nothing in the way of modern medical equipment at his service, scarcely anything, in fact, that a doctor even of the twentieth or twenty-first century would have regarded as modern. He had to make do with primitive things, medieval equipment. An X-ray scan could have told him in a couple of seconds whether she had a fungus infestation. But where would he get an X-ray scanner? On Hydros there was so little contact with the greater universe beyond the sky, and no import-export trade whatever. They were lucky to have any medical equipment here at all. Or any doctors, even half-baked ones like him. The human settlement here was inherently impoverished. There were so few people, such a shallow reservoir of skills.

Stripped to the waist, she stood beside his examining table, watching him as he slipped the stethoscope's collar around his neck. She was very slender, almost too thin; her arms were long, muscular the way a thin woman's arms are muscular, with flat, hard little muscles; her breasts were small and high and far apart. Her features were compressed in the center of her wide strong-boned face, small mouth, thin lips, narrow nose, cool gray eyes. Lawler wondered why he had thought she was attractive. Certainly there was nothing conventionally pretty about her. It's the way she carries herself, he decided: the head thrust forward a little atop the long neck, the strong jaw outthrust, the eyes quick, alert, busy. She seemed vigorous, even aggressive. To his surprise he found himself aroused by her, not because her body was half bare—there was nothing uncommon about nudity, partial or otherwise, on Sorve Island—but because of the vitality and strength she projected.

It was a long time since he had been involved in any way with any woman. These days the celibate life seemed ever so much the simplest way, free of pain and mess once you got past the initial feelings of isolation and bleakness, if you could, and he eventually had. He had never had much luck with liaisons, anyway. His one marriage, when he was twenty-three, had lasted less than a year. Everything that had followed had been fragmentary, casual, incidental. Pointless, really.

The little flurry of endocrine excitement passed quickly. In a moment he was professional again, Dr. Lawler making an examination.

He said, "Open your mouth, very very wide."

"There isn't all that much to open."

"Well, do your best."

She gaped at him. He had a little tube with a light on it, something handed down to him by his father; the tiny battery had to be recharged every few days. He put it down her throat and peered through it.

"Am I full of red wires?" she asked, when he withdrew it.

"Doesn't look that way. All I see is a little soreness in the vicinity of the epiglottis, nothing very unusual."

"What's the epiglottis?"

"The flap that guards your glottis. Don't worry about it."

He put the stethoscope's end against her sternum and listened.

"Can you hear the wires growing in there?"

"Shh."

Lawler moved the cylinder slowly around in the hard, flat area between her breasts, listening to her heart, and then out along the rib cage.

"I'm trying to pick up audible evidence of inflammation of the pericardium," he told her. "Which is the sac surrounding the heart. I'm also listening for the sounds produced in the air tubes and sacs of your lungs. Take a deep breath and hold it. Try not to cough."

Instantly, unsurprisingly, she began to cough. Lawler held the stethoscope to her as the coughing went on and on. Any information was information. Eventually the coughing stopped, leaving her red-faced and weary again.

"Sorry," she said. "It was like when you said, Don't cough, that it was a signal of some kind to my brain and I—"

She began to cough again.

"Easy," he said. "Easy."

This time the attack was shorter. He listened, nodded, listened again. Everything sounded normal.

But he had never had a case of killer-fungus infestation to handle. All Lawler knew about it was what he had heard from his father long ago or learned by talking to doctors on other islands. Would the stethoscope really be able to tell him, he wondered, what might or might not have taken up residence in her lungs?

"Turn around," he said.

He listened to the sounds of her back. He had her raise her arms and pressed his fingers against her sides, feeling for alien growths. She wriggled as though he were tickling her. He drew a blood sample from her arm, and sent her behind the screen in the corner of the room to give him a urine specimen. Lawler had a microscope of sorts, which Sweyner the toolmaker had fashioned for him. It had no more resolution than a toy, but perhaps if there were something living within her he would be able to see it anyway.

He knew so little, really.

His patients were a daily reproach to his skills. Much of the time he simply had to bluff his way. His medical knowledge was a feeble mix of hand-me-downs from his eminent father, desperate guesswork, and hard-won experience, gradually accumulated at his patients' expense. Lawler had been only halfway through his medical education when his father died and he, at not quite twenty, found himself doctor to the island of Sorve.

Nowhere on Hydros was there real medical training to be had, or anything that could remotely be considered a modern medical instrument, or any medicines other than those he could compound himself out of marine life-forms, imagination, and prayers. In his late and great father's time some charitable organization on Sunrise had dropped packages of medical supplies once in a while, but the packages were few and far between and they had to be shared among many islands. And they had stopped coming long ago. The inhabited galaxy was very large; nobody thought much about the people living on Hydros any more. Lawler did his best, but his best often wasn't good enough. When he had the chance, he consulted with doctors on other islands, hoping to learn something from them. Their medical skills were just as muddy as his, but he had learned that sometimes by exchanging ignorances with them he could generate a little spark of understanding. Sometimes.

"You can put your shirt back on," Lawler said.

"Is it the fungus, do you think?"

"All it is is a nervous cough," he told her. He had the blood sample on the glass slide, now, and was peering at it through the single eyepiece. What was that, red on red? Could they be scarlet mycelial fibers coiling through the crimson haze? No. No. A trick of his eye. This was normal blood. "You're perfectly all right," he said, looking up. She was still bare-breasted, her shirt over her skinny arm, frozen in suspense. Her expression was a suspicious one. "Why do you need to think you've got a horrible disease?" Lawler asked. "All it is is a cough."

"I need to think I *don't* have a horrible disease. That's why I came to you."

"Well, you don't." He hoped to God he was right. There was no real reason to think he wasn't.

He watched her as she dressed, and found himself wondering whether there might actually be something going on between her and Gabe Kinverson. Lawler, who had little interest in island gossip, hadn't considered that possibility before, and, considering it now, he was startled to observe how uncomfortable he was with it.

He said, "Have you been under any unusual stress lately?"

"Not that I'm aware of, no."

"Working too hard? Sleeping badly? Love affair that isn't going well?"

She shot him a peculiar look. "No. On all three."

"Well, sometimes we get stressed out and we don't even notice it. The stress becomes built in, part of our routine. What I'm saying is that I think this is a nervous cough."

"That's all?" She sounded disappointed.

"You *want* it to be a killer-fungus infestation? All right, it's a killer-fungus infestation. When you reach the stage where the wiry red threads are coming out your ears, cover your head in a sack so you don't upset your neighbors. They might think they were at risk, otherwise. But of course they won't be, not until you begin giving off spores, and that'll come much later."

She laughed. "I didn't know you were such a comedian."

"I'm not." Lawler took her hand in his, wondering whether he was trying to be provocative or simply being avuncular, his Good Old Doc Lawler persona. "Listen," he said, "I can't find anything wrong with you physically. So the odds are the cough is just a nervous habit you picked up somehow. Once you start doing it, you irritate the throat linings, the mucosa and such, and the cough starts feeding on itself and gets worse and worse. Eventually it'll go away of its own, but eventually can be a long time. What I'm going to give you is a neural damper, a tranquilizer drug, something to calm your cough reflex down long enough to let the mechanical irritation subside, so that you'll stop sending cough signals to yourself."

That came as a surprise to him too, that he would share the numbweed with her. He had never said a word about it to anyone, let alone prescribed it for a patient. But giving her the drug seemed to be the right thing to do. He had enough to spare.

He took a small dry storage gourd from his cabinet, poured a couple of centiliters of the pink fluid into it, and capped it with a twist of sea-plastic.

"This is a drug I derived myself from numbweed, which is one of the algae that grows in the lagoon. Give yourself five or six drops of it every morning, no more, in a glass of water. It's strong stuff." He studied her with a close, searching look. "The plant is full of potent alkaloids that could knock you for a loop. Just nibble one little frond of it and you'd be unconscious for a week. Or maybe forever. This is a highly diluted extract, but be careful with it anyway."

"You had a little of it yourself, didn't you, right when we first came in here?"

So she'd been paying attention after all. Quick eyes, a sharp observer. Interesting.

"I get nervous too now and then," Lawler said.

THE FACE OF THE WATERS

"Do I make you nervous?"

"All my patients do. I don't really know much about medicine, and I'd hate for them to find that out." He forced a laugh. "No, that isn't true. I don't know as much about medicine as I should, but I know enough to manage. But I find that the drug calms me when I'm not having a good morning, and today didn't start off particularly well for me. It had nothing to do with you. Here, you might as well take your first dose right now."

He measured it out for her. She sipped carefully, uneasily, and made a wry face as the curious sweet taste of the alkaloids registered on her.

"You feel the effect?" Lawler asked.

"Right away! Hey, good stuff!"

"Too good, maybe. A little insidious." He made notes on her dossier. "Five drops in a glass of water every morning, no more, and you don't get a refill until the first of the month."

"Aye, aye, sir!"

Her entire facial expression had changed; she looked much more relaxed now, the cool gray eyes warmer, almost twinkling, the lips not so tightly pursed, the tense cheek muscles allowed a little slack. She looked younger. She looked prettier. Lawler had never had a chance before to observe the effects of numbweed on anyone else. They were unexpectedly dramatic.

She said, "How did you discover this drug?"

"The Gillies use numbweed as a muscle relaxant when they're hunting meatfish in the bay."

"The Dwellers, you mean?"

The prissy correction caught Lawler by surprise. "Dwellers" was what the dominant native life-forms of Hydros called themselves. But "Gillies" was what anyone who had been on Hydros more than a few months called them, at least around here. Maybe the usage was different on the island where she was from, he thought, off in the Azure Sea. Or perhaps it was what the younger people were saying now. Usages changed. He reminded himself that he was ten years older than she was. But most likely she used the formal term out of respect, because she fancied herself a student of Gillie culture. What the hell: whichever way she liked it, he'd try to be accommodating.

"The Dwellers, yes," he said. "They tear off a couple of strands and wrap them around a chunk of bait and toss it to the meatfish, and when the meatfish swallow them they go limp and float helplessly to the surface. Then the Dwellers move in and harvest them without having to worry about those knifeblade-tipped tentacles. An old sailor named Jolly told me about it when I was a boy. Later on I remembered it and went out to the harbor and watched them doing it. And collected some of the weed and experimented with it. I thought I might be able to use it as an anesthetic."

"And could you?"

"For meatfish, yes. I don't do much surgery on meatfish, though. What I found when I used it on humans was that any dose that was strong enough to be any good as an anesthetic also turned out to be lethal." Lawler smiled grimly. "My trial-and-error period as a surgeon. Mostly error. But I eventually discovered that an extremely dilute tincture was an extremely potent tranquilizer. As you now see. It's terrific stuff. We could market it throughout the galaxy, if we had any way of shipping anything anywhere."

"And nobody knows about this drug but you?"

"And the Gillies," he said. "Pardon me. The Dwellers. And now you. I don't get much call for tranquilizers here." Lawler chuckled. "You know, I woke up this morning with some wild notion of trying to talk the Dwellers into letting us tack water-desalinization equipment onto their new power plant, if they ever get it going. Giving them a long heartfelt number about interspecies collaboration. It was a dumb idea, the sort of thing that comes to you in the night and goes away like mist when the sun rises. They'd never have gone for it. But what I really ought to do is mix up a big batch of numbweed and get them good and plastered on it. They'll let us do anything we want then, I bet."

She didn't look amused.

"You're joking, aren't you?"

"I suppose I am."

"If you aren't, don't even think of trying it, because you won't get anywhere. This is no time for asking the Dwellers for favors. They're pretty seriously annoyed with us."

"What about?" Lawler asked.

"I don't know. But something's definitely making them itchy. I went down to their end of the island last night and they were having a big conference. When they saw me, they weren't at all friendly."

"Are they ever?"

"With me they are. But they wouldn't even talk with me last night. They wouldn't let me near them. And they were holding themselves in the posture of displeasure. You know anything about Dweller body language? They were stiff as boards."

The divers, he thought. They must know about the divers. That has to be it. But it wasn't something that Lawler wanted to discuss right now, not with her, not with anyone.

"The thing about aliens," he said, "is that they're *alien*. Even when we think we understand them, we really don't understand a damned thing. And I don't see any way around that problem. Listen, if the cough doesn't go away in two or three days, come back here and I'll run some more tests. But stop fretting about killer fungus in your lungs, okay? Whatever it is, it isn't that."

"That's good to hear," she said. She went over to the shelf of artifacts again. "Are all these little things from Earth?"

"Yes. My great-great-grandfather collected them."

"Really? Actual Earth things?" Gingerly she touched the Egyptian statuette and the bit of stone that had come from some important wall, Lawler forgot where. "Actual things that came from Earth. I've never seen any before. Earth doesn't even seem real to me, you know? It never has."

"It does to me," Lawler said. "But I know a lot of people who feel the way you do. Let me know about that cough, okay?"

She thanked him and went out.

AND NOW FOR BREAKFAST, LAWLER TOLD HIMSELF. FINALLY. A NICE whipfish filet, and algae toast, and some freshly squeezed managordo juice.

But he had waited too long. He didn't have much appetite, and he simply nibbled at his meal.

A little while later a second patient appeared outside the vaargh. Brondo Katzin, who ran the island's fish market, had picked up a not-quite-dead arrowfish the wrong way and had a thick, glossy black spine five centimeters long sticking right through the middle of his left hand from one side to the other. "Imagine, being so dumb," the barrel-chested, slow-witted Katzin kept saying. "Imagine." His eyes were bugging with pain and his hand, swollen and glossy, looked twice its normal size. Lawler cut the spine loose, swabbed the wound all the way through to get the poison and other irritants out, and gave the fish-market man some gemberweed pills to ease the pain. Katzin stared at his puffed-up hand, ruefully shaking his head. "So dumb," he said again.

Lawler hoped that he had cleaned out enough of the trichomes to keep the wound from getting infected. If he hadn't, there was a good chance Katzin would lose the hand, or the whole arm. Practicing medicine was probably easier, Lawler thought, on a planet that had some land surface, and a spaceport, and something in the way of contemporary technology. But he did his best with what he had. Heigh-ho! The day was under way.

4

*A*T MIDDAY LAWLER CAME OUT OF HIS VAARGH TO TAKE A LITTLE break from his work. This had been his busiest morning in months. On an island with a total human population of just seventy-eight, most of them pretty healthy, Lawler sometimes went through whole days, or even longer, without seeing a single patient. On such days he might spend the morning wading in the bay, collecting algae of medicinal value. Natim Gharkid often helped him, pointing out this or that useful plant. Or sometimes he did nothing at all, strolled or swam or went out on the bay in a fishing boat or sat quietly watching the sea. But this wasn't one of those days. First there was Dana Sawtelle's little boy with a fever, then Marya Hain with cramps after eating too many crawlie-oysters last night, Nimber Tanamind suffering from a recurrence of his usual tremors and megrims, young Bard Thalheim with a badly sprained ankle as a result of some unwise hijinks on the slippery side of the sea-wall. Lawler uttered the appropriate spells and applied the most likely ointments and sent them all away with the customary reassurances and prognostications. Most likely they'd feel better in a day or so. The current Dr. Lawler might not be much of a practitioner, but Dr. Placebo, his invisible assistant, generally managed to take care of the patients' problems sooner or later.

Now, though, there was no one else waiting to see him and a little fresh air seemed like a good prescription for the doctor himself. Lawler stepped out into the bright noontime sun, stretched, did a few pinwheels with his extended arms. He peered downslope toward the waterfront. There was the bay, friendly and familiar, its calm enclosed waters rippling gently. It looked wonderfully beautiful just now: a glassy sheet of luminous gold, a glowing mirror. The dark fronds of the varied sea-flora waved lazily in the shallows. Farther out, occasional shining fins breached the glistening surface. A couple of Delagard's ships lolled by the shipyard pier, swaying gently to the rhythm of the easy tide. Lawler felt as though this moment of summer noon could go on forever, that night and winter would never come again. An unexpected feeling of peace and well-being infiltrated his soul: a gift, a bit of serendipitous joy.

"Lawler," a voice said from his left.

A dry frayed croak of a voice, a boneyard voice, a voice that was all ashes and rubble. It was a dismal burned-out unrecognizable wreck of a voice that Lawler recognized, somehow, as that of Nid Delagard.

He had come up along the southern path from the waterfront and was standing between Lawler's vaargh and the little tank where Lawler kept his current stock of freshly picked medicinal algae. He was flushed and rumpled and sweaty and his eyes looked strangely glassy, as though he had had a stroke.

"What the hell has happened now?" Lawler asked, exasperated.

Delagard made a wordless gaping movement with his mouth, like a fish out of water, and said nothing.

Lawler dug his fingers into the man's thick, meaty arm. "Can you speak? Come on, damn you. Tell me what's happened."

"Yeah. Yeah." Delagard moved his head from side to side in a slow, ponderous, poleaxed way. "It's very bad. It's worse than I ever imagined."

"What is?"

"Those fucking divers. The Gillies are really furious about them. And they're going to come down on us very hard. Very very *very* hard. It's what I was trying to tell you about this morning in the shed, when you walked out on me."

Lawler blinked a couple of times. "What in God's name are you talking about?"

"Give me some brandy first."

"Yeah. Yeah. Come inside."

He poured a strong jolt of the thick sea-colored liquor for Delagard, and, after a moment's consideration, a smaller drink for himself. Delagard put his away in a single gulp and held out the cup. Lawler poured again.

After a little while Delagard said, picking his way warily through his words as if struggling with some speech impediment, "The Gillies came to visit me just now, about a dozen of them. Walked right up out of the water down at the shipyard and asked my men to call me out for a talk."

Gillies? At the human end of the island? That hadn't happened in decades. Gillies never went farther south than the promontory where they had built their power plant. Never.

Delagard gave him a tortured look. " 'What do you want,' I said. Using the politest gestures, Lawler, everything very very courteous. I think the ones that were there were the big Gillie honchos, but how can you be sure? Who can tell one of them from the next? They looked important, anyway. They said, 'Are you Nid Delagard' as if they didn't know. And I said I was, and then they grabbed me."

"*Grabbed* you?"

"I mean, physically grabbed me. Put their little funny flippers on me. Pushed me up against the wall of my own building and restrained me."

"You're lucky you're still around to talk about it."

"No kidding. I tell you, doc, I was scared shitless. I thought they were going to gut me and filet me right there. Look, look here, the marks of their claws on my arm." He showed fading reddish spots. "My face is swollen, isn't it? I tried to pull my head away and one of them bumped me, maybe by accident, but look. Look. Two of them held me and a third one put his nose in my face and started telling me things, and I mean *telling* me, big booming noises, *ooom whang hoooof theeeezt, ooom whang hooof theeeezt.* At the beginning I was so shaken up I couldn't understand any of it. But then it came clear. They said it again and again until they made sure I understood. An ultimatum, it was." Delagard's voice dropped into a lower register. "We've been thrown off the island. We have thirty days to clear ourselves out of here. Every last one of us."

Abruptly Lawler felt the ground disappearing beneath his feet.

"*What?*"

The other man's hard little brown eyes had taken on a frantic glitter. He signaled for more brandy. Lawler poured without even looking at the cup. "Any human remaining on Sorve when the time's up will be tossed into the lagoon and not allowed back up on shore. Any structures we've erected here will be demolished. The reservoir, the shipyard, these buildings here in the plaza, everything. Things we leave behind in the vaarghs go into the sea. Any oceangoing vessels we leave in the harbor will be sunk. We are terminated, doc. We are ex-residents of Sorve Island. Finished, done for, gone."

Lawler stared, incredulous. A quick cycle of turbulent emotions ran through him: disorientation, depression, despair. Confusion assailed him. Leave Sorve? *Leave Sorve?*

He began to tremble. With an effort he got himself under control, fighting his way back to inner equilibrium.

Tightly he said, "Killing some divers in an industrial accident is definitely not a good thing to have done. But this is too much of an overreaction. You must have misunderstood what they were saying."

"Like shit I did. Not a chance. They made themselves very very clear."

"We all have to go?"

"We all have to go, yes. Thirty days."

Am I hearing him correctly? Lawler wondered. Is any of this really happening?

"And did they give a reason?" he asked. "Was it the divers?"

"Of course it was," Delagard said in a low husky voice clotted by shame. "It was just like you said this morning. The Gillies always know everything that we do."

"Christ. Christ." Anger was beginning to take the place of shock. Delagard had casually gambled with the lives of everyone on the island, and he had lost. The Gillies had warned him: *Don't ever do that again, or we'll throw you out of here.* And he had done it again anyway. "What a contemptible bastard you are, Delagard!"

"I don't know how they found out. I took precautions. We brought them in by night, we kept them covered until they were in the shed, the shed itself was locked—"

"But they knew."

"They knew," Delagard said. "They know everything, the Gillies. You screw somebody else's wife, the Gillies know about it. But they don't care. Not about that. You kill a couple of divers and they care like crazy."

"What did they tell you, the last time you had an accident with divers? When they warned you not to use divers again in your work, what did they say they'd do if they caught you?"

Delagard was silent.

"What did they tell you?" Lawler said again, pressing harder.

Delagard licked his lips. "That they'd make us leave Sorve," he mut-

tered, once again looking down at his feet like a schoolboy being repri-
manded.

"And you did it anyway. You did it anyway."

"Who would believe them? Jesus, Lawler, we've lived here for a hundred fifty years! Did they mind when we moved in? We dropped out of space
and squatted right down on their fucking islands and did they say, 'Go
away, hideous repellent four-limbed hairy alien beings?' No. No. They
didn't give a crap."

"There was Shalikomo," Lawler said.

"A long time ago, that was. Before either of us was born."

"The Gillies killed a lot of people on Shalikomo. Innocent people."

"Different Gillies. Different situation."

Delagard pressed his knuckles together and made a little popping
sound with them. His voice began to rise in pitch and volume. He seemed
very swiftly to be casting off the guilt and the shame that had engulfed him.
That was a knack he had, Lawler thought, the rapid restoration of his own
self-esteem. "Shalikomo's an exception," he said. The Gillies had thought
there were far too many humans on Shalikomo, which was a very small
island, and had told some of them to go; but the humans of Shalikomo had
been unable to agree on who should go and who could stay, and hardly
anyone left the island, and in the end the Gillies decided how many humans
they would allow to live there among themselves and killed the rest. "It's
ancient history," Delagard said.

"It was a long time ago, yes," said Lawler. "But what makes you think
it can't all happen again?"

Delagard said, "The Gillies have never been particularly hostile anywhere else. They don't *like* us, but they don't stop us from doing whatever
we want to do, so long as we stay down at our end of the island and don't get
too numerous. We harvest kelp, we fish as much as we like, we build
buildings, we hunt for meatfish, we do all sorts of things that aliens might
be expected to resent, and not a word out of them. So if I was able to train a
few divers to help me in ocean-floor metals recovery, which could only
benefit the Gillies as well as us, why do you suppose I would think that
they'd become so exercised over the death of a few animals in the line of
work that they—they would—"

"The last straw, maybe," Lawler said. "The one that broke the camel's
back."

"Huh? What the fuck are you saying?"

"Ancient Earth proverb. Never mind. What I'm saying is that for whatever reason, the diver thing pushed them over the edge and now they want us out of here."

Lawler closed his eyes a moment. He imagined himself packing up his things, getting aboard a boat bound for some other island. It wasn't easy.

We are going to have to leave Sorve. We are going to have to leave Sorve. We are going to—

He realized that Delagard was talking.

"It was a stunner, let me tell you. I never expected it. Standing there up against the wall with two big Gillies holding my arms and another one smack up in front of my nose saying, *You all have to clear out in thirty days, you will vanish from this island or else.* How do you think I felt about that, doc? Especially knowing I was the one responsible for it. You said this morning I didn't have any conscience, but you don't know a damned thing about me. You think I'm a boor and a lout and a criminal, but what do you know, anyway? You hide away in here by yourself and drink yourself silly and sit there judging other people who have more energy and ambition in one finger than you have in your entire—"

"Knock it off, Delagard."

"You said I had no conscience."

"Do you?"

"Let me tell you, Lawler, I feel like shit, bringing this thing down on us. I was born here too, you know. You don't have to give me any snot-nose condescending First Family stuff, not me. My family's been here from the beginning just like yours. We practically built this island, we Delagards. And now to hear that I'm being tossed out like a bunch of rotten meat, and that everyone else has to go too—" The tone of Delagard's voice changed yet again. The anger melted; he spoke more softly, earnestly, sounding almost humble. "I want you to know that I'll take full responsibility for what I've done. What I'm going to do is—"

"Hold it," Lawler said, raising one hand to cut him off. "You hear noise?"

"Noise? What noise? Where?"

Lawler inclined his head toward the door. Sudden shouts, harsh cries, were coming from the long three-sided plaza that separated the island's two groups of vaarghs.

Delagard said, nodding, "Yeah, now I hear it. An accident, maybe?"

But Lawler was already moving, out the door, heading for the plaza at a quick loping trot.

THERE WERE THREE WEATHERBEATEN BUILDINGS—SHACKS, REALLY, shanties, bedraggled lean-tos—on the plaza, one on each side of it. The biggest, along the upland side, was the island school. On the nearer of the two downslope sides was the little café that Lis Niklaus, Delagard's woman, ran. Beyond it was the community center.

A small knot of murmuring children stood outside the school, with their two teachers. In front of the community center half a dozen of the older men and women were drifting about in a random, sunstruck way, moving in a ragged circle. Lis Niklaus had emerged from her café and was staring openmouthed at nothing in particular. On the far side were two of Delagard's captains, squat, blocky Gospo Struvin and lean, long-legged Bamber Cadrell. They were at the head of the ramp that led into the plaza from the waterfront, holding on to the railing like men expecting an immediate tidal surge to strike. Between them, bisecting the plaza with his mass, the hulking fish merchant Brondo Katzin stood like a huge stupefied beast, gazing fixedly at his unbandaged right hand as though it had just sprouted an eye.

There was no sign of any accident, any victim.

"What's going on?" Lawler asked.

Lis Niklaus turned toward him in a curiously monolithic way, swinging her entire body around. She was a tall, fleshy, robust woman with a great tangle of yellow hair and skin so deeply tanned that it looked almost black. Delagard had been living with her for five or six years, ever since the death of his wife, but he hadn't married her. Perhaps he was trying to protect his sons' inheritance, people supposed. Delagard had four grown sons, living on other islands, each of them on a different one.

She said hoarsely, sounding half strangled, "Bamber and Gospo just came up from the shipyard—they say the Gillies were here—that they said—they told us—they told Nid—"

Her voice trailed off in an incoherent sputter.

Shriveled little Mendy Tanamind, Nimber's ancient mother, said in a piping tone, "We have to leave! We have to leave!" She giggled shrilly.

"Nothing funny about it," Sandor Thalheim said. He was just as ancient as Mendy. He shook his head vehemently, making his dewlaps and wattles tremble.

"All because of a few animals," Bamber Cadrell said. "Because of three dead divers."

So the news was out already. Too bad, Lawler thought. Delagard's men should have kept their mouths shut until we figured out a way to handle this.

Someone sobbed. Mendy Tanamind giggled again. Brondo Katzin broke from his stasis and began bitterly to mutter, over and over, "The fucking stinking Gillies! The fucking stinking Gillies!"

"What's the trouble here?" Delagard asked, finally coming stumping up along the path from Lawler's vaargh.

"Your boys Bamber and Gospo took it upon themselves to carry the news," Lawler said. "Everybody knows."

"What? What? The bastards! I'll kill them!"

"It's a little too late for that."

Others were entering the plaza now. Lawler saw Gabe Kinverson, Sundira Thane, Father Quillan, the Sweyners. And more right behind them. They came crowding in, forty, fifty, sixty people, practically everybody. Even five or six of the Sisters were there, standing close together, a tight little female phalanx. Safety in numbers. Dag Tharp appeared. Marya and Gren Hain. Josc Yanez, Lawler's seventeen-year-old apprentice, who was going to be the island's next doctor someday. Onyos Felk, the mapkeeper. Natim Gharkid had come up from his algae beds, his trousers soaked to the waist. The news must have traveled through the whole community by this time.

Mostly their faces showed shock, astonishment, incredulity. Is it true? they were asking. Can it be?

Delagard cried out, "Listen, all of you, there's nothing to worry about! We're going to get this thing smoothed over!"

Gabe Kinverson came up to Delagard. He looked twice as tall as the shipyard owner, a great slab of a man, all jutting chin and massive shoulders and cold, glaring sea-green eyes. There was always an aura of danger about Kinverson, of potential violence.

"They threw us out?" Kinverson asked. "They really said we had to leave?"

Delagard nodded.

"Thirty days is what we have, and then out. They made that very clear. They don't care where we go, but we can't stay here. I'm going to fix everything, though. You can count on that."

"Seems to me you've fixed everything already," Kinverson said. Delagard moved back a step and glared at Kinverson as if bracing for a fight. But the sea-hunter seemed more perplexed than angry. "Thirty days and then get out," Kinverson said, half to himself. "If that don't beat everything." He turned his back on Delagard and walked away, scratching his head.

Perhaps Kinverson really didn't care, Lawler thought. He spent most of his time far out at sea anyway, by himself, preying on the kinds of fish that didn't choose to come into the bay. Kinverson had never been active in the life of the Sorve community; he floated through it the way the islands of Hydros drifted in the ocean, aloof, independent, well defended, following some private course.

But others were more agitated. Brondo Katzin's delicate-looking little golden-haired wife Eliyana was sobbing wildly. Father Quillan attempted to comfort her, but he was obviously upset himself. The gnarled old Sweyners were talking to each other in low, intense tones. A few of the younger women were trying to explain things to their worried-looking children. Lis Niklaus had brought a jug of grapeweed brandy out of her café and it was passing rapidly from hand to hand among the men, who were gulping from it in a somber, desperate way.

Lawler said quietly to Delagard, "How exactly are you going to deal with all this? You have some sort of plan?"

"I do," Delagard said. Suddenly he was full of frenetic energy. "I told you I'd take full responsibility, and I meant it. I'll go back to the Gillies on my knees, and if I have to lick their hind flippers I will, and I'll beg for forgiveness. They'll come around, sooner or later. They won't actually hold us to this goddamned absurd ultimatum."

"I admire your optimism."

Delagard went on, "And if they won't back off, I'll volunteer to go into exile myself. Don't punish everyone, I'll tell them. Just me. I'm the guilty one. I'll move to Velmise or Salimil or anyplace you like, and you'll never see my ugly face on Sorve again, that's a promise. It'll work, Lawler. They're reasonable beings. They'll understand that tossing an old lady like Mendy here off the island that's been her home for eighty years isn't going to serve any rational purpose. I'm the bastard, I'm the murderous diver-killing villain, and I'll go if I have to, though I don't even think it'll come down to that."

"You may be right. Maybe not."

"I'll crawl before them if I have to."

"And you'll bring one of your sons over from Velmise to run the shipyard if they make you leave here, won't you?"

Delagard looked startled. "Well, what's wrong with that?"

"They might think you weren't all that sincere about agreeing to leave. They might think one Delagard was the same as the next."

"You say it might not be good enough for them if I'm the only one to go?"

"That's exactly what I'm saying. They might want something more than that from you."

"Like what?"

"What if they told you they'd pardon the rest of us provided you left and agreed that you *and* your family would never set foot on Sorve again, and that the entire Delagard shipyard would be torn down?"

Delagard's eyes grew very bright. "No," he said. "They wouldn't ask that!"

"They already have. And more."

"But if I go, if I really go—if my sons pledge never to harm a diver again—"

Lawler turned away from him.

For Lawler the first shock was past; the simple phrase *We are going to have to leave Sorve* had incorporated itself in his mind, his soul, his bones. He was taking it very calmly, all things considered. He wondered why. Between one moment and the next the existence on this island that he had spent his entire life constructing had been yanked from his grasp.

He remembered the time he had gone to Thibeire. How deeply disquieting it had been to see all those unfamiliar faces, to be unaware of names and personal histories, to walk down a path and not know what lay at the end of it. He had been glad to come home, after just a few hours.

And now he would have to go somewhere else and stay there for the rest of his life; he would have to live among strangers; he would lose all sense that he was a Lawler of Sorve Island and would become just anybody, a newcomer, an off-islander, intruding in some new community where he had no place and no purpose. That should have been a hard thing to swallow.

And yet after that first moment of terrifying instability and disorientation he had settled somehow into a kind of numbed acceptance, as though he were as indifferent to the eviction as Gabe Kinverson seemed to be, or Gharkid, that perversely free-floating man. Strange. Maybe it simply hasn't sunk in yet, Lawler told himself.

Sundira Thane came up to him. She was flushed and there was a sheen of perspiration on her forehead. Her whole posture was one of excitement and a kind of fierce self-satisfaction.

"I told you they were annoyed with us, didn't I? Didn't I? Looks like I was right."

"So you were," Lawler said.

She studied him for a moment. "We're really going to have to leave. I don't have the slightest doubt of it." Her eyes flashed brilliantly. She seemed to be glorying in all this, almost intoxicated by it. Lawler remembered that this was the sixth island she had lived on so far, at the age of thirty-one. She didn't mind moving around. She might even enjoy it.

He nodded slowly. "Why are you so sure of that?"

"Because Dwellers don't ever change their minds. When they say something they stick to it. And killing divers seems to be a more serious thing to them than killing meatfish or bangers. The Dwellers don't mind our going out into the bay and hunting for food. They eat meatfish themselves. But the divers are, well, different. The Dwellers feel very protective toward them."

"Yes," Lawler said. "I guess they do."

She stared straight into his eyes. She was nearly on eye-level with him. "You've lived here a long time, haven't you, Lawler?"

"All my life."

"Oh. I'm sorry. This is going to be rough for you."

"I'll deal with it," he said. "Every island can use another doctor. Even a half-baked doctor like me." He laughed. "Listen, how's that cough doing?"

"I haven't coughed once since you gave me that dope."

"I didn't think you would."

Delagard suddenly was at Lawler's elbow again. Without apologizing for breaking in on his conversation with Sundira, he said, "Will you come with me to the Gillies, doc?"

"What for?"

"They know you. They respect you. You're your father's son and that gives you points with them. They think of you as a serious and honorable man. If I have to promise to leave the island, you can vouch for me, that I mean it when I say I'll go away and never come back."

"They'll believe you without my help, if you tell them that. They don't expect any intelligent being to tell lies, even you. But that still won't change anything."

"Come with me all the same, Lawler."

"It's a waste of time. What we need to be doing is starting to plan the evacuation."

"Let's try it, at least. We can't be sure if we don't try."

Lawler considered that. "Right now?"

"After dark," Delagard said. "They don't want to see any of us now. They're too busy celebrating the opening of the new power plant. They got it going about two hours ago, you know. They've got a cable running from the waterfront to their end of the island and it's carrying juice."

"Good for them."

"I'll meet you down by the sea-wall at sunset, all right? And we'll go and talk to them together. Will you do that, Lawler?"

IN THE AFTERNOON LAWLER SAT QUIETLY IN HIS VAARGH, TRYING TO comprehend what it would mean to have to leave the island, working at the concept, worrying at it. No patients came to see him. Delagard, true to his promise of the early morning, had sent some flasks of grapeweed brandy over, and Lawler drank a little, and then a little more, without any particular effect. Lawler thought of allowing himself another dose of his tranquilizer, but somehow that seemed not to be a good idea. He was tranquil enough as it was, right now: what he felt wasn't his usual restlessness, but rather a sodden dullness of spirit, a heavy weight of depression, for which the pink drops weren't likely to be of any use.

I am going to leave Sorve Island, he thought.

I am going to live somewhere else, on an island I don't know, among people whose names and ancestries and inner natures are absolute mysteries to me.

He told himself that it was all right, that in a few months he'd feel just as much at home on Thibeire, or Velmise, or Kaggeram, or whatever island it was that he ultimately settled on, as he did on Sorve. He knew that that wasn't true, but that was what he told himself all the same.

Resignation seemed to help. Acceptance, even indifference. The trouble was that he couldn't stay on that numbed-down level consistently. From time to time a sudden flare of shock and bewilderment would hit him, a sense of intolerable loss, even of out-and-out fear. And then he had to start all over again.

When it began to grow dark Lawler left his vaargh and headed down to the sea-wall.

Two moons had risen, and a faint sliver of Sunrise had returned to the sky. The bay was alive with twilight colors, long streaks of reflected gold and purple, fading quickly into the gray of night as he watched. The dark shapes of mysterious sea-creatures moved purposefully in the shallow waters. It was all very peaceful: the bay at sundown, calm, lovely.

But then thoughts of the voyage that awaited him crept into his mind. Lawler looked outward beyond the harbor to the vastness of the unfriendly, inconceivable sea. How far would they have to sail before they found an island willing to take them in? A week's journey? Two weeks? A month? He had never been to sea at all, not even for a day. That time he had gone over to Thibeire, it had been a simple journey by coracle, just beyond the shallows to the other island that had come up so close by Sorve.

Lawler realized that he feared the sea. The sea was a great world-sized mouth, which he sometimes imagined must have swallowed up all of Hydros in some ancient convulsion, leaving nothing but the little drifting islands that the Gillies had created. It would swallow him too, if he set out to cross it.

Angrily he told himself that this was foolishness, that men like Gabe Kinverson went out into the sea every day and survived it, that Nid Delagard had made a hundred voyages between islands, that Sundira Thane had come to Sorve from an island in the Azure Sea, which was so far away that he had never heard of it. It would be all right. He would board one of Delagard's ships and in a week or two it would bring him to the island that would be his new home.

And yet—the blackness, the immensity, the surging power of the terrible world-spanning sea—

"Lawler?" a voice called.

He looked around. For the second time this day Nid Delagard stepped out of the shadows behind him.

"Come on," the shipyard owner said. "It's getting late. Let's go talk to the Gillies."

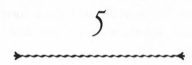

5

*T*HERE WERE ELECTRIC LIGHTS GLOWING IN THE GILLIE POWER
plant, just a little way farther along the curve of the shore. Other
lights, dozens of them, maybe hundreds, could be seen blazing in
the streets of Gillie-town beyond. The unexpected catastrophe of the expulsion had completely overshadowed the other big event of the day, the
inauguration of turbine-driven electrical generation on Sorve Island.

The light coming from the power plant was cool, greenish, faintly
mocking. The Gillies had a technology of sorts, which had reached an
eighteenth or nineteenth century Earth-equivalent level, and they had
invented a kind of light bulb, using filaments made from the fibers of the
exceedingly versatile sea-bamboo plant. The bulbs were costly and difficult
to make, and the big voltaic pile that had been the island's main source of
power was clumsy and recalcitrant, producing electricity only in a sluggish,
intermittent fashion and constantly breaking down. But now—after how
many years of work? Five? Ten?—the island's bulbs were being lit from a
new and inexhaustible source, power from the sea, warm water from the
surface converted to steam, steam making the generator's turbines turn,
electricity streaming forth from the generator to light the lamps of Sorve
Island.

The Gillies had agreed to let the humans at the other end of the island
draw off some of the new power in return for labor—Sweyner would make
light bulbs for them, Dann Henders would help with the stringing of cable,

and so forth. Lawler had been instrumental in setting up that arrangement, along with Delagard, Nicko Thalheim, and one or two others. That was the one little triumph of interspecies cooperation that the humans had been able to manage in recent years. It had taken about six months of slow and painstaking negotiation.

Only this morning, Lawler remembered, he had hoped to work out another such cooperative enterprise with them entirely by himself. That seemed a million years ago. And here they were at nightfall, setting forth to beg just to be allowed to continue living on the island at all.

Delagard said, "We'll go straight to the honcho cabin, okay? No sense not starting at the top for this one."

Lawler shrugged. "Whatever you say."

They walked around the power plant and headed into Gillie territory, still following the shore of the bay. The island widened rapidly here, rising from the low bayfront levels behind the sea-wall to a broad circular plateau that contained most of the Gillie settlement. On the far side of the plateau there was a steep drop where the island's thick wooden sea-bulwark descended in a straight sheer line to the dark ocean far below.

The Gillie village was arrayed in an irregular circle, the most important buildings in the center, the others strung raggedly along the periphery. The main difference between the inner buildings and the outer ones seemed to be one of permanence: the inner ones, which appeared to have ceremonial uses, were constructed of the same wood-kelp timber that the island itself was built from, and the outer ones, in which the Gillies lived, were slapdash tentlike things made of moist green seaweed wrapped loosely over sea-bamboo poles. They gave off a ghastly odor of rot as the sun baked them, and when they reached a certain degree of dryness the seaweed coverings were stripped away and replaced with fresh ones. What appeared to be a special caste of Gillies was constantly at work tearing down the huts and building new ones.

It would take about half a day to walk completely across the Gillie end of the island. By the time Lawler and Delagard had entered the inner circle of the village, Sunrise had set and the Hydros Cross was bright in the sky.

"Here they come," Delagard said. "Let me do the talking, first. If they start getting snotty with me, you take over. I don't mind if you tell them what a shit you think I am. Whatever works."

"Do you really think anything's going to work?"

"Shh. I don't want to hear you talking like that."

Half a dozen Gillies—males, Lawler guessed—were approaching them from the innermost part of the village. When they were ten or twelve meters away they halted and arranged themselves in front of the two humans in a straight line.

Delagard raised his hands in the gesture that meant, "We come in peace." It was the universal humans-to-Gillies greeting. No conversation ever began without it.

The Gillies now were supposed to reply with the funereal wheezing sounds that meant, "We accept you as peaceful and we await your words." But they didn't say a thing. They simply stood there and stared.

"I don't have a good feeling about this, do you?" Lawler said quietly.

"Wait. Wait."

Delagard made the peace gesture again. He went on to make the hand-signals that meant, "We are your friends and regard you with the highest respect."

One of the Gillies emitted what sounded like a fart.

Their glittering little yellow eyes, set close together at the base of their small heads, studied the two humans in what seemed like an icy and indifferent way.

"Let me try," Lawler murmured.

He stepped forward. The wind was blowing from behind the Gillies: it brought him their damp heavy musky smell, mingled with the sharp reek of rotting seaweed from their ramshackle huts.

He made the We-come-in-peace sign. That produced no response, nor did the cognate We-are-your-friends one. After an appropriate pause he proceeded to make the signal that meant, "We seek an audience with the powers that reign."

From one of the Gillies came the farting sound again. Lawler wondered if it was the same Gillie that had rumbled and snorted at him so menacingly in the early hours of the day, down by the power plant.

Delagard offered I-ask-forgiveness-for-an-unintended-transgression. Silence: cold indifferent eyes remotely watching.

Lawler tried How-may-we-atone-for-departure-from-right-conduct. He got nothing back.

"The lousy fuckers," Delagard muttered. "I'd like to put a spear right through their fat bellies."

"They know that," Lawler said. "That's why they don't want to dicker with you."

"I'll go away. You talk to them by yourself."

"If you think it's worth trying."

"You have a clean record with them. Remind them who you are. Who your father was and what he did for them."

"Any other suggestions?" Lawler asked.

"Look, I'm just trying to be helpful. But go on, do it any way you like. I'll be at the shipyard. Stop off there when you get back and let me know how it goes."

Delagard slipped off into the darkness.

LAWLER TOOK A FEW STEPS CLOSER TO THE SIX GILLIES AND BEGAN ALL over with the initiating gesture. Next he identified himself: Valben Lawler, doctor, son of Bernat Lawler the doctor. The great healer whom they surely remembered, the man who had freed their young ones from the menace of fin-rot.

He felt the strong irony of it: this was the opening of the speech he had spent half the night rehearsing in his sleepless mind. He was getting a chance to deliver it after all. In the context of a very different situation, though.

They looked at him without responding.

At least they didn't fart this time, Lawler thought.

He signaled, "We are ordered to leave the island. Is this so?"

From the Gillie on the left came the deep soughing tone that meant an affirmative.

"This brings us great sorrow. Is there any way that we can cause this order to be withdrawn?"

Negative, boomed the Gillie on the right.

Lawler stared at them hopelessly. The wind picked up, flinging their heavy odor into his face by the bucketful, and he fought back nausea. Gillies had never seemed other than strange and mysterious to him, and a little repellent. He knew that he should take them for granted, simply one aspect of the world where he had always lived, like the ocean or the sky. But for all their familiarity they remained, to him, creatures of another creation. Star-things. Aliens: us and them, humans and aliens, no kinship. Why was that? he wondered. I'm as much a native of this world as they are.

He held his ground and told them, "It was simply an unfortunate accident that those divers died. There was no malice involved."

Boom. Wheeze. Hwsssh.

Meaning: "We are not interested in why it happened, only that it happened at all."

Behind the six Gillies, bleak greenish lights flashed on and off, illuminating the curious structures—statues? machines? idols?—that occupied the open space at the center of the village, strange lumps and knobs of metals that had been patiently extracted from the tissues of small sea-creatures and assembled into random-looking, rust-caked heaps of junk.

"Delagard promises never to use divers again," Lawler told the Gillies, cajoling them now, looking hopefully for an opening.

Wheeze. Boom. Indifference.

"Won't you tell us how we can make things good again? We regret what happened. We regret it intensely."

No response. Cold yellow eyes, staring, aloof.

This is idiocy, Lawler thought. It's like arguing with the wind.

"Damn it, this is our *home!*" he cried, matching the words with furious equivalent gestures. "It always has been!"

Three rumbling tones, descending in thirds.

"Find another home?" Lawler asked. "But we love this place! I was born here. We've never done harm to you before, any of us. My father—you knew my father, he was helpful to you when—"

The farting sound again.

It meant exactly what it sounded like, Lawler thought.

There was no sense in going on. He understood fully the futility of it. They were losing patience with him. Soon would come the rumbling, the snorting, the anger. And then anything might happen.

With a wave of a flipper one of the Gillies indicated that the meeting was at its end. The dismissal was unmistakable.

Lawler made a gesture of disappointment. He signaled sadness, anguish, dismay.

To which one of the Gillies replied, surprisingly, with a quick rolling phrase that might almost have been one of sympathy. Or was that only his optimistic imagination? Lawler couldn't be sure. And then, to his amazement, the creature stepped out of the line and came shuffling toward him with unexpected speed, its flipper-arms extended. Lawler was too startled to move. What was this? The Gillie loomed over him like a wall. Here it comes, he thought, the onslaught, the casual lethal outburst of irritation. He stood as though rooted. Some frantic impulse toward self-preservation

shrieked within him, but he couldn't find the will to try to flee. The Gillie
caught him by one arm and pulled him close and enfolded him with its
flippers in a tight, smothering embrace. Lawler felt the sharp curved claws
lightly digging into his flesh, gripping him with strange, mystifying
delicacy. He remembered the red marks Delagard had shown him.

All right. Do whatever you want. I don't give a damn.

Lawler had never been this close to a Gillie before. His head was pressed
against the Gillie's huge chest. He heard the Gillie heart beating in there,
not the familiar human *lub-dub* but more of a *thum-thum-thum, thum-thum-
thum*. A baffling Gillie brain was only a few centimeters from his cheek.
Gillie reek flooded his lungs. He felt dizzy and sick—but, weirdly, not at
all frightened. There was something so overpowering about having been
swept into this bizarre Gillie-hug that there was no room in him for fear
just now. The alien's nearness stirred some kind of whirling in his mind. A
sensation as powerful as a winter storm, as powerful as the Wave itself, came
raging up through the roots of his soul. The taste of seaweed was in his
mouth. The salt sea was coursing through his veins.

The Gillie held him for a time, as if communicating something—
something—that couldn't be expressed in words. The embrace was neither
friendly nor unfriendly. It was beyond Lawler's understanding entirely. The
grip of the strong arms was tight and rough, but apparently not meant to
injure him. Lawler felt like a small child being hugged by some ugly,
strange, unloving foster mother. Or like a doll clasped to the great beast's
bosom.

Then the Gillie released him, pushing him away with a brusque little
shove, and went shuffling back to rejoin the others. Lawler stood frozen,
trembling. He watched as the Gillies, taking no further notice of him,
swung ponderously about, moved away, set out on their return to their
village. He stood looking after them for a long while, understanding
nothing. The rank sea smell of the Gillie still clung to him. It seemed to
him just then that the odor would stay with him forever.

They must have been saying good-bye, he decided finally.

That's it, yes. A Gillie farewell, a tender parting hug. Or not so tender,
but a kiss-off, all the same. Does that make sense? No, not really. But
neither does anything else. Let's call it a gesture of farewell, Lawler
thought. And leave it at that.

•   •   •

THE NIGHT WAS FAR ALONG. SLOWLY LAWLER PICKED HIS WAY BACK
along the shore, past the power plant once again, down to the shipyard,
toward the rickety little wooden house where Delagard lived. Delagard
disdained living in vaarghs. He liked to be close to the yard at all times, he
said.

Lawler found him alone, awake, drinking grapeweed brandy by the
fitful light of a smoky fire. The room was small, cluttered, full of hooks and
line, netting, oars, anchors, stacked rugfish hides, cases of brandy. It looked
like a storeroom, not a dwelling. The house of the richest man on the island,
this was.

Delagard sniffed. "You stink like a Gillie. What were you doing,
letting them fuck you?"

"You guessed it. You ought to try it. You might learn a thing or two."

"Very funny. But you *do* stink of Gillie, you know. Did they try to
rough you up?"

"One of them brushed against me as I was leaving," Lawler said. "I
think it was an accident."

Shrugging, Delagard said, "All right. You get anywhere with them?"

"No. Did you really think I would?"

"There's always hope. A gloomy guy like you may not think so, but
there always is. We've got a month to make them come around. You want a
drink, doc?"

Delagard was already pouring. Lawler took the cup and drank it off
quickly.

"It's time to knock off the bullshit, Nid. Time to dump this fantasy of
yours about making them come around."

Delagard glanced upward. By the pallid flickering light his round face
seemed heavier than it actually was, the shadows highlighting rolls of flesh
around his throat, turning his tanned, leathery-looking cheeks to sagging
jowls. His eyes seemed small and beady and weary.

"You think?"

"No question of it. They really want to be rid of us. Nothing we could
say or do will change that."

"They tell you that, did they?"

"They didn't need to. I've been on this island long enough to understand that they mean what they say. So have you."

"Yes," Delagard said thoughtfully. "I have."

"It's time to face reality. There's not a chance in hell that we can talk them into taking back their decree. What do you think, Delagard? Is there? For Christ's sake, *is there?*"

"No. I don't suppose there is."

"Then when are you going to stop pretending there is? Do I have to remind you what they did on Shalikomo when they said to go and people didn't go?"

"That was Shalikomo, long ago. This is Sorve, now."

"And Gillies are Gillies. You want another Shalikomo here?"

"You know the answer to that, doc."

"All right, then. You knew from the first that there wasn't any hope of changing their minds. You were just going through the motions, weren't you? For the sake of showing everybody how concerned you were about the mess that you had single-handedly created for us."

"You think I've been bullshitting you?"

"I do."

"Well, it isn't so. Do you understand what I feel like, having brought all this down on us? I feel like garbage, Lawler. What do you think I am, anyway? Just a heartless bloodsucking animal? You think I can just shrug and tell the town, Tough tittie, folks, I had a good thing going there for a while with those divers and then it just didn't work out, so we have to move, sorry for the inconvenience, so long, see you around? Sorve is my home community, doc. I felt I had to show that I'd at least try to undo the damage I caused."

"Okay. You tried. We both tried. And got nowhere, as we both expected all along. Now what are you going to do?"

"What do you want me to do?"

"I told you before. No more windy talk about kissing the Gillies' flippers and begging them to forgive. We have to begin figuring out how we're going to get away from here and where we're going to go. Start making plans for the evacuation, Delagard. It's your baby. You caused all this. Now you have to fix it."

"As a matter of fact," Delagard said slowly, "I've already been working on doing just that. Tonight while you were parleying with the Gillies I sent word to the three ships of mine that are currently making ferry trips that they should turn around and get back here right away to serve as transport vessels for us."

"Transporting us where?"

"Here, have another drink." Delagard filled Lawler's glass again without waiting for a response. "Let me show you something."

He opened a cabinet and took a sea-chart from it. The chart was a laminated plastic globe about sixty centimeters in diameter, made of dozens of individual strips of varying colors fitted together by some master craftsman's hand. From within it came the ticking sound of a clockwork mechanism. Lawler leaned toward it. Sea-charts were rare and precious things. He had rarely had a chance to see one at such close range.

"Onyos Felk's father Dismas made this, fifty years ago," Delagard said. "My grandfather bought it from him when old Felk thought he wanted to go into the shipping trade and needed money for building ships. You remember the Felk fleet? Three ships. The Wave sank them all. Hell of a thing, pay for your ships by selling your sea-chart, then lose the ships. Especially when it's the best chart ever made. Onyos would give his left ball to have it, but why should I sell? I let him consult it once in a while."

Circular purple medallions the size of a thumbnail were moving slowly up and down along the chart, some thirty or forty of them, perhaps even more, driven by the mechanism within. Most went in a straight line, heading from one pole toward the other, but occasionally one would glide almost imperceptibly into an adjacent longitudinal strip, the way an actual island might wander a little to the east or to the west while riding the main current carrying it toward the pole. Lawler marveled at the thing's ingenuity.

Delagard said, "You know how to read one of these? These here are the islands. This is Home Sea. This island here is Sorve."

A little purple blotch, making its slow way upward near the equator of the globe against the green background of the strip on which it was traveling: an insignificant speck, a bit of moving color, nothing more. Very small to be so dear, Lawler thought.

"The whole world is shown here, at least as we understand it to be. These are the inhabited islands, in purple—inhabited by humans. This is the Black Sea, this is the Red Sea, this is the Yellow Sea over here."

"What about the Azure Sea?" Lawler asked.

Delagard seemed a little surprised. "Way up over here, practically in the other hemisphere. What do you know about the Azure Sea, doc?"

"Nothing much. Someone mentioned it to me recently, that's all."

"A hell of a trip from here, the Azure Sea. I've never been there."

Delagard turned the globe to show Lawler the other side. "Here's the Empty Sea. This big dark thing down here is the Face of the Waters. Do you remember the great stories old Jolly used to tell about the Face?"

"That grizzly old liar. You don't actually believe he got anywhere near it, do you?"

Delagard winked. "It was a terrific story, wasn't it?"

Lawler nodded and let his mind wander for a moment back close to thirty-five years, thinking of the weather-beaten old man's oft-repeated tale of his lonely crossing of the Empty Sea, of his mysterious and dreamlike encounter with the Face, an island so big you could fit all the other islands of the world into it, a vast and menacing thing filling the horizon, rising like a black wall out of the ocean in that remote and silent corner of the world. On the sea-chart, the Face was merely a dark motionless patch the size of the palm of a man's hand, a ragged black blemish against the otherwise blank expanse of the far hemisphere, down low almost in the south polar region.

He turned the globe back to the other hemisphere and watched the islands slowly moving about.

Lawler wondered how a sea-chart made so long ago could predict the current positions of the islands in any useful way. Surely they were deflected from their primary courses by all sorts of short-term weather phenomena. Or had the maker of the chart taken that all into account, using some sort of scientific magic inherited from the great world of science in the galaxy beyond? Things were so primitive on Hydros that Lawler was always surprised when any kind of mechanism worked; but he knew that it was different on the other inhabited worlds of space, where there was land, and a ready supply of metals, and a way to move from world to world. The technological magics of Earth, of the old lost mother world, had carried over to those worlds. But there was nothing like that here.

He said, after a moment, "How accurate do you imagine this chart is? Considering that it's fifty years old, and all."

"Have we learned anything new about Hydros in the past fifty years? This is the best sea-chart we have. Old Felk was a master craftsman, and he talked to everyone who went to sea, anywhere. And checked his information against observations made from space, on Sunrise. It's accurate, all right. Damned accurate."

Lawler followed the movements of the islands as though mesmerized by them. Maybe the chart really did give reliable information, maybe not: he was in no position to tell. He had never understood how anyone at sea ever could find his way back to his own island, let alone reach some distant one, considering that both the ship and the island were in motion all the time. I ought to ask Gabe Kinverson about that sometime, Lawler thought.

"All right. What's your plan?"

Delagard pointed toward Sorve on the chart. "You see this island southwest of us, coming up out of the next strip? That's Velmise. It's drifting north and east, moving at a higher velocity than we are, and it'll pass within relatively easy reach about a month from now. At that time it'll be maybe a ten-day journey from here, maybe even less. I'm going to put through a message to my son there and ask him if they'd be willing to take us in, all seventy-eight of us."

"And if they aren't? Velmise is pretty damned small."

"We have other choices. Here's Salimil moving up from the other side. It'll be something like two and a half weeks from us when we have to leave here."

Lawler considered the prospect of spending two and a half weeks in a ship on the open sea. Under the blazing eye of the sun, in the constant parching blast of the salt sea-breeze, eating dried fish, pacing back and forth on a little deck with nothing to see but ocean and more ocean.

He reached for the brandy bottle and filled his cup again himself.

Delagard said, "If Salimil won't take us, we've got Kaggeram down here, or Shaktan, or Grayvard, even. I have kin on Grayvard. I think I can arrange something. That would be an eight-week journey."

Eight weeks? Lawler tried to imagine what that would be like.

He said, after a time, "Nobody's going to have room for seventy-eight people on thirty days' notice. Not Velmise, not Salimil, not anybody."

"In that case we'll just have to split up, a few of us going here, a few of us going there."

"No!" Lawler said with sudden vehemence.

"No?"

"I don't want that. I want the community to stay together."

"What if it can't be done?"

"We have to find a way. We can't take a group of people who have been together all their lives and scatter them all over the goddamned ocean. We're a family, Nid."

"Are we? I guess I don't think of it that way."

"Think of it that way now."

"Well, then," Delagard said. He sat quietly, frowning. "I guess as a last resort we could simply present ourselves on one of the islands that isn't currently inhabited by humans and ask the Gillies living there for sanctuary. It's happened before."

"The Gillies there would know that we were thrown out by our Gillies here. And why."

"Maybe it wouldn't matter. You know Gillies as well as I do, doc. A lot of them are pretty tolerant of us. To them we're just one more example of the inscrutable way of the universe, something that simply happened to wash up on their shores out of the great sea of space. They understand that it's a waste of breath questioning the inscrutable way of the universe. Which I suppose is why they simply shrugged and let us move in on them when we first came here."

"The wisest ones think that way, maybe. The rest of them detest us and don't want a damned thing to do with us. Why the hell should the Gillies of some other island take us in when the Sorve Gillies have tossed us out as murderers?"

"We'll be all right," Delagard said serenely, not reacting in any visible way to the ugly word. He nursed his brandy cup with both hands, staring into it. "We'll go to Velmise. Or Salimil, or Grayvard if we have to, or someplace completely new. And we'll all stay together and make a new life for ourselves. I'll see to that. Count on it, doc."

"Do you have enough ships to carry us?"

"I've got six. Thirteen to a ship and we'll make it without even feeling crowded. Stop worrying, doc. Have another drink."

"I have one already."

"Mind if I do, then?"

"Suit yourself."

Delagard laughed. He was getting drunk, now. He caressed the sea-chart as though it were a woman's breast; and then he lifted it delicately and stowed it once again in the cabinet. The brandy bottle was nearly empty. Delagard produced another one from somewhere and poured himself a stiff shot. He swayed as he did it, caught himself, chuckled.

He said, slurring his words, "I assure you of one thing, doc, which is that I'm going to bust my ass to find us a new island and get us there safely. Do you believe me when I tell you that, doc?"

"Sure I do."

"And can you forgive me in your heart for what I did to those divers?" Delagard asked woozily.

"Sure. Sure."

"You're a liar. You hate my guts."

"Come off it, Nid. What's done is done. Now we simply have to live with it."

"Spoken like a true philosopher. Here, have another."

"Right."

"And another for good old Nid Delagard too. Why not? Another for good old Delagard, yeah. Here you are, Nid. Why, thank you, Nid. Thank you very much. By damn, this is fine stuff. Fine—stuff—" Delagard yawned. His eyes closed, his head descended toward the table. "Fine— stuff—" he murmured. He yawned again, and belched softly, and then he was asleep. Lawler finished his own cup and left the building.

IT WAS VERY SILENT OUT THERE, ONLY THE LAPPING OF THE WAVELETS OF the bay against the shore, and Lawler was so used to that that he scarcely heard it. Dawn was still an hour or two away. The Cross burned overhead with terrible ferocity, cutting through the black sky from horizon to horizon like a luminous four-armed framework that was up there to keep the world from tumbling freely through the heavens.

A kind of crystalline clarity possessed Lawler's mind. He could practically hear his brain ticking.

He realized that he didn't mind leaving Sorve.

The thought astonished him. You're drunk, he told himself.

Maybe so. But somehow, somewhere in the night, the shock of the expulsion had fallen away from him. Altogether gone or simply temporarily misplaced, Lawler couldn't say. But at least for now he was able suddenly to look the idea of leaving in the eye, without flinching. Leaving here was something he could handle. It was more than that, even. The prospect of going from here was—

Exhilarating? Could that be it?

Exhilarating, yes. The pattern of his life had been set, frozen—Dr. Lawler of Sorve, a First Family man, a Lawler of the Lawlers, getting a day older every day, do your daily work, heal the sick as best you can, walk along the sea-wall, swim a little, fish a little, put in the required time teaching your craft to your apprentice, eat and drink, visit with old friends, the same old old friends you'd had when you were a boy, then go to sleep, wake up and start all over, come winter, come summer, come rain, come drought. Now that pattern was going to change. He would live somewhere else. He might *be* someone else. The idea fascinated him. He was startled to realize that he was even a little grateful. He had been here so long, after all. He had been himself for so long.

You are very very drunk, Lawler said to himself again, and laughed. Very very very very.

The idea came to him to stroll through the sleeping settlement, a sentimental journey to say his farewells, looking at everything as though this were his last night on Hydros, reliving everything that had happened to him here and there and here and there, every episode of his life. The places where he had stood with his father looking out at the sea, where he had listened to old Jolly's fantastic tales, where he had caught his first fish, where he had embraced his first girl. Scenes associated with his friendships, and with his loves, such as they had been. The side of the bay where he'd been the time he'd come close to spearing Nicko Thalheim. And the place back of the boneyard where he'd spied on gray-bearded Marinus Cadrell screwing Damis Sawtelle's sister Mariam, who was a nun in the convent now. Which reminded him of the time he'd screwed Mariam himself, a few years later, down in Gillie country, the two of them living dangerously and loving it. Everything came flooding back. The shadowy figure of his mother. His brothers, the one who had died much too young and the one who had gone off to sea and floated out of his life forever. His father, indefatigable, formidable, remote, revered by all, drilling him endlessly in matters of medical technique when he'd much rather have been splashing in the bay: those boyhood days that hadn't seemed like a boyhood at all, so many hard grim hours of enforced study, cutting him off from the games and fun. *You will be the doctor someday*, his father saying again and again. *You will be the doctor.* His wife Mireyl getting aboard the Morvendir ferry. Time was ticking backward. Tick, and it was the day of his trip to Thibeire Island. Tick, and he and Nestor Yanez were running, dizzy with laughter and fear, from the furious female Gillie that they had pelted with ginzo eggs. Tick, and here was the long-faced delegation that had come to tell him that his father was dead, that he was the doctor now. Tick, and he was finding out what it was like to deliver a baby. Tick, and he was dancing drunkenly along the bulwark's topmost point in the middle of a three-moon night with Nicko and Nestor Lyonides and Moira and Meela and Quigg, a young merry Valben Lawler who seemed to him now like someone else he had once known, long long ago. The whole thing, his forty-plus years on

Sorve viewed in reverse. Tick. Tick. Tick. Yes, I'll take a nice long walk through the past before the sun comes up, he thought. From one end of the island to another. But it seemed like a good idea to go back to his vaargh before setting out, though he wasn't sure why.

He tripped going through the low entrance and fell sprawling. And was still lying there when morning sunlight came in, hours later, to wake him.

For a moment Lawler couldn't quite remember what he had said or done in the night. Then it all came back. Being hugged by a Gillie. The scent of it was still on him. Then Delagard, brandy, more brandy, the prospect of a voyage to Velmise, Salimil, maybe even Grayvard. And that strange moment of exhilaration at the thought of leaving Sorve. Had it been real? Yes. Yes. He was sober now, and it was still there.

But—my God—my head!

How much brandy, he wondered, had Delagard succeeded in pouring into him last night?

A child's high voice from outside the vaargh said, "Doctor? I hurt my foot."

"Just a second," Lawler said, in a voice like a file.

6

THERE WAS A MEETING THAT EVENING IN THE COMMUNITY center to discuss the situation. The air in the center was thick and steamy, rank with sweat. Feelings were running high. Lawler sat in the far corner opposite the door, his usual place. He could see everything from there. Delagard hadn't come. He had sent word of pressing business at the yard, messages awaited from his ships at sea.

"It's all a trap," Dann Henders said. "The Gillies are tired of us being here, but they don't want to bother killing us themselves. So they're going to force us to go out to sea and the rammerhorns and sea-leopards will kill us for them."

"How do you know that?" Nicko Thalheim asked.

"I don't. I'm just guessing. I'm trying to figure why they're making us leave the island over a trivial thing like three dead divers."

"Three dead divers aren't so trivial!" Sundira called out. "You're talking about intelligent creatures!"

"Intelligent?" Dag Tharp said mockingly.

"You bet they are. And if I were a Gillie and I found out that the goddamned humans were killing off divers, I'd want to be rid of them too."

Henders said, "Well, whatever. I say that if the Gillies succeed in throwing us out of here, we'll find the whole goddamned ocean rising up against us once we're out to sea. And not by any accident. The Gillies control the sea animals. Everybody knows that. And they'll use them against us to wipe us out."

"What if we simply don't *let* the Gillies throw us out?" Damis Sawtelle asked. "What if we fight back?"

"Fight?" said Bamber Cadrell. "Fight how? Fight with what? You out of your mind, Damis?"

They were both ferry-captains, solid practical men, friends since boyhood. Right now they were looking at each other with the dull, glowering look of lifelong enemies.

"Resistance," Sawtelle said. "Guerrilla warfare."

"We sneak down to their end of the island and grab something that looks important from that holy building of theirs," Nimber Tanamind suggested. "And refuse to give it back unless they agree to let us stay."

"That sounds dumb to me," Cadrell said.

Nicko Thalheim said, "To me too. Stealing their jujus won't get us anywhere. Armed resistance is the ticket, just like Damis says. Guerrilla warfare, absolutely. Gillie blood flowing in the streets until they back down on the expulsion order. They don't even have the concept of war on this planet. They won't know what the hell we're doing if we put up a fight."

"Shalikomo," somebody said from the back. "Remember what happened there."

"Shalikomo, yes," another voice called. "They'll slaughter us the same way they did them. And there won't be a damned thing we can do to stop it."

"Right," Marya Hain said. "We're the ones who don't have the concept of war, not them. They know how to kill when they want to. What are we going to attack them with, scaling knives? Hammers and chisels? We aren't fighters. Our ancestors were, maybe, but we don't even know what the idea means."

"We have to learn," said Thalheim. "We can't let ourselves be driven from our homes."

"Can't we?" Marya Hain asked. "What choice do we have? We're here only by their sufferance. Which they have now withdrawn. It's their island. If we try to resist, they'll pick us up one by one and throw us into the sea, the way they did on Shalikomo."

"We'll take plenty of them with us," Damis Sawtelle said, with heat in his voice.

Dann Henders burst into laughter. "Into the sea? Right. Right. We'll hold their heads under water until they drown."

"You know what I meant," Sawtelle grumbled. "They kill one of us, we kill one of them. Once they start dying they'll change their minds pretty damn fast about making us leave."

"They'll kill us faster than we could kill them," said Poilin Stayvol's wife Leynila. Stayvol was Delagard's second most senior captain, after Gospo Struvin. He was off sailing the Kentrup ferry just then. Leynila, short and fiery, could always be counted on to speak up against anything that Damis Sawtelle favored. They had been that way since they were children. "Even one for one, where's that going to get us?" Leynila demanded.

Dana Sawtelle nodded. She crossed the room to stand next to Marya and Leynila. Most of the women were on one side of the room and the handful of men who constituted the war faction were on the other. "Leynila's right. If we try to fight we'll all be killed. What's the sense of it? If there's a war and we fight like terrific heroes and at the end of it we're all dead, how will we be better off than if we had simply gotten into a ship and gone somewhere else?"

Her husband swung around to face her. "Keep quiet, Dana."

"The hell I will, Damis! The hell I will! You think I'm going to sit here like a child while you people talk about launching an attack on a physically superior group of alien beings who outnumber us about ten to one? We *can't* fight them."

"We have to."

"No. No."

"This is all foolishness, this talk of fighting. They're only bluffing," Lis Niklaus said. "They won't really make us go."

"Oh, yes, they will—"

"Not if Nid has anything to say about it!"

"It's your precious Nid that got us into this in the first place!" Marya Hain yelled.

"And he'll get us out of it. The Gillies are angry just now, but they won't—"

"What do you think, doc?" someone called out.

Lawler had kept silent during the debate, waiting for emotions to play themselves out. It was always a mistake to jump into these things too soon.

Now he rose. Suddenly it was very quiet in the room. Every eye was on him. They wanted The Answer from him. Some miracle, some hope of reprieve. They were confident he'd deliver it. Pillar of the community, descendant of a famous Founder; the trusted doctor who knew everyone's body better than they did themselves; wise and cool head, respected dispenser of shrewd advice.

He looked around at them all before he began to speak.

"I'm sorry, Damis. Nicko. Nimber. I think all this talk of resistance gets us nowhere useful. We need to admit to ourselves that that isn't an option." There was grumbling at once from the war faction. Lawler silenced it with a cool glare. "Trying to fight the Gillies is like trying to drink the sea dry. We've got no weapons. We've got maybe forty able-bodied fighters at best, against hundreds of them. It isn't even worth thinking about." The silence became glacial. But he could see his calm words sinking in: people exchanging glances, heads nodding. He turned toward Lis Niklaus. "Lis, the Gillies aren't bluffing and Nid doesn't have any way of getting them to take back their order. He spoke to them and so did I. You know that. If you still think the Gillies are going to change their minds, you're dreaming."

How solemn they all looked, how somber! The Sweyners, Dag Tharp, a cluster of Thalheims, the Sawtelles. Sidero Volkin and his wife Elka, Dann Henders, Martin Yanez. Young Josc Yanez. Lis. Leo Martello. Pilya Braun. Leynila Stayvol. Sundira Thane. He knew them all so well, all but just a few. They were his family, just as he had told Delagard that boozy night. Yes. Yes. It was so. Everyone on this island.

"Friends," he said, "we'd better face the realities. I don't like this any more than you do, but we have no choice. The Gillies say we have to leave? Okay. It's their island. They have the numbers, they have the muscle. We're going to be living somewhere else soon and that's all there is to it. I wish I could offer something more cheery, but I can't. Nobody can. Nobody."

He waited for some fiery rejoinder from Thalheim or Tanamind or Damis Sawtelle. But they had nothing more to say. There wasn't anything anyone could say. All this talk of armed resistance had been only whistling in the wind. The meeting broke up inconclusively. There was no choice but to submit: everyone saw that now.

LAWLER WAS STANDING BY THE SEAWALL BETWEEN DELAGARD'S SHIP-yard and the Gillie power plant, looking out at the changing colors in the bay late one afternoon in the second week since the ultimatum, when Sundira Thane went swimming by below. In midstroke she glanced up quickly and nodded to him. Lawler nodded back and waved. Her long slender legs flashed in a scissor-kick, and she surged forward, torso bending in a sudden swift surface-dive.

For a moment Lawler saw Sundira's pale boyish buttocks gleaming above the water; then she was traveling rapidly just beneath the surface, a lean naked tawny wraith swimming away from shore in steady, powerful strokes. Lawler followed her with his eyes until she was lost to his sight. She swims like a Gillie, he thought. She hadn't come up for air in what felt to him like three or four minutes. Didn't she need to breathe at all?

Mireyl had been a strong swimmer like that, he thought.

Lawler frowned. It surprised him to have his long-ago wife come floating up unsummoned out of the past like this. He hadn't thought of her for ages. But then he remembered that he had thought of her only last night, in his drunken ramble. Mireyl, yes. Ancient history.

HE COULD ALMOST SEE HER NOW. SUDDENLY HE WAS TWENTY-THREE again, the young new doctor, and there she was, fair-haired, fair-skinned, compact, wide through the shoulders and the hips, a low center of gravity: a powerful little projectile of a woman, round and muscular and sturdy. Her face wasn't clear to him, though. He couldn't remember her face at all, somehow.

She was a wonderful swimmer. In the water she moved like a javelin. She never appeared to tire and she could remain submerged for ever and ever. Strong and active as he was, Lawler was always hard pressed to keep up with her when they swam. She would turn, finally, laughing, and wait for him, and he would swim up against her, clasp her tight, hold her close against him.

They were swimming now. He came up to her and she opened her arms to him. There were little glistening things swimming around them in the water, lithe and friendly.

"We should get married," he said.

"Should we?"

"We should, yes."

"The doctor's wife. I never thought I'd be the doctor's wife." She laughed. "But somebody has to be."

"No, nobody has to be. But I want you to be."

She wriggled away from him and started swimming. "Catch me and I'll marry you!"

"No fair. You had a head start."

"Nothing's ever fair," she called to him.

He grinned and went after her, swimming harder than he ever had before, and this time he caught up with her, halfway across the bay. He couldn't tell whether it was because he had been swimming beyond his capabilities or because she had deliberately let him catch her. Probably both, he decided.

The doctor had a wife, then.

"Are you happy?" he would ask.

"Oh, yes, yes."

"So am I."

A strong marriage. So he supposed, anyway. But she was restless. She had come to Sorve from another island in the first place, and now she wanted to move along, she wanted to see the world, but he was tied to Sorve by his profession, by his staid disciplined temperament, by a million invisible bonds. He didn't understand how much of a wanderer she really was: he had thought this longing for other islands was only a phase, that she would grow out of it as she settled into married life with him on Sorve.

Another scene, now. Down at the harbor, eleven months after their wedding. Mireyl getting aboard a Delagard interisland ferry bound for Morvendir, pausing to glance behind her at the pier, waving to him. But not smiling. Neither was he, uncertainly returning her wave. And then she turned her back and was gone.

Lawler had never heard anything from her or about her again. That had been twenty years ago. He hoped she was happy, wherever she was.

FAR OFF IN THE DISTANCE LAWLER SAW SCHOOLS OF AIR-SKIMMERS breaking from the water and launching themselves into their fierce finny flights. Their scales glinted in tones of red and gold, like the precious gems in the storybooks of his childhood. He had never seen actual gems— nothing of the sort existed on Hydros—but it was hard to imagine how they could be more beautiful than air-skimmers in flight at sunset. Nor could he imagine a scene more beautiful than Sorve Bay when it showed its evening colors. What a glorious summer evening! There were other times of the year when the air wasn't this soft and mild—the seasons when the island was in polar waters, hammered by black gales, swept by knife-sharp sleet. Times would come when the weather was too stormy to allow anyone to venture even so far as the edge of the bay for fish and plants, and they all ate dried fish-meat, powdered algae-meal, and dried seaweed strands, and huddled in their vaarghs waiting miserably for the time of warmth to return. But summer! Ah, summer, when the island moved in tropical waters! There was nothing better. Being evicted from the island in midsummer like this made the expulsion all the more painful: they were being cheated out of the finest season of the year.

But that's been the story of mankind from the beginning, hasn't it? he thought. One eviction after another, starting with Eden. Exile after exile.

Looking now at the bay in all its beauty, Lawler felt a sharp new pang of loss. His life on Sorve was fleeing irretrievably from him moment by moment. That strange exhilaration at the thought of starting a new life somewhere else that he had felt the first night still was with him. But not all the time.

He wondered about Sundira. What it would be like to sleep with her. There was no sense trying to pretend he wasn't attracted to her. Those long sleek legs, that agile, slender, athletic frame. Her energy, her crisp confident manner. He imagined his fingers moving along the inside of her thighs, over smooth, cool skin. His head nuzzling into the hollow between her shoulder and her throat. Those small hard breasts in his hands, the little nipples rising against his palms. If Sundira made love with half the vigor that she put into swimming, she'd be extraordinary.

It was strange to be wanting a woman again. Lawler had been self-sufficient so long: to give way to desire meant forfeiting some of his carefully constructed armor. But the prospect of leaving the island had churned up all manner of things that had been lying quiescent in his soul.

AFTER A WHILE LAWLER BECAME AWARE THAT AT LEAST TEN MINUTES had gone by, maybe even more, and he hadn't seen Sundira come up for air. Not even a strong swimmer could manage that, not if she was human. Suddenly worried, Lawler scanned the water for her.

Then he saw her walking toward him along the sea-wall promenade to his left. Her dark moist hair was pulled tight behind her head, and she had put on a blue crawlweed wrap that was hanging casually open in front. She must have circled around to the south and come ashore by the sea-ramp just next to the shipyard without his noticing it.

"Mind if I join you?" she asked.

Lawler made an open-handed gesture. "Plenty of room here."

She came up alongside him and took the same position as his, leaning forward, looking out toward the water, elbows against the railing.

She said, "You looked so serious when I came swimming past here a little while back. So deep in thought."

"Did I?"

"Were you?"

"I suppose."

"Thinking the big thoughts, doctor?"

"Not really. Just thinking." He wasn't quite up to telling her what had been on his mind a moment before. "Trying to come to terms with leaving here," he said, improvising quickly. "Having to go into exile again."

"Again?" she said. "I don't understand. What do you mean, again? Did you have to leave some island before this one? I thought you've always lived on Sorve."

"I have. But this is the second exile for all of us, isn't it? I mean, first our ancestors were exiled from Earth. And now we're exiled from our island."

She swung around to face him, looking puzzled. "We aren't exiles from Earth. Nobody who was born on Earth ever settled on Hydros. Earth was destroyed a hundred years before the first humans ever came here."

"That doesn't matter. We were all from Earth originally, if you go back to the starting point. And we lost it. That's a kind of exile. I mean everyone, all the humans living on all the worlds of space." Suddenly the words came pouring out of him. "Look, we had a mother world once, we had a single ancestral planet, and it's gone, ruined, destroyed. Finished. Nothing but a memory, a very hazy memory at that, nothing left but a handful of tiny fragments like the ones that you saw in my vaargh. My father used to tell us that Earth was one tremendous wonderful place of miracles, the most beautiful planet that ever existed. A garden world, he said. A paradise. Maybe it was. There are some who say it wasn't anything like that at all, that it was a horror of a place, a place that people fled from because they couldn't stand living there, it was so awful. I don't know. It's all become mythology now. But either way it was our home, and we went away from it and then the door was closed behind us for good."

"I don't ever think about Earth at all," Sundira said.

"I do. All the other galactic races have a home world, but not us. We have to live scattered across hundreds of worlds, five hundred of us living here and a thousand of us there, settling in strange places. Tolerated, more or less, by the various alien creatures on whose planets we've managed to find a bit of a foothold. That's what I mean by exile."

"Even if Earth still existed, we wouldn't be able to go back to it. Not from Hydros. Hydros is our home, not Earth. And nobody's exiling us from Hydros."

"Well, they are from Sorve. At least you can't argue that away."

Her expression, which had grown quizzical and a little impatient, softened. "It seems like exile to you because you've never lived anywhere else. To me an island is just an island. They're all more or less alike, really. I live on one for a while, and then somehow I feel like moving along, and I go somewhere else." Sundira let her hand rest on his for an instant. "I know it must be different for you. I'm sorry."

Lawler found himself desperately wanting to change the subject.

This one was all wrong. He was getting her pity now, which meant that she was responding to what she must see as his own self-pity. The conversation had gotten off on the wrong foot and kept on marching. Instead of talking about going into exile, and about the poignant plight of the poor homeless humans strewn like scattered grains of sand across the galaxy, he should simply have told her how terrific she had looked to him when she did that ass-high jackknife dive in the water, and would she like to come up to his vaargh right now for a little jolly grappling before dinner? But it was too late to start off on that tack now. Or was it?

He said, after a while, "How's the cough?"

"It's fine. But I could use some more of your medicine. I've got just a couple of days' worth left."

"Come up to the vaargh when it's all gone and I'll give you some more."

"I will," she said. "And I'd like to look at those things from Earth that you have, too."

"If you want to, sure. If they interest you, I'll tell you what I know about them. Such as it is. But most people lose interest fast when I do."

"I didn't realize you were so fascinated by Earth. I've never known anyone who gave it much of a thought. To most of us Earth is just the place where our ancestors used to live long ago. But it's beyond our comprehension, really. Beyond our reach. We don't think about it any more than we think about what our great-great-great-great-great-grandparents might have looked like."

"I do," Lawler said. "I can't tell you why. I think of all sorts of things that are beyond my reach. Like what it is to live on a land world, for instance. A place where there's black soil underneath your feet, and plants growing out of it, right there in the open air, plants twenty times as tall as a man."

"Trees, you mean?"

"Trees, yes."

"I know about trees. What fantastic things they are. Stems so thick you can't put your arms all the way around them. Hard rough brown skin all up and down them. Incredible."

"You talk as if you've seen some," Lawler said.

"Me? No, how could I? I'm Hydros-born just like you. But I've known people who lived on land worlds. When I was on Simbalimak, I spent a lot of time with a man from Sunrise, and he told me about forests, and birds, and mountains, and all the other things we don't have here. Trees. Insects. Deserts. It all sounded amazing."

"I imagine so," Lawler said. This conversation was making him no happier than the last. He didn't want to hear about forests or birds or mountains, or about the man from Sunrise with whom she had spent a lot of time on Simbalimak.

She was looking at him oddly. There was a long sticky pause, a pause with a subtext, though he was damned if he knew what it was.

Then she said, in a new abrupt tone, "You've never been married, have you, doctor?" The question was as unexpected as a Gillie turning handsprings.

"Once. Not for very long. It was quite a while ago, a bad mistake. And you?"

"Never. I don't understand how to do it, I guess. Tying yourself down to one person forever—it seems so strange to me."

"They say it's possible," Lawler remarked. "I've seen it done, right before my very eyes. But of course I've had very little personal experience of it."

She nodded vaguely. She seemed to be wrestling with something. So was he, and he knew what it was: his reluctance to step across the self-imposed boundaries that he had drawn around his life after Mireyl had left him, his unwillingness to expose himself to the risks of renewed pain. He had grown accustomed to his monastic, disciplined life. More than accustomed: it seemed to be what he wanted, it seemed to be what met his deepest needs. Nothing ventured, nothing lost. Was she waiting for him to make his move? So it appeared, yes. So it appeared. But would he? Could he? He had trapped himself in inflexible indifference and there seemed to be no way that he could allow himself to get out of it.

The mild summer breeze, coming up from the south, brought the fragrance of her sea-moist hair to him, and fluttered her wrap, reminding Lawler that she was naked underneath it. The orange light of the setting sun, gleaming against her bare skin, turned the faint, fine, almost invisible hairs that covered it to gold, so that her breasts glistened where they showed through the open front. Her body was still damp from her swim. Her small pale nipples were hard in the evening's gentle coolness. She looked supple, trim, enticing.

He wanted her, no doubt of that.

Okay. Go on, then. You aren't fifteen years old any more. The thing to do is to say to her, "Instead of waiting for morning, come on up to my vaargh right now, and I'll give you the medicine. And afterward let's have dinner together and a drink or two. You know. I'd like to get to know you better." And take it from there. Lawler could hear the words in the air almost as though he had actually spoken them already.

But just then Gabe Kinverson came up the path, fresh from his day at sea. He was still wearing his fishing gear, heavy tentlike garments designed to protect him against the slash of meatfish tentacles. Under one arm he carried a folded-up sail. He paused and stood looming for a moment, a dozen or so meters away, a bulky presence, rugged as a reef, emanating that curious ever-present sense of great strength contained with the greatest difficulty, of hidden violence, of danger.

"There you are," he said to Sundira. "Been looking for you. Evening, doc." His tone was calm, bland, enigmatic. Kinverson never sounded as threatening as he looked. He beckoned to her, and she went to him without hesitation.

"Nice talking to you, doctor," Sundira said, looking back over her shoulder at Lawler.

"Right," he said.

Kinverson just wants her to mend that sail for him, Lawler told himself.

Sure. Sure.

•   •   •

ONE OF THE EARTH-DREAMS CAME TO HIM AGAIN. THERE WERE TWO OF them, one very painful and the other one not so bad. Lawler had one of them at least once a month, sometimes both.

This was the easier one, the one where he was actually on Earth himself, walking on solid soil. He was barefoot and there had been rain just a little while before and the ground was soft and warm, and when he wiggled his toes and dug them into it he saw tendrils of soil come spurting up between them, the way sand did when he walked in the shallows of the bay. But the soil of Earth was darker stuff than sand, and much heavier. It yielded slightly underfoot in a way that was very strange.

He was walking through a forest. Trees rose about him on all sides, things like wood-kelp plants with long trunks and dense crowns of leaves far overhead, but they were much more massive than any wood-kelp he had ever seen, and the leaves were so far above him that he was unable to make out their shapes. Birds fluttered in the treetops. They made odd melodic sounds, a music he had never heard before and could never remember when he awakened. All manner of strange creatures loped through the forest, some walking on two legs like a human, some crawling on their bellies, some standing on six or eight little stilts. He nodded to them and they acknowledged his greeting as they went by, these creatures of Earth.

He came to a place where the forest opened up and he saw a mountain rising before him. It looked like dark glass, speckled with mirror-bright irregularities, and in the warm golden sunlight it had a wonderful brilliance. The mountain filled half the sky. Trees were growing on it. They looked so small that he could pick one up in his hand, but he knew that they only seemed that way because the mountain was so far from him, that in fact those trees were at least as big as the ones in the forest he had just left, perhaps even bigger.

Somehow he walked around the mountain's base. There was a long sloping place on the other side, a valley, and beyond the valley he saw a dark sprawling thing that he knew was a city, full of people, more people than he could easily imagine. He went toward it, thinking that he would go among the people of Earth and tell them who he was and where he had come from, and ask them about the lives they led, and whether they knew his great-great-grandfather Harry Lawler or maybe Harry Lawler's father or grandfather.

But though he walked and walked, the city never grew any closer. It remained forever on the horizon, down there at the far side of the valley. He walked for hours; he walked for days; he walked for weeks. And always the city was out of reach, forever retreating from him as he walked toward it; and when he woke at last he was weary and cramped, as though from a great exertion, and he felt as though he had had no sleep at all.

IN THE MORNING JOSC YANEZ, LAWLER'S YOUNG APPRENTICE, CAME TO his vaargh for the regular instruction session. The island had a strict apprentice system: no skill must be allowed to die out. This was the first time since the beginning of the settlement that the apprentice doctor had been anyone but a Lawler. But the Lawler line was going to end with him; some other family would have to carry the responsibility after he was gone.

"When we leave," Josc asked, "will we be able to take all the medical supplies with us?"

"As much as there's room for aboard the ships," Lawler told him. "The equipment, most of the drugs, the book of recipes."

"The patients' records?"

"If there's room. I don't know."

Josc was seventeen, tall and gangling. A sweet-souled boy with an easy smile, an open face, a good way with people. He seemed to have an aptitude for doctoring. He loved the long hours of studying in a way that Lawler himself, fidgety and rebellious as a boy, never really had. This was the second year of Josc's instruction and Lawler suspected he already knew half of the basic technical principles; the rest, and the skill of diagnosis, would be his in time. He came from a family of sailors; his older brother Martin was one of Delagard's ferry captains. It was very much like Josc to worry about the patients' medical records. Lawler doubted that they'd be able to take them along: those ships of Delagard's didn't seem to have much space for cargo, and there were other things with higher priority than old medical records. He and Josc between them would have to commit everyone's medical history to memory before they left the island. But that wouldn't be a big problem. Lawler had most of it in his memory already. And so, he suspected, did Josc.

"I hope I get to go on the same ship you do," the boy said. Lawler, next to his brother Martin, was Josc's greatest hero.

"No," Lawler told him. "We'll have to be on separate ships. If the one I'm on is lost at sea, at least you'll still be around to be the doctor."

Josc looked thunderstruck. At what? At the idea that Lawler's ship might be lost at sea and his hero would perish? Or at the idea that he was really going to be the community doctor someday, and perhaps someday very soon?

Probably that was it. Lawler remembered how he had felt when it had first come home to him that his own apprenticeship actually had a serious purpose, this grueling, endless study and drilling: that he would one day be expected to take his father's place in this office and do all the things that his father did. He had been about fourteen then. And by the time he was twenty his father was dead and he was the doctor.

"Listen, don't worry about it," Lawler said. "Nothing's going to happen to me. But we have to think of worst possible cases, Josc. You and I, we have all the medical knowledge this settlement has, between us. We have to protect it."

"Yes. Of course."

"Okay. That means we travel in separate ships. You see what I'm saying?"

"Yes," the boy said. "Yes, I understand. I'd prefer to be with you, but I understand." He smiled. "We were going to talk about inflammations of the pleura today, weren't we?"

"Inflammations of the pleura, yes," said Lawler. He unfolded his worn, blurred anatomical chart. Josc sat forward, alert, attentive, eager. The boy was an inspiration. He reminded Lawler of something he had begun lately to forget, that his profession was more than a job: it was a calling. "Inflammations and pleural effusions, both. Symptomatology, causation, therapeutic measures." He could hear his own father's voice, deep, measured, inexorable, tolling in his mind like a great gong. "A sudden sharp pain in the chest, for example—"

DELAGARD SAID, "I'M AFRAID THE NEWS ISN'T SO GOOD."

"Oh?"

They were in Delagard's office in the shipyard. It was midday, Lawler's usual break from doctoring. Delagard had asked him to stop in. There was an open bottle of grapeweed brandy on the wood-kelp table, but Lawler had

declined a drink. Not during working hours, he said. He had always tried
to keep his mind clear when he was doctoring, except for the numbweed;
and he told himself that the numbweed did no harm in that way. If
anything it made his mind more clear.

"I've got some results. So far they aren't good results. Velmise isn't
going to take us in, doc."

It was like a kick in the belly.

"They told you that?"

Delagard shoved a sheet of message-parchment across the table. "Dag
Tharp brought me this about half an hour ago. It's from my son Kendy, on
Velmise. He says they had their council meeting last night and they voted
us down. Their immigration quota for the year is six, and they're willing to
stretch it to ten, considering the unusual circumstances. But that's all
they'll take."

"Not seventy-eight."

"Not seventy-eight, no. It's the old Shalikomo thing. Every island
afraid of having too many people and getting the Gillies upset. Of course,
you could say that ten is better than none. If we send ten to Velmise, and ten
to Salimil, and ten more to Grayvard—"

"No," Lawler said. "I want us all to stick together."

"I know that. All right."

"If we don't go to Velmise, what's the next best possibility?"

"Dag's talking to Salimil right now. I've got a son there, too, you know.
Maybe he's a little more persuasive than Kendy. Or maybe the Salimil
people aren't quite as tight-assed. Christ, you'd think we were asking
Velmise to evacuate their whole goddamned town to make room for us.
They could fit us in. It might be tough for a time, but they'd manage.
Shalikomos don't happen twice." Delagard riffled through a sheaf of parch-
ment sheets in front of him and handed them across to Lawler. "Well, fuck
Velmise. We'll come up with something. What I want is for you to look at
these."

Lawler glanced at them. Each page held a list of names, scrawled in
Delagard's big, bold script.

"What are these?"

"I told you a couple of weeks ago, I've got six ships, and that divides out
to thirteen to a ship. Actually, the way it works out, we'll have one ship with
eleven, two each with fourteen, the other three with thirteen apiece. You'll

see why in a minute. These are the passenger manifests I've drawn up."
Delagard tapped the top one. "Here. This is the one that ought to interest
you the most."

Lawler scanned it quickly. It read:

> ME AND LIS
>
> GOSPO STRUVIN
>
> DOC LAWLER
>
> QUILLAN
>
> KINVERSON
>
> SUNDIRA THANE
>
> DAG THARP
>
> ONYOS FELK
>
> DANN HENDERS
>
> NATIM GHARKID
>
> PILYA BRAUN
>
> LEO MARTELLO
>
> NEYANA GOLGHOZ

"Nice?" Delagard asked.

"What is this?"

"I told you. The passenger manifest. That's our ship, the *Queen of
Hydros*. I think it's a pretty good group."

Lawler stared at Delagard in astonishment. "You bastard, Nid. You
really know how to look after yourself."

"What are you talking about?"

"I'm talking about the terrific job you've done ensuring your own safety
and comfort while we're at sea. You aren't even embarrassed to show this to
me, are you? No, I bet you're proud of it. You've got the only doctor in the
community on your own ship, and the most skilled communications man,
and the closest thing we have to an engineer, and the mapkeeper. And
Gospo Struvin's the number-one captain of your fleet. Not a bad basic crew,
for a voyage of God knows how long taking us to God knows where. Plus
Kinverson the sea-hunter, who's so strong he doesn't even seem human and
knows his way around the ocean the way you do around your shipyard.
That's a damned fine team. And no annoying children, no old people,
nobody who's in poor health. Not bad, friend."

Anger showed for a moment, but only a moment, in Delagard's glittering little eyes.

"Look, doc, it's the flagship. This may not be such an easy voyage, if we wind up having to go all the way to Grayvard. We need to survive."

"More than the others?"

"You're the only doctor. You want to be on all the ships at once? Try it. I figured, you have to be on one ship or another, you might as well be on mine."

"Of course." Lawler ran his finger along the edge of the sheet. "But even applying the Delagard-first rule, I can't figure a few of these choices. What good is Gharkid to you? He's a complete cipher of a human being."

"He knows seaweed. That's the one thing he does know. He can help us in finding food."

"Sounds reasonable." Lawler glanced at Delagard's plump belly. "We wouldn't want to go hungry out there, would we? Eh? Eh?" Looking at the list again, he said, "And Braun? Golghoz?"

"Hard workers. Mind their own business."

"Martello? A *poet*?"

"He isn't just a poet. He knows what to do aboard a ship. Anyway, why not a poet? This is going to be like an odyssey. A fucking odyssey. A whole island emigrates. We'll have somebody to write down our story."

"Very nice," said Lawler. "Bring your own Homer along so posterity gets to hear all about the great voyage. I like that." He checked the list again. "I notice you've got only four women here, to ten men."

Delagard smiled. "The proportion of women to men isn't much in my control. We've got thirty-six females on this island and forty-two males. But eleven of the ladies belong to the fucking Sisterhood, don't forget. I'm sending them off on a ship by themselves. Let them figure out how to sail it, if they can. So we've got only twenty-five women and girls otherwise, five ships, mothers need to stay with their children, et cetera, et cetera. I calculated we had room for four on our ship."

"Picking Lis I understand. How'd you choose the other three?"

"Braun and Golghoz have both worked in my crews already, on the Velmise and Salimil runs. If I'm going to have women on board, I might as well have women who can do what needs to be done."

"And Sundira? Well, she's a skilled equipment mender. That makes sense."

"Right," Delagard said. "And also she's Kinverson's woman, isn't she? If she's useful, and they're a couple besides, why separate them?"

"They aren't a couple, as far as I know."

"Aren't they? Looks that way to me," Delagard said. "I see them together a hell of a lot. Anyway, there's our shipload, doc. In case the fleet gets separated at sea, we've got some good people with us to see us through. Now, ship number two, the *Sorve Goddess,* we'll have Brondo Katzin and his wife, all the Thalheims, the Tanaminds—"

"Wait a second," said Lawler. "I'm not through with this first one. We haven't talked about Father Quillan yet. Another very useful choice. You picked him to keep yourself on the safe side with God, I suppose?"

Delagard was impervious to the thrust. He let loose a thunderous guffaw. "Son of a bitch! No, that never crossed my mind. That would be a good idea, yeah, take a priest along with you. If anyone's got any pull upstairs, it would be him. But the reason I picked Father Quillan was just that I enjoy his company so much. I find him a terrifically interesting man."

Of course, Lawler thought.

It was always a mistake to expect Delagard to be consistent about anything.

IN THE NIGHT CAME THE OTHER EARTH-DREAM, THE ONE THAT HURT, the one he always wished he could hide from. It was a long time since he had had the two dreams on consecutive nights, and he was caught by surprise, for he had thought that last night's dream would exempt him from having the other one for some time to come. But no; no. There was no escaping it. Earth would pursue him always.

There it was in the sky above Sorve, a wondrous radiant blue-green ball, slowly turning to display its shining seas, its splendid tawny continents. It was beautiful beyond all measure, a huge jewel gleaming overhead. He saw the mountains running along the spines of the continents like jagged gray teeth. There was snow, white and pure, along their crests. He stood at the top ridge of the wooden sea-wall of his little island and let himself float up into the sky, and kept on floating until he had left Hydros and was well out in space, hovering over the blue-green ball that was Earth, looking down at it like a god. He saw the cities now: building after building, not pointy-topped like vaarghs but broad and flat, one next to another to another across immense distances, with wide pathways between them. And people moving along the pathways, thousands of them, many thousands, walking swiftly, some of them riding in little carriages that were like boats that traveled on land. Above them in the sky were the winged creatures called birds, like air-skimmers and the other fish of Hydros that he knew that were capable of bursting up out of the water for short spurts of flight, but these stayed aloft forever, soaring splendidly, circling and circling the planet in great tireless sweeps. Among the birds were machines, too, that were able to fly. They were made of metal, sleek and bright, with little wings and long tubular bodies. Lawler saw them coming up from Earth's surface and moving at unthinkable speeds across great distances, carrying the people of Earth from island to island, from city to city, from continent to continent, a commerce so vast that it made his soul spin to contemplate it.

He drifted through the darkness, high above the shining blue-green world, watching, waiting, knowing what would happen next, wondering if perhaps this time it wouldn't happen.

But of course it did. The same thing as before, the thing he had lived through so many times, the thing that brought sweat bursting from his pores and made his muscles writhe with shock and anguish. There was never any warning. It simply began: the hot yellow sun suddenly swelling, growing brighter, becoming misshapen and monstrous—the jagged tongues of fire licking out across the sky—

The flames rising from the hills and valleys, from the forests, from the buildings. The boiling seas. The charred plains. The clouds of black ash darkening the air. The blackened land splitting open. The gaunt naked mountains rising above the ruined fields. The death, the death, the death, the death.

He always wished he could wake up before that moment came. But he never did, not until he had seen it all, not until the seas had boiled, not until the green forests had turned to ash.

THE FIRST PATIENT THE NEXT MORNING WAS SIDERO VOLKIN, ONE OF Delagard's shipwrights, who had taken a flameworm's prong in the calf of his leg while standing in shallow water trimming excess sea-finger growth from the keel of one of the ships. Something like a third of Lawler's work involved wounds that people got while in the gentle, shallow waters of the bay. Those gentle, shallow waters all too often were visited by creatures that liked to sting, bite, slice, stab, infiltrate, or otherwise bedevil human beings.

"Son of a bitch swam right up to me alongside the ship and reared up and looked me in the eye," Volkin said. "I went for its head with my hatchet and its tail came around from the other side and pronged me. Son of a bitch. I cut it in half, but a fucking lot of good that does me now."

The wound was narrow but deep, and already infected. Flameworms were long wriggling creatures that seemed to be nothing more than tough, flexible tubes with a nasty little mouth on one end and a vicious stinger on the other. It didn't much matter which end they got you with: they were full of microorganisms that were symbiotic with the flameworm and hostile to humankind, and the bugs the worms carried caused immediate distress and complication when they encountered human tissue. Volkin's leg was bloated and reddened, and delicate, fiery-looking traceries of inflammation ran outward along the skin from the point of entry like the cicatrices of some sinister cult.

"This is going to hurt," Lawler said, dipping a long bamboo needle into a bowl of strong antiseptic.

"Don't I know it, doc."

Lawler probed the wound with the needle, pricking it here and there, getting as much of the antiseptic into the swollen flesh as he thought Volkin could endure. The shipwright remained motionless, cursing under his breath once in a while, as Lawler poked around in him with what must surely be agonizing effect.

"Here's some pain-killer," Lawler said, offering him a packet of white powder. "You'll feel lousy for a couple of days. Then the inflammation will subside. You'll be feverish this afternoon, too. Take the day off from work."

"I can't. Delagard won't let me. We've got to get those ships ready to go. There's hell of a lot that needs to be done on them."

"Take the day off," Lawler said again. "If Delagard gives you any shit, tell him I'm the one he ought to complain to. In half an hour you'll be too dizzy to do any worthwhile work anyway. Go on, now."

Volkin hesitated a moment at the door of Lawler's vaargh.

"I sure appreciate this, doc."

"Go on. Get off that leg before you fall down."

Another patient was waiting outside: another of Delagard's people, Neyana Golghoz. She was a placid, stocky woman of about forty, with hair of an unusual orange color and a broad flat face covered with reddish freckles. Originally she was from Kaggeram Island, but she had come to Sorve five or six years back. Neyana worked in some maintenance capacity on board the ships of Delagard's fleet, constantly journeying back and forth between the neighboring islands. Six months ago a skin cancer had sprouted between her shoulderblades, and Lawler had removed it chemically, by slipping solvent-bearing needles under it until the malignancy dissolved and could be lifted away. The process hadn't been fun for either of them. Lawler had ordered her to return every month so that he could see whether any recurrence had developed.

Neyana stripped off her work-shirt and turned her back to him, and Lawler investigated the scar with his fingers. It was probably still tender, but she didn't react at all. Like most of the islanders, she was stolid and patient. Life on Hydros was simple, sometimes harsh, never very amusing for its human population. There weren't many choices, not a lot of options about what you did, who you married, where you could live. Unless you felt like trying your luck on some other island, most of the essential facts of your life were defined for you by the time you reached adulthood. If you went somewhere else, you were likely to find that your choices there were limited by many of the same factors. That tended to breed a certain stoicism.

"Looks fine," Lawler told her. "You keeping out of the sun, Neyana?"

"Damn right I am."

"Putting the ointment on?"

"Damn right."

"You won't have any problem with this again, then."

"You're one hell of a good doctor," Neyana told him. "I knew someone once on the other island, he had a cancer like this and it ate right through his skin and he died. But you look out for us, you watch over us."

"I do what I can." It always embarrassed Lawler when the patients were grateful. Most of the time he felt like a butcher, hacking away at them with such prehistoric methods, when on other planets—so he had heard from those who had come to Hydros from elsewhere—doctors had all manner of absolutely miraculous treatments at their command. They used sound waves and electricity and radiation and all sorts of things he scarcely understood, and they had drugs that could cure anything in five minutes. Whereas he had to make do with home-made salves and potions compounded from seaweed, and improvised tools made of wood and the odd bit of iron or nickel. But he had told her the truth, at least: he did what he could.

"Any time I can do something for you, doc, just ask."

"That's very kind of you," Lawler said.

Neyana went out and Nicko Thalheim came in. Thalheim was Sorve-born like Lawler. Like Lawler, too, he was First Family, a five-generation pedigree, right back to the penal-colony days: one of the island leaders, a bluff, ruddy-faced man with a short, thick neck and powerful shoulders. He and Lawler had been boyhood playmates and they were still good friends. Seven of the island's people all told were Thalheims, a tenth of the entire population: Nicko's father, his wife, his sister, his three children. Families rarely had as many as three children. Thalheim's sister had joined the group of women down at the far end of the island a few months before: she was known as Sister Boda now to everyone. Thalheim hadn't been pleased when she joined.

Lawler said, "That abscess still draining okay?"

Thalheim had an infection in his left armpit. Lawler thought he had probably been stung by something in the bay, but Thalheim denied it. The abscess was a messy one, pus constantly pouring out. Lawler had lanced it three times already and tried to clean it, but it had reinfected each time. The last time, he had had the weaver Harry Travish make up a little catch-tube of sea-plastic and had stitched it to Thalheim's side to collect the pus and carry it away from the trouble-spot.

Lawler lifted the dressing now, snipped the stitches that held the catch-tube in place, and peered at the infection. The skin all around it was red, and hot to the touch.

"Hurts like a bastard," Thalheim said.

"Looks pretty lousy, too. You putting the medicine I gave you on it?"

"Sure I am."

He didn't sound convincing. Lawler said, "You can do it or not, as it pleases you, Nicko. But if that infection spreads down your arm, I may wind up having to take the arm off you. You think you can work okay with just one arm?"

"It's only my left one, Val."

"You don't really mean that."

"No. No, I don't." Thalheim grunted as Lawler touched the wound again. "I might have missed a day or two with the medicine. I'm sorry, Val."

"You'll be sorrier in a little while."

Coolly, unsparingly, Lawler cleaned the site as though he were carving a piece of wood. Thalheim remained silent and motionless as Lawler worked.

As Lawler was reattaching the catch-tube, Thalheim said suddenly, "We've known each other a long time, haven't we, Val?"

"Close to forty years, yes."

"And neither of us ever felt like going to some other island."

`"It never occurred to me," Lawler said. "And in any case I was the doctor."

"Yes. And I just liked it here."

"Yes," Lawler said. Where was all this leading?

"You know, Val," Thalheim said, "I've been thinking about this business of having to go. I hate it. It's making me absolutely sick inside."

"I don't like it much myself, Nicko."

"No. But you seem resigned to it."

"What other choice do I have?"

"Maybe there is one, Val."

Lawler looked at him, waiting.

Thalheim said, "I heard what you said at the town meeting. When you told us that trying to fight the Gillies wouldn't work. I didn't agree with you that night, but when I thought things over I saw you were right. Still, I've been wondering if maybe there's some way a few of us can stay here."

"What?"

"I mean, say ten or twelve of us hide out down at the far end where the Sisters have been living. You, me, my family, the Katzins, the Hains— that's a dozen. A pretty decent group, too, no frictions, everybody friends. We lay low, keep out of the way of the Gillies, do our fishing off the back side of the island, and try to go on living the way we lived before."

The idea was so wild that it caught Lawler in an unprotected place. For a crazy fraction of a second he actually was tempted. Stay here after all? Not have to give up the familiar paths, the familiar bay? The Gillies never went down to the far end. They might not notice if just a few of the island's people remained behind when—

No.

The nonsensical nature of the plan came crashing in like the fist of the Wave. The Gillies wouldn't need to go down to the far end to know what was happening there. The Gillies somehow always knew everything that happened anywhere on the island. They would find them in five minutes and toss them over the rear bulwark into the sea, and that would be that. Besides, even if a few people did manage to evade Gillie surveillance, how could they think that they could live as they had lived before, with most of the community somewhere else? No. No. Impossible, absurd.

"What do you think?" Thalheim asked.

Lawler said, after a moment's pause, "Forgive me, Nicko. But I think it's as goofy as Nimber's notion the other night about stealing one of their idols and holding it for ransom."

"Do you?"

"Yeah."

Thalheim was silent, studying the swelling under his arm as Lawler bandaged it.

Then he said, "You always did have a practical way of looking at things. Kind of cold-blooded, Val, but practical, always practical. You just don't like taking risks, I guess."

"Not when the odds are a million to one against me."

"You think it's that bad?"

"It can't work, Nicko. No way. Come on: admit it. Nobody puts anything over on the Gillies. The idea's poison. It's suicide."

"Maybe so," Thalheim said.

"Not maybe."

"It sounded pretty good for a moment."

"We wouldn't stand a chance," said Lawler.

"No. No. We wouldn't, would we?" Thalheim shook his head. "I really want to stay here, Val. I don't want to go. I'd give everything I have not to have to go."

"Me too," Lawler said. "But we're going. We have to."

SUNDIRA THANE CAME TO SEE HIM WHEN HER SUPPLY OF THE NUMB-weed tranquilizer was all gone. Her vivid, energetic presence filled the little reception room of his vaargh like a trumpet-blast.

But she was coughing again. Lawler knew why, and it wasn't because alien fungi had invaded her lungs. She looked drawn, tense. The brightness that gave her eyes such intense life was the brightness of anxiety today, not simply that of inner force.

Lawler filled the little storage gourd he had given her with a new supply of the pink drops, enough to last her until the day of departure. After that, if the cough was still with her when they were out at sea, she could share his supply.

She said, "One of those crazy women from the Sisterhood was in town just now, did you know? She was telling everyone that she's cast our horoscope and none of us will survive the voyage to the new island. Not a single one, she said. Some of us are going to be lost at sea and the rest are going to sail right off the edge of the world and end up in heaven."

"That's Sister Thecla, I'd guess. She claims to be clairvoyant."

"And is she?"

"She once did a horoscope on me, back in the days before the Sisterhood when she was still speaking to men. She said I'd live to a ripe old age and have a happy, fulfilled life. Now she says we're all going to die at sea. One of those two horoscopes has to be wrong, wouldn't you think? Here, open your mouth. Let me stare at your larynx for a minute."

"Maybe Sister Thecla meant that you would be one of the ones who's going to sail straight to heaven."

"Sister Thecla is not a reliable source of information," Lawler said. "Sister Thecla is a seriously disturbed woman, as a matter of fact. Open up."

He looked down her throat. There was a little mild irritation of the tissues, nothing special: just about what an occasional psychosomatic cough would be expected to produce.

"If Delagard knew how to sail to heaven, he'd have done it already," Lawler said. "He'd be running a ferry service back and forth. He'd have shipped the Sisters there a long time ago. As for your throat, it's the same story as before. Tension, nervous coughing, irritation. Just try to relax. Keeping away from Sisters who want to forecast your future for you would be a good idea."

Sundira smiled. "Those poor silly women. I feel sorry for them." Though the consultation was over, she seemed in no hurry to leave. She wandered over to the shelf where he kept his little collection of Earth artifacts and studied them for a moment. "You said you'd tell me what these things are."

He came up alongside her. "The metal statuette's the oldest one. It's a god that they worshiped in a land called Egypt, thousands of years ago. Egypt was a land beside a river, one of the most ancient places on Earth, where civilization started. He's either the sun-god or the god of death. Or both. I'm not certain."

"Both? How can a sun-god also be a death-god? The sun's the source of life, it's bright and warm. Death is something dark. It's—" She paused. "But Earth's sun was the bringer of death, wasn't it? You mean to say they knew that in this place called Egypt thousands of years before it happened?"

"I doubt it very much. But the sun dies every night. And is reborn the next morning. Maybe that was the connection." Or maybe not. He was only guessing. He knew so little.

She picked up the small bronze figurine and held it in her palm as though weighing it.

"Four thousand years. I can't imagine four thousand years."

Lawler smiled. "Sometimes I hold it the way you're holding it now, and I try to let it take me back to the place where it was made. Dry sand, hot sun, a blue river with trees along its banks. Cities with thousands of people. Huge temples and palaces. But it's so hard to keep the vision clear. All I can really see in my mind is an ocean and a little island."

She put the statuette down and pointed to the potsherd. "And this piece of hard painted material, that's from Greece, you said?"

"Greece, yes. It's pottery. They made it out of clay. Look, you can see a bit of a picture on it, a figure of a warrior, and a spear that he must have been holding."

"How beautiful the outline is. It must have been a marvelous piece of work. But we'll never know, will we? When was Greece? After Egypt?"

"Much later. But still very ancient. They had poets and philosophers there, and great artists. Homer was a Greek."

"Homer?"

"He wrote *The Odyssey. The Iliad.*"

"I'm sorry. I don't—"

"Famous poems, very long ones. One was about a war and one about a sea voyage. My father used to tell me stories that came from them, the bits and pieces that he remembered from *his* father. Who learned them from his grandfather Harry, whose grandfather was born on Earth. It was only seven generations ago that Earth still existed. Sometimes we forget that: sometimes we forget that Earth ever existed at all. You see that round brown medallion there? That's a map of Earth. The continents and seas."

Of all his treasures, Lawler often thought that was the most precious. It was neither the most ancient nor the most beautiful; but the portrait of Earth itself was inscribed on it. He had no idea who had made it, or when, or why. It was a flat hard disk, larger than his coin from the United States of America but still small enough to fit in the palm of his hand. There was lettering around its edges that nobody was able to understand, and in the center were two overlapping circles in which the map of Earth had been engraved, two continents in one hemisphere and two in the other, with a fifth continent at the bottom of the world in both circles and some large islands breaking the great expanse of the seas. Perhaps they were continents too, some of them: Lawler didn't quite understand where the boundary was between being an island and being a continent.

He pointed to the left-hand circle. "Supposedly Egypt was here, in the middle of this place. And Greece somewhere up here. And this may have been the United States of America, over on the other side, up here. This little metal piece is a coin that they used there, in the United States of America."

"For what?"

"Money," Lawler said. "Coins were money."

"And this rusted thing?"

"A weapon. A gun, it was called. It fired little darts called bullets."

She made a little shivering gesture. "You have just these six things of Earth, and one of them has to be a weapon. But they were like that, weren't they? Making war on each other all the time? Killing each other, hurting each other?"

"Some of them were like that, especially in the ancient days. Later it changed, I think." Lawler indicated the rough chunk of stone, his final artifact. "This was from some wall they had, a wall between countries, because there was war. That would be like a wall between islands here, if you can imagine such a thing. Eventually peace came and they tore the wall down and everyone celebrated, and pieces of it were saved so no one would forget it had once existed." Lawler shrugged. "They were people, that's all. Some were good and some weren't. I don't think they were that different from us."

"But their world was."

"Very different, yes. A strange and wonderful place."

"There's a special look that comes into your eyes when you speak about Earth. I saw it the other night, down by the bay, when you were talking of how we all live in exile. A kind of glow; a look of longing, I guess. You said that some people think Earth was a paradise, and some that it was a place of horror that everyone wanted to escape from. You must be one of those who think it was a paradise."

"No," Lawler said. "I told you. I don't know what kind of place it really was. I suppose it was pretty crowded and shabby and dirty toward the end, or there wouldn't have been such a big emigration from it. But I can't say. I suppose we'll never know the truth." He paused and looked at her closely. "The only thing I know is that it was our home once. We should never forget that. Our real and true home. However much we try to fool ourselves into believing that Hydros is our home, we're all really just visitors here."

"Visitors?" Sundira said.

She was standing very close to him. Her gray eyes were bright, her lips were moist. It seemed to Lawler that her breasts were rising and falling more rapidly than usual beneath her light wrap. Imagination? Or was she coming on to him?

"Do you feel at home on Hydros?" Lawler asked her. "Really, really, feel at home?"

"Of course. Don't you?"

"I wish I did."

"But you were born here!"

"So?"

"I don't underst—"

"Am I a Gillie? Am I a diver? Am I a meatfish? They feel at home here. They *are* at home here."

"So are you."

"You still don't understand," he said.

"I'm trying, though. I want to."

This was the moment to reach out to her, Lawler thought. Pull her close, caress her, do this and that, hands, lips, make things happen. She wants to understand you, he told himself. Give her her chance.

And then he heard Delagard's voice in his head, saying, *And also she's Kinverson's woman, isn't she? If she's useful, and they're a couple besides, why separate them?*

"Yes," he said, his tone suddenly short. "Lots of questions, not many answers. Isn't it always that way?" Abruptly he wanted to be alone. He tapped the flask of numbweed tincture. "This supply should last you another couple of weeks, right up to the time we leave. If the cough doesn't clear up again, let me know."

She looked a little startled at the brusque dismissal. But then she smiled and thanked him and went out.

Shit, he thought. Shit. Shit. Shit.

DELAGARD SAID, "THE SHIPS ARE JUST ABOUT IN SHAPE, AND WE'VE still got a week. My people have really been breaking their balls getting them ready."

Lawler, at the shipyard, glanced out toward the water, where the entire Delagard fleet was at anchor in the harbor except for one ship that was up in drydock having its hull patched. Two carpenters were busy at it. Three men and four women were at work aboard the two nearest sea-borne vessels, hammering and planing. "I assume you mean that figuratively, of course."

"What? Oh. Oh. Very funny, doc. Listen, everybody who works for me has balls, even the women. It's just my vulgar way of speaking. Or one of my quaint little figures of speech, whichever you prefer. Do you want to see what we've been doing?"

"I've never been aboard a ship, you know? Only little fishing boats, coracles, things like that."

"There's always a first time. Come on. I'll show you the flagship."

It looked smaller, once Lawler was aboard, than Delagard's ships seemed when riding at anchor in the bay. Still, it looked big enough. It was almost like a miniature island. Lawler could feel it rolling lightly beneath his feet, even here in the shallows. Its keel was made of the same tough hard yellow wood-kelp timber as the island itself, long sturdy fibers tightly lashed together and caulked with pitch. The exterior of the hull had a different sort of caulking. Just as the island's bulwarks wore a covering mesh of live sea-finger weed that constantly repaired and rewove itself as the ocean battered against the island wall, just as the wooden timbers of the bay floor were reinforced by a layer of protective algae, so too did a dense green network of sea-finger festoon the sides of the hull, coming clear up almost to the railing. The stubby little blue-green tubules of the weed, which had always looked more like tiny bottles than fingers to Lawler, gave the ship a thick bristling coating, jutting out in intricate tangles just below the waterline. The deck was a flat, tight expanse of some lighter wood, carefully sealed to keep the interior of the ship dry when waves came over the bow. Two masts rose at middeck. Hatches fore and aft led to mysterious deeper regions.

Delagard said, "What we've been doing is resealing the deck and resurfacing the hull. We want to be watertight all around. We may see some ugly storms and we'll sure as hell be run down by the Wave somewhere out there. On an interisland voyage we can try to steer around lousy weather, and if things go the right way for us we can hope to avoid the worst of the Wave, but we may not have it so easy on this trip."

"Isn't this an interisland voyage?" Lawler asked.

"It may not be inter the islands we'd prefer. Sometimes, a voyage like this, you have to take the long way around."

Lawler didn't quite follow that, but Delagard didn't amplify and he let the point go by. Delagard hauled him briskly around the ship, reeling off technical terms: this is the cabinhouse, this the deckhouse, the bridge, the forecastle, the quarterdeck, the bowsprit, the windlass, the water-strider, the gantry and reel. These are gaffing rods, this is the wheel box, that's the binnacle. Down below we have the crew quarters here, the hold, the magnetron room, the radio room, the carpenter's shop, the this, the that. Lawler was scarcely listening. Most of the terms meant nothing to him. What struck him mainly was how everything below was so incredibly close together, one thing jammed up against another. He was accustomed to the privacy and solitude of his vaargh. They would all be in each other's pockets here. He was trying to imagine himself living on this crowded boat for two, three, four weeks, out there on the open ocean with no land anywhere in sight.

Not a boat, he told himself. A ship. An oceangoing sailing ship.

"What's the latest word from Salimil?" Lawler asked, when Delagard finally led him up from the claustrophobic depths.

"Dag's talking to them right now. They were supposed to have the council meeting this morning. My guess is we're in like a breeze. They've got plenty of room there. My son Rylie called me from Salimil last week and told me that four members of the council are definitely for us and two more are leaning our way."

"Out of how many?"

"Nine."

"Sounds good," Lawler said. So they would go to Salimil, then. All right. All right. So be it. He summoned an image of Salimil Island as he imagined it to be—much like Sorve, of course, but somehow bigger, grander, more lavish—and pictured himself arranging his medical equipment in a vaargh by the Salimil shore that his colleague, Dr. Nikitin of Salimil, had made ready for him. Lawler had spoken with Nikitin many times by radio. He wondered what the man actually looked like. Salimil, yes. Lawler wanted to believe that Rylie Delagard knew what he was talking about, that Salimil was going to take them in. But Lawler remembered that Delagard's other son Kendy, who lived on Velmise, had been just as confident that Velmise would accept the refugees from Sorve.

Sidero Volkin came limping up on deck and said to Delagard, "Dag Tharp's here. He's in your office."

Delagard grinned. "Here's our answer. Let's go ashore."

But Tharp was already on his way down to the edge of the water to meet them as they clambered off the ship, and the moment Lawler saw the stricken look on the little radio operator's red sharp-featured face he knew what the answer from Salimil had been.

"Well?" Delagard asked, all the same.

"Turned us down. Five-to-four vote. They're low on water, they said. Because the summer's been so dry. Offered to take six people, though."

"The bastards. Well, fuck them."

"That what you want me to tell them?" Tharp asked.

"Don't tell them anything. I wouldn't waste the time on them. We aren't going to send them six. It's all or none, wherever we go." He looked at Lawler.

"What's next?" Lawler asked. "Shaktan? Kaggeram?" The island names came easily to his lips. But he had no idea where they were, or what they might be like.

"They'll give us the same crap," Delagard said.

"I could try Kaggeram anyway," said Tharp. "They're pretty decent over there, I remember. I was there about ten years ago, when—"

"Fuck Kaggeram," Delagard said. "They've got one of those council deals too. They'll need a week to debate it, and then a public meeting, and a vote, and all that. We don't have that much more time." Delagard seemed to disappear into thought. He might have been a world away. He had the look of someone who was making abstruse calculations with the most intense mental effort. Delagard's eyes were half shut, his thick black brows were close together. A heavy shell of silence surrounded him. "Grayvard," he said finally.

"But Grayvard's eight weeks from here," said Lawler.

"Grayvard?" Tharp said, looking startled. "You want me to call Grayvard?"

"Not you. Me. I'll make the call myself, right from this ship." Delagard was silent again a moment. Once more he seemed very distant, working out mental sums. Then he nodded as if satisfied with his answer and said, "I've got cousins on Grayvard. I know how to bargain with my own cousins, for Christ's sake. What to offer. They'll take us. You can be damn sure of that. There won't be any problem. Grayvard it is!"

Lawler stood watching as Delagard went striding back toward the ship. Grayvard? Grayvard?

He knew almost nothing about it: an island at the far edge of the island group in which Sorve moved, an island that spent as much time in the adjacent Red Sea as it did in Home Sea. It was about as distant as an island could be and still have any sort of real relationship with Sorve.

Lawler had been taught in school that forty of the islands of Hydros had human settlements on them. Maybe the official number was up to fifty or sixty by now: he didn't know. The true total was probably a good deal higher than that, since everyone lived in the shadow of the Shalikomo massacre that had happened in the time of the third generation, and whenever an island's population began to grow too large, ten or twenty people would leave to seek a new life somewhere else. The settlers who moved to those new islands didn't necessarily have the means to establish radio contact with the rest of Hydros. So it was easy to lose count. Say, eighty islands with humans, by this time, or even a hundred. Scattered over an entire planet, a planet said to be bigger than Earth itself had been. Communication between the islands was spotty and difficult beyond one's own little island group. Hazy interisland alliances formed and dissolved as the islands traveled around the world.

Once, long ago, some humans had attempted to build an island of their own, so they wouldn't have to live all the time under the eyes of Gillie neighbors. They had figured out how it was done and had begun weaving the fibers, but before they got very far the island was attacked by huge sea-creatures and destroyed. Dozens of lives were lost. Everyone assumed the monsters had been sent by the Gillies, who obviously hadn't liked the idea of humans setting up a little independent domain of their own. No one had ever tried it again.

Grayvard, Lawler thought. Well, well, well.

One island is as good as another, he told himself. He'd manage to adapt, somehow, wherever they landed. But would they be really welcome on Grayvard? Would they even be able to find it, somewhere out there between Home Sea and the Red Sea? What the hell. Let Delagard worry about it. Why should he care? It was all out of his hands.

GHARKID'S VOICE, THIN AND HUSKY AND PIPING, CAME TO LAWLER AS he was walking slowly back up to his vaargh.

"Doctor? Doctor-sir?"

He was heavily laden, staggering under the weight of two immense dripping baskets stuffed with algae that he carried in a shoulder-harness.

Lawler halted to wait for him. Gharkid came lurching toward him and let the baskets slide from his shoulders practically at Lawler's feet.

Gharkid was a small wiry man, so much shorter than Lawler that he had to crane his head far back in order to look at him straight on. He smiled, showing brilliant white teeth against the dusky backdrop of his face. There was something earnest and very appealing about him. But the childlike simplicity that the man affected, that cheerful peasant innocence, could be a little cloying sometimes.

"What's all this?" Lawler asked, looking down at the tangle of weeds spilling out of the baskets, green ones and red ones and yellow ones streaked with gaudy purple veins.

"For you, doctor-sir. Medicines. For when we leave, to take with us."

Gharkid grinned. He seemed very pleased with himself.

Lawler, kneeling, poked through the sopping mess. He was able to recognize some of the seaweeds. This bluish one was the painkiller, and this with the dark strap-shaped lateral leaves yielded the better of the two antiseptics, and this one—yes, this one was numbweed. Unquestionably numbweed. Good old Gharkid. Lawler looked up and as his gaze met Gharkid's there was for just a moment a flash of something not all that naive and childlike in Gharkid's dark eyes.

"To take with us on the ship," Gharkid said, as though Lawler hadn't comprehended before. "These are the good ones, for the drugs. I thought you'd want them, some extras."

"You've done very well," Lawler said. "Here. Let's carry this stuff up to my vaargh."

It was a rich haul. The man had gathered some of everything that had any medicinal use. Lawler had been putting it off and putting it off and at last Gharkid had simply gone out into the bay and loaded up on the whole pharmacopoeia. Well done indeed, Lawler thought. Especially the numbweed. There'd be just enough time to process all this before they sailed, get it all refined down into powders and salves and ointments and tinctures. And then the ship would be nicely stocked with medicinals for the long pull to Grayvard. He knew his algae, Gharkid did. Once again Lawler wondered if Gharkid was really as much of a simpleton as he seemed, or if that was merely some sort of defensive pose. Gharkid often seemed like a blank soul, a tabula rasa on which anyone was free to write anything at all. There had to be more to him than that, somewhere inside. But where?

• • •

THE FINAL DAYS BEFORE SAILING WERE BAD ONES. EVERYONE ADMITTED the necessity to go, but not everybody had believed it would really happen, and now reality was closing in with terrible force. Lawler saw old women making piles of their possessions outside their vaarghs, staring blankly at them, rearranging them, carrying things inside and bringing other things out. Some of the women and a few of the men cried all the time, some of them quietly, some not so quietly. The sounds of hysterical sobbing could be heard all through the night. Lawler treated the worst cases with numbweed tincture. "Easy, there," he kept saying. "Easy, easy." Thom Lyonides was drunk three days straight, roaring and singing, and then he started a fight with Bamber Cadrell, saying that nobody was going to make him get on board one of those ships. Delagard came by with Gospo Struvin and said, "What the fuck is this," and Lyonides jumped at him, snarling and screeching like a lunatic. Delagard hit him in the face, and Struvin caught him around the throat and throttled him until he calmed down. "Put him on his ship," Delagard said to Cadrell. "Make sure he stays there until we sail."

On the next-to-last day, and the last day also, parties of Gillies came right down to the border between their territory and the human settlement and stood there watching in their inscrutable way, as if making sure the humans were making ready to clear out. Everyone on Sorve knew now that there would be no reprieve, no revocation of the order of expulsion. The last doubters, the last deniers, had had to cave in under the pressure of those fishy, staring, implacable eyes. Sorve was lost to them forever. Grayvard would be their new home. That much was settled.

JUST BEFORE THE END, HOURS FROM DEPARTURE, LAWLER CLIMBED THE island to its rearmost point, on the side opposite the bay, where the high bulwark faced the ocean. It was noon, and the water was ablaze with reflected light.

From his vantage point on the bulwark Lawler looked out across the open sea and imagined himself sailing on it, far from any shore. He wanted to find out if he still feared it, that endless world of water on which he would embark not very long from now.

No. No. All the fear seemed to have gone from him that drunken night at Delagard's place. It hadn't returned. Lawler stared into the distance and saw nothing but ocean, and that was all right. There wasn't anything to fear. He would be exchanging the island for a ship, which was nothing more than a miniature island, really. What was the worst-case possibility, then? That his ship would sink in a storm, he supposed, or be smashed by the Wave, and he'd die. All right: he had to die sooner or later. That wasn't news. But ships weren't lost at sea all that often. The odds were that they would reach Grayvard safely. He would go ashore once again and begin a new life.

What Lawler still felt, rather than fear of the voyage that lay ahead, was the occasional sharp stab of grief for all he would be leaving behind. The longing arose quickly and just as quickly went, unsatisfied.

But now, strangely, the things he was leaving behind began to leave him. As Lawler stood with his back to the settlement, staring into the great dark expanse of the water, they all seemed to depart on the breeze that was blowing past him out to sea: his awesome father, his gentle elusive mother, his almost forgotten brothers. His whole childhood, his coming of age, his brief marriage, his years as the island doctor, as the Dr. Lawler of his generation. Everything going away, suddenly. Everything. He felt weirdly light, as if he could simply mount the breeze and float through the air to Grayvard. All the shackles seemed to have broken. Everything that held him here had fallen from him in a moment. Everything.

Part Two

To the EMPTY SEA

1

THE FIRST FOUR DAYS OF THE VOYAGE HAD BEEN PLACID, ALMOST suspiciously so. "Real strange is what it is," said Gabe Kinverson, and solemnly shook his head. "You'd expect some troubles by now, this far out in the middle of nowhere," he said, looking out over the slow, calm blue-gray swells. The wind was steady. The sails were full. The ships stayed close together, moving serenely across a glassy sea on their route toward the northwest, toward Grayvard. A new home; a new life; for the seventy-eight voyagers, the castaways, the exiles, it was like a second birth. But should any birth, a first one or a second, be as easy as this? And how much longer would it be this easy?

ON THE FIRST DAY, WHEN THEY WERE STILL CROSSING THE BAY, LAWLER had found himself wandering astern again and again to look back at Sorve Island as it receded into invisibility.

In those early hours of the voyage Sorve had risen behind them like a long tawny mound. It still seemed real and tangible then. He was able to make out the familiar central spine and the outcurving arms, the gray spires of the vaarghs, the power plant, the rambling buildings of Delagard's shipyard. He thought he could even see the somber line of Gillies who had come down to the shore to watch the six vessels depart.

Then the water began to change color. The deep rich green of the shallow bay gave way to the ocean color, which here was a dark blue tinged with gray. That was the true mark of cutting loose from shore, when you had left the bay behind. To Lawler it felt as if a trapdoor had been sprung, catapulting him into free fall. Now that the artificial bottom had dropped away beneath them Sorve began rapidly to shrink, becoming nothing but a dark line on the horizon, and then nothing at all.

Farther out the ocean would be other colors, depending on the micro-organisms in it, the surrounding climate, the upwellings of particulate matter from the depths. The different seas were named according to their prevailing hue: the Red Sea, the Yellow, the Azure, the Black. The one to fear was the Empty Sea, the sea that was pale ice-blue, a desert sea. Great tracts of the ocean were like that and almost nothing lived in them. But the route of the expedition would pass nowhere near any of that.

The ships were traveling in a tight pyramid-shaped formation that they would try to hold to day and night. Each vessel was under the command of one of Delagard's ferry captains except for the one on which the eleven women of the Sisterhood sailed all by themselves. Delagard had offered to give them one of his men to be their pilot, but they had refused, as he had expected them to do. "Sailing a ship's no problem," Sister Halla told him. "We'll watch what you do and we'll do the same thing."

Delagard's flagship, the *Queen of Hydros,* was in the lead, at the apex of the pyramid, with Gospo Struvin in charge. Then came two side by side, the *Black Sea Star* commanded by Poilin Stayvol and the *Sorve Goddess* under Bamber Cadrell, and behind them the other three ships in a broader line, the Sisterhood in the middle aboard the *Hydros Cross* flanked by the *Three Moons* under Martin Yanez and the *Golden Sun* commanded by Damis Sawtelle.

Now, with Sorve altogether gone from view, there was nothing in sight anywhere but sky and sea, the flat horizon, the gentle ocean swells. A curious sort of peace descended over Lawler. He found it surprisingly easy to submerge himself in the vastness of it all, to lose himself completely. The sea was calm and seemed likely to stay that way forever. Sorve could no longer be seen, that was true. Sorve had disappeared. What of it? Sorve no longer mattered.

He moved forward along the deck, savoring the force of the wind against his back as it pushed the ship steadily onward, every minute carrying him farther and farther from anything he had ever known.

Father Quillan was standing by the foremast. The priest wore a dark gray wrap of some unusual light woven material, airy and soft, something he must have brought with him from another world. There were no such fabrics available on Hydros.

Lawler paused by his side. Quillan gestured broadly toward the sea. It was like an enormous blue jewel, sparkling with fierce brilliance, its great glassy curve reaching outward on all sides as if the entire planet were a single shining polished sphere. "Looking at all that, you wouldn't believe that anything but water exists anywhere in the world, would you?"

"Not here, no."

"Such an enormous ocean. Such emptiness everywhere."

"Makes you think there has to be a god, doesn't it? The immensity of it all."

Quillan looked at him, startled.

"Does it?"

"I don't know. I was asking you."

"Do you believe in God, Lawler?"

"My father did."

"But not you?"

Lawler shrugged. "My father had a Bible. He used to read it to us. It got lost, somewhere, a long time back. Or stolen. I remember a little of it. 'And God said, let there be a firmament in the midst of the waters, and let it divide the waters from the waters. And God called the firmament Heaven.' That's heaven up there, right, Father Quillan? Behind the sky? And the waters that are supposed to be above it, that's the ocean of space, isn't it?" Quillan was staring at him in astonishment. " 'And God said, Let the waters under the heaven be gathered together unto one place, and let the dry land appear, and it was so. And God called the dry land Earth; and the gathering together of the waters called the Seas.' "

Quillan said, "You know the whole Bible by heart, do you?"

"Only this little bit. It's the first page. I couldn't make any sense out of the rest of it, all those prophets and kings and battles and such."

"And Jesus."

"That part was in the back. I never read it that far." Lawler looked toward the endlessly retreating horizon, blue curving away under blue toward infinity. "Since there's no dry land here, obviously God meant to create something different on Hydros from what He created on Earth. Wouldn't you say? 'God called the dry land Earth.' And He called the wet land Hydros, I guess. What a job it must have been, creating all those different worlds. Not just Earth, but every single world in the galaxy. Iriarte, Fenix, Megalo Kastro, Darma Barma, Mentirosa, Copperfield, Nabomba Zom, the whole bunch of them, the million and one planets. With a different purpose in mind for each world, or else why bother creating so many? It was all the same god that created them all, wasn't it?"

"I don't know," Quillan said.

"But you're a priest!"

"That doesn't mean I know everything. That doesn't even mean I know anything."

"Do you believe in God?" Lawler asked.

"I don't know."

"Do you believe in anything at all?"

Quillan was silent for a time. His face went completely dead, as if his spirit had momentarily left his body.

"I don't think so," he said.

THE SEA SEEMED FLATTER HERE, FOR SOME REASON, THAN IT DID ON THE island. Darkness came suddenly, falling almost with a crash. The sun plummeted through the western sky, hovered for a moment just above the sea, and sank. Virtually at once the world turned black behind them and the Cross began to glow overhead.

"Mess call, first watch," Natim Gharkid yelled, banging on a pan.

The working crew of the *Queen of Hydros* was divided into two watches, four hours on and four hours off. The members of each watch took their meals together. The first watch was Leo Martello, Gabe Kinverson, Pilya Braun, Gharkid, Dag Tharp, and Gospo Struvin; the second watch was Neyana Golghoz, Sundira Thane, Dann Henders, Delagard, Onyos Felk, Lis Niklaus, and Father Quillan. There was no special officers' mess: Delagard and Struvin, the owner and captain, took their meals in the galley with the others. Lawler, who had no fixed duty schedule himself but was on call round the clock, was the only one outside the watch system entirely. That suited Lawler's biological rhythms: he took his morning mess with the second watch at dawn, his evening mess with the first watch at sundown. But it gave him an oddly free-floating sense of not really being part of things. Even here in the earliest days of the voyage the two watches were beginning to develop a kind of team spirit, and he belonged to neither team.

"Greenweed stew tonight," Lis Niklaus said, as the first watch filed into the galley. "Baked sentryfish fins. Fish-meal cakes, suppleberry salad." It was the third night of the voyage. The menu had been the same each night; each night Lis had made the same jovial announcement, as though expecting them all to be delighted. She did most of the cooking, with help from Gharkid and occasionally Delagard. The meals were spare, and not likely to get much better later on: dried fish, fish-meal cakes, dried seaweed, seaweed-meal bread, supplemented by Gharkid's latest haul of fresh algae and whatever live catch had been brought in that day. So far the catch had been nothing but sentryfish. Schools of the alert, eager-looking spear-nosed creatures had been following the fleet ever since Sorve. Kinverson, Pilya Braun, and Henders were the chief fishers, working from the gantry-and-reel fishing station aft.

Struvin said, "Easy day today."

"Too easy," grunted Kinverson, leaning into his plate.

"You want storms? You want the Wave?"

Kinverson shrugged. "I don't trust an easy sea."

Dag Tharp, spearing another fish-meal cake, said, "How are we doing on our water tonight, Lis?"

"One more squirt apiece and that's it for this meal."

"Shit. This is thirsty food, you know?"

"We'll be thirstier later if we drink up all our water the first week," Struvin said. "You know that as well as I do. Lis, bring out some raw sentryfish filets for the radio man."

Before leaving Sorve the villagers had loaded the ships with as many casks of fresh water as they had room for. But even so there was only something like a three-week supply on hand at the time of departure, figuring cautious use. They would have to depend on encountering rain as they went; if there was none, they'd have to find other means of meeting their freshwater needs. Eating raw fish was one good way. Everybody knew that. But Tharp wasn't having any.

He looked up, scowling. "Skip it. Fuck raw sentryfish."

"Takes away your thirst," Kinverson said quietly.

"Takes away your appetite," Tharp said. "Fuck it. I'd rather go thirsty."

Kinverson shrugged. "Suit yourself. You'll feel different about it in a week or two."

Lis put a plate of pale greenish meat on the table. The moist slices of uncooked fish had been wrapped in strips of fresh yellow seaweed. Tharp stared morosely at the plate. He shook his head and looked away. Lawler, after a moment, helped himself. Struvin had some also, and Kinverson. The raw fish was cool against Lawler's tongue, soothing, almost thirst-quenching. Almost.

"What do you think, doc?" Tharp asked, after a time.

"Not half bad," Lawler said.

"Maybe if I just took a lick of it," said the radio man.

Kinverson laughed into his plate. "Asshole."

"What did you say, Gabe?"

"You really want me to repeat it?"

"Go on deck if you're going to have a fight, you two," Lis Niklaus said, disgusted.

"A fight? Me and Dag?" Kinverson looked astonished. He could have picked Tharp up with one hand. "Don't be silly, Lis."

"You want to fight?" Tharp cried, his sharp-featured little red face turning even redder. "Come on, Kinverson. Come on. You think I'm afraid of you?"

"You ought to be," Lawler told him softly. "He's four times your size." He grinned and looked toward Struvin. "If we've used up our water quota for this evening, Gospo, how about brandy all around? That'll fix our thirst."

"Right. Brandy! Brandy!" Struvin yelled.

Lis handed him the flask. Struvin studied it for a moment with a sour expression on his face. "This is the Sorve brandy. Let's save it until we get really desperate. Give me the stuff from Khuviar, will you? Sorve brandy is piss." From a cupboard Lis took a different flask, long and rounded, with a deep sheen. Struvin ran his hand along its side and grinned appreciatively. "Khuviar, yes! They really understand brandy on that island. And wine. You ever been there, any of you? No, no, I can see you haven't. They drink all day and all night. The happiest people on this planet."

"I was there once," Kinverson said. "They were drunk all the time. They did nothing at all but drink and vomit and drink some more."

"But what they drink," said Struvin. "Ah, what they drink!"

"How do they get anything done," Lawler asked, "if they're never sober? Who does the fishing? Who mends the nets?"

"Nobody," Struvin said. "It's a miserable filthy place. They sober up just long enough to go out into the bay and find a batch of grapeweed, and then they ferment it into wine or distill it into brandy and they're drunk again. You wouldn't believe the way they live. Their clothing is rags. They live in seaweed shacks, like Gillies. The reservoir holds brackish water. It's a disgusting place. But who says all islands have to be alike? Every place is different. One island is nothing like another. That's the way it always has seemed to me: each island is itself, and noplace else. And on Khuviar what they understand is drinking. Here, Tharp. You say you're thirsty? Have some of my fine Khuviar brandy. My guest. Help yourself."

"I don't like brandy," Tharp said, sounding sullen. "You know that damned well, Gospo. And brandy'll only make you thirstier, anyway. It dries out the mouth membranes. Doesn't it, doc? You should realize that." He let out his breath in an explosive sigh. "What the fuck, give me the raw fish!"

Lawler passed him the platter. Tharp speared a slice with his fork, studied it as if he had never seen a piece of raw fish before, and finally took a tentative bite of it. He moved it around in his mouth with his tongue, swallowed, pondered. Then he took a second bite.

"Hey," he said. "That's all right. That isn't bad at all."

"Asshole," Kinverson said again. But he was smiling.

WHEN THE MEAL WAS OVER EVERYONE WENT UP ON DECK FOR THE change of watch. Henders, Golghoz, and Delagard, who were scrambling around in the rigging, came down and Martello, Pilya Braun, and Kinverson took their places.

The brilliant gleam of the Cross cut the black sky into quarters. The sea was so still that its reflection could be seen, like a taut line of cool white fire lying across the water and stretching off into the mysterious distances, where it blurred and was lost. Lawler stood by the rail and looked back toward the soft flickering points of light that marked the presence of the other five ships, moving along in their steady tapering formation behind them. Here was Sorve, right out there on the water, the whole little island community packed up in those ships, Thalheims and Tanaminds and Katzins and Yanezes and Sweyners and Sawtelles and all the rest, the familiar names, the old, old names. After dark every night each ship mounted running lights along its rails, long smoldering dried-algae flambeaus that burned with a smoky orange glow. Delagard was fanatically concerned that the fleet should keep together at all times, never breaking formation. Each vessel had its own radio equipment and they stayed in constant touch all through the night, lest any of them stray.

"Breeze coming!" someone called. "Let go the foretack!"

Lawler admired the art of turning the sails to catch the wind. He wished he understood a little more about it. Sailing seemed almost magical to him, an arcane and bewildering mystery. On Delagard's ships, more imposing than the little fishing skiffs that the islanders had used in the bay and on their wary journeys just beyond its mouth, each of the two masts bore a great triangular sail made of tightly woven strips of split bamboo, with a smaller quadrangular sail rigged above it, fastened to a yard. Another small triangular sail was fixed between the masts. The mainsails were tied to heavy wooden booms; arrangements of ropes fitted with threaded beads and pronged jaws held them in place, and they were manipulated by halyards running through block-and-tackle devices.

Under ordinary conditions it took a team of three to move the sails around, and a fourth at the helm to give the orders. The Martello-Kinverson-Braun team worked under Gospo Struvin's command, and when the other watch was on duty it was Neyana Golghoz, Dann Henders, and Delagard himself handling the sails, with Onyos Felk, the mapkeeper and navigator, taking Struvin's place in the wheel box. Sundira Thane worked relief on Struvin's watch, and Lis Niklaus on Felk's. Lawler would stand to one side, looking on as they ran about shouting things like "Square the braces!" and "Wind abaft the beam!" and "Hard alee! Hard alee!" Again and again, as the wind changed, they lowered the sails, swung them around, rehoisted them in their new positions. Somehow, no matter whether the wind was blowing toward the ship or against it, they managed to keep the vessel heading in the same direction.

The only ones who never took part in any of this were Dag Tharp, Father Quillan, Natim Gharkid, and Lawler. Tharp was too light and flimsy to be of much use on the ropes, and most of the time he was busy belowdecks anyway, operating the communications network that kept the ships of the fleet in contact. Father Quillan was generally regarded as exempt from all shipboard labor; Gharkid's responsibilities were limited to galley duty and trawling for drifting seaweed; and Lawler, though he would gladly have lent a hand in the rigging, felt abashed about asking to be taught the art and hung back, waiting for an invitation that didn't get offered.

As he stood by the rail watching the crew at work in the rigging something came whirring through the air out of the dark sea and struck him in the face. Lawler felt a stinging blow on his cheek, a painful hot rasping sensation as of rough scales scraping against his skin. An intense, unpleasantly sour sea-fragrance, becoming bitter and painful as it got deeper in his nostrils, rose up about him. There was a flopping sound at his feet.

He looked down. A winged creature about the length of his hand was flailing around on the deck. Lawler had thought in the first moment of impact that it might have been an air-skimmer, but air-skimmers were graceful elegant things, rainbow-hued, taut-bodied, streamlined for maximum aerodynamic lift, and they never went aloft after dark. This little night-flying monstrosity was more like a worm with wings, pallid and slack and ugly, with small beady black eyes and a writhing ridge of short, stiff red bristles along its upper back. It had been the bristles that had scraped Lawler as the creature smacked into him.

The wrinkled sharp-angled wings that sprouted from the thing's sides moved in a disagreeable pulsing way, slower and slower. It was leaving a wet trail of blackish slime behind it as it jerked about. Loathsome though it was, it seemed harmless enough now, pitiful, dying here on board.

The very hideousness of it fascinated Lawler. He knelt to give the thing a close look. But an instant later Delagard, just down from the rigging, came up next to him and hooked the tip of one booted foot under the creature's body. In a single deft motion he scooped it up atop his boot and with a quick kick flipped it on a high arc over the rail into the water.

"Why'd you do that?" Lawler asked.

"So it couldn't jump up and bite your silly nose, doc. Don't you know a hagfish when you see one?"

"Hagfish?"

"A baby one, yes. They get about this big when they're full grown, and they're mean sons of bitches." Delagard held his hands about half a meter apart. "If you don't know what something is, doc, don't get within biting range of it. Good rule out here."

"I'll keep it in mind."

Delagard leaned back against the rail and gave him a toothy grin, perhaps meant to be ingratiating. "How are you enjoying life at sea so far?" He was sweaty from his stint aloft, flushed, keyed up in some way. "Isn't the ocean a wonderful place?"

"It's got its charm, I suppose. I'm working hard at trying to find it."

"Not happy, are you? Cabin too small? Company not stimulating enough? Scenery dull?"

Lawler wasn't amused.

"Piss off, why don't you, Nid?"

Delagard rubbed a little patch of hagfish slime off his boot.

"Hey," he said. "Just trying to have a little friendly conversation."

LAWLER WENT BELOW AND MADE HIS WAY TOWARD HIS CABIN IN THE stern. A narrow musty passage lit by the greasy, sputtering light of fish-oil lamps mounted in bone sconces ran the length of the ship on this level. The thick smoky air caused his eyes to sting. He could hear the thud of surface swells lapping against the hull, echoing through the ship's ribs in a distorted, resonant way. From overhead came the heavy sound of the masts creaking in their sockets.

As ship's doctor Lawler was entitled to one of the three small private cabins near the stern. Struvin had the cabin next to his on the port side. Delagard and Lis Niklaus shared the biggest of the three cabins, farther over against the starboard bulkhead. Everyone else lived in the forecastle, jammed together in two long compartments that were usually used to house passengers when the ship was serving as an interisland ferry. The first watch had been given the port compartment, the second watch parked their gear on the starboard side.

Kinverson and Sundira had landed in different watches, and therefore bunked in different compartments. Lawler was surprised at that. Not that it mattered much who slept where, really: there was so little privacy in those crowded bunks that anybody interested in a bit of screwing around would have to go creeping down into the cargo hold on the next level below and do their coupling sandwiched between the crates. But were they a couple, as Delagard had said, or not? Apparently not, Lawler was beginning to realize. Or if they were, they were a damned loose-knit one. They had hardly even seemed to notice each other since the start of the voyage. Perhaps whatever had happened between them on Sorve, if anything had, had been nothing more than a quick meaningless fling, a random casual meeting of bodies, a way of passing the time.

He pushed open the door of his cabin with his shoulder and went inside. The cabin wasn't much bigger than a closet. It held a bunk, a basin, and a little wooden chest in which Lawler kept the few personal possessions he had brought with him from Sorve. Delagard hadn't let them bring much. Lawler had taken a few articles of clothing, his fishing gear, some pots and pans and plates, a mirror. The artifacts from Earth had come with him, too, of course. He kept them on a shelf opposite his bunk.

The rest of his things, such as they were, his modest furniture and his lamps and some ornaments that he had fashioned out of pretty sea-drift, he had bequeathed to the Gillies. His medical equipment and most of his supplies and his meager library of handwritten medical texts were up front, off the galley, in a cabin that was serving as the ship's infirmary. The main medical stores were below, in the cargo hold.

He lit a taper and examined his cheek in the mirror. It was a rough, lumpy piece of sea-glass that Sweyner had made for him years ago, and it provided a rough, lumpy reflection, cloudy and indistinct. Glass of high quality was a rarity on Hydros, where the only source of silica was the heaped-up shells of diatoms from the bottom of the bay. But Lawler was fond of the mirror, bubbled and murky though it was.

The collision with the hagfish didn't seem to have done any serious damage. There was a little abraded patch just above his left cheekbone, mildly sore where a few of the reddish bristles had broken off in his skin, and that was all. Lawler swabbed it down with a little of Delagard's grapeweed brandy to protect himself against infection. His medical sixth sense told him that there was nothing to worry about.

The numbweed flask stood next to the brandy. He pondered it for a moment or two.

He had had his usual ration of it already today, before breakfast. He didn't need any more just now.

But what the hell, he thought. What the hell.

LATER LAWLER FOUND HIMSELF WANDERING UP TO THE CREW COMPART-ments, looking for companionship, he wasn't sure whose.

The shift had changed again. The second watch was on duty now, and the starboard compartment was empty. Lawler peered into the other compartment and saw Kinverson asleep on his bunk, Natim Gharkid sitting up crosslegged with his eyes closed as though in some kind of meditation, and Leo Martello scribbling away, writing by feeble lamplight with his pages spread out on a low wooden chest. Working on his interminable epic poem, Lawler supposed.

Martello was about thirty, strongly built, full of energy, usually jigging around as if on springs. He had large brown eyes and a lively, open face, and liked to keep his head shaved. His father had come voluntarily to Hydros, a self-exiled drop-capsule man. He had turned up on Sorve when Lawler was a boy and had married Jinna Sawtelle, Damis's elder sister. They were both gone now, swept away by the Wave while out in a small boat at the wrong time.

Since he was fourteen or so Martello had worked in Delagard's shipyard, but his chief claim to distinction was the immense poem he claimed to be writing, a retelling of the great migration from doomed Earth to the worlds of the galaxy. He had been busy with it for years, so he said. No one had ever seen more than a few lines of it.

Lawler stood in the doorway, not wanting to disturb him.

"Doctor," Martello said. "Just the man I want to see. I need some sunburn medicine. I did a really good job on myself today."

"Let's have a peek at it."

Martello shrugged out of his shirt. Though deeply tanned, he was reddened now beneath the tan. Hydros' sun was stronger than the one under which the ancestral race of humans had evolved. Lawler was kept busy all the time treating skin cancers, sun poisoning, all sorts of dermatological miseries.

"Doesn't look so terrible," Lawler told him. "Come around to my cabin in the morning and I'll take care of it, all right? If you think you'll have trouble sleeping, I can give you something now."

"I'll be okay. I'll sleep on my belly."

Lawler nodded. "How's the famous poem going?"

"Slowly. I've been rewriting Canto Five."

A little to his own surprise Lawler heard himself say, "Can I have a look?"

Martello seemed surprised too. But he pushed one of the curling algae-paper sheets toward him. Lawler held it open with both hands to read it. Martello's handwriting was boyish and crude, all great looping whorls and swirls.

> *Now speared the long ships outward*
> *Into the dark of darks*
> *Golden worlds gleaming, calling*
> *As our fathers went forth.*

"And our mothers too," Lawler pointed out.

"Them too," Martello said, looking a little annoyed. "They get a canto of their own a little further on."

"Right," Lawler said. "It's very powerful poetry. Of course, I'm no real judge. You don't like poems that rhyme?"

"Rhyme's been obsolete for hundreds of years, doctor."

"Has it? I didn't know that. My father used to recite poems sometimes, ones from Earth. They liked using rhymes back then. *It is an ancient Mariner / And he stoppeth one of three. / 'By thy long grey beard and glittering eye, / Now wherefore stopp'st thou me?'* "

"What poem was that?" Martello asked.

"It's called *The Rime of the Ancient Mariner*. It's about a sea voyage—a very troubled voyage. *The very deep did rot: O Christ! / That ever this should be! / Yea, slimy things did crawl with legs / Upon the slimy sea.*"

"Powerful stuff. Do you know the rest of it?"

"Just stray fragments here and there," Lawler said.

"We ought to get together and talk about poetry sometime, doctor. I didn't realize you knew any." Martello's sunny expression darkened for a moment. "My father loved the old poems too. He brought a book of Earth poetry with him from the planet where he lived before he came here. Did you know that?"

"No," Lawler said, excited. "Where is it?"

"Gone. It was with him when he and my mother drowned."

"I would have wanted to see it," said Lawler sadly.

"There are times I think I miss that book as much as I do my mother and father," Martello said. He added ingenuously, "Is that a horrible thing to say, doctor?"

"I don't think so, I think I understand what you mean." *Water, water, every where*, Lawler thought. *And all the boards did shrink.* "Listen, come around to see me first thing after your morning shift, will you, Leo? I'll fix up that sunburned back of yours then."

Water, water, every where / Nor any drop to drink.

STILL LATER LAWLER FOUND HIMSELF ALONE ON DECK AGAIN, UNDER the night sky, throbbing blackness above him, a cool steady breeze blowing out of the north. It was past midnight. Delagard, Henders, and Sundira were in the rigging, calling arcane cryptic things to one another. The Cross was perfectly centered overhead.

Lawler looked up at it, neatly arranged there in its crisscross way, thousands of unthinkably huge balls of exploding hydrogen lined up so very cleanly in the sky, one row this way and one row that. Martello's unskillful verses were still in his mind. *Now speared the long ships outward / Into the dark of darks.* Was one of the suns in that formidable constellation the sun of Earth? No. No. They said you couldn't see that star from Hydros. These were other stars, the ones that made up the Cross. But somewhere farther out in the darkness, hidden from his view by the great right-angled blast of light that was the Cross, lay that smallish yellow sun under whose mild rays the whole human saga had begun. *Golden worlds gleaming, calling / As our fathers went forth.* And our mothers, yes. That sun whose swift unexpected ferocity, in a few minutes of cosmic cruelty, had canceled out that earlier gift of life. Turning ultimately against its own creations, sending implacable gusts of hard radiation, instantly transforming humanity's mother world to a blackened crisp.

He had dreamed about Earth all his life, ever since his grandfather first had told him tales of the ancestral world, and yet it was still a mystery to him. And always would be, he knew. Hydros was too isolated, too backward, too remote from whatever centers of scholarship might still exist. There was no one here to teach him what Earth had been like. He understood hardly anything about it, its music, its books, its art, its history. Only dribbets and drabbets of data had come down to him, usually only the container, not the thing contained. Lawler knew that there had been a thing called opera, but it was impossible for him to visualize what it had been like. People singing a story? With a hundred musicians playing at the same time? He had never seen a hundred human beings in one place all at once, ever. Cathedrals? Symphonies? Suspension bridges? Highways? He had heard the names of those things; the things themselves were unknown to him. Mysteries, all mysteries. The lost mysteries of Earth.

That little ball—significantly smaller than Hydros, so they said—which had spawned empires and dynasties, kings and generals, heroes and villains, fables and myths, poets, singers, great masters of the arts and the sciences, temples and towers, statues and walled cities. All those glorious mysterious things whose nature he could barely imagine, living as he had all his life on pitiful impoverished watery Hydros. Earth, which had spawned *us,* and had sent us forth after centuries of striving into the dark of darks, toward the remote worlds of the indifferent galaxy. And then the door had been slammed shut behind us in one blast of furious radiation. Leaving us stranded out here, lost among the stars.

Golden worlds gleaming, calling—

And here we are now, aboard a little wandering white speck in the great sea, on a planet which itself is no more than a speck in the larger black sea that engulfs us all.

Alone, alone, all, all alone, / Alone on a wide wide sea!

Lawler couldn't remember the next line. Just as well, he suspected. He went belowdecks to see about getting some sleep.

A NEW DREAM CAME TO HIM, AN EARTH-DREAM BUT NOT ONE LIKE THE ones he had had for so many years. This time he dreamed not of the death of Earth but of the leaving of it, the great diaspora, the flight to the stars. Once again he hovered above the familiar blue-green globe of his dream; and as he looked down he saw a thousand slender shining needles rising from it, or perhaps a million, too many for him to begin to count, all of them climbing toward him, surging outward, outward, streaming into space, a steady outward flow of them, myriad tiny points of light penetrating the blackness that surrounded the blue-green planet. They were the ships of the spacefarers, he knew, the ones who had chosen to leave Earth, the explorers, the wanderers, the settlers, going forth into the great unknown, making their way outward from the mother world to the innumerable stars of the galaxy. He followed their courses across the heavens, tracking them to their destinations, to the many worlds whose names he had heard, worlds as mysterious and magical and unattainable to him as Earth itself: Nabomba Zom where the sea is scarlet and the sun is blue, and Alta Hannalanna where the great sluggish worms with nuggets of precious yellow jade in their foreheads tunnel through the spongy ground, and Galgala the golden, and Xamur where the air is perfume and the electrified atmosphere shimmers and crackles with beauty, and Marajo of the sparkling sands, and Iriarte, and Mentiroso, and Mulano of the double suns, and Ragnarok, and Olympus, and Malebolge, and Ensalada Verde, and Sunrise—

And even Hydros, the dead-end world, from which there was no returning—

The starships pouring outward from Earth went everywhere that there was to go. And somewhere along the way the light that was Earth winked out behind them. Lawler, tossing in turbulent sleep, saw yet again that terrible last blaze of fire, and after it the final blackness closing in, and he sighed for the world that had been. But no one else seemed to notice its passing: they were too busy moving outward, outward, outward.

THE NEXT DAY WAS THE DAY WHEN GOSPO STRUVIN, MAKING HIS WAY along the deck, kicked at an untidy pile of what looked like damp yellow rope and said, "Hey, who left this net here?"

"I told you," Kinverson said afterward, a dozen times that day. "I don't trust an easy sea."

And Father Quillan said, "Yea, though I walk through the valley of the shadow of death, I will fear no evil."

2

*S*TRUVIN'S DEATH HAD BEEN TOO SUDDEN, AND IT HAD COME TOO
soon in the voyage, for it to be in any way acceptable or even
comprehensible. On Sorve death had always been a possibility: you
took a fishing boat too far out into the bay and a storm came out of nowhere,
or you were strolling along the waterfront rampart of the island and the
Wave rose up without warning and got you, or you found some nice tasty-
looking shellfish growing in the shallows and they turned out not to be so
nice after all. The ship, though, had seemed to offer a little zone of
invulnerability. Perhaps because it *was* so vulnerable, perhaps because it was
nothing more than a tiny hollow wooden shell, a mere speck floating in the
midst of an unthinkable immensity, they had all perversely come to believe
they were safe aboard it. Lawler had expected that there would be difficulties, and strain and privation, and a serious injury or two somewhere
along the way to Grayvard, a challenge to his sometimes tenuous medical
skills. But a *death*? Here in these calm waters? The death of the *captain*? And
only five days out of Sorve. Just as the eerie tranquillity of the first few days
had been troublesome and suspicious, Struvin's death seemed ominous, a
terrible foretaste of more calamities inescapably to come.

The voyagers closed around it the way pink new skin closes around a
wound. Everyone became resolutely positive-minded, studiedly hopeful,
ostentatiously considerate of the boundaries of everybody else's overstressed
psyche. Delagard announced that he would take command of the ship

himself. To even out the shifts, Onyos Felk was moved to the first watch: he would direct the Martello-Kinverson-Braun team in the rigging, and Delagard would direct the new team of Golghoz-Henders-Thane.

After that first lapse of control upon hearing of Struvin's death, Delagard presented now a facade of cool competence, utter undauntedness. He stood staunch and upright on the bridge, looking on as the watch of the day mounted the rigging. The wind stood fair from the east. The voyagers continued onward.

FOUR DAYS LATER THE PALMS OF LAWLER'S HANDS WERE STILL SMARTING from the sting of the net-creature, and his fingers continued to be very stiff. The elaborate pattern of red lines had faded to a dull brown now, but perhaps Pilya was right that he'd have scars after all. That part didn't bother him much: there were scars aplenty on him already, from this bit of carelessness or that over the years. But the stiffness troubled him. He needed delicacy in his fingers, not only for the surgery that he was occasionally required to perform, but because of the judicious probing and palpating of his patients' flesh that was an inherent part of the process of diagnosis. He couldn't read the messages of their bodies with fingers that were like sticks.

Pilya seemed worried about Lawler's hands also. As she came up on deck for her turn in the rigging she saw him and took them gently in hers, as she had in the moments after Gospo Struvin's death.

"They don't look good," she said. "Are you putting on your salve?"

"Faithfully. Although they're healed beyond the point where the salve can do much good."

"And the other medicine, the pink drops? The pain-killer?"

"Oh, yes. Yes. I wouldn't think of being without it."

She rubbed her fingers lightly over his. "You are such a good man, such a *serious* man. If anything happened to you it would break my heart. I was frightened for you when I saw you fighting with that thing that killed the captain. And when I knew that your hands were hurt."

A look of purest devotion spread like a sunrise over her sharp-planed snub-nosed face. Pilya's features were coarse and unbeautiful, but her eyes were warm and shining. The contrast between her golden hair and her sleek olive-toned skin was very appealing. She was a strong, uncomplicated girl, and the emotion she was projecting now was the strong and uncomplicated one of unconditional love. Warily, not wanting to rebuff her too cruelly, Lawler withdrew his hands from her grasp while at the same time giving her a benevolent, noncommittal smile. It would have been easy enough to accept what she was offering, find some secluded nook in the cargo hold, enjoy the simple pleasures that he had denied himself so long. He was no priest, he reminded himself. He had taken no vow of celibacy. But he had lost faith somehow in his own emotions. He was unwilling to trust himself even in so unthreatening an adventure as this one would probably turn out to be.

"Do you think we will live?" she asked him suddenly.

"Live? Of course we'll live."

"No," she said. "I still am afraid that we will die at sea, all of us. Gospo was only the first."

"We'll be all right," said Lawler. "I told you that the other day and I'll tell you again. Gospo had bad luck, that's all. There's always someone whose luck is bad."

"I want to live. I want to get to Grayvard. There will be a husband waiting for me on Grayvard. Sister Thecla told me that, when she read my future, before we left. She said that when I come to the end of the voyage I will find my husband."

"Sister Thecla told a lot of people a lot of crazy things about what was going to happen to us at the end of the voyage. You mustn't pay any attention to fortune-tellers. But if a husband is what you want, Pilya, I hope that Sister Thecla told the truth for you."

"An older man is what I want. Someone wise and strong, who will teach me things as well as love me. No one ever taught me anything, you know. Except how to work on a ship, and so I have worked on ships, and sailed here and there and here and there for Delagard, and I have never had a husband. But now I want one. It is my time. I am nice to look at, is that not so?"

"Very nice," Lawler said.

Poor Pilya, he thought. He felt guilty for not loving her.

She turned away from him, as if recognizing that they were not heading in the direction she wanted this conversation to go. After a moment she said, "I was thinking about the little things from Earth that you showed me, the things you have in the cabin. The beautiful little things. How pretty they were! I told you I wanted one, and you said no, you couldn't give me one, but now I have changed my mind anyway. I don't want one. They are the past. I want only the future. You live in the past too much, doctor."

"It's a bigger place than the future, for me. There's more room to look around."

"No. No. The future is very big. The future goes on forever and ever. You wait and see if I am not right. You should throw those old things away. I know that you will never do it, but you should." She gave him a shy, tender smile. "I need to go aloft now," she said. "You are a very fine man. I thought I should tell you that. I just want you to know that you have a friend if you want one." And then she turned and darted away.

Lawler watched her climb the rigging. Poor Pilya, he thought again. What a sweet girl you are. I could never love you, not in the way I would need to love you. But in your own way you are very fine.

She climbed lithely and swiftly, and in a moment she was high overhead. She climbed like one of the monkeys he remembered from his childhood storybooks, those books so full of tales of the incomprehensible land-world that Earth had been, that place of jungles, deserts, glaciers, monkeys and tigers, camels and swift horses, polar bears, walruses, goats that skipped from crag to crag. What were crags? What were goats? He had had to invent them for himself, from the sketchy hints in the stories. Goats were shaggy and lanky, with enormously long legs that had the spring of steel in them. Crags were rough upturned slabs of rock, which was something like wood-kelp timber only unimaginably harder. Monkeys were like ugly little men, brown and hairy and sly, and scrambled through the treetops, screeching and chattering. Well, Pilya was nothing at all like that. But she moved about up there as though it were her natural element.

It struck Lawler then that he wasn't able to remember what it had been like making love to Pilya's mother Anya, back there twenty years in the past. He recalled only that he had. But all the rest, the sounds Anya made, the way she moved, the shape of her breasts—gone. As gone as Earth itself, those sounds of hers. As though nothing had ever happened between them. Anya had had the same golden hair and dark smooth skin as Pilya, he recalled, but it seemed to him that her eyes had been blue. Lawler had been miserable then, bleeding from a thousand wounds after Mireyl's disappearance, and Anya had wandered along and offered a little comfort. Like mother, like daughter. Did mothers and daughters make love the same way also, driven unconsciously by some power of the genes? Would Pilya, in his arms, shift and blur and transform herself in his eyes into her own mother? If he embraced Pilya, would he recapture his lost memories of Anya? Lawler pondered that, wondering if it was worth making the experiment to find out. No, he decided. No.

"Studying the water-flowers, doctor?" Father Quillan said, just at his side.

Lawler glanced around. Quillan had an odd slithery way of approaching: he would materialize out of the air as though he were a thing of ectoplasm and move up the rail toward you without seeming to move at all. And then he was there beside you, shimmering with metaphysical uneasiness.

"Water-flowers?" Lawler said abstractedly, half amused at having been caught in the midst of such lascivious speculations. "Oh. There. Yes, I see."

How could he not have seen? On this brilliant sunny morning bobbing water-flowers were strewn everywhere on the bosom of the ocean. They were erect fleshy stalks about a meter high with bright fist-sized sporing structures at their top ends, very gaudily colored, bright scarlet with yellow petals striped with green, and curious swollen black air-bladders below. The air-bladders hung just below the surface, keeping the water-flowers afloat. Even when slapped by a passing high swell the plants would pop up immediately, back into the perpendicular like tireless clowns that could be knocked down again and again without ever failing to rebound.

"A miracle of resilience," Quillan said.

"A lesson to us all, yes," said Lawler, suddenly inspired to a sermon. "We must try at all times to emulate them. In this life we get hit and hit and hit and each time we have to bounce right back. The water-flower should be our model: invulnerable to everything, completely resistant, capable of enduring all blows. But in fact we aren't as bouncy as water-flowers, are we, Father?"

"I'd say that you are, doctor."

"Am I?"

"You're very highly regarded, do you know that? Everyone I've spoken to has great praise for your patience, your endurance, your wisdom, your strength of character. Especially your strength of character. They tell me that you're one of the toughest and strongest and most resilient people in the community."

It sounded like a description of someone else entirely, someone far less brittle and inflexible than Valben Lawler. Lawler chuckled. "I may seem that way from the outside, I suppose. How wrong they all are."

"I've always believed that a person is what he seems to others to be," the priest said. "What you happen to think about yourself is completely unreliable and irrelevant. Only in the estimation of others can your true worth be validly determined."

Lawler flicked an astonished glance at him. His long, austere face looked absolutely serious.

"Is *that* what you believe?" Lawler asked. He noticed that a note of irritation had crept into his voice. "I haven't heard anything quite so crazy in a long time. But no, no, you're just playing games with me, aren't you? You like playing games of that sort."

The priest offered no response. They fell silent, side by side in the cool morning sunlight. Lawler stared into the emptiness beyond. It lost focus and became a great blur of bobbing colors, an aimless ballet of water-flowers.

Then after a few moments he looked more closely at what was going on out there.

"I guess even the water-flowers aren't completely invulnerable, eh?" he said, pointing out across the water. Some huge submerged creature's mouth was visible on the far side of the field of flowers now, moving slowly among them just below the surface, creating a gaping dark cavern into which the bright-hued plants were tumbling by the dozens. "You can be as resilient as you like, but there's always something coming along eventually to gobble you up. Isn't that so, Father Quillan?"

Quillan's reply was lost in a sudden gusting breeze.

There was another long cool silence. Lawler could still hear Quillan saying, *A person is what he seems to others to be. What you happen to think about yourself is completely unreliable and irrelevant.* Total nonsense, wasn't it? Wasn't it? Of course it was.

And then Lawler heard his own voice saying, without giving him any warning, "Father Quillan, why did you decide to come to Hydros in the first place?"

"Why?"

"Yes, why. This is a damned inhospitable planet, if you happen to be human. It wasn't designed for us and we manage to live here only in uncomfortable circumstances and it isn't possible to leave once you get here. Why would you want to maroon yourself forever on a world like that?"

Quillan's eyes became curiously animated. With some fervor he said, "I came here because I found Hydros irresistibly attractive."

"That's not really an answer."

"Well, then." There was a new edge on the priest's voice, as though he felt that Lawler was pushing him into saying things he would just as soon not say. "Let's put it that I came because it's a place where all galactic refuse ultimately winds up. It's a world populated entirely by discards, rejects, the odds and ends of the cosmos. That's what it is, isn't it?"

"Of course not."

"All of you are the descendants of criminals. There aren't any criminals in the rest of the galaxy any more. On the other worlds everyone is sane now."

"I doubt that very much." Lawler couldn't believe that Quillan was serious. "We're the descendants of criminals, yes, some of us. That isn't any secret. People who were said to be criminals, at any rate. My great-great-grandfather, for instance, was sent here because he had some bad luck, that was all. He accidentally killed a man. But let's say that you're right, that we're merely so much debris and the descendants of debris. Why would you want to live among us, then?"

The priest's chilly blue eyes gleamed. "Isn't it obvious? This is where I belong."

"So you could do your holy work among us, and lead us to grace?"

"Not in the slightest. I came here for my needs, not yours."

"Ah. So you came here out of pure masochism, some kind of need to punish yourself. Is that it, Father Quillan?" Quillan was silent. But Lawler knew that he must be right. "Punishment for what? A crime? You just told me there aren't any more criminals."

"My crimes have been directed against God. Which makes me one of you, fundamentally. An outcast, an exile by my inherent nature."

"Crimes against God," Lawler said, musing. God was as remote and mysterious a concept to him as monkeys and jungles, crags and goats. "What kind of crime could you possibly commit against God? If he's omnipotent, presumably he's invulnerable, and if he isn't omnipotent how can he be God? Anyway, you told me only a week or two ago that you didn't even know whether or not you believed in God."

"Which in itself is a crime against Him."

"Only if you believe in him. If he doesn't exist, you certainly can't do him any injury."

"You have a priest's way with a sneaky argument," Quillan said approvingly.

"Were you serious, that other time, when you said you weren't sure of your faith?"

"Yes."

"Not playing verbal games with me? Not just offering me a little dollop of quick cheap cynicism for the sake of a moment's quick amusement?"

"No. Not at all. I swear it." Quillan reached out and put his hand across Lawler's wrist, an oddly intimate, confiding sort of gesture which at another time Lawler might have regarded as an unacceptable encroachment but which now seemed almost endearing. In a low, clear voice he said, "I dedicated myself to the service of God when I was still a very young man. That sounds pretty pompous, I know. But in practice what it's meant has been a lot of hard and disagreeable work, not just long sessions of prayer in cold drafty rooms at unlikely hours of the morning and night, but also the doing of chores so nasty that only a doctor, I suppose, would understand. The washing of the feet of the poor, so to speak. All right, so be it. I knew that that was what I was volunteering for, and I don't want any medals for it. But what I didn't know, Lawler, what I never remotely imagined at the outset, was that the deeper I got into serving God through serving suffering humanity, the more vulnerable I'd become to periods of absolute spiritual deadness. To long stretches when I felt cut off from all connection with the universe about me, when human beings became as alien to me as aliens are, when I didn't have the slightest shred of belief in the higher Power to which I had pledged to devote my life. When I felt so completely alone that I can't even begin to describe it to you. The harder I worked, the more pointless it all became. A very cruel joke: I was hoping to earn God's grace, I suppose, and instead He's given me some good stiff doses of His absence. Are you following me, Lawler?"

"And what causes this deadness in you, do you think?"

"That's what I came here to find out."

"Why here, though?"

"Because there's no Church here. Because there are only the most fragmentary human communities. Because the planet itself is hostile to us. And because it's a place of no return, like life itself." Something beyond Lawler's comprehension was dancing in Quillan's eyes now, something as baffling as a candle flame that burned downward instead of up. He seemed to be staring at Lawler out of some deep annihilating eternity from which he knew he had come and to which he yearned to return. "I wanted to lose myself here, do you see? And in that way maybe to find myself. Or at least to find God."

"God? Where? Someplace down there at the bottom of this enormous ocean?"

"Why not? He doesn't seem to be anywhere else, does He?"

"I wouldn't know," Lawler began to say. But then from high overhead came a startling cry.

"Land ho!" Pilya Braun sang out. She was in the foremast rigging, standing on the yard. "Island to the north! Island to the north!"

THERE *WERE* NO ISLANDS IN THESE WATERS, NEITHER TO THE NORTH OR south, nor to the east or west. If there were, everyone aboard would have been looking forward to the sighting for days. But no one had said a word about islands here.

Onyos Felk, in the wheel box, let loose a bellow of disbelief. Shaking his head, the mapkeeper came stumping toward Pilya on his short bandy legs. "What are you saying, girl? What island? What would an island be doing in this part of the sea?"

"How would I know?" Pilya called. She held to the ropes with one hand and swung herself far out over the deck. "Did I put it there?"

"There can't be an island."

"Come up here and see for yourself, you dried-up old fish!"

"What? What?"

Lawler shaded his eyes and peered into the distance. All he saw were bobbing water-flowers. But Quillan tugged eagerly at his arm. "There! Do you see?"

Did he? Yes, yes, Lawler thought he saw something: a thin yellow-brown line, perhaps, on the northern horizon. An island, though? How could he tell?

Everyone was on deck, now, milling around. In the midst of it all was Delagard, carrying the precious sea-chart globe cradled in one arm and a stubby spyglass fashioned of a yellowish metal in the other. Onyos Felk went scurrying up to him and reached for the globe. Delagard gave him a poisonous look and shook him off with a hiss.

"But I need to look at—"

"Keep your hands away, will you?"

"The girl says there's an island. I want to prove to her that that's impossible."

"She sees something, doesn't she? Maybe it is one. You don't know everything, Onyos. You don't know anything." With furious demonic energy Delagard pushed his way past the gawping mapkeeper and began to mount the rigging, climbing with his elbows and his teeth, still cradling the globe in his right arm and gripping the spyglass with the left. He reached the yard somehow, wedged himself in, put the glass to his eye. There was a tremendous silence below him on the deck. After an infinitely long time Delagard looked down and said, "Damned if there isn't!" The ship-owner handed the spyglass to Pilya and feverishly pored over the globe, tracing the movements of neighboring islands with exaggerated elbows-out excursions of his fingers. "Not Velmise, no. Not Salimil. Kaggeram? No. No. Kentrup?" He shook his head. Everyone was watching him. It was quite a performance, Lawler thought. Delagard passed the sea-chart to Pilya, took back the glass from her, gave her a little pat on the rump. He stared again. "God fuck us all! A new one, that's what it is! They're building it right now! Look at that! The timbers! The scaffolding! God fuck us all!" He tossed the spyglass toward the deck. Dann Henders caught it deftly before it struck and put it to his eye, while the others crowded around him. Delagard was on his way down from the rigging, muttering to himself. "God fuck us all! God fuck us all!"

The spyglass went from hand to hand. In a few minutes, though, the ship was close enough to the new island so that it could be seen without the aid of the glass. Lawler stared, fascinated and awed.

It was a narrow structure, perhaps twenty or thirty meters wide and a hundred meters long. Its highest point rose just a couple of meters out of the water, a ridge that looked like the humped spine of some colossal sea-creature basking just below the surface. Gillies, about a dozen of them, were moving ponderously about on it, hauling logs into place, bracing them up, cutting notches with strange Gillie tools, wrapping fibrous bindings about them.

The sea nearby was boiling with life and activity. Some of the creatures in it were Gillies, Lawler saw, Gillies by the score. The little domes of their heads were popping up and down in the tranquil waves like the tops of water-flowers. But he recognized also the long, sleek, shining forms of divers moving among them. They were fetching wood-kelp timbers up from the depths, it seemed, delivering them to the Gillies in the water, who were hewing them, squaring them off, passing them along an underwater chain to the shore of the new island, where other Gillie workers dragged them up into the air and set about preparing them for installation.

The *Black Sea Star* had pulled up to starboard. Figures were moving around on its deck, pointing, waving. On the other side, the *Sorve Goddess* was coming up fast, with the *Three Moons* not far behind it.

"That's a platform over there," Gabe Kinverson said. "North side of the island, to the left."

"Jesus, yes!" Delagard cried. "Will you look at the size of it!"

Immobile just beyond the island, drifting alongside it as though moored, was what looked like a second island but which was in fact the enormous sea-creature that the island itself had for a moment seemed to be. Platforms were the largest animals of the seas of Hydros that any human had ever heard of, larger even than the all-devouring whale-like beasts known as mouths: huge flat blocky things, vaguely rectangular in shape, so inert they might just as well have been islands. They drifted casually in all seas, passively straining microorganisms from the water through screenlike apertures around their perimeters. How they managed to take in enough food in the course of a day to sustain themselves, even feeding round the clock as they did, was beyond anyone's comprehension. Lawler imagined that they must be as sluggish as driftwood, metabolically—mere giant lumps of barely sentient meat. And yet their vast purple eyes, set in triple rows of six along their backs, each one wider across than a man's shoulders, seemed to hold some sort of somber intelligence. Now and then a platform had come wandering into Sorve Bay, floating with its belly just above the submerged planks of the bay floor. One time Lawler, out in the bay fishing from a small boat, had rowed unknowingly right over one, and found himself looking down in utter amazement into a set of those great sad eyes that stared back up at him through the transparent water with a sort of godlike detachment and even, he imagined, a weird kind of compassion.

This platform seemed to be in use as nothing more or less than a worktable. Bands of Gillies were toiling industriously on its back. They were moving about in knee-deep water, coiling and twining long strands of algae fibers that were being pushed up onto the platform from below by shining green tentacles. The tentacles were as thick as an arm, very supple, with fingerlike projections at their ends. No one, not even Kinverson, had any idea what kind of creature they might belong to.

Father Quillan said, "How marvelous it is, the way they all work together, those different animals!"

Lawler turned to the priest. "No one's ever seen an island under construction before, not that I've ever heard of. So far as we've known, all the islands are hundreds or even thousands of years old. So this is how they do it! What a sight!"

"Some day," Quillan said, "this whole planet will have real land like other worlds. The sea floor will rise, millions of years from now. By building these artificial islands and coming up out of the sea to live, the Gillies are preparing themselves for their next evolutionary phase."

Lawler blinked. "How do you know that?"

"I studied geology and evolution at the seminary on Sunrise. Don't you think priests are taught anything but rituals and scriptures? Or that we take the Bible literally? This place has a very quiet geological history, you know. There weren't any dynamic crustal movements that pushed mountain ranges and whole continents up out of the primordial sea the way it happened on land worlds, and so everything remained on the same level, most of it submerged. In time the sea was able to erode away any land formations that did project above the water. But all that's due to change. Pressure's building up at the planet's core. Internal gravitational stresses are slowly creating turbulence, and in thirty million years, forty million, fifty—"

"Hold it," Lawler said. "What's happening over there?"

Delagard and Dag Tharp were yelling at each other, suddenly. Dann Henders was mixed up in it too, red-faced, a vein standing out on his forehead. Tharp was a jittery, excitable man, always quarreling with somebody about something; but the sight of the usually soft-spoken Henders in a high temper got Lawler's attention right away.

He went over to them.

"What's going on?"

Delagard said, "A little insubordination, that's all. I can take care of it, doc."

Tharp's beak of a nose had turned crimson. The baggy flesh of his throat was quivering.

"Henders and I have suggested sailing over to the island and asking the Gillies to give us refuge," he said to Lawler. "We can anchor nearby and help them build their island. It'll be a partnership right from the start. But Delagard says no, no, we're going to go on all the way to Grayvard. Do you know how long it'll take to get to Grayvard? How many tricksy net-things can crawl up on board before we reach it? Or God knows what else that's out here? Kinverson says we've been tremendously lucky so far, not encountering anything hostile to speak of, but how much longer can we—"

"Grayvard is where we're going," said Delagard icily.

"You see? You see?"

Henders said, "We should at least put it to a vote, don't you think, doc? The longer we remain at sea, the greater the risks are of our running into the Wave, or some of the nasty critters that Gabe's been telling us about, or some killer storm, or almost anything else. Here's an island actually under construction. If the Gillies are using divers and what-all else to help them build it, even a platform, why wouldn't they accept human help besides? And be grateful for it? But he won't even consider it!"

Delagard gave the engineer a truculent glare. "Since when have Gillies ever wanted our help? You know how it was on Sorve, Henders."

"This isn't Sorve."

"It's all the same everywhere."

"How can you be sure of that?" Henders snapped. "Listen, Nid, we've got to talk to the other ships, and that's all there is to it. Dag, you go call Yanez and Sawtelle and the rest, and—"

"Stay right where you are, Dag," Delagard said.

Tharp looked from Delagard to Henders and back again, and didn't move. His wattles shook with anger.

Delagard said, "Listen to me! Do you want us to have to live on a miserable little flat island that's months or years away from being finished? In what? Seaweed huts? Do you see any vaarghs there? Is there any bay that we can bring up useful materials from? And they won't take us, anyway. They know we were tossed out of Sorve on our asses. Every Gillie on this planet knows that, believe me."

"If these Gillies don't want us," said Tharp, "how can you be so sure the Grayvard Gillies will?"

Delagard's face crimsoned. For a moment he seemed stung by that. Lawler realized that Delagard hadn't said anything at all up till now about having cleared their arrival on Grayvard with the real owners of the island. It was only the human settlers on Grayvard that had agreed to provide sanctuary.

But Delagard made a quick recovery. "Dag, you don't know what the fuck you're talking about. Since when do we have to ask permission of

Gillies for emigration between islands? Once they let humans onto an island, they don't give a shit which humans they are. They can hardly tell one batch of us from another as it is. So long as we don't slop over onto the Gillie part of Grayvard, there won't be any problem."

"You're very sure of yourself," Henders said. "But why go all the way to Grayvard if we don't have to? We still don't know that it's impossible for us to latch on at some closer island that doesn't have a human settlement yet. These Gillies here might just be willing to take us in. And yes, maybe they'd be glad to get a little help from us building it, too."

"Sure," said Delagard. "They'd especially like to have a radio operator and an engineer. That would be just what they need. Okay: you two want to live on that island? Swim for it, then. Go on! The two of you, over the side, right now!" He grabbed Tharp by the arm and began to tug him toward the rail. Tharp gaped at him, pop-eyed. "Go on! Get going!"

"Hold it," Lawler said quietly.

Delagard let go of Tharp and leaned forward, rocking on the balls of his feet. "You have an opinion, doc?"

"If they go over the side, I go too."

Delagard laughed. "Fuck, doc! Nobody's going over the side! What the hell do you think I am?"

"You really want an answer to that, Nid?"

"Look," Delagard said, "what this comes down to is one simple thing. These are my ships. I'm the captain of this ship now and I'm also the head of the whole expedition, and nobody's going to dispute that. Out of the generosity of my spirit and the greatness of my heart I've invited everyone who used to live on Sorve to sail with me to our new home on Grayvard Island. That's where we're going. A vote on whether we ought to try to settle on this little sliver of a new island here is altogether out of line. If Dag and Dann want to live there, fine, I'll escort them over to it myself in the water-strider. But there won't be any votes and there won't be any change in the basic plan of the voyage. Is that clear? Dann? Dag? Is that clear, doc?"

Delagard's fists were balled. He was a fighter, all right.

Henders said, "As I remember it, you were the one who got us into this fix in the first place, Nid. Was that out of the generosity of your spirit and the greatness of your heart too?"

"Shut up, Dann," Lawler said. "Let me think."

He glanced toward the new island. They were so close to it now that he could make out the yellow glint of Gillie eyes. The Gillies appeared to be going about their business without taking the slightest note of the approaching flotilla of human-occupied ships.

Lawler realized suddenly that Delagard was right and Henders and Tharp were wrong. Glad though he'd be to end the voyage right here and now, Lawler knew that trying to settle here wasn't an idea worth thinking about. The island was tiny, a mere sliver of wood barely rising above the waves. Even if the Gillies were willing to let them in, there would be no room for them here.

Quietly he said, "All right. For once I'm with you, Nid. It isn't any place for us, this little island."

"Good. Good. Very sensible of you. I can always count on you to take a reasonable position, can't I, doc?" Delagard cupped his hand to his mouth and shouted up to Pilya, in the rigging. "Cut to windward! Let's get out of here!"

"We should have voted," Dag Tharp said sullenly, rubbing his arm.

"Forget it," Lawler told him. "This is Delagard's party. We're only his guests."

3

*T*HE WEATHER BEGAN TO CHANGE IN A FUNDAMENTAL WAY AT
the beginning of the week that followed. As the ships followed
their northwesterly course toward Grayvard they were starting to
leave tropical waters behind, and the strong sun and clear blue skies of the
perpetual summer that reigned in the middle latitudes. These were temperate seas here. The water was cool, and dank chilling fogs rose from it when
warm breezes blew from the equator. By midday the fog was gone; but the
broad vault of the sky was often dappled with fleecy patches of cloud much
of the time, or even a dull, lingering low overcast. One thing remained the
same, though. There was still no rain. There had been none since the little
fleet had left Sorve, and that was becoming cause for concern.

The look of the sea itself was different here. Home Sea's familiar waters
were well behind them now. This was the Yellow Sea, set off from the blue
waters to the east by a sharp line of demarcation. A thick disagreeable scum
of microscopic algae, puke-yellow with long red streaks running through it
like dark gouts of blood, covered the surface in every direction as far as the
horizon.

It was ugly stuff, but fertile. The water swarmed with life, much of it
new and strange. Bulky ungraceful broad-headed fishes as big as a man,
with dull blue scales and black blind-looking eyes, nosed around the ships
like floating logs. Occasionally a beautiful velvety sea-leopard would come
up with terrific velocity from straight below and swallow one in a single

lunging gulp. One afternoon a stocky tubular thing twenty meters long with a jaw like a hatchet appeared from nowhere between the flagship and the bow of Bamber Cadrell's ship and went slamming thunderously across the flagship's wake, rising up and pounding the water frenziedly with its chin, and when it had passed by there were severed chunks of the broad-headed blue fish scattered everywhere on the yellow waves. Smaller versions of the hatchet-jaw now emerged from below and began to feed. Meatfish abounded here too, swimming in whirling circles with their sharp-tipped tentacles flashing like blades, but they stayed maddeningly out of the reach of Kinverson's fishing-lines.

Armies made up of millions of little many-legged things with glistening transparent bodies cut through the yellow scum like scythes, opening wide boulevards that closed immediately behind them. Gharkid brought up a net-load of them—they scrambled and thrashed wildly against the meshes, panicky in the open sunlight, trying to get back to the water—and when Dag Tharp, not at all serious, suggested that they might be good to eat, Gharkid promptly stewed a batch of them in their own yellow-stained seawater and ate them with a show of complete unconcern.

"Not so bad," he said. "Try some."

Two hours later he still seemed to be all right. Others took the risk, Lawler among them. They ate them legs and all. The little crustaceans were crunchy, vaguely sweet, apparently nourishing. No one reacted badly to them. Gharkid spent the day at the gantry, pulling them up in his net by the thousand, and that night there was a great feast.

Other life-forms of the Yellow Sea were less rewarding. Ambulatory green jellyfish, harmless but messy, found a way of crawling up the sides of the hull onto the deck in great numbers, where they rotted within minutes. They all had to be swept back over the side, a task that took nearly an entire day. In one region the rigid black fruiting-towers of some large alga rose to heights of seven or eight meters above the water in the mornings and exploded in the warmth of midday, bombarding the ships with thousands of hard little pellets that sent people scattering for cover. And there were hagfish in these waters, too. By tens and twenties platoons of the wormlike things went whizzing and buzzing above the waves on flights of a hundred meters or so, desperately flapping their sharp-angled leathery wings with a weird dreadful purposefulness until at last they fell back into the water. Sometimes they passed close enough to the ship so that Lawler could see the ridges of hard red bristles on their backs, and he would touch his hand to his left cheek, where some abrasions still lingered from his own encounter with one.

"Why do they fly like that?" he asked Kinverson. "Are they trying to catch something that lives in the air?"

"Isn't anything that lives in the air," Kinverson said. "Something's trying to catch *them,* more likely. They see a big mouth opening behind them and they take off. It's a pretty good way to escape. The other time they fly is when they're mating. The females go up ahead a ways, and the males come flying after them. The guys that fly the fastest and longest are the ones that get the girls."

"Not a bad selection system. If you're breeding for speed and endurance."

"Let's hope we don't get to see it in action. The fuckers come out by the thousands. They can really fill the air, and they're absolutely crazed."

Lawler indicated the rough place on his cheek. "I can imagine. A little one smacked into me right here last week."

"How little?" Kinverson said incuriously.

"Maybe fifteen centimeters."

"Lucky thing for you it was so small," Kinverson said. "Lot of real bitchy things out there."

YOU LIVE IN THE PAST TOO MUCH, DOCTOR, PILYA HAD SAID. BUT HOW could he not? The past lived in him. Not only Earth, that remote and mythical place; but Sorve, especially Sorve, where his blood and body and mind and soul had been put together. The past rose up in him all the time. It rose up in him now, as he stood by the rail looking out at the strangeness of the Yellow Sea.

HE WAS TEN YEARS OLD, AND HIS GRANDFATHER HAD CALLED HIM TO his vaargh. His grandfather had retired from doctoring three years before and spent his days walking by the sea-wall, and he was shrunken and yellowish-looking now and it was clear that he didn't have much longer to live. He was very old, old enough to remember even some of the first-generation settlers, even his own grandfather, Harry Lawler, Harry the Founder.

"I have something for you, boy," his grandfather said. "Come here.

Come closer. You see that shelf, there, Valben? Where the Earth things are? Bring them over to me."

There were four Earth things there, two flat round metal ones, and a large rusted metal one, and a painted piece of pottery. Once there had been six, but the other two, the little statuette and the piece of rough stone, were in Valben's father's vaargh now. Valben's grandfather had already begun passing his possessions on.

"Here, boy," his grandfather said. "I want you to have this. It belonged to my grandfather Harry, who got it from *his* grandfather, who brought it with him from Earth when he went to space. And now it's yours." And he gave him the piece of pottery, painted orange and black.

"Not my father? Not my brother?"

"This is for you," his grandfather said. "To remember Earth by. And to remember me by. You'll be careful not to lose it, won't you? Because there are only six Earth things that we have, and if we lose them, we won't be getting any more. Here. Here." He pressed it into Valben's hand. "From Greece, it is. Maybe Socrates once owned it, or Plato. And now it's yours."

That was the last time he ever spoke to his grandfather.

For months afterward he carried the piece of painted pottery with him wherever he went. And when he rubbed its jagged rough-edged surface it seemed to him that Earth was alive again in his hand, that Socrates himself was speaking to him out of the bit of pottery, or Plato. Whoever they might have been.

HE WAS FIFTEEN. HIS BROTHER COIREY, WHO HAD RUN OFF TO SEA, WAS home for a visit. Coirey was nine years older than he was, the oldest of what once had been three brothers, but the middle one, young Bernat, had died so long ago that Valben scarcely remembered him. Coirey was to have been the island's next doctor someday; but Coirey had no interest in doctoring. Doctoring would tie him down to a single island. The sea, the sea, the sea, that was what Coirey wanted. And so Coirey had gone off to sea, and letters had come from him from places that were only names to Valben, Velmise and Sembilor and Thetopal and Meisa Meisanda; and now Coirey himself was here, just for a short while, stopping off at Sorve on a voyage to a place called Simbalimak, in a sea known as the Azure Sea that was so far away it seemed like another world.

Valben hadn't seen him in four years. He didn't know what to expect.

The man who came in had the same face as his father, the face that he was beginning to have also, with strong features, a powerful jaw, a long straight nose; but he was so tanned by sun and wind that his skin looked like an old piece of rugfish hide, and there was an angry slash across his cheek, a purpling scar that ran from the corner of his eye to the corner of his mouth. "Meatfish got me," he said. "But I got him, too." He punched Valben's arm. "Hey, you're big! Just as big as I am, you are. But lighter. You need some flesh on your bones." Coirey winked. "Come with me to Meisa Meisanda sometime. They know food there. It's a feast day every day. And the women! The women, boy!" He frowned and said, "You go for women, don't you? Sure, of course you do. Right? Right. What about it, Val? When I get back from Simbalimak, will you take a trip to Meisa Meisanda with me?"

"You know I can't leave here, Coirey. I have studying to do."

"Studying."

"Father's teaching me doctoring."

"Oh. Right. Right. I forgot that, didn't I? You're going to be the next Dr. Lawler. But you can come away to sea with me for a little while first, can't you?"

"No," Valben said. "No, I can't."

And then he understood why his grandfather had given the little bit of pottery from Earth to him, and not to his older brother Coirey.

His brother never returned to Sorve again.

HE WAS SEVENTEEN, AND DEEP IN HIS MEDICAL STUDIES.

"High time you did an autopsy with me, Valben," his father said. "It's all just theory for you so far. But you've got to find out what's inside the package sooner or later."

"Maybe we ought to wait until I've finished my anatomy lessons," he said. "So I have a better idea of what I'm seeing."

"This is the best kind of anatomy lesson there is," his father said.

And took him inside, to the surgical room, where someone was lying on the table under a light blanket of water-lettuce cloth. He drew the blanket aside and Valben saw that it was an old woman with gray hair and flabby breasts that fell aside toward her armpits; and then a moment later he realized that he knew her, that he was looking at Bamber Cadrell's mother, Samara, the wife of Marinus. Of course he would know her, he realized:

there were only sixty people on the island, and how could any of them be strangers? But still—Marinus's wife, Bamber's mother—naked like this, lying dead on the surgical table—

"She died this morning, very quickly, just fell down in her vaargh. Marinus brought her in. Most likely her heart, but I want to see for certain, and you should see too." His father picked up his case of surgical tools. Then he said, softly, "I didn't enjoy my first autopsy either. But it's a necessary thing, Valben. You've got to know what a liver looks like, and a spleen, and lungs, and a heart, and you can't learn it by reading about them. You have to know the difference between healthy organs and diseased ones. And we don't get that many bodies to work on here. This is an opportunity I can't let you pass up."

He selected a scalpel, showing Valben the proper grip, and made the first incision. And began to lay bare the secrets of Samara Cadrell's body.

It was bad at first, very bad.

Then he found he could tolerate it, that he was getting used to the awfulness of it, the shock of taking part in this bloody violation of the sanctuary of the body.

And after a time it actually became fascinating, when he had managed to forget that this was a woman he had known all his life, and was thinking of her only as an arrangement of internal organs of various colors and textures and shapes.

But that night, when he was done with the last of his studying and was out behind the reservoir with Boda Thalheim and sliding his hands across her smooth flat belly, he couldn't keep from thinking that behind this tight drum of taut lovely skin there also was an arrangement of internal organs of various colors and textures and shapes very much like those he had seen this afternoon, the shining coils of intestines and all the rest, and that within these firm round breasts were intricate glands scarcely different from those within the flabby breasts of Samara Cadrell, which his father had demonstrated for him a few hours before with deft strokes of his scalpel. And he pulled his hands back from Boda's sleek body as though it had turned into Samara's under his caresses.

"Is something wrong, Val?"

"No. No."

"Don't you want to?"

"Of course I do. But—I don't know—"

"Here. Let me help you."

"Yes. Oh, Boda. Oh, yes!"

And in moments everything was all right. But he wondered if he would ever touch a girl again without having vivid images of her pancreas and kidneys and fallopian tubes rise unbidden and unwanted in his mind, and it occurred to him that being a doctor was a very complex business indeed.

IMAGES OUT OF BYGONE TIMES. PHANTOMS THAT WOULD NEVER LEAVE him.

THREE DAYS LATER LAWLER WENT DOWN TO THE CARGO HOLD IN THE ship's belly for some medical supplies, carrying only a small taper to light his way. In the dimness he nearly walked into Kinverson and Sundira, who were coming out from between the crates. They looked sweaty and disheveled and a little surprised to see him, and there wasn't much doubt of what they had been up to.

Kinverson, unabashed, looked at him straight on and said, "Morning, doc."

Sundira didn't say a thing. She tugged her wrap together in front, where it was parted, and went on past, expressionless, meeting Lawler's eyes only for a moment and quickly looking away. She seemed not so much embarrassed as simply retreating into a self-containing sphere. Stung, Lawler nodded as if this were a completely neutral encounter in a completely neutral part of the ship, and continued forward to the medical storage area.

It was the first real evidence he had ever had that Kinverson and Thane were lovers, and it hit him harder than he would have expected. Kinverson's words about the mating habits of hagfish, a few days earlier, came back to him now. He wondered whether they had been aimed at him in some sly, mocking way. *The guys that fly the fastest get the girls.*

No. No. Lawler knew that he had had plenty of opportunities of his own back on the island to get something going with Sundira. He had chosen not to, for reasons that had seemed to make sense at the time.

So why was he so hurt now?

You want her more than you'll admit even to yourself, don't you?

Yes. He did. Especially right now.

Why? Because she's involved with somebody else?

What did it matter? He wanted her. Lawler had known that before, and had done nothing about it. Maybe it was time to start thinking harder about why he hadn't.

HE SAW THEM TOGETHER AGAIN LATER IN THE DAY IN THE STERN, UP BY the gantry bridge. From the looks of things Kinverson had caught something unusual, and he was showing it to her, the proud huntsman displaying his catch to his woman.

"Doc?" Kinverson called, poking his head over the edge of the bridge. He smiled in a way that was either blandly amiable or casually condescending, Lawler wasn't sure which. "Come up here for a minute, will you, doc? Something here that might interest you."

Lawler's first impulse was to shake his head and keep on going. But he didn't want to give them the satisfaction of avoiding them. What was he afraid of? That he'd see Kinverson's paw-prints all over her skin? He told himself not to be so stupid and scrambled up the little ladder to the gantry.

Kinverson had all manner of fishing equipment bolted to the deck, gaffs and hooks and lines and such. Here, too, were the nets Gharkid used in trawling for algae.

A graceful greenish creature that looked a little like a diver, but smaller, was lying limply on the gantry-bridge floor in a yellow puddle, as though Kinverson had just pulled it aboard. Lawler didn't recognize it. Some sort of a mammal, most likely. Air-breathing, like so many other inhabitants of Hydros' ocean.

"What's that you have there?" he asked Kinverson.

"Well, now, we're not so sure, doc."

It had a low, sloping forehead, an elongated muzzle tipped with stubby gray whiskers, and a slender streamlined body ending in a three-vaned tail. There was a pronounced spinal ridge. Its forelimbs were flattened into narrow flippers somewhat like those of Gillies. Curved gray claws, short and sharp, protruded from them. Its eyes, black and round and shining, were open.

It didn't appear to be breathing. But it didn't look dead, either. The eyes held an expression. Fear? Bewilderment? Who could say? They were alien eyes. They seemed to be worried ones.

Kinverson said, "This was fouled in one of Gharkid's nets, and I pulled it in to clear it. You know, you can spend your whole life out on this ocean and even so you never stop seeing new critters." He prodded the animal's side. It responded with a weak, faint motion of its tail. "This one's a goner, wouldn't you say? Pretty little thing."

"Let me have a closer look," Lawler said.

He knelt beside it and cautiously put his hand on its flank. The skin was warm, clammy, perhaps feverish. He was able now to detect the sounds of faint breathing. The animal rolled its eyes downward to follow what Lawler was doing, but without any sign of great interest. Then its mouth sagged open and Lawler was startled to see a peculiar woody network just within it, a spherical structure of loosely tangled white fibrous strands blocking the animal's entire mouth and gullet. The strands coalesced into a thick stem that disappeared down the creature's throat.

He pressed his hands along the animal's abdomen and felt rigidity within, lumps and bumps where all should have been smooth. His hands had finally begun to lose their stiffness by this time, and he was able to read the topography of the creature's interior as though he had laid it bare with a scalpel. Wherever he touched it he could feel the signs of something invasive growing inside. He rolled the creature over and saw strands of the same woody network emerging from its anus, just above the tail.

Suddenly the animal uttered a dry, hacking, ratcheting sound. Its mouth opened wider than Lawler would have believed possible. The woody tangle within it rose into view, jutting far out of the animal's mouth as if on a pedestal, and started to weave from side to side. Quickly Lawler rose to a standing position and stepped back. Something that looked like a little pink tongue detached itself from the fibrous sphere and zipped madly about on the deck, darting back and forth with manic energy. Lawler brought his boot down on it just as it went past him heading toward Sundira. A second autonomous tongue erupted from the sphere. He smashed that too. The sphere waggled around sluggishly as if gathering the energy to emit a few more.

To Kinverson he said, "Throw this thing into the sea, fast."

"Huh?"

"Pick it up and heave it. Go on."

Kinverson had been watching the examination in a baffled, remote way. But the urgency of Lawler's tone got through to him. He slipped one big hand under the animal's middle, lifted, tossed, all in one swift movement. The creature went plummeting inertly toward the water like a mere inanimate sack. At the last moment it managed to right itself and hit the surface smoothly, head first, as though by inherent reflexes still partially functioning. It managed one powerful kick of its tail and glided out of sight underwater in an instant.

"What the hell was that all about?" Kinverson asked.

"Parasite infestation. That animal was loaded from its snout to its tail with some kind of plant growth. Its mouth was full of it, didn't you see? And all the way down its body. It's been completely taken over by it. And those little pink tongues—my guess is that they were offshoots looking for new hosts."

Sundira shivered. "Something like killer-fungus?"

"Something like that, yes."

"You think it could have infected us?"

"It sure was going to try," Lawler said. "In an ocean the size of this one, the parasites can't afford to be host-specific. They'll take root in whatever they can." He stared over the side, half expecting to see scores of parasite-ridden animals drifting helplessly all about the ship. But there was nothing down there except yellow scum streaked with red. Turning back to Kinverson, he said, "I want you to suspend all fishing operations until we get clear of this part of the sea. I'll go find Dag Tharp and tell him to send the same order to the other ships."

"We need fresh meat, doc."

"You want to have the personal responsibility of examining everything that's caught to see if it's carrying that parasitic plant?"

"Hell, no!"

"Then we don't haul anything in around here. It's that simple. I'd rather live on dried fish for a while than have one of those things growing in my gut, wouldn't you?"

Kinverson nodded solemnly.

"Such a pretty little thing, it was."

A DAY LATER, STILL SAILING THROUGH THE YELLOW SEA, THEY RAN INTO their first tidal surge. The only surprise was that it had been so long in coming, considering that they had been at sea for several weeks now.

It was impossible to escape the surges altogether. The planet's three moons, small and fast-moving, swung round and round in intricately intersecting orbital patterns, and at regular intervals they were lined up in such a way as to exert a powerful combined gravitational effect on the great ball of water they orbited. That lifted a great tidal bulge which continually traveled around Hydros' midsection as the planet turned. Smaller tidal effects, the products of the gravitational fields of the individual moons, moved at angles to it. The Gillies had designed their islands to withstand those inevitable times when a tidal surge would come their way. On certain exceptional occasions the lesser tidal surges crossed the path of the great one, setting up the massive turbulence known as the Wave. The Gillie islands were built to resist even the Wave; but individual boats and ships were helpless against it. The Wave was what every mariner feared more than anything.

This first tidal surge was one of the mild ones. The day was leaden and humid, the sun pale, indistinct, bloodless. The first watch was on duty, Martello, Kinverson, Gharkid, Pilya Braun. "Choppy sea ahead," Kinverson called from aloft. Onyos Felk, in the wheel-box, reached for his spyglass. Lawler, who had just emerged on deck after his morning medical call to the other ships, felt the deck plunge and buck beneath him as if the vessel had put its foot down on something solid. Yellowish spray came whirling up into his face.

He looked up toward the wheel-box. Felk was signaling to him with brusque gestures.

"Surge coming," the mapkeeper called. "Get inside!"

Lawler saw Pilya and Leo Martello securing the ropes that held the sails. A moment later they dropped down out of the rigging. Gharkid had already gone below. Kinverson came trotting past, beckoning. "Come on, doc. You don't want to be out here now."

"No," Lawler said. But still he lingered a moment more by the rail. He saw it, now. It was heading toward them out of the northwest like a little message of welcome from distant Grayvard—a fat gray wall of water that lay at a sharp angle across the horizon, rolling down on them with impressive speed. Lawler imagined some sort of rod sweeping through the sea just beneath the surface, pushing up this inexorable distended ridge. A cold salty wind preceded it, a cheerless harbinger.

"Doc," Kinverson said again, from the hatch. "Sometimes they sweep the deck when they hit."

"I know," said Lawler. But the power of the oncoming surge fascinated him and held him. Kinverson vanished with a shrug into the ship's interior. Lawler was alone now on deck. He realized they might well close the hatch and leave him out here. He took one last look at the surge, and then he ran for it. Below, everyone but Henders and Delagard was gathered in the companionway, bracing themselves against the imminent impact.

Kinverson slammed the hatch shut behind him and dogged it.

An odd grinding sound rose from the depths of the ship, somewhere to aft.

"Magnetron's coming on," Sundira Thane said.

Lawler turned to her. "You've been through these before?"

"Too often. But this one won't be much."

The grinding sound grew louder. The magnetron sent down a shaft of force that pressed against the ball of molten iron at the world's core and provided a lever capable of lifting the ship a meter or two out of the water, or a bit more if necessary, just enough to carry it over the worst force of the surge. The magnetic displacement field was the one piece of super-technology that the humans of Hydros had managed to bring with them from the worlds of the galaxy. Dann Henders once had said that a device as powerful as the magnetron would have other applications far more useful to the settlers than keeping Delagard's ferries afloat on turbulent seas, and very probably Henders was right about that; but Delagard kept the magnetrons sealed aboard his ships. They were his private property, the crown jewels of the Delagard maritime empire, the foundation of the family fortune.

"Are we up yet?" Lis Niklaus asked uneasily.

"When the grinding stops," Neyana Golghoz said. "There. Now."

All was silent.

The ship was floating just above the crest of the surge.

Only for a moment: the magnetron, potent though it was, had its limits. But a moment was long enough. The surge passed by and the ship drifted gently over it and down its far side, landing lightly in the pocket of displaced water beyond. As it resumed its place in the water it swayed and shuddered and shook. The impact of the descent was greater than Lawler had expected, and he had to fight to keep from being thrown down.

Then it was all over. They were afloat on an even keel again.

Delagard emerged from the hatch that led to the cargo hold, grinning in warm self-congratulation. Dann Henders was right behind him.

"That's it, folks," the ship-owner announced. "Back to your posts. Onward we go."

The sea, in the wake of the surge, was gently perturbed, rocking like a cradle. When he went back up on deck Lawler could see the surge itself retreating to the southeast, a diminishing ripple cutting across the scummy surface of the water. He saw the yellow flag of the *Golden Sun,* the red one of the *Three Moons,* the green and black of the *Sorve Goddess.* Farther beyond he was able to make out the remaining two vessels, safe and apparently sound.

"Wasn't so bad," he said to Dag Tharp, who had come up just behind him.

"Wait," Tharp said. "Just wait."

4

THE SEA CHANGED AGAIN. A FAST COLD CURRENT WAS SWEEPING
through it here, coming out of the south, cutting a swath through
the yellow algae. At first there was only a narrow band of clear
water through the scum, then a wider strip, and then, as the flotilla entered
the main body of the current, all the water around them was a pure, clean
blue again.

Kinverson asked Lawler if he thought the marine life here would be free
of the parasitic plant. The voyagers had had no fresh fish for days. "Bring
something up and let's see," Lawler told him. "Just be careful when you get
it on deck."

But there was no catch for Kinverson to be careful with. His nets came
up empty, his hooks went untaken. Fish lived in these waters, plenty of
them. But they kept their distance from the ship. Sometimes schools of
them could be seen, swimming vigorously away. The other ships reported
the same thing. They might as well have been sailing through desert
waters.

At mealtimes there was grumbling in the galley.

"I can't cook 'em if nobody catches 'em," Lis Niklaus said. "Talk to
Gabe."

Kinverson was indifferent. "I can't catch 'em if they won't come near
us. You don't like it, go out there and swim after them and grab 'em with
your hands. Okay?"

•   •   •

THE FISH CONTINUED TO STAY AWAY, BUT NOW THE SHIPS ENTERED A
zone that was rich with algae of several new kinds, floating masses of an
intricate tightly woven red species mingled with long strips of a wide-
leafed, highly succulent blue-green type. Gharkid had a glorious time with
them. "They will be fine to eat," he announced. "This I know. We will get
much nourishment from them."

"But if you've never seen these kinds before—" Leo Martello objected.

"I can tell. These will be good for eating."

Gharkid tested them on himself in that innocent unfearing way of his
that Lawler found so extraordinary. The red alga, he reported, would be
suitable for salads. The blue-green one was best cooked in a little fish oil.
He spent his days on the gantry bridge, reeling in load upon load, until half
the deck was covered with piles of soggy seaweed.

Lawler went up to him as he sat sorting through the slimy mess, which
still was streaming with water. Small creatures that had come up in the net
wandered amidst the tangled algae: little snails and crablets and tiny
crustaceans with very bright red shells that looked like fairy castles.
Gharkid seemed unperturbed by the possibility that any of these minute
passengers might have poisonous stingers, little jaws that could deliver
big nips, toxic excretions, perils of unknown sorts. He was brushing them
away from his algae with a comb made of reeds, and using his hands where
that was quickest. As Lawler approached, Gharkid gave him a broad
smile, white teeth shining brilliantly against the dark background of his
face, and said, "The sea has been good to us today. It has sent us a fine
harvest."

"Where'd you learn all that you know about the sea plants, Natim?"

Gharkid looked puzzled. "In the sea, where else? From the sea comes
our life. You go into it, you find what is good. You try this and you try that.
And you remember." He plucked something from a knotted clump of the
red weed and held it up delightedly for Lawler to inspect. "So sweet, it is.
So delicate." It was a kind of sea-slug, yellow with little red speckles,
almost like an animated chunk of the yellow scum in the sea that lay behind
them. A dozen curiously intense black eyes the size of fingertips waved on
stubby stalks. Lawler failed to see either sweetness or delicacy in the blobby
yellow thing, but Gharkid seemed charmed by it. He brought it close to his
face and smiled at it. Then he flipped it over the side into the water.

"The sea's blessed creature," Gharkid said, in a tone of such all-loving benevolence that it made Lawler feel sour and irritable.

"You wonder what purpose it was made for," he said.

"Oh, no, doctor-sir. No, I never wonder. Who am I to ask the sea why it does what it does?"

From his reverent tone it seemed almost as though he regarded the sea as his god. Perhaps he did. One way or another it was a question that required no answer, an impossible question for anyone of Lawler's cast of mind to deal with. He had no wish to patronize Gharkid and certainly none to offend him. Feeling almost unclean in the face of Gharkid's innocence and delight, Lawler smiled quickly and moved along. Farther up the deck he caught sight of Father Quillan studying them from a distance.

"I've been watching him work," the priest said as Lawler came by. "Picking through all that seaweed, pulling it apart, stacking it up. He never stops. He seems so gentle, but there's a fury inside that man somewhere. What do you know about him, anyway?"

"Gharkid? Not very much. Keeps to himself, doesn't say a lot. I'm not sure where he lived before he showed up on Sorve a few years back. Nothing seems to interest him except algae."

"A mystery."

"Yes, a mystery. I used to think he was a thinker, working out the Lord only knows what philosophical problem in the privacy of his own head. But now I'm not so sure that anything goes on in there except contemplating the different kinds of seaweed. It's easy enough to mistake silence for profundity, you know. I'm coming around these days to the view that he's every bit as simple as he appears to be."

"Well, that could be," the priest said. "But I'd be very surprised. I've never actually met a truly simple man."

"Do you mean that?"

"You may think they are, but you're always wrong. In my line of work you eventually get a chance to see into people's souls, when they finally come to trust you, or when they finally begin to believe that a priest is nothing but a thin curtain that stands between them and God. And then you discover that even the simple ones aren't simple at all. Innocent, perhaps, but never simple. The human mind at its most minimal is too complex ever to be simple. So forgive me, doctor, if I suggest that you return to your first hypothesis about Gharkid. I believe that he thinks. I believe that he is a seeker after God, just like all the rest of us."

Lawler smiled. Believing in God was one thing, seeking after God something else entirely. Gharkid might well be a believer, on some basic unquestioning level, for all Lawler knew. But it was Quillan who was the seeker. It always amused Lawler the way people projected their own needs and fears on the world about them and elevated them to the status of fundamental laws of the universe.

And was finding God really what they were all trying to do, every one of them? Quillan, yes. He had a professional need, so to speak. But Gharkid? Kinverson? Delagard? Lawler himself?

Lawler took a long close look at Quillan. By this time he had learned how to read the priest's face. Quillan had two modes of expression. One was the pious and sincere one. The other was the cold, dead, cynical, God-empty one. He shifted from one to the other in accordance with whatever spiritual storms were raging within his troubled mind. Right now Lawler suspected he was getting the pious Quillan, the sincere Quillan.

He said, "You think I'm a seeker after God too?"

"Of course you are!"

"Because I can quote a few lines of the Bible?"

"Because you think that you can live your life in His shadow and not for a moment accept the fact of His existence. Which is a situation that automatically calls its own opposite into being. Deny God and you are doomed to spend your life searching for Him, if only for the sake of finding out whether you're right about His nonexistence."

"Which is your situation exactly, Father."

"Of course."

Lawler glanced down the deck toward Gharkid, who was patiently sorting through his latest catch of algae, trimming away the dead strands and flinging them over the side. He was singing to himself, a little tuneless song.

"And if you neither deny God nor accept him, what then?" Lawler asked. "Wouldn't you then be a truly simple person?"

"I suppose you would, yes. But I'm yet to find any person like that."

"I suggest you have a chat with our friend Gharkid, then."

"Oh, but I have," the priest said.

STILL THERE WAS NO RAIN. THE FISH DECIDED TO COME BACK WITHIN reach of Kinverson's fishing gear, but the skies remained unyielding. The voyage was well into its third week and the water they had brought with them from Sorve was seriously depleted now. What was left of it had begun to take on a dank, brackish taste. Rationing was second nature to them all, but the prospect of struggling through the entire eight-week journey to Grayvard on what was presently in their storage tubs was a grim one.

It was still too soon to start living on the eyeballs and blood and spinal fluid of sea-creatures—techniques that Kinverson cited as things he had done during long solitary rainless voyages—and the situation wasn't yet critical enough to get out the equipment by which fresh water could be distilled from the sea. That was a last resort, inefficient and wearisome, a matter of the slow, steady accumulation of single drops, good only for a desperation supply.

But there were other things they could do. Raw fish, full of moisture and relatively low in salt, was part of everyone's daily diet now. Lis Niklaus did her best to clean and trim it into neat appealing filets; but even so it quickly became a tiresome regimen and sometimes a nauseating one. Wetting one's skin and clothing down with seawater was useful also. It was a way of reducing body temperature and thereby cutting back on the internal need for water. And it was the only way to keep clean, since the fresh water on board was too precious to use for washing.

Then one afternoon the sky darkened unexpectedly and a cloudburst broke over them. "Buckets!" Delagard yelled. "Bottles, casks, flasks, anything! Get them out on deck!"

Like demons they ran up and down the ladders, hauling out anything that might hold water until the deck was covered with receptacles of all sorts. Then they stripped, every one of them, and danced naked in the rain like lunatics, washing the salt crusts from their skins and from their clothes. Delagard cavorted on the bridge, a burly satyr with a hairy chest as fleshy as a woman's. With him was Lis, laughing and shouting and jumping beside him, her long yellow hair pasted to her shoulders, her big globular breasts bouncing like planets threatening to leave their orbits. Emaciated little Dag Tharp danced with sturdy Neyana Golghoz, who looked strong enough to flip him over her shoulder. Lawler was savoring the downpour by himself near the rear mast when Pilya Braun came dancing by, eyes shining, lips drawn back in a fixed grin of invitation. Her olive skin was glossy and splendid in the rain. Lawler danced with her for a minute or so, admiring her strong thighs and deep bosom, but when by her motions Pilya seemed to indicate dancing off with him to some snug place belowdecks, Lawler pretended not to understand what she was trying to communicate, and after a time she moved away.

Gharkid capered on the gantry-bridge next to his pile of seaweed. Dann Henders and Onyos Felk had joined hands and were prancing around near the binnacle. Father Quillan, bony and pale with his robe cast aside, seemed to be in a trance, head turned to the sky, eyes glassy, arms outstretched, shoulders working rhythmically. Leo Martello was dancing with Sundira, the two of them looking good together, slim, agile, vigorous. Lawler glanced around for Kinverson and found him up by the bow, not dancing at all, just standing matter-of-factly naked in the rain letting the water stream down his powerful frame.

The storm lasted no more than fifteen minutes. Lis calculated afterward that it had provided them with half a day's additional supply of water.

THERE WAS CONSTANT DOCTORING FOR LAWLER TO DO, THE SHIPBOARD accidents, the blisters, the sprains, some mild dysentery, one day a broken collarbone aboard Bamber Cadrell's ship. Lawler felt the strain of trying to spread himself over the entire fleet. Much of what he had to do he did by radio, crouching in front of Dag Tharp's incomprehensible jumble of equipment in the *Queen of Hydros'* radio room. But broken bones couldn't be set by radio. He went by water-strider to Cadrell's *Sorve Goddess* to handle the job.

Riding in the strider was an uneasy business. The thing was a lightweight human-powered hydrofoil, as flimsy as one of the long-legged giant crabs that Lawler sometimes had seen delicately picking their way across the floor of Sorve Bay: a mere shell made of laminated strips of the lightest of wood, equipped with pedals, pontoon floats, underwater outrigger wings to provide lift, and a high-efficiency propeller. A semi-live coating of slimy microorganisms that minimized frictional drag grew on its skin.

Dann Henders rode with Lawler on his trip over to the *Sorve Goddess*. The strider was lowered into the water by davits and they descended to it by ropes, hand over hand. Lawler's feet rested at a distance of no more than centimeters from the surface of the sea when he took his place on the frontmost of the strider's two seats. The fragile little vehicle rocked lightly on the gentle swells. It felt as though only a thin film protected him from a yawning abyss. Lawler imagined tentacles rising from the depths, mocking eyes big as platters staring at him out of the waves, silvery jaws opening to bite.

Henders settled in behind him. "Ready, doc? Let's go."

Together, pedaling flat out, they were just strong enough to get the strider up to takeoff speed. The first moments were the hardest. Once they had come up to speed the uppermost set of hydrofoils that had launched them on their way rose up out of the water, reducing drag, and the smaller pair of high-speed foils beneath was able to carry them swiftly along.

But there was no easing off once they had begun. Like any swift vessel, the strider had to climb constantly through its own bow wave: if they slackened the pace even a moment, wave drag would carry them under. No tentacles slithered toward them during the short journey, though. No toothy jaws nibbled at their toes. Friendly ropes were waiting to pull them onto the deck of the *Sorve Goddess*.

The broken collarbone belonged to Nimber Tanamind, an egregious hypochondriac whose medical problem this time, for once, was unequivocably genuine. A falling boom had cracked his left clavicle, and the whole upper side of his stocky body was swollen and blue. For once, also, Nimber wasn't uttering any complaints. Perhaps it was shock, perhaps fear, perhaps he was dazed by the pain; he sat quietly against a heap of netting, looking stunned, his eyes out of focus, his arms trembling, his fingers doing odd little jerking things. Brondo Katzin and his wife Eliyana stood beside him, and Nimber's wife Salai was nearby, fretfully pacing.

"Nimber," Lawler said, with some affection. They were almost the same age. "You damned idiot, Nimber, what have you done to yourself now?"

Tanamind raised his head a little. He looked frightened. He said nothing, only moistened his lips. A glossy line of sweat lay across his forehead, though the day was cool.

"How long ago did this happen?" Lawler asked Bamber Cadrell.

"Maybe half an hour," the captain said.

"He's been conscious the whole time?"

"Yes."

"You give him anything? A sedative?"

"Just a little brandy," Cadrell said.

"All right," said Lawler. "Let's get to work. Lay him out on his back— that's it, stretch him out flat. Is there a pillow or something we can stick under him? There, yes, right between his shoulderblades." He took a paper packet of pain-killer from his kit. "Get me some water to put this in. I need some cloth compresses, too. Eliyana? About this long, and heat them in warm water—"

Nimber groaned only once, when Lawler spread his shoulders out so that his clavicle would flex and the fracture drop back into its proper place. After that he closed his eyes and seemed to disappear into meditation while Lawler did what he could to reduce the swelling and immobilize Nimber's arm to keep him from reopening the break.

"Give him some more brandy," Lawler said when he was done. He turned to Nimber's wife. "Salai, you'll have to be the doctor now. If he starts running a fever, let him have one of these every morning and night. If the side of his face swells up, call me. If he complains about numbness in his fingers, let me know that too. Anything else that might bother him is likely not to be very important." Lawler looked toward Cadrell. "Bamber, I'll have a little of that brandy myself."

"Everything going well for you guys?" Cadrell asked.

"Other than losing Gospo, yes. And here?"

"We're doing just fine."

"That's good to hear."

It wasn't much of a conversation. But the reunion had been a strangely stilted one from the moment he had come on board. How are you, doc, nice to see you, welcome to our ship, yes, but nothing in the way of real contact, no exchange of inner feelings offered or solicited. Even Nicko Thalheim, coming on deck a little belatedly, had simply smiled and nodded. It was like being among strangers. These people had become unfamiliar to him in just a few weeks. Lawler realized how thoroughly he had become embedded in the insular life of the flagship. And they in the microcosm of the *Sorve Goddess*. He wondered what the island community was going to be like when it finally reconstituted itself in its new home.

His return to the flagship was uneventful. He went straight to his cabin.

Seven drops of numbweed tincture. No, make it ten.

THOUGHTS OF LOST EARTH CAME TO LAWLER OFTEN AS HE STOOD BY THE rail by night, listening to the heavy mysterious sounds of the sea and staring into the empty impenetrable darkness that pressed down on them.

His obsession with the mother world seemed to be growing as the six ships made their daily way across the vast face of the water-planet. For the millionth time he tried to imagine what it was like when it was alive. The large islands called countries, ruled by kings and queens, wealthy and powerful beyond all comprehension. The fierce wars. Spectacular weapons, capable of wrecking worlds. And then that great migration into space, when they had sent the myriad starships outward, bearing the ancestors of all the human beings who lived anywhere in the galaxy today. Everyone. All had sprung from a single source, that one small world that had died.

Sundira, wandering the deck by night, appeared beside him.

"Pondering the destiny of the cosmos again, doctor?"

"As usual. Yes."

"What's tonight's theme?"

"Irony. All those years that the Earth people worried about destroying themselves in one of their feverish nasty little wars. But they never did. And then their own sun went and did it for them in a single afternoon."

"Thank God we were already out here settling among the stars."

"Yes," said Lawler, with a cool glance at the dark monster-infested sea. "How fine for us that was."

LATER IN THE NIGHT SHE RETURNED. HE HADN'T MOVED FROM HIS place by the rail.

"That you still there, Valben?"

"Still me, yes." She had never called him by his first name before. It seemed odd to him for her to be doing it now: inappropriate, even. He couldn't remember when anyone had last addressed him as "Valben."

"Can you tolerate some company again?"

"Sure," he said. "Can't get to sleep?"

"Haven't tried," she said. "There's a prayer meeting going on down below, did you know that?"

"And who are the holy ones taking part in it?"

"The father, naturally. Lis. Neyana. Dann. And Gharkid."

"Gharkid? Finally coming out of his shell?"

"Well, he's just sitting there, actually. Father Quillan's doing all the talking. Telling them how elusive God is, how difficult it is for us to sustain our faith in a Supreme Being who never speaks to us, never gives us any proof that he's really there. What an effort it is for anyone to have faith, and that that's not right, it shouldn't be an effort at all, we ought to be able to simply to make a blind leap and accept God's existence, only that's too hard for most of us. Et cetera, et cetera. And the others are drinking it all in. Gharkid listens and now and then he nods. A strange one, he is. You want to go below and hear what the father's saying?"

"No," Lawler said. "I've already had the privilege of hearing him hold forth on the topic, thanks."

They stood together in silence for a time.

Then after a while Sundira said, apropos of nothing at all, "Valben. What kind of name is Valben?"

"An Earth name."

"No, it isn't. John, Richard, Elizabeth, those are Earth names. Leo, he's got an Earth name. I never heard of any name like Valben."

"Does that mean it isn't an Earth name, then?"

"I just know that I know what Earth names are like, and I never heard of a Valben."

"Well, maybe it isn't an Earth name, then. My father said it was. He could have been wrong."

"Valben," she said, playing with the sound of it. "A family name, maybe, a special name. It's a new one to me. Would you prefer that I call you Valben?"

"Prefer? No. Call me Valben if you want to. But in fact nobody does."

"What do they call you that you like, then? Doc, isn't it?"

He shrugged. "Doc's okay. Some call me Lawler. A few call me Val. Just a very few."

"Val. I like the sound of that better than Doc. Is it all right if I call you Val?"

Only his oldest friends called him Val, men like Nicko Thalheim, Nimber Tanamind, Nestor Yanez. It didn't sound at all right on her lips. But why should that matter? He could get used to it. And "Val" was better than "Valben," at least.

"Whatever you like," he said.

ANOTHER TIDAL SURGE ARRIVED THREE DAYS LATER, THIS ONE COMING from due west. It was stronger than the first one, but the magnetrons had no problem dealing with it. Up and over, and down the far side, a little bump upon landing, and that was that.

The weather stayed cool and dry. The voyagers went onward.

IN THE DEPTHS OF THE NIGHT THERE WAS A LOUD MUFFLED THUMP against the hull, as though the ship had struck a reef. Lawler sat up in his bunk, yawning, thumbing his eyes, wondering if he had dreamed it. Everything was silent for a moment. Then came another thump, a harder one. No dream, then. He was still half asleep, yes, but he was half awake also. He counted off a minute, a minute and a half. Another thump. He heard the timbers of the hull creak and shift.

He wrapped something around his middle and went out toward the companionway, fully awake now. Lights had been lit; people were streaming out of the portside cabin, blurry-faced, a couple of them still naked, no doubt just as they had slept. Lawler went up on deck. The night watch—Henders, Golghoz, Delagard, Niklaus, Thane—was running around in an agitated way, speeding from one side of the ship to the other as though following the movements of some enemy attacking from below.

"Here they come again!" someone called.

Thump. Up here, the impact was greater—the ship seemed to shiver and jump to one side—and the sound of the hull's being struck was sharper, a clear startling hard-edged sound.

Lawler found Dag Tharp near the rail.

"What's going on?"

"Look out there and you'll see."

The sea was calm. Two moons were aloft, at opposite ends of the sky, and the Cross had begun its nightly slide toward dawn, hanging in an off-center position a little toward the east. The six ships of the flotilla had wandered somewhat from their usual three-ranks formation and were arrayed in a wide loosely-drawn circle. Perhaps a dozen long streaks of brilliant blue phosphorescence were visible in the open water in the center of the group, like fiery arrows of light cutting through the ocean not far below the surface. As Lawler watched, perplexed, one of the phosphorescent streaks extended itself at a startling pace, shooting swiftly in a straight line toward the ship just to the left of theirs, traveling on a collision course, a bright needle in the darkness. From somewhere came an ominous high-pitched pinging sound, steadily growing in intensity as the streak of light approached the vessel.

The collision came. Lawler heard the crack of impact and saw the other ship heel over a little way. Faintly across the water came the sound of shouts.

The phosphorescent streak backed off, sped away, back toward the open central water.

"Rammerhorns," Tharp said. "They're trying to sink us."

Lawler grasped the rail and looked down. His eyes were more accustomed to the dark now. He could see the attackers clearly by the light of their own phosphorescence.

They looked like living missiles, narrow-bodied, ten or fifteen meters long, propelled by strong double-fluked tails. From their blunt foreheads sprouted a single thick yellow horn, perhaps five meters in length and sturdy as a kelp-trunk, that terminated in a blunt but dangerous-looking point. They were swimming at a furious rate across the open zone between the ships, getting up to immense speeds by furious lashing movements of their tails and bashing their horns into the sides of the vessels in the obvious hope of breaching them. Then, with a kind of insane persistence, they turned around, swam off to a distance, and charged again even more fiercely. The faster they swam the more intense was the luminescence that streamed from their flanks, and the louder was the sharp pinging sound that they emitted.

Kinverson appeared from somewhere, lugging something that looked like a heavy iron kettle bound in algae fiber. "Give me a hand with this, will you, doc?"

"Where are you taking it?"

"The bridge. It's a sonic."

The kettle, or whatever it was, was almost too heavy for Kinverson to manage by himself. Lawler caught hold of it by a knotted cord that dangled from the side nearest him. Together he and Kinverson were able to struggle it down the deck toward the bridge. Delagard joined them there and the three of them hauled it up to the higher level.

"Fucking rammerhorns," Kinverson muttered. "I knew they were bound to turn up sooner or later."

There was another thump below. Lawler saw a streak of dazzling blue light rebound from the ship and go scuttering off in the other direction.

Of all the strange creatures that the sea had sent against them thus far in the voyage, these things that were blindly battering into them seemed to

Lawler to be the most frightening. You could stomp some, duck others, keep a watchful eye on odd-looking netting. But how could you deal with these spears coming at you from below in the night, these huge creatures determined to sink you, and capable of doing it?

"Are they strong enough to pierce the hull?" Lawler asked Delagard.

"It's been known to happen. Jesus. Jesus!"

Kinverson's giant form, outlined by the moonlight, rose high above the big kettle, which he had installed by this time at the front end of the bridge. He had unfastened a long padded stick that had been tied to the kettle's side and now he grasped it in both hands and brought it down on the kettle's drum-like top. A heavy booming sound rumbled out across the waters.

He struck again, again, again.

"What's he doing?" Lawler asked.

"Sending a countersonic. Rammerhorns can't see. They do it all by bouncing sound waves off their target. Gabe's screwing up their directional senses."

Kinverson pounded on his drum with phenomenal energy and zeal. The air was thick with the booming sounds that he made. Could they penetrate the water? Apparently so. Down below, the rammerhorns were rushing back and forth in the space between the ships even more swiftly than before, so that the dazzling streaks of blue light that marked their trails were intricately interwoven. But the patterns were getting erratic. A chaotic jerkiness seemed to be entering the movements of the rammerhorns as Kinverson continued to beat his drum. They moved in wild lunging leaps, now and then breaking the surface of the water, soaring aloft for a moment or two, landing with great splashing impacts. One of them struck the ship, but it was only a weak glancing blow. The pingings they made grew arrhythmic and discordant. For a moment Kinverson paused, as though he were getting tired, and it appeared as if the rammerhorns might regroup. But then he resumed his booming with even more fervor than before, hammering away with his stick, on and on and on. Suddenly there was a great flurry down below and two of the huge attackers leaped from the water at the same moment. By the light of the others, swimming in ragged circles around them, Lawler saw that the horn of one had penetrated the gill-slits of the other, was in fact impaled deep within the other rammerhorn's skull; and both creatures, falling back to the water still linked in that terrible way, now began to sink. Their path into the depths was revealed for a moment or two more by the trail of phosphorescence that they left behind. Then they could no longer be seen.

Kinverson struck the drum three last slow blows, widely spaced—boom—boom—*boom*—and lowered his arm.

"Dag? Dag, where the hell are you?" It was Delagard's voice, coming out of the darkness. "Start calling around the fleet. Make sure nobody's sprung a leak."

All was dark and quiet in the water. But when Lawler closed his eyes it seemed to him that searing streaks of blue light were flashing back and forth against his lids.

THE NEXT TIDAL SURGE WAS THE MOST POWERFUL ONE YET. IT CAME upon them two days before they were expecting it, evidently because Onyos Felk had got his numbers wrong; and it struck with great enthusiasm and really jubilant malevolence, whacking the ships broadside as they lolled becalmed in a sleepy sea where drifting gray weeds belched a strangely seductive perfume upward into the air. Lawler was working belowdecks to reorganize his inventory of medicines. He thought at first that the rammerhorns had returned, so sharp was the impact. But no, no, this was nothing like the single point-source of a rammerhorn blow: it was more like the flat of a giant hand striking the hull and pushing the ship backward along its own course. He heard the magnetron kick in and waited for the sensation of lift, the sudden silence that meant they were riding the displacement field above the angry water. But the silence didn't come, and Lawler had to make a quick desperate grab for the side of his bunk as the ship heeled up at a startling angle, throwing him toward the bulkhead. Things fell from his shelves and sped in one quick whoosh along the floor, fetching up in a scrambled heap on the far side of the cabin.

Was this it? The Wave, at last? And would they be able to withstand it?

He held tight and waited. The ship rocked back, fell with what sounded like a colossal crash into the cavity that the surge had left behind, and heeled over the other way, sending everything that had fallen from the shelves sliding back across the cabin. Then it righted itself. All was still. He picked up the Egyptian god and the Greek potsherd and put them back where they had been.

More? Another blow?

No. Still and steady.

Are we sinking, then?

Apparently not. Cautiously Lawler made his way out of the cabin and cocked an ear. Delagard was yelling something. They were all right, he said. It had been a good hard smack, but they were all right.

The force of the big surge had carried them along with it, though, and it had pulled them off course, sweeping them eastward half a day's journey. But all six vessels had been swept, miraculously, as a single unit. There they were, out of formation but still within sight of one another, drifting on the now tranquil sea. It took an hour to rebuild the formation, six hours more to regain the position they had held when the surge had hit them. Not so bad, really. They went onward.

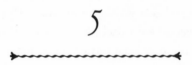

5

N IMBER TANAMIND'S COLLARBONE SEEMED TO BE HEALING
properly. Lawler didn't go back over to the *Sorve Goddess* to
check it out, since nothing that Nimber's wife Salai told him
about his condition indicated that problems were developing. Lawler de-
scribed to her how she should change the bandage and what to look for in
the vicinity of the fracture.

Martin Yanez of the *Three Moons* called in to say that old Sweyner the
glassblower had been struck in the face by a fast-flying hagfish, and now his
neck was so sore that he couldn't hold his head straight. Lawler told Yanez
what to do about that. From the Sisterhood ship, the *Hydros Cross,* came a
rare query: Sister Boda was having shooting pains in her left breast. There
was no point in going to see her. The Sisters, he knew, weren't likely to let
him examine her. He suggested painkillers and asked them to call back after
Sister Boda's next menstrual period. That was the last he heard of Sister
Boda's sore breast.

Someone on the *Black Sea Star* fell from the rigging and dislocated her
arm. Lawler led Poilin Stayvol step by step through the process of relocating
it for her. Someone on the *Golden Sun* was vomiting black bile. It turned out
that he had been experimenting with eating arrowfish caviar. Lawler ad-
vised a more cautious diet. Someone on the *Sorve Goddess* complained of
recurring nightmares. Lawler suggested a nip of brandy before going to
sleep. For Lawler it was business as usual.

Father Quillan, perhaps envious, observed that it must be wonderfully gratifying to him to be needed in this way, to be so essential to the life of an entire community, to be able to heal the suffering ones, more often than not, when they turned to him in pain.

"Gratifying? I suppose so. I've never actually bothered to think much about it. It's simply my job."

And so it was. But Lawler realized that there was something to what the priest had said. His power over Sorve Island had been almost godlike, or at least priestly. What did it mean, after all, to have been the doctor there for twenty-five years? Why, that he had had every man's balls in his hand at one time or another, that he had had his arm up every woman's cunt, that just about everyone on Sorve under the age of twenty-five was someone he had pulled out into the air, bloody and kicking, and given a first slap on the rump. All that tended to create a certain bond. It gave the doctor a certain claim on them, and they on him. No wonder people anywhere will worship their doctor, Lawler thought. To them he is the Healer. The Doctor. The Magician. The one who protects, the one who gives comfort and surcease from pain. It had been going on that way since the days of the cave dwellers, back there on poor damned doomed lost Earth. He was only the latest in a long long line. And, unlike the hapless Father Quillan and others of his profession, whose thankless task it was to proffer the blessings of an invisible god, he was actually in a position where he could sometimes deliver tangible benefits. So yes, yes, he was a powerful figure in the community by virtue of his vocation, the man with the power of life and death, respected and needed and probably feared, and he supposed that that was gratifying. Very well. He was gratified. He didn't see where that made much of a difference.

THEY WERE IN THE GREEN SEA NOW, WHERE DENSE COLONIES OF A lovely aquatic plant made it almost impossible for the ships to move forward. The plant was succulent, with thick glossy spoon-shaped leaves sprouting from a brown central stem and a central sporing stalk topped by brilliant yellow-and-purple reproductive bodies. Air-filled bladders kept the plants afloat. Feathery gray roots twined like tentacles below the surface, tangled together in dark mats. The plants were so closely inter-woven below the water-line that they formed what was virtually an unbro-ken carpet covering the sea. The ships butted bow-first into them and came to a standstill.

Kinverson and Neyana Golghoz went out in the water-strider with machetes to hack them apart.

"Useless," Gharkid said, to no one in particular. "I know these plants. You cut them up, each one turns into five new ones."

Gharkid was right. Kinverson chopped at the pretty weeds with might and main while Neyana pedaled the strider forward by sheer brute force; but no opening appeared. It wasn't possible for one man, no matter how strong, to cut a big enough hole in the plant-mass to create any real channel. The sundered pieces of each plant took up independent lives immediately: you could almost see them growing themselves back, sealing off the cut place, putting out new roots, sending up shiny new spoons and showy new sporing stalks.

"Let me check my medical supplies," said Lawler. "I might have something we can sprinkle on them that they won't enjoy."

He went below, to the cargo hold. What he had in mind was a tall flask of a black viscous oil sent to him long ago by his colleague Dr. Nikitin of Salimil Island in return for a favor. Supposedly Dr. Nikitin's oil was useful in killing fireflower, an unpleasant stinging plant that occasionally caused problems for human swimmers, though Gillies didn't seem to mind its presence at all. Lawler had never needed to make use of the oil: the last fireflower infestation in Sorve Bay had occurred when he was still a young man. But it was the only thing in his collection of drugs, medicines, ointments, and potions that was intended to do injury to some form of plant life. Maybe it would be effective against the one they were encountering here. He saw no harm in trying.

The instructions on the label, closely written out in Dr. Nikitin's meticulous hand, said that a concentration of one part to a thousand parts of water would be sufficient to clear a hectare of bay from fireflower. Lawler mixed it in a concentration of one part to a hundred and had himself swung out over the water in the davits to spray it on the weeds around the *Queen of Hydros'* bow.

The weeds seemed unbothered by it. But as the diluted oil trickled down through the clotted plants and spread out through the water around them an undersea commotion began, and quickly became a turmoil. From the deep came fish, thousands of them, millions, little nightmare creatures with huge gaping jaws, slim serpentine bodies, broadly flaring tails. Vast numbers of them must have been nesting down there under the plants and now the whole colony was rising as though with one accord. They smashed their way upward through the matted clumps of roots and went into a wild mating frenzy at the surface. Dr. Nikitin's oil, harmless though it was to the weeds, appeared to have a potent aphrodisiac effect on the creatures that lived in the water below them. The wild writhing of vast numbers of the snaky little things set the sea into such turbulence that the tight clusters of interwoven weeds were ripped apart and the ships were able to make their way through the channels that appeared. In short order all six vessels were past the zone of congestion, moving freely in open water.

"What a clever bastard you are, doc," Delagard said.

"Yes. Except I didn't know that was going to happen."

"You didn't?"

"Not a clue. I was simply trying to poison those plants. I had no idea those fish were underneath them. Now you see how a lot of great scientific discoveries get made."

Delagard frowned. "And how is that?"

"By sheer accident."

"Ah, yes," said Father Quillan. Lawler saw that the priest was in his cynic/unbeliever mode. With a mock-solemn intonation Quillan exclaimed, "God moves in a mysterious way His wonders to perform."

"Indeed," Lawler said. "So he does."

A COUPLE OF DAYS BEYOND THE WATER-PLANT ZONE THE SEA BECAME shallow for a time, hardly any deeper than Sorve Bay, with utterly transparent water. Gigantic contorted heads of coral, some of it green, some of it ochre, much of it a brooding dark shade of blue that was practically black, could be seen rising from a sea-floor of brilliant white sand that looked close enough to touch. The green coral sprouted in fantastic baroque spires, the blue-black was in the form of umbrellas and long thick arms, the ochre had the shape of great flaring flattened horns, branching and rebranching. There was also a huge scarlet coral that grew as single isolated globular masses, vivid against the white sand, which had the wrinkled, involuted shape of human brains.

In places the coral had expanded its reach so exuberantly that it breached the surface. Little whitecaps licked around it at the waterline. The clumps that had been exposed longest to the air were dead, bleaching to whiteness in the hard sunlight, and just below them was a layer of dying coral that was taking on a dull brown color.

"The beginning of land on Hydros," Father Quillan observed. "Let the sea level change a little and all this coral will be sticking out of the water. Then it'll decompose into soil, seed-producing air-dwelling plants will evolve and start sprouting, and away we'll go. Natural islands first, then the sea-floor rises a little more, and we get continents."

"And how long do you think it'll be before that happens?" Delagard asked.

Quillan shrugged. "Thirty million years? Forty, maybe. Or maybe a lot more than that."

"Thank God!" Delagard bellowed. "Then we don't have to worry about it for a while!"

What they did have to worry about, though, was this coral sea. The ochre coral heads, the horn-shaped ones, looked sharp as razors, and in places their upper edges lay only a few meters deeper than keel-depth. There might be other places where there was even less clearance. A ship that passed over one could find itself laid open from bow to stern.

So it was necessary to move warily, searching for safe channels within the reefs. For the first time since they had left Sorve there could be no night sailing at all. By day, when the sun was a beacon striking patterns of sparkling lines on the shimmering white sea-floor, the voyagers wove a cautious path between the coral outcroppings, staring down in wonder at the unthinkable swarms of gilded fish that clustered around the coral, swiftly and silently going about their business, great hordes of them threading down every passageway as they fed on the reef's rich population of microlife. By night the six ships anchored close by one another in some safe open sector, waiting for the dawn. Everyone came up on deck and leaned out, calling to friends on the other ships, even conducting shouted conversations. It was the first real contact most of them had had since their departure.

The night spectacle was even more dazzling than the daytime one: under the cold light of the Cross and the three moons, with Sunrise adding its own measure of brilliance, the coral creatures themselves came to life, emerging from a billion billion tiny caverns in the reefs: long whips, scarlet here, subtle rose there, a sulfurous yellow on this kind of coral, a glaucous bright aquamarine on that one, everything uncoiling and reaching forth, all of them frantically flagellating the water to harvest the even tinier beings that hung suspended in it. Down the aisles of the reef came stunning serpentine things, all eyes and teeth and shining scales, that slithered diligently along the bottom, leaving elegant belly-tracks in the sand. A pulsing green luminescence flowed from them. And out of a myriad dark dens appeared the apparent kings of the reef, swollen red octopoid creatures with plump, baggy, prosperous-looking bodies held secure within long swirling coiling tentacles from which emanated a throbbing, terrifying bluish-white light. By night every coral head became the throne for one of these great octopoids: there it sat, glowing smugly, quietly surveying its kingdom with gleaming yellow-green eyes that were larger across than a man's outstretched hand. There was no escaping the gaze of those eyes as you peered over the rail in the darkness to look down at the wonderworld beneath. They stared at you confidently, complacently, revealing neither curiosity nor fear. What those great eyes seemed to be saying was, *We are masters here, and you are not at all important. Come, swim down to us, and let us put you to some good use.* And sharp yellow beaks would open suggestively. *Come down to us. Come down to us.* It was a temptation.

The coral outcroppings began to thin out, grew more and more sparse, finally vanished altogether. The sea-floor remained shallow and sandy a while longer; then, abruptly, the brilliant white sand could no longer be seen, and the turquoise water, which had been so clear and serene, turned once more into the opaque dark blue of deep waters, with a choppy covering of light rippling swells.

Lawler began to feel as if the voyage would never end. The ship had become not just his island but his entire world. He would simply go on and on aboard it forever. The other ships traveled alongside it like neighboring planets in the void.

The odd thing was that he saw nothing much wrong with that. He was fully caught up in the rhythm of the voyage now. He had learned to enjoy the constant rocking of the ship, accepting the little privations, even relishing the occasional visitations of monsters. He had settled down. He had adapted. Was he mellowing? Or was it, perhaps, that he had simply become an ascetic, not really needing anything, not caring much about temporal comforts? It could be. He made a note to ask Father Quillan about that when he had a chance.

DANN HENDERS HAD GASHED HIS FOREARM ON A GAFF WHILE HELPING Kinverson bring on board some enormous flopping man-sized fish, and Lawler, his supply of bandages depleted, went down to the cargo hold to get more from his reserve stores. He was always uneasy when he went down there, ever since his encounter with Kinverson and Sundira; he assumed they were still slipping off there together and the last thing he wanted was to stumble upon them again.

But Kinverson was on deck just then, busy gutting his fish. Lawler rummaged around amidships for a time in the dark musty depths of the hold. Then he turned to start making his way back up and practically collided with Sundira Thane, coming toward him down the same narrow, badly lit passageway that he had just entered.

She seemed as surprised to find Lawler there as he was to see her, and the surprise appeared genuine. "Val?" she said. Her eyes went wide and she took a hasty awkward step back from him just in time to avoid crashing into him.

Then the ship lurched sharply and flung her forward again, right into his arms.

It had to be an accident: she would never have done anything so blatant. Bracing himself against the stack of packing crates behind him, Lawler let his stack of folded bandages drop and caught her as she came whirling into him like a discarded doll that some petulant little girl had thrown. He held her, steadying her on her feet. The ship started to lurch back the other way and he tightened his grip to keep her from being hurled against the far wall. They stood nose to nose, eye to eye, laughing.

Then the ship righted itself and Lawler became aware that he was still holding her. And enjoying it.

So much for his alleged asceticism. What the hell. What the hell, indeed.

His lips went to hers, or perhaps hers went to his: he was never quite sure afterward which it had been. But the kiss was a long and active and interesting one. After that, though the ship's motions had become much less extreme, there was nothing really to be gained by letting go of her. His hands moved, though, one roaming the small of her back, the other sliding downward to her taut muscular rump, and he pulled her even closer against him, or she pushed herself closer: that too was an uncertain thing.

Lawler was wearing only a twist of yellow cloth around his waist. Sundira had on a light hip-length gray wrap. It was easy enough to untwist and unwrap. The whole thing was happening in a simple, orderly, predictable way, though it was not at all dull for being so predictable: it had the clear, crisp, lucid inevitability of a dream, and a dream's infinitely promising mysteriousness. Dreamily Lawler explored her skin. It was smooth and warm. Dreamily Sundira ran her fingers across the back of his neck. Dreamily he moved his right hand from her back to her front, down between their close-pressed bodies, past the valley between her small firm breasts where he had probed with his stethoscope what seemed several hundred years before, and on downward over her flat belly to the juncture of her thighs. He touched her. She was wet. She began to take the lead away from him now, pushing him backward, not in any unfriendly way but just trying, so it seemed, to guide him into a place between the packing crates where they would have room to lie down, or at least almost to lie down. After a moment he understood that.

It was close, cramped quarters. They both were long-legged people. But somehow they managed things, without even having rehearsed them. Neither of them said a word. Sundira was lively and active and quick. Lawler was vigorous and eager. It took just a moment for them to synchronize their rhythms and then it was smooth sailing all the way. Somewhere in the middle of things Lawler found himself trying to calculate how long it had actually been since he had last done this, and he dictated an angry memorandum to himself that got his attention back where it belonged.

Afterward they lay laughing and gasping in a sweaty heap, their legs still intertwined in a complicated fashion that might have been a challenge for the octopoids of the coral reef to bring off. Lawler sensed that this was not the time to be saying anything that might be construed as sentimental or romantic.

But he had to say something, eventually.

"You didn't follow me down here, did you?" he asked, finally breaking the long silence.

She looked at him with surprise and amusement mingling in her look.

"Why would I have done that?"

"How would I know?"

"I came down here to get some rope-mending tools. I didn't know you were here. The next thing was the ship jumping around and then I was in your arms."

"Yes. You don't regret that, do you?"

"No," she said. "Why should I? Do you?"

"Not at all."

"Good," she said. "We could have done this a long time back, you know."

"Could we?"

"Of course we could. Why did you wait so long?"

He studied her by the light of the dim, smoky taper. Her cool gray eyes held a glint of amusement, definite amusement, but he saw no mockery there. Even so, it seemed to him that she was taking this rather more lightly than he was.

"I could ask the same thing," he said.

"Good point." Then, after a moment: "I gave you some opportunities. You very carefully didn't take them."

"I know."

"Why not?"

"It's a long story," he said. "Also very boring. Does it matter?"

"Not really."

"Good."

They fell into another spell of silence.

After a little while the thought came to him that it might be a good idea to make love again, and he began idly stroking her arm and her thigh as they lay entangled on the floor of the hold. He detected the first little tremors of response in her, but with a remarkable display of control and tact she contrived to abort the process before it had gone too far to halt and gently disengaged herself from his grasp.

"Later," she said in a friendly way. "I really did have a reason for coming down here, you know."

She rose and put her wrap back on and gave him a cool, cheerful grin and a wink, and disappeared into the storeroom in the stern.

Lawler was startled by her imperturbability. Certainly he had no right to expect that what had just happened would be as unsettling to her as it had been for him after his long period of self-imposed celibacy. She had seemed to welcome it, yes. She had definitely seemed to enjoy it. All the same, had it really been nothing more than a casual random event for her, a mere fortuitous consequence of the lurching of the ship? So it would seem.

FATHER QUILLAN, ONE TORPID AFTERNOON, DECIDED TO MAKE A CATH-olic out of Natim Gharkid. At least that was what he appeared to be doing, with great intensity, as Lawler wandered past them and glanced down from the bridge. The priest, looking sweaty and inflamed, was offering the little brown-skinned man a voluble conceptual flow; and Gharkid was listening intently in his usual impassive way. "Father, Son, and Holy Ghost," Quillan said. "A single Godhead, but a triple entity." Gharkid nodded solemnly. Lawler, an unseen listener, blinked at the strange term "Holy Ghost." Whatever could that be? But Quillan had moved onward from there. Now he was explaining something called the Immaculate Conception. Lawler's attention wandered and he strolled on, but when he came back that way fifteen minutes later Quillan was still at it, speaking now of redemption, renewal, essence and existence, the meaning of sin and how it can exist in a creature that is the image of God, and why it had become necessary to send to the world a Savior who by His death would take upon Himself the evils of mankind. Some of it made sense to Lawler, some seemed the wildest gibberish; and after a time the proportion of gibberish to sense struck him as so high that he was offended by Quillan's intense dedication to such an absurd creed. Quillan was too intelligent, Lawler thought, to give any veracity to these notions of a god who first must create a world populated by a flawed version of himself and then send an aspect of himself to that world to redeem it from its built-in flaws by letting himself be killed. And it angered him to think that Quillan, after keeping his religion to himself so long, was fastening now on the hapless Gharkid as his first convert.

He went up to Gharkid later and said, "You mustn't pay attention to the things Father Quillan was saying. I'd hate to see you falling for that pile of nonsense."

In Gharkid's unreadable eyes appeared a momentary glint of surprise. "You think I am falling?"

"You seemed to be."

Gharkid laughed softly. "Ah, that man understands nothing," he said. And he walked away.

LATER IN THE DAY QUILLAN SOUGHT LAWLER OUT AND SAID TESTILY, "I'D be grateful if you'd avoid offering your opinions about things you hear in the conversations you eavesdrop on. All right, doctor?"

Lawler reddened. "What do you mean?"

"You know very well what I mean."

"Ah. I suppose."

"If you've got something to contribute to the dialogue, come sit with Gharkid and me and let's hear it. But don't snipe at me from behind my back."

Nodding, Lawler said, "Sorry."

Quillan gave him a long frosty look.

"Are you?"

"Do you think it's fair, trying to sell your beliefs to a simple soul like Gharkid?"

"We've been through this before. He's less simple than you think."

"Perhaps so," Lawler said. "He told me he wasn't very impressed with your dogmas."

"He isn't. But at least he's approaching them with an open mind. Whereas you—"

"All right," Lawler said. "So I'm by nature not a religious man. I can't help that. Go ahead and turn Gharkid into a Catholic. I don't really care. Make him an even better Catholic than yourself. That wouldn't be hard. Why should I care, after all? I've already said I was sorry for butting in. And I am. Will you accept my apology?"

"Of course," Quillan answered, after a moment.

But things remained strained between them for some time. Lawler made a point of keeping away whenever he saw the priest and Gharkid together. It was evident, though, that Gharkid wasn't making any more sense out of Quillan's teachings than Lawler could, and his dialogues with the priest eventually came to an end. Which pleased Lawler more than he had anticipated.

AN ISLAND CAME INTO VIEW, THE FIRST THEY HAD SEEN ON THE ENTIRE voyage, unless you counted the one that the Gillies were constructing. Dag Tharp hailed it by radio, but no answer came back.

"Are they just unsociable," Lawler said to Delagard, "or is it a Gillie island?"

"Gillies," Delagard said. "Nobody but fucking Gillies over there. Trust me. That's not one of ours."

Three days later there was another, in the shape of a crescent moon, lying like a sleeping animal on the northern horizon. Lawler, borrowing the helmsman's spyglass, thought he could see signs of a human settlement at the island's eastern end. Tharp started down to the radio room, but Delagard called him back, telling him not to bother.

"This one a Gillie island, too?" Lawler asked.

"Not this time. But there's no sense putting in a call. We aren't going to pay them a visit."

"Maybe they'd let us fill up on water. We're running pretty damned low."

"No," Delagard said. "That's Thetopal over there. My ships don't have landing rights on Thetopal. I don't get along well with the Thetopali at all. They wouldn't let us have a bucket of stale piss."

"Thetopal?" Onyos Felk said, looking puzzled. "You sure?"

"Sure I'm sure. What else can it be? That's Thetopal."

"Thetopal," Felk said. "All right. Thetopal, then. If you say so, Nid."

Once they had passed Thetopal, the sea was devoid of islands again. There was nothing but water to be seen in all directions. It was like traveling through an empty universe.

LAWLER CALCULATED THAT THEY WERE ABOUT HALFWAY TO GRAYVARD by now, though it was only a guess. Surely they had been at sea at least four weeks, but the ship's isolation and the unvarying daily routines made it difficult for him to work out any very clear sense of how rapidly time was passing.

For three days running a cold, hard wind raked down on the fleet from the north and stirred the wrath and fury of the sea all about them. The first sign was an abrupt transformation of the atmosphere, which in the region of the coral reefs had been soft and almost tropically mild. Suddenly now the air turned clear and tight-strung, so that the sky arched high above the ship, vibrating and pale, like an immense metallic dome. Lawler, who was something of an amateur meteorologist, was troubled by that. He brought his fears to Delagard, who took them seriously and gave orders to batten down. A little while later came a distant drumroll that heralded the first strong winds, a prolonged deep booming; and then the winds themselves arrived, quick nervous short-lived bursts of chilly air that licked and jabbed at the sea, stirring it as though with a pestle. With them came sparse rattling scatterings of dry hail, but no rain.

"Worse to come," Delagard muttered. He was on deck constantly as the weather worsened, scarcely taking the time to sleep. Father Quillan was often beside him, the two of them standing together like old cronies, peering into the wind. Lawler saw them talking, pointing, shaking their heads. What did these two have to say to each other, anyway, that coarse raucous man of blunt appetites and the austere, melancholic, God-haunted priest? There they were, anyway, together in the wheel-box, together by the binnacle, together on the quarterdeck. Was Quillan trying to convert Delagard now? Or were they trying to pray the storm away?

It came on anyway. The sea became an immense waste of broken water. Spray as fine as white smoke filled the air. The full wind struck with a hammering rush, burning past their ears and leaving a confused clamor echoing behind. They shortened the sails to it, but the ropes pulled free nevertheless and the heavy yards went whirling from side to side.

All hands were on deck. Martello, Kinverson, and Henders moved about precariously in the rigging, lashing themselves in to keep from being whirled off into the water. The rest yanked on the ropes while Delagard furiously shouted orders. Lawler worked alongside the rest: no more doctor's exemption for him, not in a gale like this.

The sky was black. The sea was blacker, except where it was tipped with white foam, or when a mammoth wave rose beside them like a giant wall of green glass. The ship wallowed forward into it, boring down instead of rising as it should, pitching headlong into dark smooth hollows, rolling as some great wave backed off to leeward with a terrible sucking sound, then came crashing toward them again to send cataracts of water tumbling across the deck. The magnetron was useless for this: the winds were coming in from contrary directions, colliding, surrounding them with unruly water that slammed against them from all sides, so that there was no rising over it. They had battened down everything, they had brought whatever they could belowdecks, but the sluicing waves found anything left behind, a bucket, a stool, a gaff, a water cask, and sent it thumping and leaping across the deck until it vanished over the side. The ship's nose dipped, rose, dipped again. Someone was vomiting; someone was screaming. Lawler caught a glimpse of one of the other ships—he had no idea which, it flew no flag—hard alongside them, caught in an oscillating wallow, now rising above them as though it planned to come crashing right down on their deck, now plummeting out of sight as if being dragged straight to the bottom.

"The masts!" someone yelled. "They're going to go! Get down! Get down!"

But the masts held firm, certain though it seemed that they would be jumped from their sockets and thrown into the sea. Their desperate vibrations shook the entire ship. Lawler found himself clinging to someone—Pilya, it was—and when Lis Niklaus came scudding down the deck at the mercy of the wind they both caught hold of her and reeled her in like a hooked fish. At any moment Lawler expected a deluge of rain to begin, and it bothered him that in all this frenzy of wind they would have no chance to put out any containers to catch the good sweet fresh water. But the winds remained dry, dry and crackling. Once he looked out over the rail and by the light of the sea-foam he saw the ocean full of little glinting staring eyes. Fantasy? Hallucination? He didn't think so. Drakken-heads, they were: an army of the things, a legion of them, long evil-looking snouts sticking up everywhere. A myriad of sharp teeth waiting for the moment when the *Queen of Hydros* capsized and its thirteen occupants went pitching into the water.

The gale blew and blew and blew, but the ship held and held and held. They lost all track of time. There was no night; there was no day; there was only the wind. Onyos Felk calculated later that it had been a three-day blow: perhaps he was right. It all came to an end as swiftly as it started, the black winds transforming themselves into a clear bright force that gleamed and cut like a knife; and then, as though some cue had been given, the storm dropped away in a moment and calmness returned with an impact much like a crash.

Stunned, Lawler moved slowly across the soaking deck in the strange new quietness. The deck was littered with torn bits of algae, clumps of jellyfish, angry flopping things, all sorts of marine detritus that the surging waves had thrown up. His hands ached where new rope-burns had awakened the pain the net-thing had inflicted. Silently Lawler took inventory: there was Pilya, there was Gharkid, there was Father Quillan, there was Delagard. Tharp, Golghoz, Felk, Niklaus. Martello? Yes, up above. Dann Henders? Yes.

Sundira?

He didn't see her. Then he did, and wished he hadn't: she was up near the forecastle, wet through and through, her clothes clinging to her skin so that she might just as well not have been wearing any, and Kinverson was with her. They were examining some creature of the deeps that he had found and was holding up to her, a sea-serpent of sorts, a long drooping comical thing with a wide but somehow harmless-seeming mouth and rows of circular green spots running down its flabby yellow body to give it a clownish look. They were laughing; Kinverson shook the thing at her, practically thrusting it into her face, and she howled with laughter and waved it away. Kinverson dangled it from its tail and watched its pathetic wrigglings; Sundira ran her hand along its sleek length, as though petting it, consoling it for its indignities; and then he flipped it back into the sea. He slipped his arm across her shoulders and they moved on out of sight.

How easy they were with each other. How casual, how playful, how disturbingly intimate.

Lawler turned away. Delagard was coming down the deck toward him. "You seen Dag?" he called out.

Lawler pointed. "Right over there." The radioman sat crumpled like a pile of rags against the starboard rail, shaking his head as though unable to believe that he had survived.

Delagard wiped strands of sopping hair out of his eyes and looked around. "Dag! Dag! Get on that fucking horn of yours, fast! We've lost the whole goddamned fleet!"

Lawler, aghast, swung about to stare at the eerily calm water. Delagard was right. Not one of the other ships was in view. The *Queen of Hydros* was all alone in the water.

"You think they sank?" he asked the ship-owner.

"Let's just pray," Delagard said.

BUT THE SHIPS WEREN'T LOST AT ALL. THEY WERE SIMPLY OUT OF VIEW. One by one they made radio contact with the flagship as Tharp tuned them in. The storm had casually scattered them like flimsy straws, carrying them this way and that over a great stretch of the sea; but they were all there. The *Queen of Hydros* held its position and the others homed in on it. By nightfall the entire fleet was reunited. Delagard ordered brandy broken out to celebrate their survival, the last of Gospo Struvin's Khuviar stock. Father Quillan, standing on the bridge, led them in a brief prayer of thanksgiving. Even Lawler found himself uttering a few quick, thankful words, a little to his own surprise.

6

WHATEVER EXISTED BETWEEN KINVERSON AND SUNDIRA
didn't seem to preclude whatever was coming into existence
between Sundira and Lawler. Lawler was unable to understand
either relationship, Sundira and Kinverson's or his own and Sundira's; but
he was wise enough in this sort of thing to know that the surest way to kill it
was to try to understand it. He would simply have to take what came.

One thing quickly became clear. Kinverson didn't care that Sundira
had taken up with Lawler. He seemed indifferent to matters of sexual
possessiveness. Sex was like breathing to him, so it appeared: he did it
without thinking about it. With anyone handy, as often as his body called
for it, purely a natural function, automatic, mechanical. And he expected
other people to look upon it the same way.

When Kinverson cut his arm and came to Lawler to have it cleaned and
bandaged, he said, while Lawler was working on him, "So you're fucking
Sundira now too, doc?"

Lawler pulled the bandage tight.

"I don't see why I need to answer that. It's none of your business."

"Right. Well, of course you're fucking her. She's a fine woman. Too
smart for me, but I don't mind that. And I don't mind what you do with
her either."

"Very kind of you," Lawler said.

"Of course I hope it works the same the other way."

"What do you mean by that?"

"It means there might be something left between Sundira and me," said Kinverson. "I hope you realize that."

Lawler gave him a long clear-eyed stare. "She's a grown woman. She can do whatever she wants with whoever she wants, whenever."

"Good. It's a small place, a ship. We wouldn't want any fuss here over a woman."

In rising irritation Lawler said, "You do what you do, and I'll do what I do, and let's not talk about it any more. You make her sound like a piece of equipment we both want to use."

"Yeah," said Kinverson. "Damned fine equipment."

ONE DAY NOT LONG AFTERWARD LAWLER WANDERED INTO THE GALLEY and found Kinverson with Lis Niklaus, the two of them giggling and groping and grappling and growling like Gillies in rut. Lis gave him a quick wink and a raucous chuckle over Kinverson's shoulder. "Hi, there, doc!" she called, sounding very drunk. Lawler looked back at her, startled, and went quickly out.

The galley was very far from being a private place: obviously Kinverson wasn't much concerned with taking precautions against Sundira's discovering—or Delagard, for that matter—that he had something running with Lis on the side. At least Kinverson was consistent, Lawler thought. He didn't care. About anything. About anyone.

Several times in the week following the windstorm Lawler and Sundira found the opportunity for a rendezvous in the cargo hold. His body, its fires so long dormant, was quickly relearning the meaning of passion. But there was nothing like passion coming from her, so far as Lawler could see, unless swift, efficient, enthusiastic but almost impersonal physical pleasure qualified as passion. Lawler didn't think so. He might have when he was younger, but not now.

They never said anything to each other while they were making love, and when they lay together afterward, returning from it, they seemed by common treaty to limit their conversation to the lightest of chatter. The new rules were established very quickly. Lawler took his cues from her, as he had from the start: she was obviously enjoying what was going on between them, and just as obviously she had no wish for any heavier transaction. Whenever Lawler encountered her on deck they spoke in the same inconsequential way, now. "Nice weather," they would say. Or, "What a strange color the sea is here."

He might say, "I wonder how soon we'll get to Grayvard."

She might say, "I don't cough at all any more, have you noticed that?"

He might say, "Wasn't that red fish we had for dinner last night marvelous?"

She might say, "Look, isn't that a diver swimming past us down there?"

Everything very bland, pleasant, controlled. He never said, "I haven't felt like this about anyone in a million years, Sundira." She never said, "I can't wait until the next time we can slip away, Val." He never said, "We're two of a kind, really, people who don't quite fit in." She never said, "The reason I kept wandering from island to island is that I was always looking for something more, wherever I was."

Instead of getting to know her better now that they were lovers he found that she was becoming more remote and indistinct to him. Lawler hadn't expected that. He wished there was more. But he didn't see how he could make there be more unless she wanted it.

She seemed to want to hold him at arm's length and take from him nothing more than she was already getting from Kinverson. Unless he had misread her, she didn't desire any other kind of intimacy. Lawler had never known a woman like that, so indifferent to permanence, to continuity, to the union of spirits, one who appeared to take each event as it came and never troubled to link it to what had gone before or what might come afterward. Then he realized that he did know someone like that.

Not a woman. Himself. The long-ago Lawler of Sorve Island, skipping from lover to lover with no thought except for the moment. But he was different now. Or so he hoped.

IN THE NIGHT LAWLER HEARD MUFFLED SHOUTS AND THUMPS COMING from the cabin next to his. Delagard and Lis were having a quarrel. It wasn't the first time, not by any means; but this one sounded louder and angrier than most.

In the morning, when Lawler went down to the galley early for breakfast, Lis was huddled over her stove with her face averted. From the side her face looked puffy; and when she turned he saw a yellow bruise along her cheekbone and another over her eye. Her lip was split and swollen.

"You want me to give you something for that?" Lawler asked.

"I'll survive."

"I heard the noise last night. What a lousy thing."

"I fell out of my bunk, is what happened."

"And went rattling around the cabin for five or ten minutes, shouting and cursing? And Nid, when he picked you up, felt like shouting and cursing too? Come off it, Lis."

She gave him a cold, sullen look. She seemed close to tears. He had never seen tough, salty Lis so close to breaking before.

Quietly he said, "Let breakfast wait a few minutes. I can clean up that cut for you and give you something to take the sting out of those bruises."

"I'm used to it, doc."

"He hits you often?"

"Often enough."

"Nobody hits anybody any more, Lis. That kind of stuff went out with the cavemen."

"Tell that to Nid."

"You want me to? I will."

Panic flared in her eyes. "No! For Christ's sake, don't say a word, doc! He'll kill me."

"You really are afraid of him, aren't you?"

"Aren't you?"

Lawler said, surprised, "No. Why should I be?"

"Well, maybe you aren't. But that's you. I figure I got off lucky. I was doing something he didn't like, and he found out, and he took it a lot harder than I ever imagined he would. Taught me a thing or two, that did. Nid's a wild man. I thought last night he was going to murder me."

"Call me, next time. Or bang on the cabin wall."

"There won't be a next time. I'm going to be good from now on. I mean it."

"You're that much afraid of him?"

"I love him, doc. Can you believe that? I love the dirty bastard. If he doesn't want me screwing around, I'm not going to screw around. He's that important to me."

"Even though he hits you."

"That tells me how important I am to him."

"You can't seriously mean that, Lis."

"I do. I do."

He shook his head. "Jesus. He slams you black and blue, and you tell me it's because he loves you so much."

"You don't understand these things, doc," Lis said. "You never did. You never could."

Lawler studied her in bewilderment, trying to comprehend. She was as alien to him as a Gillie right now.

"I guess I don't," he said.

AFTER THE WINDSTORM THE SEA WAS QUIET FOR A WHILE, NEVER exactly tranquil but not especially challenging, either. There came another zone thick with the clustering sea-plants, though these were less dense than the first one and they got through without needing Dr. Nikitin's lethal aphrodisiac oil. A little farther on was a place where close-packed clumps of mysterious lanky yellow-green algae drifted. They humped themselves up above the surface of the sea as the ship went by and emitted sad whooshing exhalations from dark waggling bladders dangling on short prickly stems: "Go back," they seemed to be saying, "go back, go back, go back." It was a disturbing and troublesome sound. This was plainly an unlucky place to be. But before long the strange algae were no longer to be seen, though it was still possible, for another half a day or so, to hear their distant melancholy murmur occasionally riding on the gusts of a following wind.

The next day another unfamiliar life-form appeared: a gigantic floating colonial creature, a whole population in itself, hundreds or perhaps thousands of different kinds of specialized organisms suspended from one huge float nearly the size of a platform or a mouth. Its fleshy transparent central body glistened up out of the water at them like a barely submerged island; and as they drew closer they could see the innumerable components of the thing quivering and whirring and churning about in their individual duties, this group of organisms paddling, this set trawling for fish, these little fluttering organs around the edges serving as stabilizers for the whole vast organism as it moved in its stately way through the sea.

When the ship came near it the creature extruded several dozen clear pipe-like structures, a couple of meters in height, that rose like thick glossy chimneys above the surface of the water.

"What are those things, do you think?" Father Quillan asked.

"Visual apparatus?" Lawler suggested. "Periscopes of some sort?"

"No, look, now there's something coming out of them—"

"Watch out!" Kinverson yelled from overhead. "It's shooting at us!"

Lawler pulled the priest down with him to the deck just as a blob of some gooey reddish substance went whistling past. The blob fell in mid-deck, two or three meters behind them. It looked like a large orange turd, shapeless and quivering. Steam began to rise from it. Half a dozen similar projectiles landed at other points along the deck, and more were arriving every moment.

"Fuck! Fuck! Fuck!" Delagard roared, stomping around wildly. "The stuff is burning the deck. Buckets and shovels! Buckets and shovels! Tack! Tack, Felk! Get us the hell out of here, damn you!"

The deck was sizzling and steaming where the blobs were eating into it. Felk, at the wheel, struggled to pull away from the bombardment, shoving and dodging and maneuvering the ship with frantic zeal. Under his hoarse commands the duty watch pulled the ropes about, swung the yards, reset the sails. Lawler, Quillan, and Lis Niklaus rushed about the deck, shoveling up the soft corrosive projectiles and tossing them overboard. Dark charred scars remained wherever one of the acid lumps had touched the pale yellow wood of the planks. The colonial creature, distant now, continued to hurl its missiles at the ship with methodical unthinking hostility, though now they dropped harmlessly into the water, stirring up puffs of vapor as they boiled downward and disappeared.

The charred marks in the deck were too deep to remove. Lawler suspected that the sticky projectiles, if they hadn't been swept up immediately, would have burned right down from deck to deck until they emerged through the hull.

The following morning Gharkid saw a gray cloud of whizzing airborne forms far off to starboard.

"Hagfish in mating frenzy."

Delagard swore and gave the order for a change of course.

"No," Kinverson said. "That won't work. There's no time to maneuver. Lower the sails."

"What?"

"Take them down or they'll act as hagfish nets when the swarm hits us. We'll be up to our asses in hagfish on deck."

Cursing mightily, Delagard ordered the sails to be struck. Soon the *Queen of Hydros* was drifting with bare poles rising into a hard white sky. And then the hagfish came.

The ugly bristle-backed winged worms, berserk with lust, were spread out by the millions, just windward of the fleet. It was a sea of hagfish: you could hardly see the water for the thrashing bodies. In surging waves they took to the air—the females in the lead, uncountable numbers of them, blotting out the sunlight. Furiously they beat their shiny sharp-angled little wings; desperately they held their snub-nosed heads aloft; onward they came, maddened platoons of them. And the males were right behind them.

It didn't matter to them that there were ships in their way. Ships were mere incidental distractions to hagfish in heat. Mountains would have been. They had their genetically programmed course to follow, and they followed it blindly, unresistingly. If it meant that they would smash head-on into the side of the *Queen of Hydros,* so be it. If it meant that they would clear the deck of the ship by a few meters and go cracking into the base of a mast or the door of the forecastle, so be it. So be it. So be it. There was no one on the ship's deck when the hagfish armada reached it. Lawler already knew what it was like to be struck by an immature one. A full-grown one in the high frenzy of its mating urge would probably be traveling with ten times the force of the one that had hit him: a collision would be fatal, most likely. A glancing blow of a wing-tip would cut through skin to the bone. The touch of those fierce bristles would leave a bloody track.

The only thing to do was hide and wait. And wait, and wait. All hands took refuge below. For hours the buzzing whoosh of their passage filled the air, punctuated by strange whining cries and the sound of brutal, abrupt impacts.

At last there was silence. Cautiously, Lawler and a couple of the others went up on deck.

The air was clear. The swarm had moved on. But dead and dying hagfish were everywhere, piled like vermin wherever some structure of the deck had created an obstacle to their flight. Broken as they were, some still had enough life left in them to hiss and nip and try to rise and fly into the faces of the cleanup crew. It took all day to get rid of them.

After the hagfish came a dark cloud that promised welcome rain, but dropped instead a coating of slime: a migrating mass of some foul-smelling little airborne microorganism that enveloped the ship in its nearly infinite multitudes and left a slick gluey brown pall on sails and rigging and masts and every square millimeter of the deck. Cleaning *that* off took three days more.

And after that came more rammerhorns, and Kinverson bestrode the deck once more, pounding on his drum to drive them into confusion.

And after the rammerhorns—

Lawler began to think of the great planetary sea as a stubborn, implacably hostile force that was tirelessly throwing one thing after another at them in an irritable response to their presence on its broad bosom. Somehow the voyagers were making the ocean itch, and it was scratching at them. Some of the scratching was pretty intense. Lawler wondered if they would manage to survive long enough to reach Grayvard.

THERE WAS A BLESSED DAY OF HEAVY RAIN, AT LAST. IT CLEANED AWAY the slime of the microorganisms and the reek that the dead hagfish had left on deck, and allowed them to refill their storage casks just when the water situation had been starting to seem critical again. In the wake of the rain a school of divers appeared and frolicked in a genial playful way alongside the ship, leaping in the foam like elegant dancers welcoming tourists to their native land. But no sooner had the divers moved on out of sight than another of the turd-throwing colonial things drifted near, or perhaps it was the same one as before, and bombarded the ship with moist incendiary missiles all over again. It was as though the ocean had belatedly become aware that by sending the rain and then the divers it was showing the voyagers too amiable a face, and wanted to remind them of its true nature.

Then for a time all was quiet again. The winds were fair, the creatures of the ocean relented from the pattern of constant assault. The six ships moved onward serenely toward their goal. Their wakes, long and straight, stretched out behind them like retreating highways through the immense solitude that they had already crossed.

In the calm of a perfect dawn—the sea almost without waves, the breeze steady, the sky shimmering, the lovely blue-green globe of Sunrise visible just above the horizon and one moon still in view also—Lawler came up on deck to find a conference taking place on the bridge. Delagard was there, and Kinverson, and Onyos Felk, and Leo Martello. After a moment Lawler saw Father Quillan too, half-hidden behind Kinverson's bulk.

Delagard had his spyglass with him. He was scanning the distance with it and reporting on something to the others, who were pointing, staring, commenting.

Lawler clambered up the ladder.

"Something going on?"

"Something sure is, yes," Delagard said. "One of our ships is missing."

"Are you serious?"

"Take a look." Delagard handed Lawler the spyglass. "An easy night. Nothing unusual between midnight and dawn, the lookouts tell me. Count the ships you can see. One, two, three, four."

Lawler put the glass to his eye.

One. Two. Three. Four.

"Which one isn't there?"

Delagard tugged at his thick, greasy coils of hair. "Not sure yet. They don't have their flags up. Gabe thinks it's the Sisters who are gone. Splitting off during the night, taking some independent course of their own."

"That would be crazy," Lawler said. "They've got no real idea how to navigate a ship."

"They've been doing all right so far," Leo Martello said.

"That's by simply following along in the convoy. But if they tried to go off on their own—"

"Well, yes," Delagard said. "It would be crazy. But they *are* crazy. Those fucking dyke bitches, I wouldn't for a moment put it past them to do something like—"

He broke off. There was the sound of footsteps on the ladder below them.

"Dag, that you?" Delagard called. To Lawler he explained, "I sent him down to the radio room to do some calling around."

Tharp's shriveled little head appeared, and then the rest of him.

"The *Golden Sun*'s the one that's missing," Tharp announced.

"Sisters are on the *Hydros Cross*," Kinverson said.

"Right," said Tharp sourly. "But *Hydros Cross* answered when I called them just now. So did the *Star,* the *Three Moons,* and the *Goddess.* All silent out of the *Golden Sun.*"

"You absolutely certain? Couldn't raise them at all?" Delagard asked. "Wasn't any way at all you could bring them in?"

"You want to try, you go and try. I called around the fleet. Four ships answered."

"Including the Sisters?" Kinverson persisted.

"I talked to Sister Halla herself, okay?"

Lawler said, "Whose ship is the *Golden Sun*? I forget."

"Damis Sawtelle's," Leo Martello replied.

"Damis would never go off on his own. He isn't like that."

"No," Delagard said, with a look of suspicion and distrust. "He isn't, is he, doc?"

THARP KEPT ON TRYING TO PICK UP THE GOLDEN SUN'S FREQUENCY ALL day long. The radio operators of the other four ships tried also.

Silence on the *Golden Sun* channel. Silence. Silence. Silence.

"A ship just doesn't vanish in the night," Delagard said, pacing ferociously.

"Well, this one seems to have," said Lis Niklaus.

"Shut your fucking mouth!"

"Oh, nice, Nid, very nice."

"Shut it or I'll shut it for you!"

"This isn't helping," Lawler said. He turned toward Delagard. "You ever lose one of your ships like this before? Just quietly disappearing, no S.O.S., nothing?"

"I never lost a ship. Period."

"They would have radioed if there was trouble, right?"

"If they could have," Kinverson said.

"What does that mean?" Delagard asked.

"Suppose a whole bunch of those net-things came crawling up on board during the night. The watch changes at three in the morning, the people in the rigging come down, the watch below goes up on deck, they all step on nets and get pulled over the side. And you've got half the ship's complement gone just like that. Damis or whoever comes down out of the wheel box while the massacre is going on to see what's what and a net gets him, too. And then the rest, one by one—"

"Gospo yelled like crazy when the net got him," Pilya Braun pointed out. "You think a whole shipload of people is going to get tangled up in those things and dragged overboard and not one person will make enough noise to warn the others of what's going on?"

"So it wasn't nets," said Kinverson. "It was something else that came on board. Or it was nets plus something else. And they all died."

"And then a mouth came along and swallowed the ship, too?" Delagard asked. "Where the fuck is the ship? Everybody on it may be gone, but what happened to the *ship*?"

"A ship under sail can drift a long way in a few hours, even in a quiet sea," Onyos Felk observed. "Ten, fifteen, twenty kilometers—who knows? And still moving. We'd never find it if we looked for a million years."

"Or maybe it sank," Neyana Golghoz said. "Something came up beneath it and drilled a hole in its bottom and it went right down just like that."

"Without even sending a signal?" Delagard asked. "Ships don't sink in two minutes. Somebody would have had time to radio to us."

"Do I know?" said Neyana. "Let's say *fifty* things came up beneath it and drilled holes. It was *full* of holes all at once. And it went down faster than you can fart. It just sank, *bam,* no time to do anything. I don't know. I'm just suggesting."

"Who was on board the *Golden Sun?*" Lawler asked.

Delagard counted up on his fingers, "Damis and Dana and their little boy. Sidero Volkin. The Sweyners. That's six."

Each name fell like an ax. Lawler thought of the gnarled old toolmaker and his gnarled old wife. How clever Sweyner had been with his hands, how adept at employing the limited materials that Hydros made available to them. Volkin, the shipwright, tough and hardworking. Damis. Dana.

"Who else?"

"Let me think. I've got the list somewhere, but let me think. The Hains? No, they're with Yanez on the *Three Moons.* But Freddo Wong was on board, and his wife—what the hell was her name—"

"Lucia," Lis said.

"Lucia, right. Freddo and Lucia Wong, and that girl Berylda, the one with the tits. And Martin Yanez's kid brother, I think. Yes. Yes."

"Josc," someone said.

Josc, yes.

Lawler felt a savage pain. That eager bright-eyed boy. The future doctor, the one who was going to take the burden of being the healer from him someday.

He heard a voice saying, "All right, that's ten. What were there, fourteen on board? So we have to account for four more."

People began to suggest names. It was hard to remember who had been on which ship, so many weeks after the departure from Sorve. But there had been fourteen on board the *Golden Sun,* everyone was agreed on that.

Fourteen deaths, Lawler thought, dazed by the enormity of the loss. He felt it in his bones. Felt personally diminished. These people had shared his life, his past. Gone. Gone without warning, forever. Nearly a fifth of the community gone in a single stroke. On Sorve Island, in a bad year, they might have had two or three deaths. In most years, none. And now fourteen all at once. The disappearance of the *Golden Sun* had ripped a ragged hole in the fabric of the community. But wasn't the community shattered already? Would they ever be able to restore on Grayvard anything resembling what they had been forced to abandon on Sorve?

Josc. The Sawtelles. The Sweyners. The Wongs. Volkin. Berylda Cray. And four others.

Lawler left them still discussing it on the bridge and went below. The numbweed flask was in his hand a moment after he entered his cabin. Eight drops, nine, ten, eleven. Let's say a dozen for this, shall we? Yes. Yes. A dozen. What the hell. A double dose: that should take the sting out of anything.

"Val?" Sundira's voice, outside the cabin door. "Are you all right?"

He let her in. Her eyes went to the glass in his hand, then back to his face.

"God, it really hurts you, doesn't it?"

"Like losing some of my fingers."

"Did they mean a lot to you?"

"Some of them did." The numbweed was hitting, now. He felt the sharp edge of the pain blurring. His voice sounded furry in his ears. "Others were just people I knew, part of the island scene, old familiar faces. One was my apprentice."

"Josc Yanez."

"You knew him?"

She smiled sadly. "A sweet boy. I was swimming, once, and he came along, and we talked for a while. Mostly about you. He worshiped you, Val. Even more than he did his brother, the sea-captain." A frown crossed her face. "I'm making it worse, not better."

"Not—really—"

His tongue was thick. He knew he had had too much numbweed.

She took the glass from his hand and put it down.

"I'm sorry," she said. "I wish I could help."

Come closer, Lawler wanted to say, but somehow he couldn't, and didn't.

She seemed to understand anyway.

•   •   •

FOR TWO DAYS THE FLEET LAY AT ANCHOR IN THE MIDDLE OF NOWHERE while Delagard had Dag Tharp run through the whole spectrum of radio frequencies, trying to bring in the *Golden Sun*. He picked up radio operators on half a dozen islands, he picked up a ship called *Empress of Sunrise* that was running ferry service in the Azure Sea, he picked up a floating mining station working somewhere in the far northeast, the existence of which came as a complete surprise, and not a welcome one, to Delagard. But from the *Golden Sun* Tharp heard not a whisper.

"All right," Delagard said finally. "If they're still afloat, maybe they'll find a way to get in touch with us. If they aren't, they won't. But we can't sit here forever."

"Will we ever find out what happened to them?" Pilya Braun asked.

"Probably not," Lawler said. "It's a big ocean full of dangerous things that we don't know a goddamned thing about."

"If we knew what it was that got them," said Dann Henders, "we'd have a better chance of guarding against it ourselves if it showed up again to try to get us."

"When whatever it was that got them shows up to get us," Lawler said, "that's when we'll find out what it was. Not before."

"Let's hope we don't find out, then," said Pilya.

7

ON A DAY OF HEAVY FOG AND ROLLING SEAS BIG UNFAMILIAR diamond-shaped creatures with thick, heavily ridged green shells covering their backs came up alongside the ship and accompanied it for a time. They looked like floating storage tanks that had equipped themselves with swimming flippers. Their armored heads were flat and squat with pointed snouts, their eyes were bleak little white slits, their underslung jaws seemed extremely unforgiving. Lawler was at the rail watching them when Onyos Felk appeared at his side and said, "Can I talk to you for a minute, doc?"

Felk was First Family, like Lawler, a distinction that meant nothing at all now that the Sorve Island community had taken to the sea. The mapkeeper was something like fifty-five years old, a dour little short-legged heavy-boned man who had never married. Supposedly he knew a great deal about the geography of Hydros and the way of the sea, and if things had gone differently over the years it could easily have been Felk and not Nid Delagard who controlled the Sorve shipyard; but the Felks had a reputation for bad luck and, sometimes, poor judgment.

"You not feeling well, Onyos?" Lawler asked.

"You won't be either, when you hear what I've got to say. Let's go down below."

From his compartment in the forecastle Felk produced a small greenish globe, a sea-chart, though nothing much like the elaborate clockwork one that belonged to Delagard. This one had to be wound up with a little wooden key and the position of its islands had to be reset by hand every time it started up: a joke, compared with Delagard's spectacular device. After a few moments spent adjusting it Felk held it out toward Lawler and said, "All right. Look closely, here. This is Sorve, over here. This is Grayvard, all the way around here to the northwest. This is the route we've been traveling."

The lettering on the chart was cramped and faded and very hard to read. The islands were so close to one another that it wasn't easy for Lawler to make clear sense of what he was seeing even where he could make out the labels. But he followed the line of Felk's pointing finger westward around the globe, and as the mapkeeper retraced the journey Lawler began to translate the symbols on the chart into an understanding of the shape of their journey.

"This is where we were when the net grabbed Struvin. Here's where we saw the Gillies building that new island. Now, this here is where we entered the Yellow Sea, and this is where we were when the rammerhorns attacked us the first time. We ran into that big tidal surge over here, and it knocked us a little way off course, like this. You following me, doc?"

"Keep going."

"This is the Green Sea here. Just beyond it is that place where the coral was growing. Here's where we passed those two islands, the Gillie one and then the one that Delagard said was Thetopal. This is where we hit the three-day windstorm that scattered the fleet. The hagfish were swarming over here. This is where we lost the *Golden Sun*." Felk's stubby finger was far around the curve of the little globe by now. "Are you beginning to notice anything a little strange?"

"Show me where Grayvard is, again?"

"Up here. Northwest of Sorve."

"Am I reading things wrong, or is there some reason having to do with the currents why we're sailing due west along the equator instead of on a northerly diagonal toward Grayvard?"

"We aren't sailing due west," Felk said.

Lawler frowned. "No?"

"The chart's very small, and it's hard to see the latitude lines unless you're used to them. But in fact we're not just going due west, we're actually veering *south*west."

"*Away* from Grayvard?"

"Away from Grayvard, yes."

"You're absolutely sure of this?"

An expression of barely suppressed fury appeared for a moment, but only for a moment, in Felk's small dark eyes. In a tightly controlled voice he said, "Let's assume for the sake of the discussion that I understand how to read a chart, all right, doc? And that when I get up in the morning and look at where the sun's coming up, I can remember where it came up the day before and the day before that and where it rose a week ago, and from that I can form at least an approximate idea of whether we're sailing northwest or southwest, okay?"

"And we've been sailing southwest all this time?"

"No. We started out on a proper northwest course. Someplace around the coral sea we leveled off back into tropical waters and began heading due west, right along the equator, getting further and further off course every day. I knew something was wrong, but I didn't realize how wrong it was until we went by those islands. Because that wasn't Thetopal at all. Not only does the real Thetopal happen to be in high temperate waters right now, up toward Grayvard way, but it's a round island. This one was curved, remember? In fact the island we passed was really Hygala. Here it is down here."

"Practically on the equator."

"Right. We should have been a long way north of Hygala if we were on a Grayvard course. But it was north of us, actually. And when Delagard recalculated our positions after the windstorm broke up the fleet, he got us going again in a sharp southerly veer. We're down below the equator now a little ways. You can tell that from the position of the Cross, if you know anything about the night sky. Maybe you haven't been looking, I guess. But for at least the last week we've been traveling precisely ninety degrees off our proper course. Would you like to see where we're heading now? Or have you already figured that out for yourself?"

"Tell me."

Felk turned the chart. "This is what we're currently sailing toward. You don't notice any islands shown here, do you?"

"We're going into the Empty Sea?"

"We're already in it. Islands have been sparse ever since we set out. We've only passed two, two and a half, on the whole trip, and since Hygala there haven't been any. There won't be any, now. The Empty Sea is empty because the currents don't bring any islands that way. If we were on course for Grayvard, we'd be all the way up here north of the equator, and we'd have passed four different islands by this time. Barinan, Sivalak, Muril, Thetopal. One, two, three, four. Whereas way down over here there's nothing at all once we're beyond Hygala."

Lawler contemplated the quadrant of the chart that Felk had turned toward him. He saw the little crescent shape that was Hygala; to the west and south of it he saw only nothingness and nothingness and more nothingness, and then, far away around the bend of the little globe, the dark splotch that was the Face of the Waters.

"You think Delagard's made a mistake in figuring our course?"

"That's the last thing I think. Delagards have been running ships around this planet since the days this was a penal colony. You know that. He isn't any more likely to set us on a southwesterly course when he wants to go northwesterly than you are to start spelling 'Lawler' wrong when you sign your name."

Lawler put his thumbs to his temples and held them there, and pressed hard.

"*Why* would Nid want to sail us into the Empty Sea, for Christ's sake?"

"I thought you might want to ask him just that very thing."

"Me?"

"Sometimes he seems almost to have a little respect for you," Felk said. "He might actually give you an honest answer. Then again he might not. But he sure as hell isn't going to tell *me* anything, is he? Is he now, doc?"

KINVERSON WAS BUSY ARRANGING HIS HOOKS AND TACKLE, GETTING ready for the day's fishing, when Lawler found him, a little while later that morning. He looked up grudgingly, regarding Lawler with the sort of absolute indifference that Lawler might have expected from an island, a hatchet, a Gillie. Then he went back to doing what he had been doing.

"So we're off course. I knew that. What's it to me, doc?"

"You knew?"

"These don't look like northern waters to me."

"You knew all along that we were heading into the Empty Sea? And you didn't say anything about it to anybody?"

"I know we're off course, but I don't necessarily know we're heading into the Empty."

"Felk says we are. He showed it to me on his chart."

"Felk isn't always right, doc."

"Let's say that this time he is."

"Well, then we're heading into the Empty," said Kinverson calmly. "So?"

"Instead of heading toward Grayvard."

"So?" Kinverson said again. He picked up a hook, pondered it, clamped it between his teeth and twisted it into a different shape.

This was getting nowhere. "Don't you give the slightest damn that we're going the wrong way?"

"No. Why the hell should I? One stinking island's just like the next one. I don't care where we wind up living."

"There aren't any islands in the Empty Sea, Gabe."

"Then we'll live on the ship. What of it? I can live okay in the Empty Sea. It isn't empty of fishes, doc, is it? It's not supposed to have much, but it's got to have some, if there's water in it. If a place has fishes, I can live there. I could have lived in my old little boat, if I had to."

"Why weren't you living in it all along, then?" Lawler asked, starting to get annoyed.

"Because I happened to be living on Sorve. But I could live in my boat just as easily. You think those islands are so fucking wonderful, doc? You walk around on hard wooden boards all the time and you live on seaweed and fish and it's too hot when the sun shines and too cold when it's raining, and that's life. At least that's *our* kind of life. It isn't much. So it's all the same to me, whether it's Sorve or Salimil or a cabin on the *Queen of Hydros* or a fucking rowboat. I just want to be able to eat when I'm hungry and get laid when I'm horny and stay alive till I die, okay?"

It was probably the longest speech Kinverson had ever made in his life. He seemed surprised himself that he had said so much. When he was done with it he stared at Lawler coldly for a moment in evident anger and irritation. Then once again he went back to his hooks and tackle.

Lawler said, "You don't mind that our great leader is leading us right into completely unknown territory and that he can't take the trouble to let us in on whatever it is he's up to?"

"No. I don't mind. I don't mind anything, except people who bother me too much. I take one day at a time. Let me alone, doc. I've got work to do, okay?"

•   •   •

DAG THARP SAID, "YOU WANT TO MAKE YOUR CALLS NOW, DOC? YOU'RE an hour early, aren't you?"

"I could be. Does it matter?"

"Whatever you like." Tharp's hands moved over his dials and knobs. "You want to call early, we'll call early. Don't blame me if nobody's ready for you out there."

"Get me Bamber Cadrell first."

"You usually call the *Star* first."

"I know that. Call Cadrell first today."

Tharp looked up, perplexed. "You got an eel up your ass this morning, doc?"

"When you hear what I have to say to Cadrell, you'll find out what I've got up my ass. Call him, will you?"

"Okay. Okay." From the bank of radio equipment came sputters and clicks. "This fucking fog," Tharp muttered. "A wonder the equipment doesn't rot. Come in, *Goddess*. Come in, *Goddess. Queen* calling. *Goddess? Goddess*, come in."

"*Queen*, this is *Goddess*." A boy's voice, high-pitched, squeaky. Nicko Thalheim's boy Bard was the radio operator aboard the *Sorve Goddess*.

"Tell him I want to talk to Cadrell," Lawler said.

Tharp spoke into the microphone. Lawler wasn't able to hear the tinny response clearly.

"What was that?"

"He says Bamber's at the helm. His watch has another two hours to run."

"Tell him to get Bamber down from the wheel and on the horn right away. This needs to be dealt with."

More sputters, more clicks. The boy seemed to be objecting. Tharp repeated Lawler's request, and there was a minute or so of silence at the other end.

Then came the voice of Bamber Cadrell: "What is it that's so god-damned urgent, doc?"

"Send the boy away and I'll tell you."

"He's my radio operator."

"Fine. But I don't want him to hear what I'm about to say."

"There's a problem, huh?"

"Is he still there?"

"I sent him outside. What's going on, doc?"

"We're ninety degrees off course, in equatorial waters, heading south-southwest. Delagard is steering us into the Empty Sea." Dag Tharp, listening at Lawler's side, caught his breath sharply in amazement. "Are you aware of that, Bamber?"

There was another long silence from the *Sorve Goddess*.

"Of course I am, doc. What the hell kind of seaman do you think I am?"

"The Empty Sea, Bamber."

"Right. I heard you."

"We're supposed to be going to Grayvard."

"I know that, doc."

"It's perfectly okay with you that we're sailing the wrong way?"

"I assume Delagard knows what he's doing."

"You *assume*?"

"These are his ships. I just work for him. When we started to veer south I figured there must be some trouble up north, a storm, maybe, something bad that he wants to get around. He's got all the good charts, doc. We're simply following the lead he sets."

"Straight into the Empty Sea?"

"Delagard isn't crazy," Cadrell said. "We'll turn north again before long. I don't have any doubt of that."

"You haven't wanted to ask him why the change of course?"

"I told you. I assume it's for a good reason. I assume he knows what he's doing."

"You assume a fucking lot," Lawler said.

THARP LOOKED UP FROM THE RADIO DESK. HIS EYES, USUALLY HOODED in wrinkled folds of flesh, were bright and big with astonishment.

"The Empty Sea?"

"Looks that way."

"But that's insane!"

"Isn't it, though. Just pretend you haven't heard a thing, for a little while, all right, Dag? Get me Martin Yanez, now."

"Not Stayvol? You always make Stayvol your first call."

"Yanez," Lawler said, and fought back the memory of Josc smiling eagerly up at him.

Some fiddling with the dials, and the *Three Moons'* radio operator's voice came squeaking through the static—she was one of the Hain girls, Lawler wasn't sure which one—and then a moment later the deep, steady voice of Martin Yanez, saying, "There's nothing to report, doc, we've got a clean bill of health over here today."

"This isn't the regular medical call," Lawler said.

"What then? You didn't hear something from the *Golden Sun,* did you?" There was sudden excitement in Yanez's voice, eagerness, hope.

"Nothing like that, no," Lawler said quietly.

"Ah."

"I wanted to find out what you think about our change of course."

"What change of course do you mean?"

"Don't give me that shit, Martin. Please."

"Since when do navigational matters concern the doctor?"

"I said don't give me that shit."

"Are you the navigator now, doc?"

"I'm an interested party. We all are. It's my life too. What's going on, Martin? Or are you so deep in Delagard's pocket that you won't tell me?"

"You sound awfully worked up," Yanez said. "We've made a detour to the south. What of it?"

"Why have we done it?"

"You ought to ask Delagard that."

"Have you?"

"I don't need to. I'm simply following his lead. He turns south, I turn south too."

"Bamber said more or less the same thing. Are you guys all such puppets that you let him jerk your strings any way he likes? Jesus, Martin, why aren't we heading for Grayvard any longer?"

"I told you. Ask Delagard."

"I mean to. First I wanted to find out how the other captains feel about sailing into the Empty Sea."

"Is that what we're doing?" Yanez asked, his voice as calm as ever. "I thought we were simply making a short-term detour to the south, for some reason that Delagard isn't talking about. So far as I know Grayvard's still our ultimate destination."

"Do you really mean that?"

"If I said I did, would you believe me?"

"I'd like to."

"It's the truth, doc. As I loved my brother, it's God's own truth.

Delagard hasn't said a word about the change, and I haven't asked, and neither have Bamber or Poilin. I assume the Sisters aren't even aware that we're off course."

"You've talked about it with Cadrell and Stayvol, though?"

"Sure."

"Stayvol's very thick with Delagard. I don't trust him much. What has he said?"

"He's as puzzled as the rest of us."

"You think he really is?"

"Yes. But what difference does it make? We're all following Delagard. You want to know what's going on, you ask him. And if he tells you, you tell me, doc."

"That's a promise."

"YOU WANT ME TO CALL STAYVOL NEXT?" DAG THARP ASKED.

"No. I think I'll skip him just now."

Tharp tugged at the wattles of his throat. "Holy shit," he said. "Holy, holy, holy shit. You think it's a conspiracy? All the captains up to something weird and not telling?"

"I believe Martin Yanez. Whatever's happening, Delagard may have let Stayvol in on it, but most likely not the other two."

"And Damis Sawtelle?"

"What about him?"

"Suppose that when he noticed this change of course he radioed Delagard and asked him what was what, and Delagard said it was none of his fucking business, and Damis got so annoyed that he just turned his ship around in the middle of the night and went shooting off toward Grayvard by himself. Damis has a pretty hot temper, you know. So there he is, a thousand kilometers north of us by now, and when we send out scanning calls trying to find him he simply ignores us, because he's seceded from the fleet."

"That's a nice theory. But does Delagard understand how to operate this radio equipment?"

"No," Tharp said. "Not that I know of."

"Then how would Damis have talked with him unless you had taken the call?"

"You've got a point there."

"Sawtelle didn't just take off and sail away by himself. I'd bet on it, Dag. The *Golden Sun*'s at the bottom of the sea, with Damis Sawtelle and everybody else that was on board it. Something that lives in this ocean came along in the night and quickly and quietly sank it, something very cute and full of tricks, and if we're lucky we're never going to find out what it was. There's no sense thinking about the *Golden Sun* right now. What we need to know is why we're heading south instead of north."

"You going to talk to Delagard, doc?"

"I think I ought to," Lawler said.

8

*D*ELAGARD HAD JUST COME OFF WATCH. HE LOOKED TIRED. HIS burly shoulders were slumped forward, his head was thrust forward wearily on his thick neck. As he started to descend the hatch that led to his quarters Lawler called to him to wait.

"What is it, doc?"

"Can we talk?"

Delagard's eyelids slid downward for a moment. "Right this minute?"

"I think so, yes."

"All right. Come on. Come on down with me."

Delagard's cabin, more than twice as spacious as Lawler's, was littered with discarded clothes, empty brandy bottles, odds and ends of ship's equipment, even a few books. Books were such rarities on Hydros that it amazed Lawler to see them scattered so casually about.

"You want a drink?" Delagard asked.

"Not just yet. Go on, help yourself." Lawler hesitated a moment. "A little problem has turned up, Nid. We seem to have accidentally gone off course."

"Have we?" Delagard didn't sound surprised.

"It appears that we're on the wrong side of the equator. We're heading south-southwest instead of north-northwest. It's a pretty considerable variation from the plan."

"That far off course?" Delagard said. It was mock wonder, very heavy-handed. "Going in the wrong direction entirely?" He toyed with his brandy cup, rubbed his right collarbone as though it ached, rearranged some of the intricate clutter on the table in front of him. "That's one hell of a navigational error, if it's true. Somebody must have sneaked up to the binnacle and turned the compass clean upside down with intent to deceive. But are you sure about all this, doc?"

"Don't fuck around with me. It's too late for that. What are you up to, Nid?"

"You don't know shit about open-sea navigation. How can you tell which direction we're going in?"

"I consulted some experts."

"Onyos Felk? That foolish old fart?"

"Yes, I talked to him. Among others. Onyos isn't always all that reliable, I agree. But the others are. Believe me."

Delagard gave Lawler a deadly look, slitted eyes, clamped jaws. Then he calmed; he drank again, and topped off his brandy cup; he disappeared into a contemplative silence.

"All right," Delagard said finally. "Here's where I let you in on it. Felk happens to be right for once. We aren't going to Grayvard."

Delagard's casual self-assurance hit Lawler hard, a sharp jolt.

"Jesus Christ, Nid. Why not?"

"Grayvard doesn't want us. It never did. They gave me the same bullshit story the other islands did, that they had room for maybe a dozen refugees tops, certainly not the whole bunch of us. I pulled all the strings I could. They stuck to their position. We were out in the cold, flat on our asses, nowhere to go."

"So you were lying right from the start of the voyage? You were planning to take us to the Empty Sea all along? What the hell were you up to? Why did you bring us here, of all places?" Lawler shook his head wonderingly. "You've really got balls, Nid."

"I didn't lie to *everybody*. I told Gospo Struvin the truth. And Father Quillan."

"Gospo I can understand, I guess. He was your top-of-the-line captain. But how come Quillan?"

"I tell him a lot of things."

"You a Catholic now? He's your confessor?"

"He's my friend. He's full of interesting ideas."

"I'm sure. And what interesting idea did Father Quillan have about the course we should take?" Lawler asked. He felt as if he were dreaming this. "Did he tell you that through the wonders of prayer and spiritual fortitude he could work a miracle for us? Did he offer to conjure up some nice unoccupied island in the Empty Sea where we could set up housekeeping, maybe?"

"He told me that we ought to head for the Face of the Waters," Delagard said coolly.

Another jolt, stronger than the last. Lawler's eyes widened. He helped himself to a deep gulp of some of Delagard's brandy, and waited a moment for it to achieve an effect. Delagard, facing him across the table, sat patiently watching, looking alert, calm, perhaps even amused.

"The Face of the Waters," Lawler said, when he felt steady enough to speak again. "That's what you said. The Face of the Waters."

"Right, doc."

"And why, can you tell me, did Father Quillan think it was such a great idea to head toward the Face?"

"Because he knew I had always wanted to go there."

Lawler nodded. He felt the serenity of complete despair coming over him. Another drink seemed like a good idea. "Sure. Father Quillan believes in the gratification of irrational impulses. And since we had no place else to go anyway, you might just as well haul the entire fucking lot of us off halfway around the world to the strangest, most remote place on Hydros, about which we know absolutely nothing at all except that even the Gillies don't have the guts to go anywhere near it?"

"That's right." Delagard shook off the sarcasm, smiling quietly.

"Father Quillan gives wonderful advice. That's why he's been such a success in the priesthood."

Eerily calm, Delagard continued, "I asked you once if you remembered the stories Jolly used to tell about the Face."

"A bunch of fairy tales, yes."

"That's more or less what you said the other time. But do you *remember* them?"

"Let's see. Jolly claimed that he made it all the way across the Empty Sea by himself and found the Face, which he said was a huge island, a lot bigger than any of the Gillie islands, a warm, lush place with strange, tall plants bearing fruit, freshwater ponds, rich waters ripe for harvesting." Lawler thought a moment, dredging into his memories. "He would have stayed there forever, it was such a sweet place to live. But one day when he was out fishing a storm blew him out to sea, and he lost his compass, and I think got caught in the Wave on top of everything else, and when he had control of his boat again, he was halfway home with no way of getting back to the Face. So he kept on going, on to Sorve, and tried to get people to go back there with him, but no one would. Everyone laughed at him. No one believed a thing he said. And eventually he went out of his mind. Right?"

"Yes," Delagard said. "That's the essential story."

"It's terrific. If I were still ten years old I'd be just thrilled out of my skull that we're going to pay a visit to the Face of the Waters."

"You ought to be, doc. It's going to be the great adventure of our lives."

"Is it, now?"

"I was fourteen years old when Jolly came back," Delagard said. "And I listened to what he had to say. I listened very carefully. Maybe he was crazy, but he didn't seem that way to me, at least not at first, and I believed him. A big, rich, fertile uninhabited island just waiting for us—and no stinking Gillies to get in our way! It sounds like paradise to me. A land of milk and honey. A place of miracles. You want to keep the community together, don't you? Then why the hell should we crowd ourselves into some unwanted little corner of somebody else's island and live like beggars on their charity? What better way can I make it up to everybody for what I did to them than by taking them around the world to live in paradise?"

Lawler stared.

"You're out of your fucking mind, Nid."

"I don't think so. The Face is up for grabs, and we can grab it. The Gillies are so superstitious about it that they won't go near it. Well, we can. And we can settle on it, we can build on it, we can farm it. We can make it give us the thing that we most want."

"And what is it, the thing that we most want?" Lawler prompted, feeling as if he had begun to drift free of the planet and was floating off into the blackness of space.

"Power," Delagard said. "Control. We want to run this place. We've lived on Hydros like pitiful pathetic refugees long enough. It's time we made the Gillies kiss our asses. I'd like to build a settlement on the Face twenty times as big as any existing Gillie island—fifty times as big—and get a real community going there, five thousand people, ten thousand, and put a spaceport on it and open up commerce with the other human-inhabited planets of this fucking galaxy, and start to live like real human beings instead of having to scrape out a miserable soggy seaweed-eating life for ourselves drifting around randomly in the ocean the way we've been doing here for a hundred-fifty years."

"You say all this so calmly, too. Such a rational tone of voice."

"You think I'm crazy?"

"Maybe I do, maybe I don't. What I do think is that you're a monstrous selfish son of a bitch. Making us all hostages to this weird fantasy of yours this way. You could have dropped a few of us off at each of five or six different islands if Grayvard wouldn't take us all."

"You yourself said that you didn't want that. Remember?"

"And is this better? Dragging us with you out here? Putting all our lives at risk while you go chasing after fairy tales?"

"Yes. It is."

"You bastard. You absolute and utter bastard. You *are* crazy, then!"

"No, I'm not," Delagard said. "I've been working this out for years, now. I've spent half my life thinking about it. I quizzed Jolly up and down, and I'm completely sure that he took the voyage he claimed to take and that the Face is what he says it is. I was planning for years to launch an expedition there. Gospo knew about it. He and I were going to go there together, maybe in another five years or so. Well, the Gillies gave me a good excuse, tossing us off Sorve the way they did, and then the other islands wouldn't take us in, and I figured, here's the moment, here's the chance. Grab it, Nid. And I did."

"So you had it in mind right from the time we left Sorve."

"Yes."

"But didn't tell your captains, even."

"Only Gospo."

"Who thought it was a perfectly swell idea."

"Correct," Delagard said. "He was with me all the way. So was Father Quillan when I told him. The father agrees with me completely."

"Of course he does. The stranger the better, for him. The farther away from civilization he can hide himself, the more he likes it. The Face is the Promised Land to him. When we get there he can set up the Church in this land of milk and honey of yours with himself as high priest, cardinal, pope, whatever he wants to call himself—while you build an empire, eh, Nid. And everybody's happy."

"Yes. You've got it exactly."

"And so it's all set up. Here we are at the edge of the Empty Sea, getting deeper in every minute."

"You don't like it, doc? You want to get off the ship? Go right ahead. We're going forward whether you like it or not."

"And your captains? You think they're going to go with you once they know what the real destination is?"

"You bet they will. They go where I say. Always have, always will. The Sisters may not follow, if they pick up any idea of what's really going on, but that's okay. What good are they anyway, those crazy bitches? They'll just make trouble for us when we get to the Face. But Stayvol will sail anywhere I want him to. And Bamber, and Martin. And poor fucking Damis would have, too. Right straight on to the Face. No question of it. We'll get there, and we'll build the biggest, richest goddamned place Hydros has ever seen, and we'll all live happily ever after. Trust me, we will. You want some more brandy, doc? Yes. Yes, I think you do. Here. Have a good stiff one. You look like you need it."

FATHER QUILLAN, STANDING AT THE RAIL STARING OUT ECSTATICALLY at an emptiness that seemed even emptier than the endless skein of sea they had already crossed, seemed to be in his high spiritual mode at the moment. His face was ruddy, his eyes were glowing.

"Yes," he said. "I told Delagard that he should make the journey to the Face."

"When was this? While we were still on Sorve?"

"Oh, no. When we were at sea. It was a little while after Gospo Struvin was killed. Delagard took Gospo's death very hard, you know. He came to me and said, Father, I'm not a religious man, but I need to talk to somebody and you're the only one available that I trust. Maybe you can help me, he said. And he told me about the Face. What it was like, why he wanted to go there. And about the plan that he and Gospo had worked out. He didn't know what to do now that Gospo was gone. He still wanted to go to the Face but he wasn't sure he could bring the voyage off. We discussed the Face of the Waters at great length. He explained its nature to me very fully, as he had heard it from that old sailor long ago. And when he had told me the story I urged him to carry through with his scheme, even without Gospo. I saw the importance of it and told him that he was the only man on this planet who could possibly achieve it. Nothing must be allowed to stand in your way, I told him. Go on: bring us to this paradise, this unspoiled island where we'll have a fresh start. And he turned the ship and started heading south."

"And why," Lawler said carefully, "do you think we're going to be able to make any sort of workable fresh start on this unspoiled island you and Delagard are taking us to? Just a handful of people settling in an unknown wilderness, where we don't know anything about anything?"

"Because," said Quillan, in a calm, flat voice hard enough to have inscribed his words on metal plates, "I believe that the Face is literally a paradise. I think it's Eden. Literally."

Lawler blinked. "You're serious? The actual Eden where Adam and Eve lived?"

"The actual Eden, yes. Eden is anywhere that has not been touched by original sin."

"So Delagard got that idea from you, about the Face being a paradise? I should have guessed. And I suppose you think God lives there too. Or is it just his vacation home?"

"I don't know. But I would like to think that He is there. He always is wherever Paradise is."

"Sure," Lawler said. "The Creator of the Universe is living right here on Hydros on a gigantic marshy island covered with a tangle of seaweed. Don't make me laugh, Father. I'm not even sure you *believe* in God. Half the time I don't think you're sure either."

"Half the time I'm not sure," the priest said.

"When you have your 'dead' times."

"Yes. The times when I find myself absolutely convinced that we evolved out of the lower animals for no purpose at all. When I think that the whole long process of rising from amoeba to man on Earth, from microorganism of any kind to sentient being of whatever sort on whichever planet, is as automatic as the movements of a planet about its sun, and just as meaningless. When I think that nothing set it in motion. That nothing keeps it going but its own innate nature."

"This is what you believe half the time."

"Not half. But sometimes. Most of the time not."

"And when it's not what you believe? What then?"

"Then I believe that there was a First Cause which set it all in motion for reasons that we may never know. And who keeps it all going, out of His great love for His creatures. For God is love, just as Jesus said, in the part of the Bible you didn't get around to reading: *He that loveth not knoweth not God, for God is love.* God is connection, God is the end of aloneness, the ultimate communion. Who will one day gather all of us, however unworthy, to His bosom, where we will live everlastingly in glory, free from pain of every sort."

"You believe this most of the time."

"Yes. Do you think you can?"

"No," Lawler said. "I wish I could. But I can't."

"So you feel that everything is without purpose?"

"Not exactly. But we'll never know what that purpose is. Or *whose* it is. Things happen, the way the *Golden Sun* happened to disappear in the night, and we don't necessarily find out why. And when we die, there'll be no bosom to welcome us, no further life in glory. There won't be anything."

"Ah," Quillan said, nodding. "My poor friend. You spend every day in the condition I reach at my moments of bleakest despair."

"Maybe so. Somehow I endure it." Lawler narrowed his eyes and looked off toward the southwest across the glaring surface of the sea, as though he expected a dark vast island to be coming into view out there at any moment. His head was throbbing. He wanted to drown the ache in numbweed tincture.

"What I pray for you is that you'll be able one day soon to yield up your pain at last," Quillan said.

"I see," Lawler said darkly.

"*Do* you see? Do you really?"

"What I see is that in your hunger for paradise you didn't think twice about selling us all out to Delagard."

"You put it very harshly," Quillan said.

"Yes. I suppose I do. I'm sorry about that. You don't think I have any reason to be annoyed, do you?"

"My child—"

"I'm not your child!"

"You are His child, at least."

Lawler sighed. Two lunatics, he thought: Delagard, Quillan. One willing to do anything for redemption's sake, the other out to conquer the world.

Quillan put his hand lightly on Lawler's hand and smiled.

"God loves you," he said gently. "God will bring you His grace, never fear."

"TELL ME WHAT YOU KNOW ABOUT THE FACE OF THE WATERS," LAWLER said to Sundira. "Everything."

They were in his cabin. She said, "It isn't a lot. I know that it's some kind of gigantic island or islandlike object, immensely bigger than any of the known and inhabited islands. It covers thousands of hectares, an enormous permanently anchored landmass."

"That much I know already. But did you learn anything about it in all those conversations you used to have with the Gillies? Pardon me: the Dwellers."

"They didn't like to talk about it. Except one, a female Dweller I used to know on Simbalimak. She was willing to answer a few of my questions."

"And?"

"She said it's the forbidden place, a place where no one may go."

"Is that all? Tell me more."

"It's pretty murky stuff."

"I imagine it is. Tell me, Sundira. Please."

"She was pretty cryptic. Deliberately so, it seemed to me. But I got the impression from her that the Face is not simply taboo, or sacred, and therefore to be avoided, but that it's literally uninhabitable—physically dangerous. 'It is the fountain of Creation,' she said. A dead Dweller is thought of as returning to the source. When a Dweller dies, she said, the phrase that they use is that it 'has gone to the Face.' I got the impression of something boiling with energy—something hot and fierce and very, very powerful. As though a nuclear reaction is going on there all the time."

"Christ," Lawler said tonelessly. Warm as it was in the humid little cabin, he felt a chill starting to move up his legs. His fingers were cold too, and twitchy. Turning, he took down the flask of numbweed tincture and poured a little dose for himself. He looked inquiringly at Sundira, but she shook her head. "Hot and fierce and powerful," he said. "A nuclear reaction."

"You understand that that wasn't her concept. It's mine, based on the vague and no doubt metaphorical phrases she was using. You know how hard it is to understand what the Dwellers say to us."

"Yes."

"But I found myself wondering, while she was talking about these things with me, whether some Dweller experiment might have taken place there long ago, maybe some kind of atomic power project that went astray, something along that line. It's only a guess, you understand. But I could see from the way she was talking, how uneasy she was, how she kept putting up walls when I asked too many questions, that she believes that there's *something* very much to be avoided on the Face. Something she doesn't even want to think about, let alone talk about."

"Shit. Shit." Lawler drank the numbweed in a single gulp and felt its steadying effect almost at once. "A nuclear wasteland. A perpetual chain reaction. That doesn't fit very well with the things that Delagard was telling me. Or Father Quillan."

"You've been talking about the Face of the Waters with them? Why? What's so interesting about the Face, suddenly?"

"It's the big topic of the moment."

"Val, will you be kind enough to tell me what's going on?"

He hesitated a moment. Then he said quietly, "We haven't been traveling in the direction of Grayvard for days. We're south of the equator and moving steadily deeper into the Empty Sea." She gave him a startled look. He went right on. "What we're heading for," he told her, "is the Face of the Waters."

"You say that as though you're actually serious."

"I am."

She pulled back from him, the sort of little reflexive jerking gesture she might have made if he had raised his hand in a menacing way.

"Is this Delagard's doing?"

"Right. He told me so himself, half an hour ago, when I braced him with some questions about the route we seemed to be following." Quickly Lawler summed it up for her: Jolly's tale of his voyage to the Face; Delagard's dream of establishing a city there and using it to gain power over the whole planet, Dwellers and all; his plan to build a spaceport, eventually, and open Hydros to interstellar commerce.

"And Father Quillan? How does he fit into this?"

"He's cheering Delagard on. He's decided, don't ask me why, that the

Face is some sort of paradise, and that God—*his* God, the one he's been trying to find all his life—makes his headquarters there when he's in the neighborhood. So he's eager to have Delagard take him there so he can finally say hello."

Sundira was staring at him with the disconcerted expression of a woman who has just discovered a small snake crawling upward along the inside of her thigh.

"Are they both crazy, do you think?"

"Anybody who talks about things like 'seizing control' and 'gaining power' seems crazy to me," Lawler said. "Likewise somebody who's concerned with a concept like 'finding God.' These are nonsensical ideas to me. Anyone who embraces nonsensical ideas is crazy, by my definition of the word. And one of them happens to be in command of this fleet."

THE SKY WAS DARKENING WHEN LAWLER RETURNED TO THE MAIN deck, and the midday watch was scampering around in the rigging, swiftly shortening sail under Onyos Felk's direction. A brisk northerly wind was blowing, already hard and strong, with the clear potential of turning into a screaming gale at any minute. A heavy storm was coming down upon them, a ragged black mass of turbulence advancing out of the south. Lawler could see it on the march far in the distance, hurling down torrents of rain, churning the bosom of the sea into wild crests of white foam. Lightning flickered across the sky, a rare sight, a terrifying forked yellow flash. It was followed almost immediately by a heavy booming roll of thunder.

"Buckets! Casks! Here comes water!" Delagard was yelling.

"Yeah, enough water to swamp us but good," Dag Tharp said under his breath, as he trotted up the deck past Lawler.

"Dag! Wait!"

The radioman turned. "What is it, doc?"

"You and I have to do some calling around the fleet when this storm is over. I've been talking to Delagard. He's taking us to the Face of the Waters, Dag."

"You've got to be joking."

"I wish I was." Lawler glanced upward at the rapidly shifting sky. It had taken on a weird metallic tone, a sinister dull grayish glow, and little hissing tongues of lightning were flickering at the edges of the great black storm-cloud that now hung just to the south of the ships. The ocean was beginning to look as fierce as it had during the three-day windstorm. "Listen, we don't have time to discuss this now. But he's got a whole raft of berserk reasons for doing what he's doing. We have to stop him."

"And how are we going to do that?" Tharp asked. A wave rose against the starboard side with whipcrack ferocity.

"We'll speak with the captains. Call a convocation of all the ships. Tell everyone what's going on, put it to a vote if necessary, depose Delagard somehow." Lawler saw the scheme clearly in his mind: a meeting of all the Sorve people, a revelation of the bizarre truth of their journey, a passionate denunciation of the ship-owner's insane ambition, a straightforward appeal to the common sense of the community. His reputation for logic and sanity staked against Delagard's grandiose vision and tempestuous headstrong nature. "We can't just let him drag us off willy-nilly into whatever lunatic place he's heading for. He has to be prevented from doing it."

"The captains are loyal to him."

"Will they stay loyal when they find out what the actual situation is?"

Another wave struck the ship, a hard back-of-the-hand blow that sent it heeling toward portside. A sudden cascade came roiling over the rail. A moment later there was a terrible lightning flash and an almost simultaneous earsplitting crack of thunder, and then the rain descended in a single drenching sheet.

"We'll talk about it," Lawler called to Tharp. "Later. When the storm blows itself out!"

The radioman went off toward the bow. Lawler clung to the rail, engulfed in water, choking as it hit him from several sides at once, the wildly leaping foaming sea and the great downward weight of the almost solid mass of rain. His mouth and nostrils were full of water, fresh water and salt water mixed. He gasped and turned his head away, feeling half-drowned, and choked and wheezed and coughed until he could breathe again. A midnight blackness had descended on the ship. The sea was invisible, except when a flash of lightning revealed vast yawning black caverns rising all around them, like secret chambers opening to swallow them up. Dark figures could still be seen moving about the deck, running frenziedly to and fro as Delagard and Felk screamed orders. The sails were down, now. The *Queen of Hydros,* rocking and heeling wildly under the full brunt of the storm, turned its bare spars to windward. Now it rose on a towering sea, now it plunged downward into a gaping hollow, striking its foaming floor with a tremendous bang. Lawler heard distant shrieks. He had an overwhelming sense of great volumes of relentless water descending from every side.

Then in the midst of the immense uproar of the storm, the terrifying percussive fury that was hammering them, the shrill cry of the wind and the rumble of the thunder and the drumming of the rain, there came a sudden sound that was more frightening than anything that had preceded it: the sound of silence, the utter absence of noise, falling as though magically like a curtain over the tumult. Everyone on the ship perceived it at the same moment, and paused and looked up, startled, bewildered, scared.

It lasted for perhaps ten seconds, that strange silence: an eternity, just then.

And after it came a sound that was even stranger—incomprehensible, even—and so overwhelmingly awesome that Lawler had to fight against the urge to drop down to his knees. It was a low roaring sound that rose swiftly in intensity from second to second, so that in a few moments it filled the air like the outcry of a throat bigger than the galaxy. Lawler was deafened by it. Someone ran by him—it was Pilya Braun, he realized afterward—and tugged furiously on his arm. She pointed windward and shouted at him. Lawler stared at her, not understanding a word; and she said it again, and this time her voice, infinitesimal against the monstrous roar that filled the heavens, reached him clearly enough.

"What are you doing on deck?" she asked. "Go below! Go below! Don't you see, it's the Wave!"

Lawler peered into the blackness and saw something long and high and glowing with a golden inner fire lying on the breast of the ocean far away: a bright line that stretched along the horizon, something higher than any wall, streaming with its own radiance. He looked at it in wonder. Two figures rushed past him, crying out warnings to him, and Lawler nodded to them: Yes, yes, I see, I understand. He was still unable to draw his eyes away from that distant onrushing thing. Why was it glowing that way? How high was it? Where had it come from? There was a kind of beauty about it: the snowy white tongues of foam along its crest, the crystalline gleam of its heart, the purity of its unbroken advancing motion. It was devouring the storm as it came, imposing a titanic order of its own on the storm's chaos. Lawler watched until there was almost no time left. Then he rushed toward the forward hatch. He paused for an instant to look back and saw the Wave looming above the ship like a god astride the sea. He dived through the opening and shut it behind him. Kinverson rose up beside him to drive home the battens. Without a word Lawler sprawled down the ladder into the heart of the ship and huddled down with his shipmates to await the moment of impact.

Part Three

The
FACE
of the
WATERS

1

The ship was on a greased track, sliding freely across the world. Beneath him Lawler could feel the long roll of the world ocean, the great swinging planetary surge of it, as the colossal wall of water on which they rode swept them resistlessly along. They were mere flotsam. They were an isolated atom tossing in the void. They were nothing at all and the immensity of the maddened sea was everything.

He had found a place amidships where he could crouch and brace himself, jammed up against one of the bulkheads with a thick wad of blankets wedging him into place. But he had no real expectation of surviving. That wall of water had been too huge, the sea too stormy, the ship too flimsy.

From sound and motion alone Lawler tried to imagine what must be happening abovedecks now.

The *Queen of Hydros* was scudding over the surface of the sea, caught up in the forward motion of the Wave and carried helplessly along by it, riding on its lower curl. Even if Delagard had managed to switch on his magnetron device in time it must have had little or no effect in shielding the ship from the impact of the oncoming surge, or from being scooped up and swept forward by it. Whatever the velocity of the Wave was, that was how fast the ship must be traveling now as the great mass of water pushed it onward. Lawler had never seen a Wave so great. Probably no one had in the brief hundred-fifty years of human settlement on Hydros. Some unique concatenation of the three moons and the sister world, most likely: some diabolical conflux of gravitational forces, it was, that had lifted this unthinkable bulge of water and sent it careening around the belly of the planet.

Somehow the ship was still afloat. Lawler had no idea why. But he was certain that it still hovered like a bobbing cork on the breast of the water, for he could feel the steady force of acceleration as the Wave drove onward. That unyielding force hammered him back against the bulkhead and pegged him to it so he was unable to move. If they had already capsized, he reasoned, the Wave would have passed on by this time, leaving them quietly sinking in its lee. But no: no. They were traveling. Within the Wave they were, spinning over and over, keel upward, keel downward, keel upward, keel downward, everything within the ship that wasn't pinned down breaking loose and rattling around. He could hear the sounds of that, things clattering as though the ship were being shaken in the grasp of a giant, which indeed it was. Over and over and over. He found himself struggling for breath, gasping as though it were he himself and not the topdeck that was constantly being submerged and allowed to rise again. Down, up, down, up. There was a pounding in his chest. Dizziness assailed him, and a kind of drunken light-headedness that stripped all possibility of panic from him. He was being whirled around too wildly to feel fear: there was no room in his mind for it.

When do we finally sink? Now? Now? Now?

Or would the Wave never release them, but carry them endlessly around the world, turning forever like a wheel under the force of its terrible power?

A time came when everything was steady again. We're free of it, he thought, we're drifting on our own. But no: no. Only an illusion. After a moment or two the whirling began again, more intense than before. Lawler felt his blood streaming from his head to his feet, his feet to his head, his head to his feet, his feet to his head. His lungs ached. His nostrils burned at every intake of breath.

There were thumps and bangs that seemed to come from within the ship, furniture flying about, and louder thumps and bangs that seemed to come from without. He heard distant voices shouting, sometimes shrieking. There was the sound of the roaring of the wind, or at least the illusion of the sound of the roaring of the wind. There was the deeper booming of the Wave itself. There was a high seething hiss, shading into a harsh snarling, that Lawler couldn't identify at all: some angry confrontation of water and sky at their meeting-place, perhaps. Or perhaps the Wave was a thing of varying densities, and its own component waters, held together helter-skelter only by the overriding momentum of the larger force, were quarreling among themselves.

Then finally came another spell of stillness, and this one seemed to last and last and last. We are sinking now, Lawler thought. We are fifty meters below the surface, and descending. We are about to drown. At any moment the pressure of the water outside will burst the little bubble that is the ship and the sea will come rushing in, and it will all be over.

He waited for that inward gush to come. A quick death, it would be. The water's fist against his chest would choke the flow of blood to his brain: he'd be unconscious in an instant. He would never know the rest of the story, the slow drifting descent, the crushed timbers cracking open, the curious creatures of the deeps wandering in to stare and ponder and eventually to feed.

But nothing happened. All was peaceful. They were drifting in a time outside of time, silent, calm. It occurred to Lawler now that they must already be dead, that this was the next life in which he had never been able to believe, and he laughed and looked around, hoping to find Father Quillan nearby so that he could ask the priest, "Is this what you thought it would be like? An endless suspended drifting? Lying here in the very place where you died, still conscious, with an enormous silence all around you?"

He smiled at his own foolishness. The next life wouldn't merely be a continuation of this one. This was still the old one. There were his familiar feet; these were his hands, with fading scars on their palms; that was the sound of his own breathing. He was still alive. The ship must still be afloat. The Wave had passed on at last.

"Val?" a voice said. "Val, are you all right?"

"Sundira?"

She came crawling toward him down the narrow passageway, cluttered now by all manner of things that had shaken loose. Her face was very pale. She looked dazed. Her eyes had a frozen glint to them. Lawler stirred, freed himself from a plank that had fallen from somewhere and landed on his chest without his being aware of it, and began to scramble out of his snug hiding-place. They met midway.

"Jesus," she said softly. "Oh, Jesus God!"

She began to cry. Lawler reached for her and realized he was crying, too. They held each other and wept together in the weird dreamlike stillness.

ONE OF THE HATCHES WAS OPEN AND A SHAFT OF LIGHT WAS COMING through it. Hand in hand they emerged into the open air.

The ship was upright, seated normally in the water as though nothing at all had happened. The deck was wet and shining as Lawler had never seen it shine before. It looked as if an army of a million deckhands had been swabbing it down for a million years. The wheel-box was still there, the binnacle, the quarterdeck, the bridge. The masts, amazingly, were still in place, though the foremast had lost one of its yards.

Kinverson was already on deck down by the gantry area, and Lawler saw Delagard up by the bow, splayfooted and motionless, stupefied by shock. He seemed rooted to the deck: it was as if he had been standing in that one place all the time that the ship had been swept along in the grip of the Wave. Beyond him to starboard was Onyos Felk, standing in that same stunned immobile way.

One by one the others were leaving their hiding places: Neyana Golghoz, Dann Henders, Leo Martello, Pilya Braun. Then Gharkid, limping a little from some misadventure belowdecks, and Lis Niklaus, and Father Quillan. They moved about cautiously, shuffling like sleepwalkers, assuring themselves in a tentative way that the ship was still intact, touching the rails, the seatings of the masts, the roof of the forecastle. The only one missing was Dag Tharp. Lawler assumed that he had stayed below to try to make radio contact with the other ships.

The other ships? They were nowhere in sight.

"Look how calm it is," Sundira said softly.

"Calm, yes. And empty."

It looked the way the world must have looked on the first day of Creation. To all sides stretched a totally featureless sea, gray-blue and tranquil, not a swell in it, not a wave, not a whitecap, not the merest ripple: a placid horizontal nothingness. The passage of the Wave had purged it of all energy.

The sky too was smooth and gray and nearly empty. A single low cloud lay across it in the distant west, with the sun setting behind it. Pale light streamed up from beyond the horizon. Of the storm that had preceded the Wave there was no trace. It had vanished as completely as the Wave itself.

And the other ships? The other ships?

Lawler walked slowly from one side of the vessel to the other and back again. His eyes searched the water for signs and portents: floating timbers, drifting fragments of sail, scattered clothing, even struggling swimmers. He saw nothing. Once before in this voyage, after that other great storm, the three-day gale, he had looked out onto a sea in which no other ship could be seen. That time the fleet had merely been strewn around by the winds, and within hours it had reassembled. Lawler was afraid that it was going to be different this time.

"There's Dag," Sundira murmured. "My God, look at his face!"

Tharp was coming up the rear hatch now, pale, blank-eyed, slack-jawed, his shoulders stooped and his arms dangling limply. Delagard, breaking from his stasis, whirled and snapped, "Well? What's the news?"

"Nothing. No news." Tharp's voice was a hollow whisper. "Not a sound. I tried and tried. Come in, *Goddess,* come in, *Star,* come in, *Moons,* come in, *Cross.* This is *Queen.* Come in, come in, come in." He sounded half out of his mind. "Not a sound. Nothing."

Delagard's jowly face went leaden. His flesh sagged.

"None of them?"

"Nothing, Nid. They won't come in. They aren't there."

"Your radio's broken."

"I picked up islands. I got Kentrup. I got Kaggeram. It was a bad Wave, Nid. Really bad."

"But my ships—"

"Nothing."

"My ships, Dag!"

Delagard's eyes were wild. He charged forward as though he meant to seize Tharp by the shoulders and shake better news out of him. Kinverson stepped between them out of nowhere and held Delagard back, steadying him while he shivered and trembled.

"Go back down," Delagard ordered the radioman. "Try again."

"It's no use," Tharp said.

"My ships! My ships!" Delagard spun about and ran to the rail. For one startling moment Lawler thought he was going to hurl himself overboard. But he simply wanted to hit something. He made clubs out of his fists and battered them against the rail, again and again, striking with such astonishing force that half a meter of the rail dented, bent, collapsed under the impact. "My ships!" Delagard wailed.

Lawler felt himself beginning to tremble now. The ships, yes. And all those who had been aboard them. He turned to Sundira and saw sympathy in her eyes. She knew what sort of pain he was feeling. But how could she possibly understand, really? They had all been strangers to her. To him, though, they represented his whole past: the substance of his life, for better or for worse. Nicko Thalheim, Nicko's old father Sandor, Bamber Cadrell, the Sweyners, the Tanaminds, Brondo, the poor crazy Sisters, Volkin, Yanez, Stayvol, everyone, everyone he had ever known, everything, his childhood, his boyhood, his manhood, the custodians of a lifetime's shared memories, all swept away at once. How could she comprehend that? Had she ever been part of a long-established community? Ever? She had left the island of her birth without giving it a second thought and wandered from place to place, never looking back. You couldn't know what it was like to lose what you had never had.

"Val—" she said softly.

"Let me be, all right?"

"If I could only help somehow—"

"But you can't," Lawler said.

Now darkness was coming on. The cross was starting to enter the sky, hanging at a curious angle, strangely askew, slanting from southwest to northeast. There was no wind. The *Queen of Hydros* wallowed languidly in the calm sea. Everyone was still on deck. No one had bothered to rig the sails again, though it was hours since the Wave had passed by. But that scarcely mattered in this stillness, these doldrums.

Delagard turned to Onyos Felk. In a lifeless voice he asked, "Where do you think we are?"

"By dead reckoning, or you want me to get my instruments out?"

"Just take a fucking guess, Onyos."

"The Empty Sea."

"I can figure that out for myself. Give me a longitude."

"You think I'm a magician, Nid?"

"I think you're a dumb prick. But you can give me a longitude, at least. Look at the fucking Cross."

"I see the fucking Cross," Felk said acidly. "It tells me that we're south of the equator and a lot further west than we were when the Wave got us. You want better than that, let me go below and try to find my instruments."

"A lot further west?" Delagard asked.

"A lot. A whole lot. We really had ourselves a ride."

"Go get your instruments, then."

Lawler watched, comprehending very little, as Felk, after a lengthy rummage in the chaos belowdecks, emerged with the tools of his trade, the crude, awkwardly fashioned navigational instruments that probably would have made a mariner of sixteenth-century Earth chuckle condescendingly. He worked quietly, muttering to himself now and then as he took a fix on the Cross, pondered, fixed again. After a time Felk glanced at Delagard and said, "We're farther west than I want to believe."

"What's our position?"

Felk told him. Delagard looked surprised. He went below himself, was gone a long while, returned eventually with his sea-chart. Lawler moved closer as Delagard ran his finger down the lines of longitude. "Ah. Here. Here."

Sundira said, "Can you see where he's pointing?"

"We're in the heart of the Empty Sea. We're almost as close to the Face of the Waters as we are to any of the settled islands behind us. It's the middle of nowhere, all right, and we're all alone in it."

2

ONE NOW WAS ANY HOPE OF CALLING A CONVOCATION OF THE ships, of focusing the will of the entire Sorve community against Delagard. The entire Sorve community had been reduced to just thirteen people. By this time everyone aboard the one surviving ship knew what the real destination of the voyage was. Some, like Kinverson, like Gharkid, seemed not to care: one destination was as good as any other, for men like that. Some—Neyana, Pilya, Lis—were unlikely to oppose Delagard in anything he wanted to do, no matter how strange. And at least one, Father Quillan, was Delagard's avowed ally in the quest for the Face.

That left Dag Tharp and Dann Henders, Leo Martello, Sundira, Onyos Felk. Felk loathed Delagard. Good. One for my side, Lawler told himself. As for Tharp and Henders, they had already had one brush with Delagard over the direction of the voyage; they wouldn't shrink from another. Martello, though, was a Delagard man, and Lawler wasn't sure where his sympathies would lie in a showdown with the ship-owner. Even Sundira was an unknown quantity. Lawler had no right to assume that she'd side with him, no matter what sort of closeness seemed to be developing between them. She might well be curious about the Face, eager to learn its true nature. By avocation she was a student of Gillie life, after all.

So it was four against all the rest, or at best six. Not even half the ship's complement. Not good enough, Lawler thought.

He began to think that the idea of bringing Delagard under control was

THE FACE OF THE WATERS   245

futile. Delagard was too powerful a force to bring under control. He was like the Wave: you might not like where it was taking you, but there wasn't much you could do about it. Not really.

In the aftermath of the catastrophe Delagard bustled with inexhaustible energy about the deck getting the ship ready for the resumption of the voyage. The masts were repaired, the sails were raised. If Delagard had been a driven, determined man before, he seemed completely demoniacal now, a relentless force of nature. The analogy with the Wave seemed like the right one, Lawler thought. The loss of his precious ships appeared to have thrust Delagard across some threshold of will into a new realm of purposefulness. Furious, volatile, supercharged with energy, Delagard functioned now at the center of a vortex of kinetic power that made him all but impossible to approach. *Do this! Do that! Fix this! Move that!* He left no space about himself for someone like Lawler to come up to him and say, "We aren't going to let you take this ship where you want to take it, Nid."

There were fresh bruises and cuts on Lis Niklaus's face the morning after the Wave. "I didn't say a thing to him," she told Lawler, as he worked to repair the damage. "He just went wild and started hitting me as soon as we got inside the cabin."

"Has that happened before?"

"Not like this, no. He's a crazy man, now. Maybe he thought I was going to say something he wouldn't like. The Face, the Face, the Face, that's all he can think about. He talks about it in his sleep. Negotiates deals, threatens competitors, promises wonders—I don't know." Big, solid woman that she was, she looked suddenly shrunken and frail, as though Delagard were drawing life out of her and into himself. "The longer I live with him, the more he scares me. You think he's just a rich shipyard owner, interested in nothing but drinking and eating and screwing and getting even richer, God knows what for. And then once in a while he lets you look a little way inside him and you see devils."

"Devils?"

"Devils, visions, fantasies. I don't know. He thinks this big island will make him like an emperor here, or maybe like a god, that everyone will obey him, not just people like us, but the other islanders, the Gillies too, even. And on other worlds. Do you know he wants to build a spaceport?"

"Yes," Lawler said. "He told me that."

"He'll do it, too. He gets what he wants, that man. He never rests, he never lets up. He thinks in his sleep. I mean it." Lis gingerly touched a purpling place between her cheekbone and her left eye. "Are you going to try to stop him, do you think?"

"I'm not sure."

"Be careful. He'll kill you if you try to get in his way. Even you, doc. He'll kill you the way he'd kill a fish."

THE EMPTY SEA SEEMED WELL NAMED, CLEAR AND FEATURELESS, NO islands, no coral reefs, no storms, hardly even a cloud overhead. The hot sun cast long orange gleams on the listless, glassy blue-gray swells. The horizon seemed a billion kilometers away. The wind was slack and fitful. Tidal surges came rarely now, and they were minor ones when they came, hardly more than a ripple on the sea's flat bosom. The ship coasted easily over them.

Nor was there much in the way of marine life either. Kinverson trawled his lines in vain; Gharkid's nets brought up scarcely any seaweed that might be of use. Occasionally some glittering school of fish went by, or larger sea-creatures could be seen sporting at a distance, but it was rare that anything came close enough to be caught. The existing supplies on board, the stocks of dried fish and algae, were running very low. Delagard ordered that the daily rations be cut. It looked to be a hungry voyage from here on in. And a thirsty one too. There had been no time to put out the usual catch-receptacles during the fantastic downpour that had struck just before the coming of the Wave. Now, under that serene cloudless sky, the level in the water-casks grew lower every day.

Lawler asked Onyos Felk to show him where they were on the chart. The mapkeeper was vague, as usual, about his geography; but he indicated a point on the chart far out into the Empty Sea, close to midway between the equator and the supposed location of the Face of the Waters.

"Can that be right?" Lawler asked. "Can we really have come so far?"

"The Wave was moving at an incredible speed. It carried us with it all day long. The miracle is that the ship didn't simply break up."

Lawler studied the chart. "We've gone too far to turn back, haven't we?"

"Who's talking about turning back? You? Me? Certainly Delagard isn't."

"If we wanted to," Lawler said. "Just if."

"We'd be better off just keeping on going," said Felk gloomily. "We've got no choice, really. There's all that emptiness behind us. If we turn back toward known waters, we'll probably starve before we get anyplace useful. About the only chance we've got now is to try to find the Face. There might be food and fresh water available there."

"You think so?"

"What do I know?" Felk said.

Leo martello said, "do you have a minute, doc? i want to show you something."

Lawler was in his cabin, sorting through his papers. He had three boxes here of medical records for sixty-four former citizens of Sorve Island who presumably had been lost at sea. Lawler had fought bitterly with Delagard for the right to bring them along when the fleet left Sorve, and for once he had managed to win. What now? Keep them? For what? On the chance that the five vanished ships would reappear with all hands on board? Save them to be used by some future historian of the island?

Martello was as close to being the island's historian as anyone was. Maybe he'd like these useless documents to work into the later cantos of his epic.

"What is it, Leo?"

"I've been writing about the Wave," Martello said. "What happened to us, and where we are now, and where we may be going, and all of that. I thought you might want to read what I've done so far."

He grinned eagerly. There was a bright glow of excitement in his glossy brown eyes. Lawler realized that Martello must be tremendously proud of himself, that he was looking for applause. He envied Martello his exuberance, his outgoing nature, his boundless enthusiasms. Here in the midst of this desperate doomed journey Martello was capable of finding poetry. Amazing.

"Aren't you getting a little ahead of yourself?" Lawler asked. "The last I heard, you had just gotten up to the emigration from Earth to the first colonized worlds."

"Right. But I figure I'll eventually reach the part of the poem that tells of our life on Hydros, and this voyage will be a big part of it. So I thought, why not write it down now while it's still fresh in my mind, instead of waiting until I'm an old man forty or fifty years from now to do it?"

Why not indeed, Lawler thought.

Martello had been letting his shaven scalp grow in, over the past few weeks: dense, rank brown hair now had sprouted. It made him look ten years younger. Martello would probably live fifty more years if anyone on this ship did. Seventy, even. Plenty of time to write poetry. But yes, it was better to get the poetic impressions down on the page right now.

Lawler extended a hand. "Okay, let's have a look at it," he said.

Lawler read a few lines of it and pretended to scan the rest. It was a long scrawled outpouring, the same awkward mawkish stuff as the other piece of the great epic that Martello had allowed him to see, though at least this segment had the vigor of personal recollection.

> *Down from the sky came a deluge of darkness*
> *Drenching us deep, soaking our bones.*
> *Then as we struggled and fought to keep upright*
> *Came a new enemy greater than the last.*
> *The Wave it was! Striking deep fear in us.*
> *Choking our throats and chilling our hearts.*
> *The Wave! Dread foe, mightiest of adversaries*
> *Rising like a death-wall on the breast of the sea.*
> *Then did we tremble, then did we falter,*
> *Then did we sink to our knees in despair—*

Lawler glanced up.

"It's very powerful stuff, Leo."

"I think it's a whole new level for me. All the historical stuff, I've had to feel my way into it from the outside, but this—it was right *here*—" He held up his hands, fingers outstretched. "I simply had to write it down, as fast as I could get the words on paper."

"You were inspired."

"That's the word, yes." Shyly Martello reached for the sheaf of manuscript. "I could leave it with you, if you'd like to go over it more carefully, doc."

"No, no, I'd just as soon wait until you've finished the whole canto. You haven't done the part about our coming out on deck afterwards and finding ourselves far out in the Empty Sea."

"I thought I'd wait," Martello said. "Until we get to the Face of the Waters. This part of the voyage isn't very interesting, is it? Nothing's happening at all. But when we get to the Face—"

He paused meaningfully.

"Yes?" Lawler said. "What do you think's going to happen there?"

"Miracles, doc. Wonders and marvels and fabulous things." Martello's eyes were shining. "I can't wait. I'll do a canto about it that Homer himself would have been glad to write. Homer himself!"

"I'm sure you will," said Lawler.

OUT OF THE EMPTINESS CAME HAGFISH YET AGAIN, SUDDENLY, RISING BY the hundreds without warning. There was no reason to expect them: if anything, the sea seemed emptier here than it had been since the voyagers had entered it.

But at torrid noon it opened and besieged the ship with hagfish. They launched themselves all at once from the water, leaping across the mid-section of the vessel in thick clouds. Lawler was on deck. He heard the first whirring sounds and ducked automatically into the shadow of the foremast. The hagfish, half a meter long and thick as his arm, came through the air like swift deadly projectiles. Their angular leathery wings were outspread, the rows of needle-sharp bristles on their backs were erect.

Some cleared the deck in a single swooping arc and landed splashing in the sea beyond. Others cracked into the masts, or the forecastle roof, or piled up in the bellying sails, or simply exhausted their trajectories amid-ships and landed in angry lashing convulsions on the deck. Lawler saw two go right past him side by side, dull eyes sparkling malevolently. Then came three flying even closer together, as if yoked; then more than he could count. There was no way to reach the safety of the hatch. He could only hide and huddle and wait.

He heard a scream from farther down the deck, and from another direction came an irritated grunt. Looking up, he caught sight of Pilya Braun in the rigging, struggling to hold herself up while beating off a swarm of them. One of her cheeks was torn and bloody.

A plump hagfish grazed Lawler's arm but did no damage: the bristly side was facing away from him. Another crossed the deck just as Delagard was emerging from the hatch. It struck him across the chest, ripping a jagged, rapidly reddening line through his shirt, and fell writhing at his feet. Savagely he brought his heel down on it.

For three or four minutes the onslaught was like a rain of javelins. Then they were gone. The air was quiet again; the sea was still and smooth, a sheet of ground glass stretching toward infinity.

"Bastards," Delagard said thickly. "I'll wipe them out! I'll exterminate every fucking one!"

When? When the Face of the Waters had made him supreme ruler of the planet?

"Let me see that cut, Nid," Lawler said to him.

Delagard shook him off. "It's just a scratch. I don't even feel it any more."

"Whatever you like."

Neyana Golghoz and Natim Gharkid appeared from belowdecks and began sweeping the dead and dying hagfish into a heap. Martello, who had taken a bad slice in the arm and had a row of hagfish bristles embedded in his back, came over to show the damage to Lawler. Lawler told him to go below and wait in the infirmary for him. Pilya descended from the rigging and showed Lawler her wounds also: a bloody slash across her cheek, another just beneath her breasts. "You'll need a few stitches, I think," he told her. "How badly are you hurting?"

"It stings a little. It burns. It burns a lot, in fact. But I'll be all right."

She smiled. Lawler could still see the affection for him, the desire, whatever it was, shimmering in her eyes. She knew he was sleeping with Sundira Thane, but that hadn't seemed to change anything for her. Maybe she actually welcomed getting chopped up by these hagfish like that: it would get her his attention, his touch would be on her skin. Lawler felt sorry for her. Her patient devotion saddened him.

Delagard, still bleeding, came by again as Neyana and Gharkid made ready to dump their pile of hagfish overboard. "Hold on, here," he said brusquely. "We haven't had fresh fish for days."

Gharkid gave him a look of sheer wonder. "You would eat hagfish, captain-sir?"

"We can try it, can't we?" Delagard said.

Baked hagfish turned out to taste like rags that had been steeped in urine for a couple of weeks. Lawler managed three mouthfuls before he gave up, gagging. Kinverson and Gharkid refused to have any; Dag Tharp, Henders, and Pilya did without their portions also. Leo Martello gamely ate half a fish. Father Quillan picked at his with obvious distaste but dogged determination, as though he had taken some vow to the Virgin to eat whatever was set before him, no matter how loathsome.

Delagard finished his entire serving, and called for another.

"You *like* it?" Lawler asked.

"Man's got to eat, don't he? Man's got to keep his strength up, doc. Don't you agree? Protein is protein. Eh, doc? What do you say, doc? Here, have some more yourself."

"Thanks," said Lawler. "I think I'll try to get along without it."

HE NOTICED A CHANGE IN SUNDIRA. THE SHIFT IN THE DIRECTION AND purpose of the voyage appeared to have released her from whatever self-imposed restraints on intimacy she had bound herself with, and no longer were their periods of lovemaking marked by long spells of brittle silence broken only by bursts of shallow chatter. Now, as they lay together in the dark and mildewed corner of the cargo hold that was their special place, she revealed herself to him in long unexpected bursts of autobiographical monologue.

"I was always a curious little girl. Too curious for my own good, I suppose. Wading in the bay, picking up things in the shallows, getting nipped and bitten. When I was about four I put a little crab in my vagina." Lawler winced; she laughed. "I don't know whether I was trying to find out what would happen to the crab or to my vagina. The crab apparently didn't mind it much. But my parents did."

Her father had been mayor of Khamsilaine Island. *Mayor*, apparently, was a term that signified the head of a government among the islanders in the Azure Sea. The human settlement on Khamsilaine was a big one, close to five hundred people. To Lawler's way of thinking that was an enormous multitude, an unimaginably complex aggregation. Sundira was vague about her mother: a scholar of some sort, perhaps a historian, a student of the human galactic migration, but she had died very young and Sundira barely remembered her. Evidently Sundira had inherited some of her mother's searching intellect. The Gillies in particular fascinated her—the *Dwellers;* she was forever careful to call them by the more formal term, which to Lawler was awkward and ponderous. When she was fourteen Sundira and an older boy had begun spying on the secret ceremonies of the Dwellers of Khamsilaine Island. She and the boy had engaged in some sexual experimentation, too, her first: she mentioned that in a matter-of-fact way to Lawler, who was surprised to find himself bitterly envying him. To have had a dazzling girl like Sundira for a lover, when you were so young? What a privilege that would have been! There had been a sufficiency of girls in Lawler's own adolescence, and then some, whenever he had managed to escape from the endless hours of medical studies that kept him penned so much of the time in his father's vaargh. But it hadn't been their questing minds that had attracted him to those girls. He wondered for a moment what his life would have been like if there had been a Sundira on Sorve Island when he had been growing up. What if he had married her instead of Mireyl? It was an astounding supposition: decades of close partnership with this extraordinary woman instead of the solitary, marginal life that he had actually chosen to lead. A family. A deep continuity.

He pushed the distracting thoughts aside. Useless fantasies, these were: he and Sundira had grown up thousands of kilometers and many years apart. And even if things had been different in this way, whatever continuity they would have built on Sorve would have been shattered by the expulsion in any case. All paths led to this point of floating exile, bobbing in a tiny ship in the midst of the Empty Sea.

Sundira's questing mind had eventually taken her into deep scandal. She was in her early twenties; her father was still mayor; she lived by herself at the edge of the human community on Khamsilaine and spent as much of her time among the Dwellers as they would allow. "It was an intellectual challenge. I wanted to learn all I could about the world. Understanding the world meant understanding the Dwellers. There was something going on here, I was sure: something that none of us were seeing."

She became fluent in the Dweller language—not a common skill, it appeared, on Khamsilaine. Her father appointed her the island's ambassador to the Dwellers: all contact with them was carried on through her. She spent as much time in the Dweller village at the island's south end as she did in her own community. Most of them merely tolerated her presence, as Dwellers customarily did; some were bluntly hostile, as Dwellers often were; but there were a few that seemed almost friendly. Sundira felt she was coming to know some of those as actual individuals, not merely as the hulking ominous undifferentiated alien creatures that Dwellers seemed to most human beings to be.

"That was my mistake, and theirs: getting too close to them. I presumed on that closeness. I remembered certain things that I had seen when I was a girl, when Tomas and I were sneaking around where we shouldn't have gone. I asked questions. I got evasive answers. Tantalizing answers. I decided I needed to go sneaking again."

Whatever it was that Sundira had seen in the secret chambers of the

Gillies, she didn't seem able to communicate its nature to Lawler: perhaps
she was being secretive with him, perhaps she simply hadn't seen enough to
comprehend anything. She hinted at ceremonies, communions, rituals,
mysteries; but the vagueness in her descriptions seemed to be centered in
her own perceptions, not in her willingness to share what she knew with
him. "I went back to the same places I had crept into with Tomas years
before. This time I was caught. I thought they were going to kill me.
Instead they took me to my father and told *him* to kill me. He promised that
he'd drown me, and they seemed to accept that. We went out in a fishing
boat and I jumped over the side. But he had arranged for a boat from
Simbalimak to pick me up, around at the back of the island. I had to swim
for three hours to get to it. I never went back to Khamsilaine. And I never
saw my father or spoke with him again."

Lawler touched her cheek gently.

"So you know something about exile too."

"Something, yes."

"You never said a word to me."

She shrugged. "What did it matter? You were hurting so much. Would
it have made you feel any better if I told you that I had had to leave my
native island too?"

"It might have."

"I wonder," she said.

A DAY OR TWO LATER AND THEY WERE IN THE HOLD AGAIN; AND AGAIN
afterward she spoke of the life she had left behind. A year on Simbalimak—
a serious love affair there, which she had alluded to once before, and further
attempts to probe the secrets of the Gillies that ended nearly as disastrously
as her illicit prowlings on Khamsilaine—and then she had moved along,
out of the Azure Sea entirely, off to Shaktan. Whether it was Gillie pressure
or the collapse of the affair that caused her to leave was a point about which
Lawler wasn't quite certain, and he didn't care to ask.

Shaktan to Velmise, Velmise to Kentrup, at last Kentrup to Sorve: a
restless life and not a particularly happy one, so it would seem. There was
always some new question beyond the last answer. More attempts to penetrate Gillie secrets; more trouble as a result. Other love affairs, coming to
nothing. An isolated, fragmentary, roving existence. Why had she come to

Sorve? "Why not? I wanted to leave Kentrup. Sorve was a place to go to. It was close, it had room for me. I would have stayed awhile and moved along."

"Is that how you expected things to be for the rest of your life? Stay somewhere a little while, and then go somewhere else, and then leave that place too?"

"I suppose so," she said.

"What were you looking for?"

"The truth."

Lawler waited, offering no comment.

She said, "I still think something's going on here that we only barely suspect. The Dwellers have a unitary society. It doesn't vary from island to island. There's a link: between one Dweller community and another, between the Dwellers and the divers, the Dwellers and the platforms, the Dwellers and the mouths. Between the Dwellers and the hagfish, for all I know. I want to know what that link is."

"Why do you care so much?"

"Hydros is where I'm going to have to spend all the rest of my life. Doesn't it make sense for me to learn as much about it as I can?"

"So you aren't troubled, then, that Delagard has hijacked us and is dragging us off like this?"

"No. The more I see of this planet, the more I can understand of it."

"You aren't afraid to sail to the Face? To go into uncharted waters?"

"No," she said. Then, after a moment: "Yes, maybe a little. Of course I'm afraid. But only a little."

"If some of us tried to stop Delagard from carrying out his plan, would you be willing to join us?"

"No," she said, without hesitation.

3

>———————————<

S OME DAYS THERE WAS NO WIND AT ALL, AND THE SHIP LAY LIKE A
dead thing in the water, altogether becalmed under a swollen sun
that grew larger all the time. The air here in these deep tropics was
dry and hot and often it was a struggle simply to breathe. Delagard
performed wonders at the helm, ordering the sails to be swung around this
way and that, that way and this, in order to catch the faintest puff of breeze,
and somehow they moved along, most of the time, making their steady
headway to the southwest, ever deeper into this barren wilderness of water.
But there were the other days too, the terrible ones, when it seemed that
there would be no gust of air again to fill the sails, not ever, and they would
sit here forever until they turned to skeletons. "As idle as a painted ship,"
Lawler said, "upon a painted sea."

"What's that?" Father Quillan asked.

"A poem. From Earth, an old one. One of my favorites."

"You've quoted from it before, haven't you? I remember the meter of it.
Something about water, water everywhere."

"Nor any drop to drink," said Lawler.

THE WATER WAS ALL BUT GONE NOW. THERE WAS NOTHING BUT STICKY
shadows left at the bottom of most of the casks. Lis measured out the supply
in dribbles.

Lawler was entitled to an extra ration, if he needed it for medicinal purposes. He wondered how to deal with the problem of administering his daily doses of the numbweed tincture. The stuff had to be taken in highly diluted form or it was dangerous; and he could hardly allow himself the luxury of that much water for a purely private indulgence. What then? Mix it with seawater? He could get away with that for a little while, at least; there'd be a cumulative effect on his kidneys if he kept it up very long, but he could always hope that some rain would come in a few days and he'd have a chance to flush himself clean.

There was always the possibility also of simply not taking the drug at all.

He tried that just as an experiment one morning. By midday his scalp felt strangely itchy. By late afternoon his skin was crawling as though infested with scale. He was trembling and sweaty with need by twilight.

Seven drops of numbweed and his agitation faded into the familiar welcome numbness.

But his supply of the drug was starting to run low. That seemed a worse problem to Lawler than the water shortage. There was always the hope that it would rain tomorrow, after all. But the numbweed plant didn't seem to grow in these seas.

Lawler had counted on finding more when the ship reached Grayvard. The ship wasn't ever going to get to Grayvard, though. He had just enough numbweed left to last him another few weeks, he estimated. Perhaps less. Before long it would all be gone.

What then? What then?

In the meantime, try mixing it with a little seawater.

SUNDIRA TOLD HIM MORE ABOUT HER CHILDHOOD ON KHAMSILAINE, HER turbulent adolescence, her later wanderings from island to island, her ambitions, her hopes, her strivings and failures. They sat together for hours in the musty darkness, stretching their long legs out before them amidst the crates, intertwining their hands like young lovers while the ship drifted placidly on the placid tropical sea. She asked Lawler about his life too, and he related the small tales of his simple boyhood and his quiet, steady, carefully self-circumscribed life as an adult on the one island he had ever known.

Then one afternoon he went belowdecks to rummage in his storage cases for fresh supplies and heard moans and gasps of passion coming from a dark corner of the hold. It was their special corner of the hold; it was a woman's voice. Neyana was in the rigging, Lis was in the galley, Pilya was off duty and lounging on deck. The only other woman on board was Sundira. Where was Kinverson? He was first watch, like Pilya: he'd be off duty too. That must be Kinverson behind those crates, Lawler realized, urging those gasps and moans out of Sundira's eager body.

So whatever it was that those two had had between them—and Lawler knew what it was—hadn't ended, not at all, not even in these new days of shared autobiographical confidences and sweetly intertwined hands.

Eight drops of numbweed helped him get through it, more or less.

He measured out what was left of his supply. Not much. Not very much at all.

FOOD WAS BECOMING A PROBLEM TOO. IT WAS SO LONG SINCE THEY'D had any fresh catch that another attack by a hagfish swarm was almost beginning to seem like an appealing prospect. They lived on their dwindling supply of dried fish and powdered algae, as though they were in the depths of an arctic winter. Sometimes they were able to pull in a load of plankton by trawling a strip of fabric behind the ship, but eating plankton was like eating gritty sand, and the taste was bitter and difficult. Deficiency diseases began to make themselves felt. Wherever he looked Lawler saw cracked lips, dulled hair, blotchy skins, gaunt and haggard faces.

"This is crazy," Dag Tharp muttered. "We've got to turn back before we all die."

"How?" Onyos Felk asked. "Where's the wind? When it blows at all here, it blows from the east."

"Doesn't matter," Tharp said. "We'll find a way. Throw that bastard Delagard overboard and swing the ship around. What do you say, doc?"

"I say we need some rain before long, and a good school of fish to come by."

"You aren't with us any more? I thought you were as hot to turn back as we are."

"Onyos has a good point," said Lawler cautiously. "The wind's against us here. With or without Delagard, we may not be able to beat our way back east."

"What are you saying, doc? That we just have to sail right on around the world until we come up on Home Sea again from the far side?"

"Don't forget the Face," Dann Henders put in. "We'll get to the Face before we start up the other side of the world."

"The Face," said Tharp darkly. "The Face, the Face, the Face! Fuck the Face!"

"The Face will fuck us first," Henders said.

THE BREEZE FRESHENED FINALLY AND CHOPPED AROUND FROM NORTH-east to east-southeast, and blew with surprising chilly vigor, while the sea grew high and confused, breaking frequently across the stern. Suddenly there were fish again, a teeming silvery mass of them, and Kinverson netted a heavy load.

"Easy there," Delagard cautioned, when they sat down at table. "Don't stuff yourselves or you'll burst."

Lis outdid herself preparing the meals, conjuring up a dozen different sauces out of what seemed like nothing at all. But there was still no water, which made eating a taxing chore. Kinverson urged them to eat their fish raw once again, to get the benefit of the moisture it contained. Dipping the fresh bleeding chunks in seawater helped to make them more palatable, although it compounded the problem of thirst.

"What'll happen to us if we drink salt water, doc?" Neyana Golghoz asked. "Will we die? Will we go crazy?"

"We already are crazy," Dag Tharp said softly.

"We can tolerate a certain amount of salt water," Lawler said, thinking of the amount he had consumed himself lately. But he wasn't going to say anything about that. "If we had any fresh water, we could actually stretch the supply by diluting it ten or fifteen percent with ocean water and it wouldn't hurt us any. In fact it would help us replace the salt we're sweating out of ourselves all the time in this hot weather. But we can't live on straight seawater very long. Our bodies would manage to filter it and turn it into pure water, but our kidneys wouldn't be able to get rid of the salt buildup without pulling water out of other body tissues to do it. We'd dry up pretty fast. Fever, vomiting, delirium, death."

Dann Henders set up a row of little solar stills, stretching clear plastic over the mouths of pots partly filled with seawater. Each pot had a cup inside it, placed carefully to catch the drops of fresh water that condensed on the underside of the plastic. But that was a tortuous business. It seemed impossible to produce enough usable water this way to meet their needs.

"What if it doesn't rain soon?" Pilya Braun asked. "What are we going to do?"

Lawler gestured toward Father Quillan. "We could try praying," he said.

LATE THE FOLLOWING EVENING WHEN THE HEAT HELD THEM AS TIGHTLY as a glove and the ship was standing almost perfectly still in the water, Lawler heard Henders and Tharp whispering in the radio room as he headed back to his cabin to go to sleep. There was something irritatingly abrasive about the scratchy sounds of their voices.

As Lawler halted in the passageway for a moment Onyos Felk came down the ladder and gave him a quick nod of greeting; then Felk went on to the radio room too. Lawler, pausing outside his cabin door, heard Felk say, "The doc's out here. You want me to ask him in?"

Lawler couldn't hear the reply. But it must have been affirmative, because Felk turned and beckoned to him and said, "Would you come over here for a minute, doc?"

"It's late, Onyos. What is it?"

"Just for a minute."

Tharp and Henders were sitting practically knee-to-knee in the tiny radio room with a guttering candle casting a somber light between them. There was a flask of grapeweed brandy on the table, and two cups. Tharp ordinarily wasn't a drinker, Lawler remembered.

Henders said, "Some brandy, doc?"

"I don't think so, thanks."

"Everything going all right?"

"I'm tired," Lawler said, not very patiently. "What's up, Dann?"

"We've been talking about Delagard, Dag and I. And Onyos. Discussing this idiotic fucked-up mess of a voyage that he's dragged us off on. What do you think of him, doc?"

"Delagard?" Lawler shrugged. "You know what I think."

"We all know what all of us think. We've all known each other too goddamned long. But tell us anyway."

"A very determined man. Stubborn, strong, completely unscrupulous. Totally sure of himself."

"Crazy?"

"That I can't say."

"I bet you could," Dag Tharp put in. "You think he's out of his fucking head."

"That's very possible. Or then again, not. Sometimes it's not easy to tell the difference between single-mindedness and insanity. A lot of geniuses have seemed like madmen, in their times."

"You think he's a genius?" Henders asked.

"Not necessarily. But he's unusual, at least. I'm not in a position to say what goes on in his mind. He may well be crazy. But he can give you perfectly rational-sounding reasons for what he's doing, I'd be willing to bet. This Face of the Waters thing may make perfect sense to him."

Felk said, "Don't pretend to be so innocent, doc. Every lunatic thinks that his lunacy makes perfect sense. Isn't a man in the world who ever believed he was crazy."

"Do you admire Delagard?" Henders said to Lawler.

"Not particularly." Lawler shrugged. "He's got his strong points, you have to admit. He's a man of vision. I don't necessarily think his visions are very admirable ones."

"Do you like him?"

"No. Not in the slightest."

"You're straightforward on that, anyway."

"Look, is there a point to all this?" Lawler asked. "Because if you're simply having a good time sitting here over a bottle of brandy telling each other what a miserable bastard Delagard is, I'd just as soon go to bed, okay?"

"We're just trying to find out where you stand, doc," Dann Henders said. "Tell us, do you want the voyage to continue the way it's been going?"

"No."

"Well, what are you prepared to do to change things?"

"Is there anything we *can* do?"

"I asked you a question. Asking me a question back doesn't amount to an answer."

"You planning on a mutiny, are you?"

"Did I say that? I don't remember saying that, doc."

"A deaf man could hear you saying it."

"A mutiny," Henders said. "Well, now, what if some of us did try to take some active role in deciding which way the ship ought to be traveling. What would you say if that were to happen? What would you do?"

"It's a lousy idea, Dann."

"You think so, doc?"

"There was a time when I was just as eager as you are to make Delagard turn the ship around. Dag knows that. I spoke to him about it. Delagard has to be stopped, I told him. You remember that, Dag? But that was before the Wave brought us way the hell out here. Since then I've had plenty of time to think about it, and I've changed my mind."

"Why?"

"Three reasons. One is that this is Delagard's ship, for better or for worse, and I don't much like the notion of taking it away from him. A moral issue, you might say. You could justify doing it on the grounds that he's risking our lives without our consent, I suppose. But even so I don't think it's a smart idea. Delagard's too tricky. Too dangerous. Too strong. He's on guard all the time. And a lot of the others on board are loyal to him, or afraid of him, which amounts to the same thing. They won't help us. They're likely to help *him*. You try any funny stuff with him and you very likely will find yourself regretting it."

Henders's expression was a wintry one. "You said you had three reasons. That was two."

Lawler said, "The third is the thing that Onyos was talking about the other day. Even if you grabbed the ship, how would you make it take us back to Home Sea? Be realistic about it. There's no wind. We're running out of food and water faster than I want to think about. Unless we can somehow pick up a westerly wind, the best we can hope for at this point is to keep on heading toward the Face on the chance that we'll be able to reprovision ourselves when we get there."

Henders gave the mapkeeper a quizzical look. "You still feel that way, Onyos?"

"We're pretty far in, yes. And right now we do seem to be becalmed most of the time. So I suppose we really don't have a lot of choice but to continue on our present course."

"That's your opinion?" Henders asked.

"I suppose it is," said Felk.

"Continuing to follow a lunatic who's leading us toward a place we know nothing about? One which very likely is full of all sorts of dangers that we can't even begin to imagine?"

"I don't like that any more than you do. But like the doctor says, we need to be realistic. Of course, if the wind should change—"

"Right, Onyos. Or if angels should come down from the skies and bring some nice cool fresh water with them." There was a long prickly silence in the small, cramped room. At length Henders looked up and said, "Okay, doc. This isn't accomplishing anything. And I don't want to take up any more of your time. We were just inviting you in for a friendly little drink, but I can see how tired you are. Good night, doc. Sleep well."

"Are you going to try it, Dann?"

"I don't see where that concerns you one way or another, doc."

"All right," Lawler said. "Good night."

"Onyos, would you stick around for a little while?" Henders said.

"Whatever you want, Dann," Felk said.

The mapkeeper sounded as though he was ready to be convinced.

A bunch of fools, Lawler thought, as he went to his bunk. Playing at being mutineers. But he doubted very much that anything would come of it. Felk and Tharp were weaklings, and Henders couldn't deal with Delagard by himself. In the end nothing would be done, and the ship would stay on course for the Face. That seemed the likeliest outcome of all this planning and scheming.

SOMEWHERE IN THE NIGHT LAWLER HEARD NOISES FROM ABOVE, shouts, some heavy pounding, the sound of feet running across the deck. There was an angry yell, muffled by the deck planking above him but nevertheless clearly a cry of rage, and he knew that he had been wrong. They were doing it after all. He sat up, blinking. Without taking the time to dress, he rose and made his way into the passageway and up the ladder.

It was almost dawn. The sky was gray-black; the Cross was low in the sky, hanging in that weirdly askew fashion that was its way in these latitudes. A strange drama was being enacted on deck, near the fore hatch. Or was it a farce?

Two frantic figures were chasing each other around the open hatch, yelling and gesticulating as they ran. After a moment Lawler focused his sleep-blurred eyes and saw that they were Dann Henders and Nid Delagard. Henders was doing the chasing, Delagard the fleeing.

Henders had one of Kinverson's gaffs clutched in his hand like a spear. As he followed Delagard around the perimeter of the hatch he stabbed the air with the weapon again and again, with the clear intent of putting it through the ship-owner's back. There had already been at least one hit. Delagard's shirt was torn; Lawler saw a thin jagged line of blood seeping through near his right shoulder, like a red thread sewn into the fabric, widening with every moment.

But Henders was going it alone. Dag Tharp stood near the rail, goggle-eyed, motionless as a statue. Onyos Felk was close by him. In the rigging were Leo Martello and Pilya Braun, frozen also, looks of astonishment and awe on their faces.

"Dag!" Henders yelled. "For Christ's sake, Dag, where are you? Give me a hand with him, will you?"

"I'm here—over here—" the radioman whispered, in a hoarse husky tone that could barely be heard five meters away. He stayed where he was.

"For Christ's sake," Henders said again, disgustedly. He shook his fist at Tharp and leaped wildly toward Delagard in a frantic lunging attempt at reaching him. But Delagard managed—only barely—to elude the sharp tip of the gaff. He looked back over his shoulder, cursing. His face glistened with sweat; his eyes were inflamed and bright with fury.

As Delagard passed near the foremast in his frenzied circular flight he looked up and called out in a whipcrack voice to Pilya, suspended just above him on the yard, "Help me! Fast! Your knife!"

Swiftly Pilya unfastened the scabbard that held the blade of sharpened bone she always wore strapped around her waist and tossed it, scabbard and all, to Delagard as he went by beneath her. He snapped it out of the air with a quick fierce swipe of his hand, pulled the blade from its holder, gripped its haft tightly in his hand. Then he swung around, unexpectedly striding straight toward the astounded Henders, who was plunging along behind him at a pace too swift to check. Henders ran right into him. Delagard brushed the long gaff to one side with a stiff, brusque motion of his forearm and came in underneath it, bringing his arm upward and sinking the blade to its hilt in Henders's throat.

Henders grunted and flung up his arms. He looked amazed. The gaff went flying aside. Delagard, embracing Henders now as though they were lovers, clamped his other hand to the back of the engineer's neck and with weird tenderness held him close up against him with the blade firmly rammed home.

Henders's eyes, wide and bulging, glistened like full moons in the gray of dawn. He made a thick sputtering sound and a spurt of dark blood shot from his mouth. His tongue came into view, swollen and lagging. Delagard held him upright, pressing hard.

Lawler found his voice, finally.

"Nid—my God, Nid, what have you done—"

"You want to be next, doc?" Delagard asked calmly. He pulled the blade out, giving it a savage twist as he withdrew it, and stepped back. A torrent of blood came springing forth once the knife was out. Henders's face had turned black. He took a shaky step, and another, like a sleepwalker. The look of astonishment still gleamed in his eyes.

Then he tottered and fell. Lawler knew he was dead before he reached the deck.

Pilya had come down from the rigging. Delagard tossed the blade across the planks to her. It landed at her feet. "Thanks," he said offhandedly. "I owe you one for that." Scooping Henders's body up as if it were weightless, one arm around the dead man's shoulders and the other under his legs, Delagard strode quickly toward the rail, lifted the body high over his head, and flung it into the sea as though it was garbage.

Tharp hadn't moved during the whole thing. Delagard went over to him and slapped him in the face, hard enough to send his head rocking back.

"You cowardly little fucker, Dag," Delagard said. "You didn't even have the guts to follow through on your own plot. I ought to throw you overboard, too, but it isn't worth the effort."

"Nid—for God's sake, Nid—"

"Shut your mouth. Get out of my sight." Delagard wheeled around and glared at Felk. "What about you, Onyos? Were you part of this thing too?"

"Not me, Nid! I wouldn't! You know that!"

" 'Not me, Nid!' " Delagard mimicked savagely. "Cocksucker! You would have been if you'd had the guts. A coward from the start. And how about you, Lawler? Will you stitch me up, or are you part of this fucking conspiracy, too? You weren't even here. What did you do, sleep late for your own mutiny?"

"I wasn't in it," said Lawler quietly. "It was a dumb idea, and I told them so."

"You knew, and you didn't warn me?"

"That's right, Nid."

"If you're not party to a mutiny, then it's your obligation to notify the captain of what's going on. Law of the sea. You didn't do that."

"That's right," Lawler said. "I didn't."

Delagard considered that for a moment. Then he shrugged and nodded. "All right, doc. I think I get your meaning." He looked around. "Somebody clean up the deck," he said. "I hate a messy ship." He gestured to Felk, who looked dazed. "Onyos, take the wheel, as long as you seem to be awake. I've got to get this cut fixed. Come on, doc. I guess I can trust you to stitch me up."

AT MIDDAY A WIND CAME UP BETWEEN ONE MOMENT AND THE NEXT, AS if Henders's death had been a sacrifice to whatever gods ruled the weather on Hydros. In the vast quiet of the long calm there abruptly appeared the deep roaring of gusts that had traveled a long way: all the way from the pole, in fact, a sharp southerly blow, cold and crisp.

The sea grew high. The ship, stilled for so long, tumbled into a trough, heeled back, dropped into another. Then the sky darkened with a suddenness that was almost startling. The wind was bringing rain with it.

"Buckets!" Delagard bellowed. "Casks!"

No one needed to be urged. The watch below came awake in an instant and the deck was alive with busy hands. Anything that could hold water was set forth to catch it, not simply the usual jars and casks and pots, but also clean rags, blankets, clothes, whatever was absorbent and could be wrung out after the storm. It had been weeks since the last rainfall; it might be weeks until the next.

The rain was a distraction, easing the shock of Henders's abortive mutiny and violent death. Lawler, naked in the cool rain, rushing back and forth like everyone else to empty the smaller vessels into the larger storage containers, was grateful for it. The nightmare scene on deck had affected him in a wholly unexpected way, stripping him of layers of hard-won defenses. It had been a long time since he had felt so naive, so callow. Spouting gouts of blood, raw torn flesh, even sudden death, they were all everyday things to him, part of his professional routine. He was accustomed to them; he took them casually. But a killing? He had never seen a murder before. He had never really even imagined the possibility of one. For all of Dag Tharp's brave talk of throwing Delagard overboard in the past couple of weeks, Lawler could hardly believe that one man might actually be capable of taking another's life. There was no question, certainly, that Delagard had killed Henders in self-defense. But he had done it coolly, matter-of-factly, remorselessly. Lawler felt humiliatingly ingenuous, confronting these ugly realities. Wise old Doc Lawler, the man who has seen everything, shivering in his boots over a bit of archaic violence? It was absurd. And yet it was real. The impact on him was intense. It had been a shattering sight.

Archaic was the right word for it. The efficiency and indifference with which Delagard had rid himself of his pursuer had been positively medieval, if not downright prehistoric: a hand had risen up out of the shadowy past, a dark act out of mankind's primeval dawn had been reenacted on the deck of the *Queen of Hydros* this morning. Lawler would hardly have been more surprised if Earth itself had appeared suspended in the sky, hanging just above the masts with blood dripping from every teeming continent. So much for all those centuries of civilization. So much for the earnest common belief that all such ancient passions were extinct, that raw violence of that bloody kind had evolved out of the race.

The rainstorm was a welcome distraction, yes, as well as a much-needed source of water. It washed the deck clean of the stain of sin. What had happened here today was something Lawler would just as soon forget as quickly as he could.

4

I N THE NIGHT CAME TROUBLING DREAMS, DREAMS FILLED NOT with murder but with powerful erotic passions.

The shadowy figures of women danced around Lawler as he slept, women without faces, mere cavorting bodies, generic receptacles for desire. They could have been anyone, anonymous, mysterious, pure female essence without specific identity, blank tablets and nothing more: a procession of swaying breasts, broad hips, full buttocks, dense thick pubic triangles. Sometimes it seemed to him that the dance was made up of disembodied breasts alone, or a succession of endlessly parting thighs, or moist shining lips. Or wriggling fingers, or flicking tongues.

He tossed restlessly, drifting toward wakefulness but always subsiding again into sleep, which brought new flurries of fevered sensuality. Clouds of women surrounded his bunk, their eyes slitted and wanton, their nostrils flaring, their bodies bare. Now there were faces to go with the bodies, the faces of the Sorve women he had known and loved and all but forgotten, a legion of them, all the escapades of his busy youth recalled to life and surrounding him now, the unformed faces of adolescent girls, the leering faces of older women who were dallying with a boy half their age, the tense, sharp-eyed faces of women stricken with a love that they knew was futile. One by one they passed within Lawler's reach, let him touch them, allowed him to pull them close, and then faded into smoke, to be replaced almost at once by another. Sundira—Anya Braun—Boda Thalheim, not yet Sister

Boda—Mariam Sawtelle—Mireyl—Sundira again—Meela—Moira—
Sundira—Sundira—Anya—Mireyl—Sundira—

Lawler felt all the torment that desire can bring, and no hope of relief
from it. His penis was huge, aching, a log. His testicles were iron weights.
A hot musky woman-smell, maddening and irresistible, covered his nose
and mouth like a smothering blanket, choking him, seeping down deep
into his throat and filling his lungs until they were fiery with discomfort.

And beneath the images, beneath the fantasies, beneath the aching
sense of distress and frustration, was something else: a strange vibration,
perhaps a sound or perhaps not, in any event a steady widening beam of
strong sensory input that came stabbing up through his body from his loins
to his skull. He could feel it entering him like an icy spear just behind his
testicles and rising through all the steaming intricacies of his guts, through
his diaphragm, his heart, piercing his throat, stabbing upward into his
brain. He was skewered on it and turning slowly like a fish grilling on a
spit; and as he turned the intensity of the erotic sensations grew and grew
and grew until there seemed to Lawler that nothing else existed in the
universe but the need to find a partner and couple with her at once.

He rose from his narrow bed, not sure whether he was awake or still
dreaming, and went out into the passageway. Up the ladder, through the
hatch, out on deck.

The night was mild and moonless. The Cross trailed across the lower
sky like a cluster of jewels that someone had carelessly tossed aside. The sea
was calm, with little rounded rippling swells glittering by starlight. There
was an easy breeze. The sails were set and full.

Figures were moving about: sleepwalkers, dreamers.

They were as vague and ghostly to Lawler as the figures of his dreams.
He understood that he knew them, but that was all. They had no names just
now. They had no selves. He saw a short thick-bodied man and another with
a bony, angular body and a tiny, emaciated one with wattles at his throat.
Men were not what he was looking for, though. Far down by the stern there
was a tall, slender dark-haired woman. He headed for her. But before he
could reach her another man appeared, a tall strapping one with big
glowing eyes, who came gliding out of the shadows and caught her by the
wrist. They sank down together on the deck.

Lawler turned. There were other women on this ship. He would find
one. He had to.

The throbbing ache between his legs was unendurable. That strange vibratory sensation still spitted him, rising the whole length of his torso, past his gullet and into his skull. It had the cold burning force of an icicle, and an icicle's knife-like insistence.

He stepped over one couple grappling on the deck: a graying older man with a compact, solid-looking body and a big hefty woman with dark skin and golden hair. Lawler thought vaguely that he might have known them once; but, as before, no names came. Beyond them a small bright-eyed man flitted by alone, and then there was another couple locked in a close embrace, the man huge and muscular, the woman lithe, youthful, vigorous.

"You!" came a voice from the shadows. "Here!"

She was sprawled below the bridge, beckoning to him, a sturdy broad-bodied woman with a flat-featured face, orange hair, a sprinkling of reddish freckles on her face and breasts. She was shiny with sweat, breathing hard. Lawler knelt by her and she drew him down and gripped him between her thighs.

"Give it to me! Give it to me!"

He slipped easily inside her. She was warm and lathered and soft. Her arms enfolded him. She crushed him down against her heavy breasts. His hips moved in urgent thrusts. It was quick, wild, fierce, a hard grunting moment of rut. Almost as soon as he began to move, Lawler felt the walls of her hot moist passage quivering and tightening on him in deep, steady spasms. He could feel the impulses of pleasure running along her nerve-channels. That was confusing, that he should be feeling what she was feeling. An instant later came his spurting response, and he could feel that in a double way, too, not only his sensations but hers as she received his fluid. That too was very strange. It was difficult to tell where his conscious-ness left off and hers began.

He rolled away from her. She reached for him, trying to pull him back, but no, no, he was on his way. He wanted another partner now. That single throbbing moment hadn't been nearly enough to ease the need that drove him. It might be that nothing could. But perhaps he could find the tall slender one next, or else that robust young sleek-limbed one who seemed to be overflowing with vital energies. Or even the big dark-skinned one with the golden hair. It made no difference which one. He was insatiable, inexhaustible.

There was the slender one, by herself once more. Lawler started toward her. Too late! The hairy thick-bodied man with fleshy breasts like a woman's seized her and claimed her. Off they went into the darkness.

Well, the big one, then—

Or the young one—

"Lawler!" a man's voice said.

"Who's that?"

"Quillan! Here! Here!"

It was the angular man, the man who seemed to have no flesh. He came out from behind the place where the water-strider was stowed and took hold of Lawler's arm. Lawler shook him off. "No, not you—it's not a man that I'm after—"

"Neither am I. Nor a woman, either. Good lord, Lawler! Have you all gone crazy?"

"What?"

"Stand here with me and watch what's going on. This lunatic orgy."

Lawler shook his head muzzily. "What? What? Orgy?"

"You see Sundira Thane and Delagard going at it over there? Kinverson and Pilya? And look, look, there's Neyana, moaning for it like a madwoman. You've just finished with her yourself, haven't you? And already you want more. I've never seen anything like this."

Lawler clutched his loins. "I feel—pain—here—"

"It's something out of the sea that's doing it to us. Affecting our minds. I feel it, too. But I'm able to control myself. Whereas you—the whole crazed lot of you—"

Lawler had great difficulty understanding what the bony man was telling him. He began to move away. Now he saw the big golden-haired woman wandering the deck, looking for her next partner.

"Lawler, come back!"

"Wait—later—we can talk later—"

As he shambled toward the woman a slender dark male figure moved past him, calling out, "Father-sir! Doctor-sir! I see it! Over here, over the side!"

"What do you see, Gharkid?" the angular one called Quillan asked.

"A big limpet, Father-sir. Attached to the hull. It must be sending out some chemical—some drug—"

"Lawler! Come look at what Gharkid's found!"

"Later—later—"

But they were merciless. They went toward him and took him by the arms, one gripping him on each side, and marched him toward the rail. Lawler peered over. Here the sensations were far more intense than anywhere else on board: Lawler felt a deep rhythmic thrumming along his backbone, a stupefying pounding in his groin. His balls tolled like bells. His rigid penis trembled and jerked upright, pointing at the stars.

He fought to clear his brain. He could barely comprehend what was happening.

A thing invading the ship, driving everybody crazy with lust.

Names returned to his mind and he matched them with faces and forms. Quillan. Gharkid. Resisting the force. And those who hadn't: he and Neyana, Sundira and Martello, Sundira and Delagard. Kinverson and Pilya. Felk and Lis. On and on in an unending change of partners, a feverish dance of pricks and cunts. Where was Lis? He wanted Lis. He had never wanted her before. He had never wanted Neyana either. But he did now. Now, Lis, yes. And then Pilya, finally. Give her what she's been after this whole voyage. And Sundira after that. Get her away from loathsome Delagard. Sundira, yes, and then Neyana again, and Lis, and Pilya—Sundira, Neyana, Pilya, Lis—fuck till dawn—fuck till noon—fuck till the end of time—

"I'm going to kill it," Quillan said. "Hand me that gaff, Natim."

"You don't feel its force?" Lawler asked. "You're immune?"

"Of course I'm not immune," the priest said.

"So your vows—"

"It isn't the vows that are holding me back. It's simple fear, Lawler." To Gharkid Quillan said, "The gaff should just about reach. Hang on to my legs so I don't go overboard."

"Let me do it," Lawler said. "My arms are longer than yours."

"Stay where you are."

The priest pulled himself up on the rail and wriggled down the outer side of the hull. Gharkid grabbed his legs. Lawler steadied Gharkid. Looking down, Lawler saw something that looked like a bright yellow plaque perhaps a meter across clinging to the ship just above the water-line. It was flat and circular with a little puckered dome in its center. Quillan reached down as far as he could and stabbed at it. Again. Again. A tiny spurt of blue fluid rose like a feeble little fountain from the creature's back. Another poke. The creature quivered convulsively.

Lawler felt the pain in his loins beginning to ease.

"Hold me tighter!" Quillan called. "I'm starting to slip!"

"No, Father-sir. No!"

Lawler clamped his hands around Quillan's upturned ankles. He felt the priest's body go taut as he bent away from the ship, reached downward, drove the gaff home with a short hard thrust. The thing clinging to the ship rippled wildly along its fleshy perimeter. Its color darkened to a deep green, then to a morbid black; sudden writhing ridges arose in its soft flesh; it drew itself up and fell back into the sea and was swept off into the ship's wake.

Almost at once Lawler felt his mind throw off the last of its fog.

"My God," he said. "What was it?"

"A limpet is what Gharkid called it," said Quillan. "Stuck to the ship, dousing us all with wild pheromones." He was quivering as though released from some unbearable tension. "Some of us were able to fight it. Some weren't."

Lawler looked updeck. Everywhere naked people were wandering slowly about, looking dazed, like newly awakened sleepers. Leo Martello stood beside Neyana, staring at her as if he had never seen her before in his life. Kinverson was with Lis Niklaus. Lawler's eyes met Sundira's. She seemed stunned. Her hand brushed again and again across her flat bare belly in an anguished scrubbing motion, as if to rub away the impress of Delagard's flesh against her own.

THE LIMPET WAS A HARBINGER. IN THESE LOW LATITUDES THE EMPTY Sea appeared to be getting less empty.

A new kind of drakken appeared, a southern species. They were much like the ones of the north, but larger and more cunning-looking, with a cheerily calculating look about them. Instead of traveling in swarms of many hundreds these drakkens moved in a pack of only a few dozen, and when their long tubular heads came jutting up out of the water they were very widely spaced, as though each member of the pack demanded and received a generous territorial allotment from its companions. They accompanied the ship for hours, kicking along untiringly beside it with their noses up in the air. Their gleaming crimson eyes never closed. It was easy enough to believe that they were waiting for darkness and an opportunity to come scrambling up on board. Delagard ordered the watch below to go on duty early, patrolling the deck armed with gaffs.

At twilight the drakkens submerged, all of them vanishing in a single moment in that sudden simultaneous way of their kind, as if they had been sucked down in one gulp by some vastness below them. Delagard wasn't convinced that they were gone and kept the patrols on deck all night. But there was no attack, and in the morning the drakkens were nowhere to be seen.

THEN LATE THAT AFTERNOON AS DARKNESS BEGAN TO FALL A GREAT amorphous soft mass of some sallow viscous stuff came drifting by the ship on the windward side. It went on and on, stretching out over hundreds of meters, perhaps more. It might almost have been an island of some strange kind, it was so big: a colossal flabby island, an island made entirely of mucus, a gigantic agglomeration of snot. When they drew closer to it they realized that this huge puckered wrinkled thing was actually alive, or at least partly so. Its pale custardy surface was lightly quivering in fitful motion, pushing up little rounded projections that almost immediately sank back down into the central mass.

Dag Tharp struck a comic pose. "Here we are, ladies and gentlemen! The Face of the Waters at last!"

Kinverson laughed. "More like the other end, is the way it looks to me."

"Look there," Martello said. "Bits of light rising from it, fluttering around in the air. How beautiful they are!"

"Like fireflies," said Quillan.

"Fireflies?" Lawler asked.

"They have them on Sunrise. Insects equipped with luminescent organs. You know what insects are? Land-dwelling six-legged arthropods, unbelievably common on most worlds. Fireflies are insects that come out at twilight and blink their little lights on and off. Very pretty, very romantic. The effect is much like this."

Lawler watched. It was a beautiful sight, yes: tiny fragments of that enormous turgid drifting mass detaching themselves and rising, borne upward on the light breeze, glowing as they rose, quick flashes of yellow brilliance, little soaring sunlets. The air was full of them, dozens, hundreds. They coasted on the wind, rose, fell, climbed again. On, off, on, off: flashing, flashing, flashing.

On Hydros beauty was almost always cause for suspicion. Lawler felt a growing uneasiness as the fireflies danced.

Then Lis Niklaus yelled, "The sail's on fire!"

Lawler glanced upward. Some of the fireflies had come drifting across the ship, and wherever they fetched up against one of the sails they clung and glowed steadily, igniting the close-woven sea-bamboo fabric. Little puffs of smoke were spiraling upward in a dozen places; little red gleams of burning threads could be seen. In fact the ship was under attack.

Delagard shouted orders for a change of course. The *Queen* pulled away as fast as it could from the bloated enemy on its flank. Anyone not needed to shift the sails was sent aloft to defend them. Lawler scrambled around in the rigging with the others, batting at the little sparklers as they came drifting into the sails, scraping away at the ones that were already affixed to them. The heat of them was insignificant but persistent: the constant warmth they emitted while stuck to the fabric was what achieved ignition. Lawler saw charred places where they had been pulled free in time, others where starlight glittered through small holes in the sails, and—high up on the foremast topsail—a scarlet tongue of flame, tipped with a black trail of smoke, where the material was ablaze.

Kinverson was climbing swiftly toward the burning place. He reached it and began to clamp his hands over the blaze to smother it. The bright flamelets disappeared one by one into his grasp as though by a conjuring trick. In moments nothing but glowing embers could be seen; and then those too were out. The firefly that had ignited the fire was already gone. It had fallen to the deck as the sail gave way around it, leaving behind a ragged, blackened hole the size of a man's head.

The ship caught the wind and moved quickly off to the southwest. Their unlovely foe, unable to travel at the same pace, soon was out of sight behind them. But its pretty offshoots, its dainty fluttering fireflies, continued to ride the breeze for hours in lessening numbers, and it was dawn before Delagard felt it was safe for the defenders in the rigging to come down.

Sundira spent the next three days mending the sails, with help from Kinverson, Pilya, and Neyana. The ship made no headway while the spars were bare. The air was still; the sun was disagreeably strong; the sea was quiet. Sometimes a fin flickered above the surface in the distance. Lawler had the feeling they were under constant surveillance now.

He calculated that he had a week's supply of numbweed left, at best.

ANOTHER FREE-FLOATING CREATURE, NEITHER AS GIGANTIC NOR AS repellent nor as hostile as the last, came by: a large featureless ovoidal thing, perfectly smooth, of a lovely emerald color, aglow with radiant luminosity. It stood up out of the water to its midsection, but the sea was so clear here that its shining lower half was easily visible. The thing was perhaps twenty meters around at its waist, and ten or fifteen meters in length from its submerged bottom to its rounded summit.

Delagard, jumpy, ready for anything, lined everyone up along the side of the ship armed with gaffs. But the ovoid drifted on past, harmless as a piece of fruit. Perhaps that was all that it was. Two more wandered along later the same day. The first was more spherical, the second more elongated, but they seemed otherwise to be of the same kind. They seemed to take no notice of the *Queen*. What these ovoids needed, Lawler decided, were huge glistening eyes, the better to stare at the ship as they floated past it. But their faces were blind, smooth, mysterious, maddeningly bland. There was a curious solemnity about them, a massive calm gravity. Father Quillan said they reminded him of a bishop he had once known; and then he had to explain to everyone what a bishop was.

After the ovoids came a species of flying fish, neither the elegant irides-cent air-skimmers of Home Sea nor the hideous hagfish of the open ocean. These were delicate-looking glossy creatures about fifteen centimeters long with filmy graceful wings that lifted them to astonishing heights. They could be seen far off, bursting almost vertically from the water and traveling for extraordinary distances before swooping back down and re-entering the ocean virtually without a splash. Moments later they were aloft again, up and down, up and down, coming closer to the ship with each cycle of flight and descent, until finally they were just off the starboard bow.

These fliers didn't seem any more dangerous than yesterday's huge floating emerald ovoids. They flew so high that there was no risk of colliding with them on deck, and so there was no need to duck and hide as would have been necessary if an overflight of hagfish had come by. They were so beautiful, gleaming brilliantly against the bright hard dome of the sky, that nearly the entire ship's complement turned out to watch their passage.

Their bodies were practically transparent. It was easy to make out their fine wiry bones, their round pulsing red-violet stomachs, their threadlike blue veins, as they went shooting by overhead. Their blood-red eyes were finely faceted, glinting as they caught the light.

Beautiful, yes. But as they coursed through the air above the ship a strange rain fell from them, a faint shimmering shower of dark glittering drops that bit deep and burned wherever they touched.

In the first few moments no one realized what was happening. The initial nipping bites of the fliers' secretions were barely perceptible annoyances. But the pain was cumulative: the acid worked its way in, and what had been an odd little mild itch turned quickly to agony.

Lawler, standing in the shadow of the foresails, was shielded against the worst of the bombardment. Some scattering outspray caught him along his forearm, not enough to provoke more than a frown. But then he saw dark mottled scars beginning to appear on the polished yellow wood of the deck just a short distance away, and he looked up to see his shipmates howling and prancing wildly around, slapping at their arms, rubbing at their cheeks.

"Get down!" he called. "Take cover! It's coming from those flying fish!"

The airborne attackers had passed over the ship now and gone on beyond. But already a second wave of the creatures was rising from the sea off to starboard.

The entire onslaught lasted close to an hour, half a dozen waves in all. Afterward, the victims lined up one by one in Lawler's infirmary to have their burns treated.

Sundira, who had been in the rigging when the fliers came, was the last one to come. She had been wearing nothing but a twist of cloth about her waist, and blisters were rising all over her body now. In silence Lawler dabbed her with ointment. She stood naked before him and his hands moved over her skin, rubbing the ointment in around her nipples, along her thighs, up her crotch to a point a fingerbreadth's length from her loins.

They hadn't made love since before the night of the limpet. But Lawler found no desire stirring in him now as he touched her, even in the most intimate places.

Sundira noticed it too. Lawler could feel her muscles tensing beneath his probing fingers. She was drawing herself up tightly, angrily.

She said finally, "You're handling me like so much meat, Val."

"I'm a medical man trying to care for a patient who's got a bunch of nasty blisters all over her skin."

"That's all I am to you now?"

"Right at this moment, yes. You think it's a good idea for a doctor to start breathing hard every time he touches an attractive patient's body?"

"I'm not just any patient, am I?"

"Of course you aren't."

"But you've been keeping away from me for days. And now you treat me like a stranger. What's the problem?"

"Problem?" He gave her a troubled look. Tapping her lightly on the hip, he said, "Turn around. I missed the ones in the small of your back. Where's there a problem, Sundira?"

"Am I right that you don't want me any more?"

He dipped his fingers into the ointment flask and rubbed the stuff on her just above her bare buttocks.

"I didn't know we had a specific schedule. Do we?"

"Of course not. But look how you're touching me now."

"I just got through telling you," Lawler said. "Let me try again. I thought you were here for medical care, not for lovemaking. Doctors learn early that it's never a good idea to mix the two. But also it might have occurred to me, not as a matter of ethics but just one of common sense, that you wouldn't want me to come on to you at a time when you happen to have painful blisters all over your skin. Okay?" This was the closest thing to a quarrel they had ever had. "Does that sound reasonable, Sundira?"

She swung around to face him. "It's because of what I did with Delagard, isn't it?"

"What?"

"You hate the idea that he had his hands on me, and more than his hands, and now you don't want anything to do with me again."

"Are you serious?"

"Yes. And I'm right, too. If you could see the expression on your face just now——"

Lawler said, "We were all out of our minds while that thing was stuck to the hull. Nobody's responsible for anything that happened that night. You think I wanted to fuck Neyana? If you want the truth, Sundira, it was you I was looking for when I first came up on deck. Not that I could even remember your name, or my own, in the condition I was in. But I saw you and I wanted you and I headed toward you, only Leo Martello got to you first. And then Neyana caught hold of me and so I went with her. I was under the influence, same as you, same as everybody. Everybody except Father Quillan and Gharkid, that is. Our two holy men." Lawler's cheeks were hot. He felt his heartbeat climbing. "Jesus, Sundira, I've known about you and Kinverson all along, and that hasn't stopped me, has it? And on the limpet night there was you and Martello first, before Delagard. Why would what you did with Delagard matter to me any more than what you've done with all the others?"

"Delagard's different. You hate him. He disgusts you."

"Does he?"

"He's a murderer and a bully. He got us all thrown off Sorve Island. Ever since then he's been running this expedition like a tyrant. He beats Lis. He killed Henders. He lies, he cheats, he does whatever he feels like doing in order to get his way. Everything about him is loathsome to you, and you can't stand the idea that he's fucked me too, now, whether or not I was in my right mind when I let him do it. So you're taking it out on me. You don't want to put your mouth where Delagard's mouth has been, let alone your cock. Isn't that so, Val?"

"You're doing an awful lot of mind reading, suddenly. I never knew you were telepathic, Sundira."

"Don't be a smart-ass. Is it so or isn't it?"

"Look, Sundira—"

"It is, isn't it?" Her tone, which had been hard and cold, softened suddenly, and she looked at him with a tenderness and longing that surprised him. "Val, Val, don't you think it disgusts me too, to know that I had that man inside me? Don't you think I've been trying to wash myself clean of him ever since? But that shouldn't be your problem. I don't have spots on my skin where he touched me. You have no right to turn against me like this, simply because some alien *thing* clamped itself to the side of our ship one night and made us commit acts that we never would have dreamed of doing otherwise." Then there was bright anger in her eyes again. "If it isn't Delagard, what is it? Tell me."

In a voice thickened by shame Lawler said, "All right. I admit it. It is Delagard."

"Oh, shit, Val."

"I'm sorry."

"Are you?"

"I don't think I even realized what was bothering me myself, not until you flung it in my face like this. But yes, yes, I suppose that on some level it's been eating away at me since that night. Delagard's hand crawling around between your legs. Delagard's blubbery mouth on your breasts." Lawler closed his eyes a moment. "It wasn't your fault. I'm acting like a stupid adolescent kid."

"You're right on all counts. You're being very silly. And I want to remind you that under normal circumstances I wouldn't have let Delagard screw me in a million years. Not if he was the last man in the galaxy."

Lawler smiled. "The devil made you do it."

"The limpet."

"Same thing."

"If you say so. But it never happened, not really. Not by any conscious act of mine. And I'm trying as hard as I know how to unhappen it. You try too. I love you, Val."

He looked at her in astonishment. That was a phrase that had never arisen between them. He had never imagined that it would. It was so long since he had last heard it that he couldn't remember who it was who had said it to him.

What now? Was he expected to say it too?

She was grinning. She wasn't expecting him to say anything. She knew him too well for that.

"Come here, doctor," she said. "I need some more intense examination."

Lawler glanced around to see if the infirmary door was locked. Then he went to her.

"Watch out for my blisters," she said.

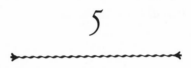

5

*T*HINGS LIKE GIANT PERISCOPES ROSE FROM THE SEA, GLISTENING stalks twenty meters high topped with five-sided blue polygons. From distances of half a kilometer or so they regarded the ship with a cool, unwavering gaze for hours. They were eye-stalks, obviously. But the eyes of what?

The periscopes slipped down into the water and didn't reappear. Next came great yawning mouths, vast creatures similar to those of the Home Sea, but even larger: large enough, it would seem, for them to swallow the *Queen of Hydros* at a single gulp. They too stayed at a distance, lighting up the sea day and night with their greenish phosphorescence. Mouths had never been known to create difficulties for ships on Hydros, but these were the mouths of the Empty Sea, capable of anything. The dark chasms of their open gullets were a threatening, troublesome sight.

The water itself grew phosphorescent. The effect was mild at first, just a little tingle of color, a faint charming glow. But then it intensified. At night the ship's wake was a line of fire across the sea. Even by day the waves looked fiery. The spray that occasionally broke across the rail had a bright sparkle.

There was a rain of stinging jellyfish. There was a display of madly frolicking divers, breaking the surface and leaping so high they seemed to be trying to take wing and fly. In one place something that looked like a collection of wooden poles tied together by a bundle of shabby cords came walking across the surface of the sea, with a tiny many-eyed globular creature in an open capsule at the center of it, as though traveling on stilts.

Then one morning Delagard, peering over the edge of the rail—he was constantly on patrol now, wary of attack from any quarter—reared back abruptly and cried out, "What the fuck? Kinverson, Gharkid, will you come here and look at this?"

Lawler joined the group. Delagard was pointing straight down. At first Lawler saw nothing unusual; but then he noticed that the ship had sprouted a skirt of some sort about twenty centimeters below the surface, an outgrowth of yellowish fibrous stuff that extended outward all along the hull for a distance of a meter or so. No, not a skirt, Lawler decided: more like a ledge, a woody shelf.

Delagard turned to Kinverson. "You ever see anything like that before?"

"Not me."

"You, Gharkid?"

"No, Captain-sir, never."

"Some sort of seaweed growing on us? A cross between a seaweed and a barnacle? What do you think, Gharkid?"

Gharkid shrugged. "It is a mystery to me, Captain-sir."

Delagard had a rope ladder flung over the rail and went over the side to inspect. Hanging from the ladder by one arm, dangling just above the surface of the water and leaning far out and down, he used a long-handled barnacle-scraper to prod at the strange excrescence. He came back up red-faced and cursing.

The problem, he said, was with the network of sea-finger weed that grew on the hull as a constantly self-repairing coating, protecting and reinforcing the ship's outer timbers. "Some local plant has hooked up with it. A related species, maybe. Or a symbiote. Whatever it is, it's clustering around the sea-finger, attaching itself as fast as it can, and it's growing like crazy. The shelf that's jutting out of us now is big enough already to be causing a perceptible drag. But if it keeps going at the rate it's expanding, in a couple of days we're going to find ourselves sealed in for good."

"What are we going to do about it?" Kinverson asked.

"You have any suggestions?"

"That somebody go out there in the water-strider and cut the damned stuff off while it can still be done."

Delagard nodded. "Good idea. I'll volunteer to take the first shift. Will you go with me?"

"Sure," Kinverson said. "Why not?"

Delagard and Kinverson climbed into the water-strider. Martello, operating the davits, lifted it and swung it far out past the rail, well beyond the new ledge, before lowering it to the surface of the water.

The trick was to pedal fast enough to keep the strider afloat, but not so fast that the man operating the barnacle-scraper would be unable to cut away the intrusive growths. That was hard to manage at first. Kinverson, holding the scraper, made the most of his long reach to lean over and chop at the ledge; but he took only a couple of strokes and then the strider went shooting past the place where he was working, and when they backed up and tried to hold it in one position for a longer time it began to lose lift and slip down into the water.

After a time they got the hang of it. Delagard pedaled, Kinverson chopped. When Kinverson became visibly weary they changed places, precariously creeping around the rocking vehicle until Delagard was in front and Kinverson was at the pedals.

"All right, next shift," Delagard called finally. He had been working with his usual manic zeal and he looked worn out. "Two more volunteers! Leo, did I hear you say you'd take the next turn? And was that you, Lawler?"

Pilya Braun worked the davits to lower Martello and Lawler over the side. The sea was fairly calm, but even so the flimsy strider bobbed and rocked constantly. Lawler imagined himself being flung out into the water by some unusually strong swell. When he looked down, he could see individual fibers of the invading sea-plant tossing on the swells just beyond the border of the shelf that had already formed. As the movements of the sea brought them against the side of the ship he was sure that he saw some of them affixing themselves to it.

He also could see small shining ribbony shapes coiling and writhing in the water. Worms, serpents, maybe eels. They looked quick and agile. Hoping for a snack, were they?

The ledge resisted chopping. Lawler had to grip the barnacle-scraper with both hands and ram it downward with all his strength. Often it slipped harmlessly aside, deflected by the toughness of the strange new growth. He nearly lost it altogether a couple of times.

"Hey!" Delagard yelled from above. "We don't have any of those things to spare!"

Lawler found a way of striking edge-on at a slight angle that allowed the scraper to get between individual strands of the fibrous mass. Chunk after huge chunk of the stuff now came loose and went drifting away. He fell into the rhythm of it, slicing and slicing. Sweat rolled down his skin. His arms and wrists began to protest. Pain spread upward toward his armpits, his chest, his shoulders. His heart pounded.

"Enough," he said to Martello. "Your turn, Leo."

Martello seemed tireless. He hacked away with a joyous vigor that Lawler found humiliating. He had thought he had done pretty well during his stint; but in Martello's first five minutes with the scraper he chopped away as much as Lawler had managed in his whole time. Lawler supposed that Martello even now was composing the Chopping Canto of his great epic in his head while he worked:

> Fiercely then we strained and strived
> Against the ever-growing foe.
> Valiantly did we smite its evil spread,
> Grimly did we strike and hack and cut—

Onyos Felk and Lis Niklaus went down next. After them it was the turn of Neyana and Sundira, and after them, Pilya and Gharkid.

"Fucking stuff grows as fast as we can cut," said Delagard sourly.

But they were making progress. Great chunks of the outgrowth were gone. In some places it had been cut back right to the original line of sea-finger weed.

The turn of Delagard and Kinverson came around once more. They chopped and slashed with diabolical fury. When they returned to the ship both men looked incandescent with exhaustion; they had passed beyond mere weariness into some transcendental state that left them glowing and exalted.

"Let's go, doc," Martello said. "It's us again."

Martello seemed determined to outdo even Kinverson. While Lawler kept the water-strider stabilized with a steady, numbing effort, Martello went after the vegetable enemy like some avenging god. Whack! Whack! Whack! He lifted the scraper high over his head, rammed it downward with a two-handed thrust, drove it deep. Whack! Whack! Huge sections of weed broke loose and floated away. Whack! Each stroke was mightier than the last. The water-strider tipped wildly from side to side. Lawler struggled to keep it upright. Whack! Whack!

Then Martello rose higher than ever before and brought the barnacle-scraper downward in a stroke of terrible force. It carved away an immense slab, clear back to the hull of the *Queen*. The stuff must have come away more easily than Martello was expecting: Martello lost first his balance and then his grip on the scraper's handle. He clawed at it, missed, and toppled forward, plunging with a heavy splash into the sea.

Lawler, still pedaling, leaned over and stretched out his hand. Martello was a couple of meters from the strider by now and flailing around desperately. But either he didn't see the reaching hand or he was too far gone in panic to understand what to do.

"Swim toward me!" Lawler called. "Over here, Leo! Here!"

Martello continued to thrash and flounder. His eyes were glazed with shock. Then he stiffened suddenly as if wounded by a dagger from below. He began to jerk convulsively.

The davits were out over the water now. Kinverson was dangling from them. "Lower," he ordered. "A little more. That's it. Over to the left. Good. Good."

He caught the struggling Martello under the arms and reeled him in as though he were a child.

"Now you, doc," Kinverson said.

"You can't lift us both!"

"Come on. Here."

Kinverson's other arm locked itself around Lawler's chest.

The davits rose. Swung inward over the rail, onto the deck. Lawler staggered free of Kinverson's grip, stumbled and pitched forward, landed hard on both his knees. Sundira was at his side at once to help him up.

Martello, dripping wet, lay face upward, limp and motionless.

"Keep back," Lawler ordered. He waved Kinverson away. "You too, Gabe."

"We got to turn him over and pump the water out of him, doc."

"It's not the water I'm worried about. Get back, Gabe." Lawler turned to Sundira. "You know where my bag of instruments is? The scalpels, and all? Bring it up on deck, will you?"

He knelt beside Martello and bared him to the waist. Martello was breathing, but he didn't seem to be conscious. His eyes were wide, expressionless, unseeing. Now and again his lips would draw back in a frightful writhing grimace of pain and his whole body would go rigid and jerk as though an electrical current had passed through him. Then he would go limp again.

Lawler put his hand on Martello's belly and pressed. He felt movement within: a trembling, a strange quivering, beneath the hard, tight band of abdominal muscle.

Something in there? Yes. This damnable ocean, invading wherever you gave it the slightest chance. But maybe it wasn't too late to save him, Lawler thought. Clean him out, seal the wound, keep the community from being diminished any further.

Shadows moved above him. Everyone was crowding in, staring. They looked fascinated and repelled, both at once.

Brusquely Lawler said, "Clear out, all of you. You won't want to see this. And I don't want you watching me."

No one moved.

"You heard the doctor," came Delagard's low growl. "Back off. Let him do his work."

Sundira put his medical kit down on the deck beside him.

Lawler touched Martello's abdomen again. Movement, yes. An unmistakable squirming. A quivering. Martello's face was flushed, his pupils were dilated, his eyes were staring into some other world entirely. Hot sweat ran from every pore.

Lawler drew his best scalpel from the bag and set it down on the deck. He put both his hands on Martello's abdomen just below the diaphragm and squeezed upward. Martello made a dull sighing sound, and a trickle of seawater and some vomit dribbled from his lips, but nothing else. Lawler tried again. Nothing. He felt motion again under his fingers: more spasms, more squirmings.

One more try. He turned Martello over and rammed his joined hands downward against the middle of Martello's back with all the strength he could find. Martello grunted. He spewed up some more thin puke. But that was all.

Lawler sat back for a moment, trying to think.

He turned Martello over again and picked up his scalpel.

"You won't want to see this," Lawler said to anyone who might be watching, without looking up, and drew a red line with the sharp iron point from left to right across Martello's abdomen. Martello barely seemed to notice. He made a soft blurry sound, the vaguest of comments. Other distractions were taking priority for him.

Skin. Muscle. The knife seemed to know where it had to go. Deftly Lawler stripped back the layers of tissue. He was cutting now through the peritoneum. He had trained himself to enter an altered state of consciousness whenever he performed surgery, in which he thought of himself as a sculptor, not as a surgeon, and of the patient as something inanimate, a wooden log, not a suffering human being. That was the only way he could bear the process at all.

Deeper. He had breached the restraining abdominal wall now. Blood mingled with the puddle of seawater around Martello on the deck.

The intestinal coils should come spilling out into view—

Yes. Yes. There they were.

Someone screamed. Someone uttered a grunt of disgust.

But not at the sight of the intestines. Something else was rising from Martello's belly, something slender and bright, slowly unreeling itself and standing up on end. Perhaps six centimeters of it was visible: eyeless, seemingly even headless, just a smooth, slippery pink strip of undifferentiated living matter. There was an opening at its top end, a mouth of sorts, through which a sharp little rasping red tongue could be seen. The supple shining creature moved with supernal grace, gliding from side to side in a hypnotic way. Behind Lawler the screaming went on and on.

He struck the thing with a quick, steady backhand flick of his scalpel that cut it neatly in half. The upper end landed on the deck next to Martello, writhing. It began heading toward Lawler. Kinverson's great boot descended at once and crushed it to slime.

"Thanks," Lawler said quietly.

But the other half was still inside. Lawler tried to coax it out with the scalpel's tip. It seemed untroubled by its bisecting; its dance continued, as graceful as before. Probing behind the heavy mound of intestines, Lawler struggled to dislodge it. He poked here, tugged there. He thought he saw the inner end of it and sliced at it, but there was more: another few centimeters still mocked him. He cut again. This time he had it all. He flipped it aside. Kinverson crushed it.

Everyone was silent now behind him.

He started to close the incision. But a new squirming motion made him stop.

Another one? Yes. Yes, one more, at least. Probably others. Martello groaned. He stirred slightly. Then he jerked with sudden force, rising a little way from the deck: Lawler got the scalpel out of the way just in time to keep from wounding him. A second eel rose into view and a third, weaving in that same eerie dance; then one of them pulled itself back in and disappeared once again into Martello's abdominal cavity, burrowing upward in the general direction of his lungs.

Lawler teased the other one out, cut it in half and in halves again, yanked the last bit of it free. He waited for the one that had gone back in to make itself visible again. After a moment he caught a glimpse of it, bright and gleaming within Martello's bloody midsection. But it wasn't the only one. He could see the slender coils of others, now, busily wriggling about, having themselves a feast. How many more were in there? Two? Three? Thirty?

He looked up, grim-faced. Delagard stared back at him. There was a look of shock and dismay and sheer revulsion in Delagard's eyes.

"Can you get them all out?"

"Not a chance. He's full of them. They're eating their way through him. I can cut and cut, and by the time I've found them all I'll have cut him to pieces, and I still won't have found them all, anyway."

"Jesus," Delagard murmured. "How long can he live this way?"

"Until one of them reaches his heart, I suppose. That won't be long."

"Can he feel anything, do you think?"

"I hope not," Lawler said.

THE AGONY WENT ON ANOTHER FIVE MINUTES. LAWLER HAD NEVER realized that five minutes could last so long. From time to time Martello would jump and twitch as some major nerve was struck; once he seemed to be trying to rise from the deck. Then he uttered a little sighing sound and fell back, and the light went out of his eyes.

"All over," Lawler announced. He felt numb, hollow, weary, beyond all grief, beyond all shock.

Probably, he thought, there had never been any chance to save Martello. At least a dozen of the eels must have entered him, very likely more, a horde of them gliding swiftly in through mouth or anus and burrowing diligently through flesh and muscle toward the center of his abdomen. Lawler had extracted nine of the things; but others were still lurking in there, at work on Martello's pancreas, his spleen, his liver, his kidneys. And when they were done with those, the delicacies, there was all the rest of him awaiting their little rasping red tongues. No surgery, no matter how speedily done or unerring, could have cleaned all of them out of him in time.

Neyana brought a blanket and they wrapped it about him. Kinverson gathered the body in his arms and moved toward the side with it.

"Wait," Pilya said. "Put this with him."

She held a sheaf of papers that she must have brought up from Martello's cabin. The famous poem. She tucked the worn and folded pages of the manuscript into the blanket and pulled its ends tight around the body. Lawler thought for a moment of objecting, but he checked himself. Let it go. It belonged with him.

Quillan said, "Now we commend our dearly beloved Leo to the sea, in the name of the Father, the Son, the Holy Ghost—"

The Holy Ghost again? Every time Lawler heard that odd phrase of Quillan's he was startled by it. It was such a strange concept: try as he might, he couldn't imagine what a holy ghost might be. He shook the thought away. He was too tired for such speculations now.

Kinverson carried the body to the rail and held it aloft. Then he gave it a little push and it went outward, downward, into the water.

Instantly creatures of some strange kind appeared as if by a conjuring spell from the depths, long slim finny swimmers covered in thick black silken fur. There were five of them, sinuous, gentle-eyed, with dark tapering snouts covered with twitching black bristles. Gently, tenderly, they surrounded Martello's drifting body and buoyed it up and began to unwrap the blanket that covered it. Tenderly, gently, they pulled it free. And then—gently, tenderly—they clustered around his stiffening form and set about the task of consuming him.

It was quietly done, no slovenly gluttonous frenzy. It was horrifying and yet eerily beautiful. Their motions stirred the sea to extraordinary phosphorescence. Martello seemed to be absorbed by a shower of cool crimson flame. Slowly he exploded in light. They made an anatomy lesson of him, peeling back the skin with utmost fastidiousness to reveal tendons, ligaments, muscles, nerves. Then they went deeper. It was a profoundly disturbing thing to watch, even for Lawler, to whom the inner secrets of the human body were no secret at all; but nevertheless the work was carried out so cleanly, so unhurriedly, so reverently, that it was impossible not to watch, or to fail to see the beauty in what they were doing. Layer by layer they put Martello's core on display, until at last only the white cage of bone remained. Then they looked up at the watchers at the rail as though for approval. There was the unmistakable glint of intelligence in their eyes. Lawler saw them nod in what could only have been a salute; and then they slipped out of sight as silently as they had come. Martello's clean skeleton had already disappeared, on its way to some unknown depth where, no doubt, other organisms were waiting to put its calcium to good use. Of the vital young man who had been Leo Martello nothing was left now except some pages of manuscript drifting on the surface of the water. And after a little while not even those could be seen.

Later, alone in his cabin, Lawler studied what was left of his numbweed supply. About two days' worth, he figured. He poured half of it into a flask and drank it down.

What the hell, he thought.

He drank the other half too. What the hell.

6

*T*HE WITHDRAWAL SYMPTOMS BEGAN THE MORNING AFTER NEXT, just before noon: the sweats, the shakes, the nausea. Lawler was ready for them, or thought he was. But they quickly grew more severe, far worse than he had expected, a test so tough he was unsure that he would pass it. The intensity of the pain, sweeping in on him in great billowing waves, frightened him. He imagined that he could feel his brain expanding, pressing against the walls of his skull.

Automatically he looked for his flask, but of course the flask was empty. He crouched on his bunk, shivering, feverish, miserable.

Sundira came to him in mid-afternoon.

"Is it what happened the other day?" she asked.

"Martello? No, that isn't it."

"Are you sick, then?"

He indicated the empty flask.

After a moment she understood. "Is there anything I can do, Val?"

"Hold me, that's all."

She cradled his head in her arms, against her breast. Lawler shook violently for a while. Then he grew calmer, though he still felt terrible.

"You seem better," she said.

"A little. Don't go away."

"I'm still here. Do you want some water?"

"Yes. No. No, just stay where you are." He nestled against her. He could feel the fever rising, falling, rising again, with sudden devastating velocity. The drug was more powerful than even he had suspected and his dependency evidently had been a very strong one. And yet—yet—the pain fluctuated; as the hours passed there were moments when he felt almost normal. That was odd. But it gave him hope. He didn't mind fighting if he had to, but he wanted to win in the end.

Sundira stayed with him all through the afternoon. He slept, and when he woke she was still there. His tongue felt swollen. He was too weak to stand.

"Did you know it would be like this?" she asked.

"Yes. I suppose I did. Maybe not quite this bad."

"How do you feel now?"

"It varies," Lawler said.

He heard a voice outside the door. "How is he?" Delagard.

"He's worried about you," Sundira said to Lawler.

"Very thoughtful of him."

"I told him you were sick."

"Not going into details?"

"No details, no."

THE NIGHT WAS A TERRIFYING ONE. LAWLER THOUGHT FOR A TIME THAT he would go out of his mind. But then in the small hours came another of those unexpected, inexplicable periods of recovery, as though something were reaching into his brain from afar and tuning down the craving for the drug. By dawn he felt his appetite return; and when he stood up—it was the first time he had risen from his bunk since the fever had started—he was able to keep his balance.

"You look okay," Sundira told him. "Are you?"

"More or less. The bad stuff will come back. This is going to be a long struggle."

But when it did come back it was less severe than it had been. Lawler was at a loss to explain the change. He had expected three, four, even five days of utter horror and then perhaps a gradual sloping off of the torment as his system gradually purged itself of the need. This was only the second day, though.

Again that sense of intervention from without, something guiding him, lifting him, pulling him free of the morass.

Then the tremors and sweats again. And then another spell of recovery, lasting nearly half a day. He went up on deck, enjoyed the fresh air, walked slowly around. Lawler told Sundira that he felt he was getting off too easy.

"Count your blessings," she said.

By nightfall he was sick again. On, off: up, down. But the basic trend was favorable. He seemed to be recovering. By the end of the week there were only occasional moments of discomfort. He looked at the empty flask and grinned.

THE AIR WAS CLEAR, THE WIND WAS STRONG. THE QUEEN OF HYDROS sped onward at a steady swift rate, following its southwesterly track around the watery globe.

The sea's phosphorescence increased in intensity day by day, even hour by hour. The whole world began to look luminous. Water and sky glowed day and night. Nightmarish creatures of half a dozen unfamiliar kinds burst from the water to soar briefly overhead and disappear with great splashes in the distance. Huge mouths yawned in the depths.

Silence reigned much of the time aboard the *Queen*. Everyone moved quietly and efficiently through his chores. There was much to do, for now only eleven remained to do the work that fourteen had performed at the beginning of the voyage. Martello, lighthearted, cheery, optimistic, had done much to set the tone for the rest: his death inevitably altered things.

But also the Face was growing nearer. That must have something to do with the newly somber mood, Lawler thought. It was impossible yet to see it on the horizon, but everyone knew it was there, not far away. Everyone felt it. It was a real presence on board. Its effects were indefinable but unmistakable. Something was there, Lawler found himself thinking, something more than a mere island. Something alert and aware. Waiting for them.

He shook his head, trying to clear it. These were nonsensical fantasies, feverish nightmare horrors, insubstantial, foolish. The drug withdrawal must still be operating on him, he told himself. He was wobbly, weary, vulnerable.

The Face continued to occupy his mind. He struggled to remember the things Jolly had told him about it long ago, but everything was vague and muddled under thirty years' layers of memories. A wild and fantastic place, Jolly had said. Full of plants unlike the ones that grew in the sea. Plants, yes. Strange colors, bright lights shining day and night, a weird realm at the far edge of the world, beautiful and eerie. Had Jolly said anything about animals, land-dwelling creatures of any sort? No, nothing that Lawler could recall. No animal life, just thick jungles.

But there was something about a city, too—

Not *on* the Face. *Near* it.

Where? In the ocean? The image eluded him. He struggled to recapture the times he had spent with Jolly, down by the water, the leathery-faced sun-darkened old man rocking back and forth, casting his fishing lines, talking, talking—

A city. A city in the sea. *Under* the sea.

Lawler caught the tip of the recollection, felt it slip away, lunged for it, could not get it, lunged again—

A city under the sea. Yes. A doorway in the ocean opening into a passageway, a gravity funnel of some sort, leading downward to a tremendous underwater city where Gillies lived, a hidden city of Gillies as superior to the island-dwelling ones as kings are to peasants—Gillies living like gods, never coming up to the surface, sealed away under the sea in pressurized vaults, living in solemn majesty and absolute luxury—

Lawler smiled. That was it, yes. A grand fable, a glorious fantasy. The finest, most flamboyant of all Jolly's tales. He could remember trying to imagine what that city had been like, envisioning tall, stately, infinitely majestic Gillies moving through lofty archways into shining palatial halls. Thinking about it now, he felt like a boy again, crouching in wonder at the old seaman's feet, straining to hear the hoarse, rasping voice.

FATHER QUILLAN HAD BEEN THINKING ABOUT THE FACE, TOO.

"I have a new theory about it," he announced.

The priest had spent an entire morning meditating, sitting beside Gharkid in the gantry area. Lawler, going past them, had stared in wonder. The two of them had seemed lost in trances. Their souls might have been on some other plane of existence entirely.

"I've changed my mind," said Quillan. "You remember I told you before that I thought the Face had to be Paradise and God Himself walked there, the First Cause, the actual Creator, He to whom we address all our prayers. Well, I don't feel that way any more."

"All right," Lawler said, indifferently. "The Face isn't God's vaargh, then. If you say so. You know more about these things than I do."

"Not God's vaargh, no. But definitely *some* god's vaargh. This is the exact reverse of my original notion about the island, you see. And of everything I have ever believed about the nature of the Divine. I begin to drop into the greatest heresy. I become a polytheist at this late stage in my life. A pagan! It seems absurd even to me. And yet I embrace it with all my heart."

"I don't understand. A god, *the* god—what's the difference? If you can believe in one god, you can believe in any number of them, as far as I can see. The trick is to believe in as many as one, and I can't even get that far."

Quillan gave him a loving smile. "You really don't understand, do you? The classical Christian tradition, which derives from Judaism and for all we know from something out of ancient Egypt, holds that God is a single indivisible entity. I've never questioned that. I've never even *thought* of questioning that. We Christians speak of Him as a Trinity, but we are aware that the Trinity is One. That may seem confusing to an unbeliever, but we know what it means. No dispute about it: one God, only one. Just in the past few days, though—the last few hours, even—" The priest paused. "Let me make use of a mathematical analogy. Do you know what Gödel's Theorem is?"

"No."

"Well, neither do I, not exactly. But I can give you an approximation of it. It's a twentieth-century idea, I think. What Gödel's Theorem asserts, and nobody has ever been able to disprove it, is that there's a fundamental limit to the rational reach of mathematics. We can prove all the assumptions of mathematical reasoning down to a certain bed-rock point, and then we hit a level where we simply can't go any farther. Ultimately we find that we've descended beyond the process of mathematical proof to a realm of unprovable axioms, things that simply have to be taken on faith if we're to make any sense out of the universe. What we reach is the boundary of reason. In order to go beyond it—in order to go on thinking at all, really— we are compelled to accept our defining axioms as true, even though we can't prove them. Are you following me?"

"I think so."

"All right. What I propose is that Gödel's Theorem marks the dividing line between gods and mortals."

"Really," Lawler said.

"This is what I mean," said Quillan. "It sets a boundary for *human* reasoning. The gods occupy the far side of that boundary. Gods, by definition, are creatures who aren't bound by the Gödel limits. We humans live in a world where reality ultimately breaks down into irrational assumptions, or at least assumptions that are non-rational because they're unprovable. Gods live in a realm of absolutes where realities are not only fixed and knowable down beyond the level of our axiomatic floor, but can be redefined and reshaped by divine control."

For the first time in this discussion Lawler felt a flicker of interest. "The galaxy is full of beings which aren't human, but their math isn't any better than ours, is it? Where do they fit your scheme?"

"Let's define all intelligent beings who are subject to the Gödel limitations as human, regardless of their actual species. And any beings that are capable of functioning in an ultra-Gödelian realm of logic are gods."

Lawler nodded. "Go on."

"Now let me introduce the concept that came to me this morning when I was sitting up there thinking about the Face of the Waters. This actually is the blackest heresy, I admit. But I've been heretical before, and survived it. Though not *this* heretical." Again Quillan smiled beatifically. "Let us suppose that the gods themselves at some point must reach a Gödel limit, a place where their own reasoning powers—that is, their powers of creation and re-creation—run up against some kind of barrier. Like us, but on a qualitatively different plane, they eventually come to a point at which they can go thus far, and no farther."

"The ultimate limit of the universe," Lawler said.

"No. Just *their* ultimate limit. It may well be that there are greater gods beyond them. The gods we're talking about are encapsulated just as we mortals are within a larger reality defined by a different mathematics to which they have no access. They look upward to the next reality and the next level of gods. And those gods—that is, the inhabitants of that larger reality—also have a Gödel wall around them, with even greater gods outside it. And so on and so on and so on."

Lawler felt dizzy. "To infinity?"

"Yes."

"But don't you define a god as something that's infinite? How can an infinite thing be smaller than infinity?"

"An infinite set may be contained within an infinite set. An infinite set may contain an infinity of infinite subsets."

"If you say so," replied Lawler, a little restless now. "But what does this have to do with the Face?"

"If the Face is a true paradise, unspoiled and virgin—a domain of the holy spirit—then it may very well be occupied by superior entities, beings of great purity and power. What we of the church once called angels. Or gods, as those of older faiths might have said."

Be patient, Lawler thought. The man takes these things seriously.

He said, "And these superior beings, angels, gods, whatever term we choose to use—these are the local post-Gödelian geniuses, do I have it right? Gods, to us. Gods to the Gillies, too, since the Face seems to be a holy place for them. But not God Himself, God Almighty, your god, the one that your church worships, the prime creator of the Gillies and us and everything else in the universe. You won't find him around here, at least not very often. That god is higher up along the scale of things. He doesn't live on any one particular planet. He's up above somewhere in a higher realm, a larger universe, looking down, checking up occasionally on how things are going here."

"Exactly."

"But even he isn't all the way at the top?"

"There is no top," Quillan said. "There's only an ever-retreating ladder of Godhood, ranging from the hardly-more-than-mortal to the utterly unfathomable. I don't know where the inhabitants of the Face are located on the ladder, but very likely it's somewhere at a point higher than the one we occupy. It's the whole ladder that is God Almighty. Because God is infinite, there can be no one level of godhood, but only an eternally ascending chain; there is no Highest, merely Higher and Higher and Even Higher, ad infinitum. The Face is some intermediate level on that chain."

"I see," said Lawler uncertainly.

"And by meditating on these things, one can begin to perceive the higher infinities, even though by definition we can never perceive the Highest of all, since to do that we'd have to be greater than the greatest of infinities." Quillan looked toward the heavens and spread his arms wide in a gesture that was almost self-mocking. But then he turned to Lawler and said in an entirely different tone of voice from the one he had used a moment before, "At last, doc, I've come to an understanding of why I failed in the priesthood. I must have been aware all along that the God I was looking for, the One Supreme Entity who watches over us, is utterly unattainable. So far as we're concerned He doesn't in fact exist. Or if He does, He exists in a region so far removed from our existence that He might just as well not exist at all. Now finally I understand that I need to go looking for a lesser god, one who's closer to our own level of awareness. For the first time, Lawler, I see the possibility that I can find some comfort in this life."

"What kind of bullshit are you two discussing?" said Delagard, who had come up behind them.

"Theological bullshit," Quillan said.

"Ah. Ah. A new revelation?"

"Sit down," said the priest. "I'll tell you all about it."

INFLAMED BY THE LOGIC OF HIS NEW REVELATION, QUILLAN WENT about the ship offering to share it with anyone who would listen. But he found few takers.

Gharkid seemed the most interested. Lawler had always suspected that the strange little man had a deep streak of mysticism in him; and now, enigmatic as always, Gharkid could be seen sitting with shining eyes in a pose of the deepest attention, drinking in everything that the priest had to say. But as ever Gharkid had no comments of his own to offer, only the occasional soft query.

Sundira spent an hour with Quillan and came to Lawler afterward looking puzzled and thoughtful. "The poor man," she said. "A paradise. Holy spirits walking around in the underbrush, offering benedictions to pilgrims. All these weeks at sea must have driven him out of his mind."

"If he was ever in it in the first place."

"He wants so badly to give himself over to something bigger and wiser than he is. He's been chasing God all his life. But I think he's really just trying to find his way back to the womb."

"What a terribly cynical thing to say."

"Isn't it, though?" Sundira laid her head on Lawler's lap. "What do you think? Did any of that mathematical mumbo-jumbo make any sense to you? Or the theology? Paradise? An island of holy spirits?"

He stroked her thick, dark hair. The weeks and months of the voyage had coarsened its texture, giving it a crisped, frizzled look. But it was still beautiful.

He said, "A certain amount. At least I can understand the metaphor he's using. But it doesn't matter, do you know? Not to me. There could be an infinity of distinct layers of gods in the universe, each one with exactly sixteen times as many eyes as the ones in the layer below it, and Quillan could have absolute irrefutable proof of the existence of the whole elaborate rigmarole, and it wouldn't mean a thing to me. I live in this world, and only in this world, and there aren't any gods here. What might be happening in the higher levels, if there are any, doesn't concern me."

"That doesn't mean the higher levels don't exist."

"No. I suppose you're right. Who knows? The old sailor who told us all about the Face in the first place also had some wild story about an underwater city of super-Dwellers just offshore. I can believe that just as easily as I can all of Quillan's theological hodge-podge, I guess. But in fact I can't believe any of it. One notion's just as crazy as the other to me."

She craned her head around to look at him. "But let's say for argument's sake that there really is a city under the sea not far from the Face, and some special kind of Dwellers live there. If that's so, it would explain why the Dwellers we know regard the Face as a holy island, and are afraid or at least unwilling to go near it. What if there *are* god-like beings living there?"

"Let's wait and see what's there when we get there, and then I'll give you an answer to that, okay?"

"Okay," Sundira said.

HALFWAY THROUGH THE NIGHT LAWLER FOUND HIMSELF SUDDENLY awake, in that kind of hyper-wakefulness that is certain to last until dawn. He sat up, rubbing his aching forehead. He felt as though someone had opened his skull while he slept and filled it with a million bright strands of fine shimmering wire, which now were rubbing back and forth against each other with every breath he took.

Someone was in his cabin. By the faint gleam of starlight that came through his single porthole he saw a tall square-shouldered figure against the bulkhead, quietly watching him. Kinverson? No, not quite big enough for Kinverson, and why would Kinverson invade his cabin in the dead of night anyway? But none of the other men on board were nearly this tall.

"Who's there?" Lawler said.

"Don't you know me, Valben?" A deep voice, resonant, wonderfully calm and self-assured.

"Who are you?"

"Take a good look, boy." The intruder turned so that the side of his face was in the light. Lawler saw a strong jaw, a thick, curling black beard, a straight, commanding nose. Except for the beard the face could have been his own. No, the eyes were different. They had a powerful gleam; their gaze was at once more stern and more compassionate than Lawler's. He knew that look. A shiver went down his back.

"I thought I was awake," he said calmly. "But now I see that I'm still dreaming. Hello, Father. It's good to see you again. It's been a long time."

"Has it? Not for me." The tall man took a couple of steps toward him. In the tiny cabin, that brought him practically to the edge of the bunk. He was wearing a dark ruffled robe of an old-fashioned kind, a robe that Lawler remembered well. "It must have been a while, though. You're all grown up, boy. You're older than I am, aren't you?"

"About the same, now."

"And a doctor. A good doctor, I hear."

"Not really. I do my best. It isn't good enough."

"Your best is always good enough, Valben, if it's truly your best. I used to tell you that, but I suppose you didn't believe me. So long as you don't shirk, so long as you honestly care. A doctor can be an absolute bastard off duty, but so long as he cares he's all right. So long as he understands that he's put here to protect, to heal, to love. And I think you understood that." He sat down on the corner of the bunk. He seemed very much at home. "You didn't have a family, did you?"

"No, sir."

"Too bad. You'd have been a good father."

"Would I?"

"It would have changed you, of course. But for the better, I think. Do you regret it?"

"I don't know. Probably. I regret a lot of things. I regret that my marriage went bad. I regret that I never married again. I regret that you died too soon, Father."

"Was it too soon?"

"For me it was."

"Yes. Yes, I suppose it was."

"I loved you."

"And I loved you too, boy. I still do. I love you very much. I'm very proud of you."

"You talk as though you're still alive. But this is all only a dream: you can say anything you like, can't you?"

The figure rose and stepped back into the darkness. It seemed to cloak itself in shadows.

"It isn't a dream, Valben."

"No? Well, then. You're dead, even so, Father. You've been dead twenty-five years. If this isn't a dream, why are you here? If you're a ghost, why did you wait until now to start haunting me?"

"Because you've never been this close to the Face before."

"What does the Face have to do with you or me?"

"I dwell in the Face, Valben."

Despite himself, Lawler laughed. "That's a thing that a Gillie would say. Not you."

"It isn't only Gillies that are taken to dwell in the Face, boy."

The flat, quiet, appalling statement hung in the air like a miasmic cloud. Lawler recoiled from it. He was starting to understand, now. Anger began to rise in him.

He gestured irritably at the phantom.

"Get out of here. Let me have some sleep."

"What way is that to talk to your father?"

"You aren't my father. You're either a very bad dream or a lying illusion coming from some telepathic sea urchin or dragon fish out there in the ocean. My father would never have said a thing like that. Not even if he came back as a ghost, which is also something he wouldn't have done. Haunting wasn't his style. Go away and leave me alone!"

"Valben, Valben, Valben!"

"What do you want with me? Why won't you leave me alone?"

"Valben, boy—"

Lawler realized suddenly that he could no longer see the tall shadowy figure.

"Where are you?"

"Everywhere around you, and nowhere."

Lawler's head was throbbing. Something was churning in his stomach. He groped in the dark for his numbweed flask. After a moment he remembered that it was empty.

"*What* are you?"

"I am the resurrection and the life. He that believeth in me, though he were dead, yet shall he live."

"No!"

"God save thee, ancient Mariner! From the fiends, that plague thee thus!—"

"This is lunacy! Stop it! Get out of here! Out!" Trembling now, Lawler searched for his lamp. Light would drive this thing away. But before he could locate it he felt a sudden sharp sense of new solitude and realized that the vision, or whatever it had been, had left him of its own accord.

Its departure left an unexpected ringing emptiness behind.

Lawler felt its absence as a shock, like that of an amputation. He sat for a time at the edge of his bunk, shivering, sweat-soaked, shaking as he had shaken during the worst of his period of withdrawal from the drug.

Then he rose. Sleep wasn't likely now. He went up on deck. A couple of moons were overhead, stained strange purples and greens by the luminescence that rose out of the western horizon and now seemed to fill the air all the time. The Hydros Cross itself, hanging off in the corner of the sky like a bit of discarded finery, was pulsing in color too, something Lawler had never seen before: from its two great arms came booming, dizzying swirls of turquoise, amber, scarlet, ultramarine.

Nobody seemed to be on duty. The sails were set, the ship was responding to a light steady breeze, but the deck looked empty. Lawler felt a quick stab of terror at that. The first watch should be on duty: Pilya, Kinverson, Gharkid, Felk, Tharp. Where were they? Even the wheel-box was untended. Was the ship steering itself?

Apparently so. And steering off course, too. Last night, he remembered now, the Cross had been off the port bow. Now it was lined up with the beam. They were no longer going west-southwest, but had swung around at a sharp angle to their former path.

He tiptoed around the deck, mystified. When he came by the rear mast he saw Pilya asleep on a pile of ropes, and Tharp nearby, snoring. Delagard would flay them if he knew. A little farther on was Kinverson, sitting against the side with his back to the rail. His eyes were open, but he didn't seem awake either.

"Gabe?" Lawler said quietly. He knelt and waggled his fingers back and forth in front of Kinverson's face. No response. "Gabe, what's going on? Are you hypnotized?"

"He's resting," came the voice of Onyos Felk suddenly, from behind. "Don't bother him. It was a busy night. We were hauling sail for hours and hours. But look now, there's the land, dead ahead. We're moving very nicely toward it."

Land? When did anyone ever speak of land, on Hydros?

"What are you talking about?" Lawler asked.

"There. Do you see it?"

Felk gestured vaguely toward the bow. Lawler looked forward and saw nothing, just the vastness of the luminous sea, and a clear horizon marked only by a few low stars and a sprawling, heavy cloud at middle height. The dark backdrop of the sky seemed weirdly ablaze, a frightful aurora fiercely blazing. There was color everywhere, bizarre color, a fantastic show of strange light. But no land.

"In the night," said Felk, "the wind shifted, and turned us toward it. What an incredible sight it is! Those mountains! Those tremendous valleys! Would you ever have believed it, doc? The Face of the Waters!" Felk seemed about to burst into tears. "All my life, staring at my sea-charts, seeing that dark mark on the far hemisphere, and now we're looking it right in the eye—the Face, doc, the Face itself!"

Lawler pulled his arms close against his sides. In the tropic warmth of the night he felt a sudden chill.

He still saw nothing at all, only the endless roll of the empty water.

"Listen, Onyos, if Delagard comes on deck early and finds your whole watch sleeping, you know what's going to happen. For God's sake, if you won't wake them up, I will!"

"Let them sleep. By morning we'll be at the Face."

"What Face? Where?"

"There, man! There!"

Lawler still didn't see. He strode forward. When he reached the bow he found Gharkid, the one missing member of the watch, sitting crosslegged, perched on top of the forecastle with his head thrown back and his eyes wide and staring like two orbs of glass. Like Kinverson he was in some other state of awareness entirely.

Bewilderedly Lawler peered into the night. The dazzling maze of colors danced before him, but he still saw only clear water and empty sky ahead. Then something changed. It was as though his vision had been clouded, and now at last it had cleared. It seemed to him that a section of the sky had detached itself and come down to the water's surface and was moving about in an intricate way, folding and refolding upon itself until it looked like a sheaf of crumpled paper, and then like a bundle of sticks, and then like a mass of angry serpents, and then like pistons driven by some invisible engine. A writhing interwoven network of some incomprehensible substance had sprung up along the horizon. It made his eyes ache to watch it.

Felk came up alongside him.

"Now do you see? Now?"

Lawler realized that he had been holding his breath a long while. He let it out slowly.

Something that felt like a breeze, but was something else, was blowing toward his face. He knew it couldn't be a breeze, for he could feel the wind also, blowing from the stern, and when he glanced up at the sails he saw them bellying outward behind him. Not a breeze, no. An emanation. A force. A radiation. Aimed at him. He felt it crackling lightly through the air, felt it striking his cheeks like fine wind-blown hail in a winter storm. He stood without moving, assailed by awe and fear.

"Do you see?" Felk said again.

"Yes. Yes, now I do." He turned to face the mapkeeper. By the strange light that was bursting upon them from the west Felk's face seemed painted, goblinish. "You'd better wake up your watch, anyway. I'm going to go down below and get Delagard. For better or for worse, he's brought us this far. He doesn't deserve to miss the moment of our arrival."

7

>——————————————◄

*I*N THE WANING DARKNESS LAWLER IMAGINED THAT THE SEA THAT lay before them was retreating swiftly, pulling back as though it were being peeled away, leaving a bare, bewildering sandy waste between the ship and the Face. But when he looked again he saw the shining waters as they had always been.

Then a little while later dawn arrived, bringing with it strange new sounds and sights: breakers visible, the crisp slap of wavelets against the bow, a line of tossing luminous foam in the distance. By the first gray light Lawler found it impossible to make out more than that. There was land ahead, not very far, but he was unable to see it. All was uncertain here. The air seemed thick with mist that would not burn off even as the sun moved higher. Then abruptly he became aware of the great dark barrier that lay across the horizon, a low hump that might almost have been the coastline of a Gillie island, except that there weren't any Gillie islands the size of this one on Hydros. It stretched before them from one end of the world to the other, walling off the sea, which thundered and crashed against it in the distance but could not impose its strength on it in any way.

Delagard appeared. He stood trembling on the bridge, face thrust forward, hands gripping the rail in eerie fervor.

"There it is!" he cried. "Did you believe me or didn't you? There's the Face at last! Look at it! *Look* at it!"

It was impossible not to feel awe. Even the dullest and simplest of the voyagers—Neyana, say, or Pilya, or Gharkid—seemed moved by its en-croaching presence, by the strangeness of the landscape ahead, by the power of the inexplicable psychic emanations that came in pulsing waves from the Face. All eleven of the voyagers stood arrayed side by side on deck, nobody bothering to sail or to steer, staring in stunned silence as the ship drifted toward the island as if caught in some powerful magnetic grip.

Only Kinverson appeared, if not untouched, then at least unshaken. He had awakened from his trance. Now he too was staring fixedly at the approaching shore. His craggy face seemed riven by strong emotion of some sort. But when Dag Tharp turned to him and asked him if he was afraid at all, Kinverson replied with a blank look, as if the question had no meaning for him, and a flat incurious glare, as though he felt no need to have it explained.

"Afraid?" he said. "No. Should I be?"

The constant motion of everything on the island struck Lawler as its most bewildering aspect. Nothing was at rest. Whatever vegetation lay along its shore, if vegetation was indeed what it was, appeared to be in a process of intense, dynamic, churning growth. There was no stillness anywhere. There were no recognizable patterns of topography. Everything was moving, everything was writhing, flailing, weaving itself into the tangled web of shimmering substance and unweaving itself again, whip-ping about in a ceaseless lunatic dance of exhausting energy that might well have been going on this way since the beginning of time.

Sundira came up alongside Lawler and laid her hand gently on his bare shoulder. They stood facing outward, scarcely daring even to breathe.

"The colors," she said softly. "The electricity."

It was a fantastic display. Light was constantly born from every milli-meter of surface. Now it was a pure white, now a brilliant red, now the deepest of violets, verging on impenetrable black. And then came colors Lawler could barely name. They were gone before he could comprehend them, and others just as potent came in their place.

It was light that had the quality of vast noise: it was an explosion, a terrible din, a flashing, pounding dazzle. The overwhelming energy of it had a perverse, demented vigor: such fury could hardly be sane. Phantasmal eruptions of cold flame danced and gleamed and vanished and were re-placed. One could not dwell on the same part of it very long; the force of those violent bursts of color forced the eye away. Even when you didn't look, Lawler thought, it pounded insistently at your brain all the same. The place was like an immense radio device that sent forth an inexorable broadcast on the biosensory wavelengths. He could feel its emanation probing him, touching his mind, slithering around inside his skull like invisible fingers caressing his soul.

He stood motionless, shivering, his arm around Sundira's waist, all his muscles clenched from scalp to toes.

Then, cutting through the crazed blazing brilliance, there came something just as violent, just as demented, but much more familiar: the voice of Nid Delagard, transformed now into something raw and harsh and weirdly rigid, but recognizable even so. "All right, back to your posts, all of you! We've got work to do!"

Delagard was panting in strange excitement. His face had a dark, stormy look, as though some private tempest was roiling his soul. In an odd frantic way he moved along the deck among them, roughly seizing them one by one, swinging them around bodily to get their eyes off the Face.

"Turn away! Turn away! That cockeyed light'll hypnotize you if you give it the chance!"

Lawler felt Delagard's fingers digging into the flesh of his upper arms. He yielded to the tugging and let Delagard pull him away from the astonishing sight across the water.

"You've got to force yourself not to look," Delagard said. "Onyos, take the wheel! Neyana, Pilya, Lawler, let's get those sails to the wind! We need to find ourselves a harbor."

SAILING WITH SLITTED EYES, WORKING HARD TO AVERT THEIR GAZE from the incomprehensible display that was erupting before them, they cruised along its turbulent shore seeking some cove or bay where they might find shelter. At first it seemed that there was none. The Face was one long headland, impenetrable, unwelcoming.

Then the ship swept unexpectedly through the line of breakers and found itself in calm waters, a placid bay encircled by two jutting limbs of the island rimmed by steep hills. But the placidity was deceptive and short-lived. Within moments of their arrival the bay began to heave and swell. In the churning water thick black strands of what might have been kelp rose into view, flailing the surface like the dark limbs of monsters, and spiky spear-like protrusions appeared menacingly between them, emitting clouds of sinister radiant yellow smoke. Convulsions of the land seemed to be taking place along the shore.

Lawler, exhausted, began to imagine images, mysterious, abstract, tantalizing. Unfamiliar shapes danced in his mind. He felt a maddening unreachable itch behind his forehead and pressed his hands to his temples, but it did no good.

Delagard paced the deck, brooding, muttering. After a time he gave orders to swing the ship around and took it out beyond the breakers again. As soon as they had left the bay it grew calm. It looked as tempting as it had before.

"Do we try again?" Felk asked.

"Not now," said Delagard dourly. His eyes flashed with cold anger. "Maybe this isn't a good place. We'll move along westward."

The coast to the west was unpromising: rough and wild and steep. A crisp acrid odor of combustion drifted on the wind. Flaming sparks floated upward from the land. The air itself seemed to be burning. Occasional waves of overpowering telepathic force came drifting toward them from the island, short sudden jolts that caused mental confusion and disarray. The midday sun was bloated and discolored. There appeared to be no inlets anywhere. After a time Delagard, who had gone below, reappeared and announced in a tight, bitter voice that he was abandoning, for the moment, his attempts to make a closer approach.

They retreated to a point well beyond the churning surf, where the sea was flat and shallow, streaming with colors that rose from a bed of glistening sand. There they cast anchor for the second time since the beginning of the voyage.

Lawler found Delagard at the rail, staring into the distance.

"Well? What do you think of your paradise now, Nid? Your land of milk and honey?"

"We'll find a way in. We just came on it from the wrong side, that's all."

"You *want* to land there?"

Delagard turned to face him. His bloodshot eyes, strangely transformed by the clashing light all around them, seemed to be dead, utterly without life. But when he spoke, his voice was as strong as ever. "Nothing that I've seen so far has changed my mind about anything, doc. This is the place I want to be. Jolly was able to make a landfall here, and so will we."

Lawler made no reply. There wasn't anything he could think of to say that wasn't likely to trigger an explosion of insane wrath in Delagard.

But then he grinned and leaned forward and clapped his hand to Lawler's shoulder amiably. "Doc, doc, doc, don't look so solemn! Of course this is a weird-looking place. Of course. Why else would the Gillies have kept away from it all this time? And of course the stuff that comes wafting out of there feels strange to us. We simply aren't used to it. But that doesn't mean we need to be afraid of it. This is just a fancy bunch of visual effects. Just decorations, just trimming on the package. They don't mean a thing. Not a fucking thing."

"I'm glad you're so sure of yourself."

"Yes. So am I. Listen, doc, have faith. We're almost there. We've made it this far, and we're going to go the rest of the way. There's nothing to worry about." He grinned again. "Look, doc, relax, will you? I found a little of Gospo's brandy hidden away last night. Come on down to my cabin in an hour or so. Everyone will be there. We'll have a party. We're going to celebrate our arrival."

LAWLER WAS THE LAST TO ARRIVE. BY CANDLELIGHT IN THE DARK cramped musky-smelling room they were all grouped in a rough semicircle around Delagard, Sundira to his left, Kinverson just on the other side of her, Neyana and Pilya beyond, then Gharkid, Quillan, Tharp, Felk, Lis. Everyone had a cup of brandy. An empty flask and two full ones were on the table. Delagard stood facing them with his back pressed up against the bulwark and his head drawn down into his shoulders in a peculiar way that seemed both defensive and aggressive at the same time. He looked possessed. His eyes were bright, almost feverish. His face, stubbly and pocked with some irritation of the skin, was flushed and sweaty. It struck Lawler suddenly that the man was on the verge of some kind of crisis: an inner eruption, a violent explosion, the release of pent-up emotion that had been too long in storage.

"Have a drink, doc," Delagard called.

"Thanks. I will. I thought we were out of this stuff."

"I thought so too," said Delagard. "I was wrong." He poured until the cup overflowed, and shoved it along the table toward Lawler. "So you remembered Jolly's story about the undersea city, eh?"

Lawler took a deep gulp of the brandy and waited until it had hit bottom.

"How did you know that?"

"Sundira told me. She said you talked to her about it."

With a shrug Lawler said, "It came floating back into my mind out of nowhere yesterday. I hadn't thought about it in years. The best part of Jolly's story, and I'd forgotten it."

"But I hadn't," Delagard said. "I was just telling the others, while we were waiting for you to come down. What do you think, doc? Was Jolly full of shit or wasn't he?"

"An underwater city? How would that be possible?"

"Gravity funnel, that's what I remember Jolly saying. Super-technology. Achieved by super-Gillies." Delagard rotated his cup, rolling the brandy around in it. He was well on his way toward being drunk, Lawler realized. "I always liked that story of his best of all, just like you," Delagard said. "How the Gillies, half a million years ago, decided to go live under the ocean. There was some landmass on this planet, that's what they told Jolly, remember? Fair-sized islands, small continents, even, and they dismantled most of that and used the material to build sealed chambers at the deep end of their gravity tunnel. And when they had everything ready they moved down below and shut the door behind them."

"And you believe this?" Lawler asked.

"Probably not. It's pretty wild stuff. But it's a nice story, isn't it, doc? An advanced race of Gillies down there, the bosses of the planet. Leaving their country cousins behind on the floating islands, serfs and peasants who run the upper world for them as a farm to provide them with food. And all the life-forms on Hydros, the island Gillies and mouths and platforms and divers and hagfish and everything else, right down to the crawlie-oysters and the raspers, are tied together in one big ecological web whose sole purpose is to serve the needs of the ones who live in the undersea city. The island Gillies believe that when they die they come here to live on the Face. Ask Sundira if you don't believe me. That must mean that they hope to go down below and live a soft life in the hidden city. Maybe the divers believe that too. And the crawlie-oysters."

"An old man's crazy fable, this city," Lawler said. "A myth."

"Maybe so. Or maybe not." Delagard offered him a cool, taut smile. His self-control was frightening in its intensity, unreal, ominous. "But let's say it isn't. What we saw this morning—this whole incredible jimbo-jambo of whirling, dancing God-knows-what—might in fact be a huge biological machine that provides the energy for the secret Gillie city. The plants that grow over there are metal. I'll bet that they are. They're parts of the machine. They've got their roots in the sea and they extract minerals and create new tissues out of them. And perform all sorts of mechanical functions. And what's on that island somewhere, maybe, is a gigantic electrical grid. In the middle of it, I'll bet, there's a solar collector, an accumulator disk that pulls in energy that all that semiliving wiring over there is pumping down to the submerged city. What we've been feeling is the surplus force of it all. It comes crackling through the air and fucks up our minds. Or would, if we let it. But we aren't going to let it. We're smart enough to stay out of its grip. What we're going to do is sail right along the coast at a safe distance until we come to the entrance to the hidden city, and then—"

Lawler said, "You're moving too fast, Nid. You say that you don't think the undersea city is anything more than an old man's fantasy, and all of a sudden you're at its entrance."

Delagard looked unfazed. "I'm just assuming it's real. For the sake of the conversation. Have some more brandy, doc. This is the last of it for sure. We might as well enjoy it all at once."

"Assuming it's real," said Lawler, "how are you going to build the great city you were talking about here, when the place is already in possession of a bunch of super-Gillies? Aren't they going to get a little annoyed? Assuming they exist."

"I imagine they will. Assuming they exist."

"Then aren't they likely to call in an armada of rammerhorns and hatchet-jaws and sea-leopards and drakkens to teach us not to come around bothering them again?"

"They won't get the chance," Delagard said serenely. "If they're there, what we'll do is go down there and conquer the shit out of them."

"We'll do *what*?"

"It'll be the easiest thing you can imagine. They're soft and decadent and old. If they're there, doc. If. They've had their own way on this world since the beginning of time and the concept of an enemy doesn't even exist in their minds. Everything on Hydros is here to serve them. And they've been down there in their hole for half a million years living in luxury we couldn't even begin to imagine. When we get down there we'll discover that they'll have no way of defending themselves at all. Why should they? Defend themselves against whom? We walk right in and tell them we're taking over, and they'll roll over and surrender."

"Eleven half-naked men and women armed with gaffs and belaying pins are going to conquer the capital city of an immensely advanced alien civilization?"

"You ever study any Earth history, Lawler? There was a place called Peru that ruled half a continent and had temples built of gold. A man named Pizarro came in with maybe two hundred men armed with medieval weapons that weren't any damned good at all, a cannon or two and some rifles you wouldn't believe, and he seized the emperor and conquered the place just like that. Around the same time a man named Cortés did the same thing in an empire called Mexico that was just as rich. You take them by surprise, you don't let yourself even allow for the possibility of defeat, you simply march in and get command of their central authority figure, and they fall down at your feet. And everything they have is yours."

Lawler stared at Delagard, wonder-struck.

"Without even lifting a finger in our own defense, Nid, we allowed ourselves to be thrown off the island where we had lived for a hundred-fifty years by the simple peasant cousins of these super-Gillies, because we knew we didn't stand a chance in a fight against them. But now you tell me with a straight face that you're going to overthrow an entire superior technological civilization with your bare hands, and you give me medieval folktales about mythical kingdoms captured by ancient culture-heroes to prove to me that it can be done. Jesus, Nid! Jesus!"

"You'll see, doc. I promise you."

Lawler looked around, appealing to the others. But they sat mute, glazed, as though asleep.

"Why are we even wasting our time on this?" he asked. "There's no such city. It's an impossible concept. You don't believe in it for a minute, Nid. Do you? Do you?"

"I've already told you, maybe I do, maybe I don't. Jolly believed in it."

"Jolly was crazy."

"Not when he first came back to Sorve. It was only later, after he'd been laughed at for years—"

But Lawler had had enough. Delagard went round and round and round and nothing he said made sense. The close, dank air in the cabin suddenly was as hard to breathe as water. Lawler felt as if he were choking. Spasms of claustrophobic nausea swept over him. He yearned powerfully for his numbweed.

He understood now that Delagard wasn't simply dangerously obsessive: he was completely crazy.

And we are all lost down here at the far end of the world, Lawler thought, with no way of escaping and no place to escape to even if we could.

"I can't listen to this garbage any more," he said in a voice half-strangled by rage and disgust, and got up and rushed from the room.

"Doc!" Delagard called. "Come back here! Damn you, doc, come back!"

Lawler slammed the door and kept on going.

AS HE STOOD ALONE ON THE DECK LAWLER KNEW EVEN WITHOUT turning around that Father Quillan had come up behind him. That was odd, knowing without looking. It must be some side effect of the furious emanations pouring over them out of the Face.

"Delagard asked me to go up and talk with you," the priest said.

"About what?"

"Your outburst down below."

"*My* outburst?" Lawler said, astonished. He turned and looked at the priest. By the strange many-colored light that crackled all about them Quillan seemed more gaunt than ever, his long face a thing of a myriad planes, his skin tanned and glossy, his eyes bright as beacons. "What about Delagard's outburst? Lost cities under the sea! Cockeyed wars of conquest modeled on mythical fables out of antiquity!"

"They weren't mythical. Cortés and Pizarro really lived, and really did conquer great empires with just a handful of troops, a thousand years ago. It's the truth. It's been documented in Earth history."

Lawler shrugged. "What happened long ago on another planet doesn't matter here."

"You say that? You, the man who visits Earth in his dreams?"

"Cortés and Pizarro weren't dealing with Gillies. Delagard's a lunatic and everything he's been saying to us today is absolute madness." Then, suddenly cautious, he said, "Or don't you agree?"

"He's a volatile, melodramatic man, full of frenzy and fire. But I don't think he's crazy."

"An undersea city at the deep end of a gravity funnel? You actually think such a thing can exist? You'll believe anything, won't you? Yes, you will. You can believe Father, Son, and Holy Ghost, so why not an undersea city?"

"Why not?" the priest said. "Stranger things than that have been found on other worlds."

"I wouldn't know," Lawler said sullenly.

"And it's a plausible explanation for why Hydros is the way it is. I've been giving this place some thought, Lawler. There are no real water-worlds in the galaxy, you know. The others that are like Hydros all have chains of natural islands, at least, archipelagoes, the tops of sunken mountains showing above the sea. Hydros is just a big ball of water, though. But if you postulate that there once was a certain amount of land, and it was cut away to build one or more enormous undersea cities, until at last all of Hydros' surface territory had disappeared into the sea and there was nothing but water left on top—"

"Maybe so. Or maybe not."

"It stands to reason. Why are the Gillies an island-building race? Because they're evolving from an aquatic form and need land to live on? That's a reasonable theory. But what if it's the other way around entirely, that they were land-dwellers to begin with, and the ones who were left behind at the surface at the time of the migration underground evolved into a semi-aquatic form when the land was taken away? That would account for—"

Wearily Lawler said, "You argue science the way you argue theology: start with an illogical notion, then pile all kinds of hypotheses and speculations on top of it in the hope of making it make sense. If you want to believe that the Gillies suddenly got bored with living outdoors, so they built themselves a hideaway in the ocean, stripped away all the land surface of the planet in the process, and left a mutated amphibious form of themselves up above just for the hell of it, go ahead and believe it. I don't care. But do you also believe that Delagard can march in and conquer them the way he says he's planning to do?"

"Well—"

"Look," Lawler said, "I don't for a moment think that this magical city exists. I used to talk to this Jolly too, and he always seemed like a crackpot to me. But even if the place is right around the next bend in the coast, we can't possibly invade it. The Gillies would wipe us out in five minutes." He leaned close to the other man. "Listen to me, Father. What we really need to do is put Delagard under restraint and get ourselves out of here. I felt that way weeks ago, and then I changed my mind, and now I see I was right the first time. The man's deranged and we have no business being in this place."

"No," said Quillan.

"No?"

"Delagard may be as disturbed as you say he is, and his schemes pure lunacy. But I won't support you in any attempt to interfere with him. Quite the contrary."

"You want to continue sniffing around the Face, regardless of the risks?"

"Yes."

"Why?"

"You know why."

For a beat or two Lawler was silent. "Right," he said finally. "It slipped my mind for the moment. Angels. Paradise. How could I have let myself forget that you were the one who encouraged Delagard to come here in the first place, for your own private reasons, which have nothing to do with his?" Lawler waved a hand contemptuously at the wild circus of gyrating vegetation across the strait on the shore of the Face. "You still think that that's the land of the angels over there? Of the gods?"

"In a way, yes."

"And you still think you can wangle some kind of redemption for yourself over there?"

"Yes."

"Redeemed by *that*? Lights and noise?"

"Yes."

"You're crazier than Delagard."

"I can understand why you'd think so," the priest said.

Lawler laughed harshly. "I can just see you marching beside him into the undersea city of the super-Gillies. He's carrying a gaff and you're carrying a cross, and the two of you are singing hymns, you in one key and him in another. The Gillies come forward and kneel, and you baptize them one by one, and then you explain to them that Delagard is now their king."

"Please, Lawler."

"Please what? You want me to pat you on the head and tell you how impressed I am with your profound ideas? And then go below and tell Delagard how grateful I am for his inspired leadership? No, Father, I'm sailing aboard a ship commanded by a madman, who with your connivance has brought us to the weirdest and most dangerous place on this planet, and I don't like it, and I want to get out of here."

"If only you'd be willing to see that what the Face has to offer us—"

"I know what the Face has to offer. Death is what it has to offer, Father.

Starvation. Dehydration. Or worse. You see those lights flashing over there? You feel that strange electrical crackling? It doesn't feel friendly to me. It feels lethal, in fact. Is that your idea of redemption? Dying?"

Quillan shot him a sudden startled, wild-eyed glance.

"Isn't it true," Lawler said, "that your church believes that suicide is one of the gravest of all sins?"

"You're the one who's talking about suicide, not me."

"You're the one who's planning to commit it."

"You don't understand what you're saying, Lawler. And in your ignorance you're distorting everything."

"Am I?" Lawler asked. "Am I, really?"

8

*L*ATE THAT AFTERNOON DELAGARD ORDERED THE ANCHOR PULLED up, and once more they moved westward along the coast of the Face. A hot, steady onshore breeze was blowing, as though the huge island were trying to gather them in.

"Val?" Sundira called. She was just above him in the rigging, fixing the stays on the fore yard.

He looked up toward her.

"Where are we, Val? What's going to happen to us?" She was shivering in the tropic warmth. Uneasily she glanced toward the island. "Looks like my idea of this place as the scene of some sort of nuclear devastation was wrong. But it's scary all the same, over there."

"Yes."

"And yet I still feel drawn to it. I still want to know what it really is."

"Something bad is what it is," Lawler said. "You can see that from here."

"It would be so easy to turn the ship toward shore—you and me, Val, we could do it right now, just the two of us—"

"No."

"Why not?" There wasn't much conviction in her question. She looked as uncertain about the island as he was. Her hands were shaking so badly that she dropped her mallet. Lawler caught it as it fell and tossed it back up to her. "What would happen to us, do you think, if we went closer to the shore?" she asked. "If we went up onto the Face itself?"

"Let somebody else find that out for us," Lawler told her. "Let Gabe Kinverson go over there, if he's so brave. Or Father Quillan. Or Delagard. This is Delagard's picnic: let him be the first to go ashore. I'll stay here and watch what happens."

"That makes sense, I suppose. And yet—yet—"

"You're tempted."

"Yes."

"There's a pull, isn't there? I feel it, too. I hear something inside me saying, *Go on across, have a look, see what's there. There's nothing else like it in the world. You have to see it.* But it's a crazy idea."

"Yes," Sundira said quietly. "You're right. It is."

She was silent for a time, concentrating on the repairs. Then she climbed down to his level in the rigging. Lawler touched his fingertips lightly, almost experimentally, to her bare shoulder. She made a soft sound and pressed herself up against him, and together they stared out at the color-stained sea, the swollen setting sun, the haze of bewildering light rising from the island across the way.

"Val, can I stay with you in your cabin tonight?" she asked.

She hadn't done that often, and not for a long time. The two of them together were too big for the tiny cabin, for his narrow bunk.

"Of course."

"I love you, Val."

Lawler ran his hands across the strong ridges of her shoulders and up to the nape of her neck. He felt more strongly drawn to her than ever before: almost as though they were two halves of some severed organism, and not just two semi-strangers who had happened to find themselves thrown together on a bizarre voyage to a perilous place. Was it the peril, he wondered, that had brought them together? Was it—God forbid!—the enforced togetherness in the middle of the ocean that made him so open to her now, so eager to be near her?

"I love you," he whispered.

They ran for his cabin. He had never felt this close to her . . . to anyone. They were allies, just the two of them against a turbulent, mystifying universe. With only each other to clutch as the mystery of the Face enveloped them.

The short night was a tangle of interwoven arms and legs, sweaty bodies slipping and sliding against one another, eyes meeting eyes, smiles meeting smiles, breath mingling with breath, soft words spoken, her name on his lips, his on hers, reminiscences exchanged, new memories forged, no sleep at all. Just as well, Lawler thought. Sleep might bring new phantoms. Better to pass the night in wakefulness. And in passion. The new day could well be their last.

HE WENT ON DECK AT DAWN. THESE DAYS HE WAS WORKING FIRST watch. During the night, Lawler saw, the ship had passed within the line of breakers again. Now it was anchored in a bay very much like the first one, though there were no hills along the shore, only low meadows densely packed with dark vegetation.

This time the bay seemed to be accepting their presence, even welcoming it. Its surface was calm, not so much as a ripple; there was no hint of the flailing kelp that had driven them almost at once from the last one.

Here, as everywhere else, the water was luminescent, sending up cascades of pink and gold and scarlet and sapphire radiance; and on shore the wild looping dance of never-resting life was going on with the usual frenzy. Purple sparks rose from the land. The air seemed to be aflame again. There were bright colors everywhere. The insane indefatigable magnificence of the place was a hard thing to face first thing in the morning after a sleepless night.

Delagard was alone on the bridge, huddling into himself in an odd way, arms locked across his chest.

"Come talk to me, doc," he said.

Delagard's eyes were bleary and reddened. He looked as if he had had no sleep, not just this night past, but for days. His jowls were grayish and sagging, his head seemed to have folded downward into his thick neck. Lawler saw a tic at work in Delagard's cheek. Whatever demon had been riding him yesterday on their first approach to the shore of the Face had returned in the night.

Hoarsely Delagard said, "I hear that you think I'm crazy."

"Does it matter a damn to you if I do?"

"Will it make you any happier if I tell you that I'm starting to come around almost to agree with you? Almost. Almost."

Lawler searched for a trace of irony in Delagard's words, of humor, of mockery. But there was none. Delagard's voice was thick and husky, with a cracked edge to it.

"Look at that fucking place," Delagard muttered. He waved his arms in loose looping circles. "Look at it, doc! It's a wasteland. It's a nightmare. Why did I ever come here?" He was shaking, and his skin was pale beneath the beard. He looked terrifyingly haggard. In a low husky voice he said, "Only a crazy man would have come this far. I see that clear as anything, now. I saw it yesterday when we pulled into that bay, but I tried to pretend it wasn't so. I was wrong. At least I'm big enough to admit that. Christ, doc, what was I thinking of when I brought us to this place? It isn't meant for us." He shook his head. When he spoke again his voice was no more than an anguished croak. "Doc, we've got to get out of here right away."

Was he serious? Or was this all some grotesque test of loyalty?

"Do you mean it?" Lawler asked him.

"Damned right I do."

Yes. He really did. He was terrified, quaking. The man seemed to be disintegrating before Lawler's eyes. It was a stupefying reversal, the last thing Lawler would have expected. He struggled to come to terms with it.

After a while he said, "What about the sunken city?"

"You think that there is one?" Delagard asked.

"Not for a second. But you do."

"Like shit I do. I had too much brandy, that's all. We've traveled a third of the way around the Face, I figure, and there hasn't been any sign of it. You'd suppose there'd be a strong coastal current if there's a gravity funnel holding the sea open up ahead. A vortex flow. But where the fuck is it?"

"You tell me, Nid. You seemed to think it was here."

"That was Jolly who thought so."

"Jolly was crazy. Jolly's brains got cooked when he took his trip around the Face."

Delagard nodded somberly. His eyelids rolled slowly down over his bloodshot eyes. Lawler thought for a moment that he had fallen asleep standing up. Then he said, still keeping his eyes closed, "I've been out here by myself all night, doc. Working things out in my mind. Trying to take a practical view of the situation. It sounds funny to you, because you think I'm crazy. But I'm not crazy, doc. Not really. I may do things that look crazy to other people, but I'm not crazy myself. I'm just different from you. You're sober, you're cautious, you hate taking chances, you just want to go along and go along and go along. That's all right. There are people like you in the universe and there are people like me, and we never really understand each other, but sometimes it happens that we get thrown together in a situation and we have to work together anyway. Doc, I wanted to come here more than anything I've ever wanted in my life. For me it was the key to everything. Don't ask me to explain. You'd never get it, anyway. But now I'm here and I see I made a mistake. There's nothing here for us. Nothing."

"Pizarro," Lawler said. "Cortés. They would at least have gone ashore before turning tail and running."

"Don't fuck around with me now," said Delagard. "I'm trying to level with you."

"You gave me Pizarro and Cortés when I tried to level with you, Nid."

Delagard opened his eyes. They were frightful: bright as coals, fiery with pain. He drew back the corner of his mouth in what might have been an attempt at a smile. "Go easy, doc. I was drunk."

"I know."

"You know what my mistake was, doc? I believed my own bullshit. And Jolly's bullshit. And Father Quillan's. Quillan fed me a lot of stuff about the Face of the Waters as a place where godly powers would be mine for the taking, or so I interpreted what he was saying. And here we are. Here lie we. Rest in peace. I stood here all night and I thought, How would I build a spaceport? With what? How could anyone live in all that chaos over there without going out of his mind in half a day? What would we eat? Could we even breathe the air? No wonder the Gillies won't come here. The miserable place is uninhabitable. And suddenly everything came clear to me, and I was standing here all by myself, face to face with myself, laughing at myself. Laughing, doc. But the joke was on me, and it wasn't very funny. This whole voyage has been sheer lunacy, hasn't it, doc?"

Delagard was swaying back and forth, now. Lawler saw abruptly that he must still be drunk. There had to be one more hidden cache of brandy on board and probably he'd been drinking all night. For days, maybe. He was so drunk that he thought he was sober.

"You ought to lie down. I can give you a sedative."

"Fuck your sedative. What I want is for you to agree with me! It's been a crazy voyage. Hasn't it, doc?"

"You know that's what I think, Nid."

"And you think I'm crazy too."

"I don't know if you are or you aren't. What I do know is that you're right on the verge of collapse."

"Well, what if I am?" Delagard asked. "I'm still the captain of this ship. I got us into this. All those people who died, they died because of me. I can't let anybody else die. I've got the responsibility for getting us out."

"What's your plan, then?"

"What we need to do now," Delagard said, speaking slowly and carefully out of some almost unfathomable depth of fatigue, "is work out a course that'll take us up into inhabited waters, and go to the first island we can reach and fucking beg them to take us in. Eleven people: they can always find room for eleven people, no matter how crowded they try to tell us they are."

"That sounds fine with me."

"I figured it would."

"Okay, then. You go get yourself some rest, Nid. The rest of us will get us out of here right now. Felk can navigate, and we'll pull the sails around, and by mid-afternoon we'll be a hundred kilometers from here and making for someplace like Grayvard as fast as we know how." Lawler nudged Delagard toward the steps leading down from the bridge. "Go on. Before you drop."

"No," Delagard said. "I told you, I'm still the captain. If we have to leave here, it'll be with me at the wheel."

"All right. Whatever you like."

"It isn't what I like. It's what I have to do. What I need to do. And there's something I need from you, doc, before we go."

"What's that?"

"Something that'll let me deal with the way things have turned out. It's been a total defeat, hasn't it? A complete fuck-up. I've never failed at anything in my life until now. But this catastrophe—this disaster—" Delagard's hand suddenly jabbed out and clutched at Lawler's arm. "I need a way of making myself able to live with it, doc. The shame. The guilt. You don't think I'm capable of feeling guilt, but what the fuck did you ever know about me, anyway? If we survive this trip everyone on Hydros is going to look at me wherever I go and say, There's the man who headed the voyage, who led six ships full of people right down the toilet. And there'll be reminders for me all the time. From now on every time I see you, or Dag, or Felk, or Kinverson—" Delagard's eyes were fixed and fiery now. "You've got some drug, don't you, that numbs out your feelings, right? I want you to give me some. I want to dose myself up on it but good, and stay dosed from here on in. Because the only other thing for me to do now is kill myself, and that's something I can't even imagine doing."

"Drugs are a form of killing yourself, Nid."

"Spare me the pious bullshit, will you, doc?"

"I mean it. Take it from somebody who spent years dosing himself with the stuff. It's a living death."

"That's still better than a dead death."

"Maybe so. But in any case I can't give you any. I used up the last of my supply before we got here."

Delagard's grasp on Lawler's arm tightened fiercely. "You're lying to me!"

"Am I?"

"I know you are. You can't live without the drug. You take it every day. Don't you think I know that? Don't you think everybody does?"

"It's all gone, Nid. Do you remember last week, when I was so sick? What I was doing was going through withdrawal. There isn't a drop left. You can search my stores if you like. But you won't find any."

"You're lying to me!"

"Go and look. You can have all you can find. That's a promise." Carefully Lawler lifted Delagard's hand from his arm. "Listen, Nid, just lie down and get yourself some rest. By the time you wake up we'll be far from here and you'll feel better, believe me, and you'll be able to start the whole process of forgiving yourself. You're a resilient man. You know how to deal with things like guilt—believe me, you do. Right now you're so damned tired and depressed that you can't see beyond the next five minutes, but once we're out in the open sea again—"

"Hold on a minute," Delagard said, looking over Lawler's shoulder. He pointed toward the gantry area in the stern. "What the fuck's happening down there?"

Lawler turned to see. Two figures were struggling, a big man and a much slighter one: Kinverson and Quillan, an unlikely pair of antagonists. Kinverson had his hands clamped on the priest's thin shoulders and was holding him at arm's length, immobilized, while Quillan fought to break free.

Lawler scrambled down the steps and hurried aft, with Delagard stumbling along behind him.

"What are you doing?" Lawler asked. "Let go of him."

"I let go, he goes across to the Face. That's what he says. You want him to do that, doc?"

Quillan looked weirdly ecstatic. He wore a sleepwalker's glazed stare. His pupils were dilated, his skin was as pale as though he had been drained of blood. His lips were drawn back in a frozen grin.

Kinverson said, "He was wandering around here like somebody who's out of his head. Going to the Face, he kept saying. Going to the Face. Started to climb over the side, and I grabbed him, and he hit me. Jesus, I never knew he was such a fighter! But I think he's quieting down a little now."

"Try letting go," Lawler said. "See what he does."

Shrugging, Kinverson released him. Quillan began at once to press onward toward the rail. The priest's eyes were shining as if with an inner light.

"You see?" the fisherman asked.

Delagard came shouldering forward. He looked groggy but determined. Order had to be maintained aboard ship. He caught the priest by his wrist. "What are you up to? What do you think you're trying to do?"

"Going ashore—the Face—to the Face—" Quillan's dreamy grin broadened until it seemed that his cheeks must split. "The god wants me— the god in the Face—"

"Jesus," Delagard said, his face mottling in exasperation. "What are you saying? You'll die if you go over there. Don't you understand that? There's no way to live over there. Look at the light coming from everything. The place is poison. Snap out of it, will you! Snap out of it!"

"The god in the Face—"

Quillan struggled to break free of Delagard's grasp, and for a moment succeeded. He took two sliding steps toward the rail. Then Delagard caught him again, yanking Quillan toward him and slapping him so hard that the priest's lip began to bleed. Quillan stared at him, stunned. Delagard raised his hand again.

"Don't," Lawler said. "He's coming out of it."

Indeed something was changing in Quillan's eyes. The glow was leaving them, and the rigid look of trance. He seemed dazed now but fully conscious, trying to blink away his confusion. Slowly he rubbed his face where Delagard had struck him. He shook his head. The motion widened into a convulsive body-long shudder, and he began to tremble. Tears glistened in his eyes.

"My God. I actually was going over there. That was what I was doing, wasn't I? It was *pulling* me. I felt it pulling."

Lawler nodded. It seemed to him that he felt it too, suddenly. A pulsation, a throbbing in his mind. Something stronger than the tempting urge, the mild tug of curiosity, that he and Sundira had felt the night before. It was a powerful mental pressure, drawing him inward, calling him toward the wild shore behind the surf line.

Angrily he brushed the idea aside. He was getting as crazy as Quillan.

The priest was still talking about the pull he had felt. "There was no way I could resist it. It was offering me the thing I'd been searching for all my life. Thank God Kinverson grabbed me in time." Quillan gave Lawler a disheveled look, terror mixed with bewilderment. "You were right, doc, what you said yesterday. It would have been suicide. I thought just then that I'd be going to God, to a god of some sort. But it was the devil, for all I know. That's hell over there. I thought it was paradise, but it's hell." The priest's voice trailed off. Then, more distinctly, he said to Delagard, "I ask you to take us away from this place. Our souls are in danger here, and if you don't believe that there is such a thing as the soul, then at least consider that it's our lives that are in peril. If we stay here any longer—"

"Don't worry," Delagard said. "We aren't going to stay. We're leaving here as fast as we can."

Quillan made an O of surprise with his lips.

Wearily Delagard said, "I've had a little revelation of my own, Father, and it agrees with yours. This voyage was a gigantic fucking miscalculation, if you'll excuse the vernacular. We don't belong here. I want to get out of here as much as you do."

"I don't understand. I thought—that you—"

"Don't think so much," said Delagard. "Thinking too much can be very bad for you."

"Did you say we're leaving?" Kinverson asked.

"That's right." Delagard looked up defiantly at the big man. His face was red with chagrin. But he seemed almost amused now by the extent of the calamity that was tumbling down upon him. He was beginning to seem himself again. Something not far from a smile played across his features. "We're clearing out."

"Fine with me," said Kinverson. "Any time you say."

Lawler glanced away, his attention caught suddenly by something very strange.

He said abruptly, "Did you hear that sound, just now? Somebody speaking to us out of the Face?"

"What? Where?"

"Stand very still and listen. It's coming from the Face. *'Doctor-sir. Captain-sir. Father-sir.'*" Lawler mimicked the high, thin, soft voice with keen accuracy. "You hear that? *'I am with the Face now, Captain-sir. Doctor-sir. Father-sir.'* It's as if he's standing right here next to us."

"Gharkid!" Quillan exclaimed. "But how—where—"

Others were coming on deck, now: Sundira, Neyana, Pilya Braun. Dag Tharp and Onyos Felk were a few paces behind them. All of them seemed astounded by what they had heard. The last to appear was Lis Niklaus, moving in a peculiar shambling, stumbling way. She jabbed her forefinger at the sky again and again, as though trying to stab it.

Lawler turned and looked up. And saw what Lis was pointing to. The swirling colors in the sky were congealing, taking shape—the shape of the dark, enigmatic face of Natim Gharkid. A gigantic image of the mysterious little man hovered above them, inescapable, inexplicable.

"Where is he?" Delagard cried, in a thick, clotted voice. "How's he doing that? Bring him here! Gharkid! Gharkid!" He waved his arms frantically. "Go find him. All of you! Search the ship! Gharkid!"

"He's in the sky," Neyana Golghoz said blandly, as if that explained everything.

"No," Kinverson said. "He's on the Face. Look there—the water-strider's gone. He must have gone across while we were busy with the Father."

Indeed the strider's housing was empty. Gharkid had taken it out by himself and crossed the little bay to the shore beyond. And had entered the Face; and had been absorbed; and had been transformed. Lawler stared in wonder and terror at the huge image in the sky. Gharkid's face, no question of that. But how? How?

Sundira came up beside him. Her arm slipped through his. She was shivering with fear. Lawler wanted to comfort her, but no words would come.

Delagard was the first to find his voice.

"Work stations, everyone! Pull that anchor up! I want to see sails! We're getting the hell out of here right now!"

"Wait a second," Quillan said quietly. He nodded toward the shore. "Gharkid's coming back."

THE LITTLE MAN'S JOURNEY TOWARD THE SHIP SEEMED TO TAKE A thousand years. No one dared move. They all stood in a row watching by the rail, frozen, appalled.

The image of Gharkid had vanished from the sky the moment the real Gharkid had come into view. But the unmistakable tone of Gharkid's voice, somehow, was still a part of the strange mental emanation that had begun to radiate steadily from the Face. The physical incarnation of the man might be returning, but something else had remained behind.

He had abandoned the water-strider—Lawler saw it now, beached in the vegetation at the edge of the shore; tendrils of new growth were already beginning to wrap themselves around it—and was swimming across the narrow bay: wading, really. He moved at an unhurried pace, obviously not regarding himself in any danger from whatever creatures might inhabit these strange waters. Of course not, Lawler thought. He was one of them now.

When he reached the deeper waters close to the ship, Gharkid put his head down and began to swim. His strokes were slow and serene, and he moved with ease and agility.

Kinverson went to the gantry and returned with one of his gaffs. His cheek was jerking with barely controlled tension. He held the sharp tool aloft like a spear.

"If that thing tries to climb up on board—"

"No," Father Quillan said. "You mustn't. This is his ship as much as yours."

"Who says? What is he? Who says he's Gharkid? I'll kill him if he comes near us."

But Gharkid had no intention, it seemed, of coming up on board. He was just off the side now, floating placidly, holding himself in one place with little motions of his hands.

He was looking up at them.

Smiling his sweet, inscrutable Gharkid-smile.

Beckoning to them.

"I'll kill him!" Kinverson roared. "The bastard! The dirty little bastard!"

"No," said Quillan again quietly, as the big man drew back the hand that held the gaff. "Don't be afraid. He won't hurt us." The priest reached up and touched Kinverson lightly on the chest; and Kinverson seemed to dissolve at the touch. Looking stunned, he let his arm sag to his side. Sundira came up alongside him and took the gaff from him. Kinverson hardly seemed to notice.

Lawler looked toward the man in the water. Gharkid—or was it the Face, speaking through what had been Gharkid?—was calling to them, summoning them to the island. Now Lawler felt the pull in earnest, no doubt of that, no illusion either but a firm unmistakable imperative coming in heavy throbbing waves; it reminded him of the strong undertows that sometimes came eddying up while he was swimming in the bay of Sorve Island. He had been able easily enough to withstand those undertows. He wondered whether he'd be able to withstand this one. It was tugging at the roots of his soul.

He became aware of Sundira's ragged breathing close beside him. Her face was pale, her eyes were bright with fear. But her jaw was set. She was determined to hold her own against that eerie summons.

Come to me, Gharkid was saying. Come to me, come to me.

Gharkid's soft voice. But it was the Face that spoke. Lawler was certain of it: an island that spoke, seductively promising everything, anything, in a word. Only come. Only come.

"I'm coming!" Lis Niklaus cried suddenly. "Wait for me! Wait! I'm coming!"

She was midway down the deck, near the mast, blank-eyed, trance-faced, moving uncertainly toward the rail with flatfooted shuffling steps. Delagard, whirling about, called out to her to stop. Lis kept on going. He cursed and began to run toward her. He caught up with her just as she reached the rail and made a grab for her arm.

In a cold, fierce voice that Lawler could barely recognize as hers Lis said, "No, you bastard. No. Keep away from me!" She shoved at Delagard and sent him tumbling to the deck. Delagard struck the planks hard and lay there on his back, looking at her incredulously. He seemed unable to rise. A moment later Lis was on the rail, and then over it, plunging in free fall toward the water, landing with a tremendous luminous splash.

Side by side, she and Gharkid swam off toward the Face.

CLOUDS OF A NEW COLOR HUNG LOW IN THE HOT, CHURNING AIR ABOVE the Face of the Waters. They were tawny above, darker below: Lis Niklaus's coloration. She had reached her destination.

"It's going to take us all," Sundira said, gasping. "We have to get away from here!"

"Yes," Lawler said. "Fast." He glanced quickly around. Delagard still lay sprawled on the deck, more stunned than hurt, perhaps, but not getting up. Onyos Felk was crouching by the foremast, talking to himself in muzzy whispers. Father Quillan was on his knees, making the sign of the Cross over and over again, muttering prayers. Dag Tharp, yellow-eyed with fear, was clutching at his belly and rocking with dry heaves. Lawler shook his head. "Who's going to navigate?"

"Does it matter? We just have to put the Face behind us and keep on going. So long as we have enough of a crew working the sails—"

Sundira circled the deck. "Pilya! Neyana! Grab those ropes! Val, do you know how to work the wheel? Oh, Jesus, the anchor's still down. Gabe! Gabe, for Christ's sake, heave the anchor up!"

"Lis is coming back now," Lawler said.

"Never mind that. Give Gabe a hand with the anchor."

But it was too late. Already Lis was halfway back to the ship, swimming powerfully, easily. Gharkid was just behind her. She paused in the water and looked up, and her eyes were new, strange, alien.

"God help us all," Father Quillan muttered. "They're both pulling on us now!" There was terror in his eyes. He was shaking convulsively. "I'm afraid, Lawler. This is what I've wanted all my life, and now that it's here, I'm afraid, I'm afraid!" The priest extended his hands toward Lawler in appeal. "Help me. Take me belowdecks. Or else I'll go over to it. I can't fight it any longer."

Lawler started toward him.

"Let him go!" Sundira cried. "We don't have time. He's no use to us anyway."

"Help me!" Quillan wailed. He was moving toward the rail in the same dreamlike shuffle Lis had used. "God is calling me and I'm afraid to go to Him!"

"That isn't God that's calling," Sundira snapped. She was running everywhere at once, trying to galvanize the others into motion, but nothing seemed to be happening. Pilya was looking up at the rigging as though she had never seen a sail before. Neyana was off by herself near the forecastle, chanting something in a low monotone. Kinverson had done nothing about the anchor: he stood stock still amidships, vacant-eyed, lost in uncharacteristic contemplation.

Come to us, Gharkid and Lis were saying. Come to us, come to us, come to us.

Lawler trembled. The pull was far more powerful now than when it had been Gharkid alone who was summoning them. He heard a splash. Someone else had gone over the side. Felk? Tharp? No, Tharp was still there, a puking little heap. But Felk was gone. And then Lawler saw Neyana too, hoisting herself over the rail, plummeting like a meteor toward the water.

One by one they all would go, he thought. One by one, they would be incorporated into the alien entity that was the Face.

He struggled to resist. He summoned all the stubbornness in his soul, all the love of solitude, all the cantankerous insistence on following his own path, and used it as a weapon against the thing that was calling him. He wrapped his lifelong aloneness around him like a cloak of invisibility.

And it seemed to work. Strong though the pull was—and getting stronger—it couldn't manage to draw him over the rail. An outsider to the last, he thought, the eternal loner, keeping himself apart even from union with that potent hungry thing that waited for them across the narrow strait.

"Please," Father Quillan said, almost whimpering. "Where's the hatch? I can't find the hatch!"

"Come with me," Lawler said. "I'll take you below."

He saw Sundira heaving desperately at the windlass, trying to get the anchor up herself. But she didn't have the strength for it: only Kinverson, of them all, was strong enough to do it alone. Lawler hesitated, caught between Quillan's need and the greater urgency of getting the ship aweigh.

Delagard, on his feet at last, came staggering toward him like a man who has had a stroke. Lawler shoved the priest into Delagard's arms.

"Here. Hang onto him, or he'll go over."

Lawler ran toward Sundira. But Kinverson suddenly stepped out into his path and pushed him back with one big hand against his chest.

"The anchor—" Lawler began. "We've got to lift anchor—"

"No. Let it be."

Kinverson's eyes were very strange. They seemed to be rolling upward in his head.

"You too?" Lawler asked.

He heard a grunt from behind him, and then another splash. He looked back. Delagard was alone by the rail, studying his fingers as if wondering what they were. Quillan was gone. Lawler saw him in the water, swimming with sublime determination. He was on his way to God—or whatever was over there—at last.

"Val!" Sundira called, still pulling at the windlass.

"No use," Lawler replied. "They're all going overboard!"

He could see figures on shore, moving steadily deeper into the throbbing thickets of baroque vegetation: Neyana, Felk. And now Quillan, scrambling up onto the land and moving after them. Gharkid and Lis had already disappeared.

Lawler counted up those who remained on board: Kinverson, Pilya, Tharp, Delagard, Sundira. And he made six. Tharp went over even as he was making the count. Five, then. Just five, out of all those who had set out from Sorve Island.

Kinverson said, "This miserable life. How I hated every stinking day of it. How I wished I'd never been born. You didn't know that? What did you know? What did anybody know? They figured I was too big and strong to hurt. Because I never said anything, nobody knew. But I did hurt, every goddamned minute of the day! And nobody knew. Nobody knew."

"Gabe!" Sundira cried.

"Get out of my fucking way or I'll fucking split you in half."

Lawler lurched over, clutched at him. Kinverson swept him aside as if he were a straw and leaped to the top of the rail in one smooth bound, and vaulted over.

Four.

Where was Pilya, though? Lawler glanced around and saw her in the rigging, naked, glistening in the sunlight, climbing higher, higher—was she going to dive from there? Yes. Yes, she was.

Splash.

Three.

"JUST US," SUNDIRA SAID. SHE LOOKED AT LAWLER AND THEN AT DE-lagard, who sat dismally propped against the base of the mainmast with his hands over his face. "We're the ones it doesn't want, I guess."

"No," said Lawler. "The only ones strong enough to fight it off."

"Hurrah for us," Delagard said gloomily, without looking up.

"Are three of us enough to sail this ship?" she asked. "What do you think, Val?"

"We can try, I suppose."

"Don't talk garbage," Delagard said. "You can't possibly run this ship with a crew of three."

"We could set the sails to the prevailing breezes and simply ride the current," Lawler said. "Maybe if we did that we'd get to some inhabited island sooner or later. It's better than staying here. What do you say, Nid?"

Delagard shrugged.

Sundira was looking toward the Face.

"Can you see any of them?" Lawler asked.

"Not a one. But I hear something. I feel something. Father Quillan, I think, coming back."

Lawler peered toward shore. "Where?" The priest was nowhere in sight. But yet, but yet—no doubt of it, Lawler, too, felt a Quillan-like presence. It was as though the priest were right here beside them on the deck. Another trick of the Face, he decided.

"No," Quillan said. "Not a trick. I *am* here."

"It isn't so. You're still on the island," said Lawler tonelessly.

"On the island, and here with you, at one and the same time."

Delagard made a hollow sound of disgust. "Son of a bitch. Why won't the thing leave us alone?"

"It loves you," Quillan said. "It wants you. *We* want you. Come and join us."

Lawler saw that their victory was only a tentative one. The pull was still there—subtler now, as if holding itself in abeyance, but ready to seize them the moment they let down their guard. Quillan was intended as a distraction—a seductive distraction.

He said, "Are you Father Quillan, or are you the Face speaking?"

"Both. I am of the Face now."

"But you still perceive yourself as the priest Father Quillan, dwelling within the entity that is the Face of the Waters?"

"Yes. Yes, exactly."

"How can that be?" Lawler asked.

"Come and see," said Quillan. "You remain yourself. And yet you become something infinitely greater."

"Infinitely?"

"Infinitely, yes."

"It's like a dream," Sundira said. "Talking to something that you can't see, and having it answer you in the voice of someone you know." She sounded very calm. Like Delagard, she seemed past all fear now, past all tumult. Either the Face would have them or it wouldn't, but it was almost at the point of being beyond their control. "Father, can you hear me too?"

"Of course, Sundira."

"Do you know what the Face is? Is it God? Can you tell us?"

"The Face is Hydros, and Hydros is the Face," said the priest's quiet voice. "Hydros is a great corporate mind, a collective organism, a single intelligent entity that spans the entire planet. This island which we have come to, this place that we call the Face of the Waters, is a living thing, the brain of the planet. And more than a brain: the central womb of everything is what the Face is. The universal mother from which all life on Hydros flows."

"Is that why the Dwellers won't come here?" Sundira asked. "Because it's sacrilege to return to the place from which you've come?"

"Something like that, yes."

"And the multitude of intelligent life-forms on Hydros," Lawler said, seeing the connection suddenly. "That came about because everything is linked to the Face, isn't that so? The Gillies and the divers and the rammerhorns and everything else? One giant conglomerate world-mind?"

"Yes. Yes. One universal intelligence."

Lawler nodded. He closed his eyes and tried to imagine what it was like to be part of such an entity. The world as a single huge clockwork mechanism, ticking, ticking, ticking, and every living thing on it dancing to the rhythm of the ticks.

Quillan was part of it now. Gharkid. Lis, Pilya, Neyana, Tharp, Felk, even poor tortured Kinverson. Swallowed up in the godhead. Lost in the immensity of the divine.

Delagard said suddenly, still not lifting his head from the posture of darkest depression in which he sat slumped, "Quillan? Tell me this, Quillan: what about the undersea city? Is there one or isn't there?"

"A myth," the voice of the unseen Quillan replied. "A fable."

"Ah," said Delagard bitterly. "Ah."

"Or a metaphor, more truthfully. Your wandering seaman had something of the fundamental idea, but he garbled it. The great city is everywhere on Hydros, under the sea and in it and at its surface. The planet is a single city; every living creature on it is a citizen of it."

Delagard looked up. His eyes were dull with exhaustion.

Quillan went on, "The beings who live here have always dwelled in the water. Guided by the Face, united with the Face. At first they were completely aquatic, and then the Face showed them how to build the floating islands, to prepare them for the time in the distant future when land would begin to rise from the depths. But there was never any secret undersea city. This is a water-world and nothing else. And everything in it is bound harmoniously within the power of the Face."

"Everything except us," said Sundira.

"Everything except the few wandering humans who have found their way to this world, yes," Quillan said. "The exiles. Who out of ignorance have continued to be exiles here. Insisting on it, even. Aliens choosing to live apart from the harmony that is Hydros."

"Because they have no business being part of that harmony," Lawler said.

"Not true. Not true. Hydros welcomes everyone."

"But only on its own terms."

"Not true," said Quillan.

"But once you cease to be yourself—" Lawler said. "Once you become part of some larger entity—"

He frowned. Something had changed just then. He felt silence all around him. The aura, the enveloping blanket of thought, that had surrounded them during their colloquy with Quillan had vanished.

"I don't think he's here any more," Sundira said.

"No, he isn't," said Lawler. "He's pulled back from us. *It* has." The Face itself, the sense of a vast nearby presence, seemed to be gone. For the moment, at least.

"How strange it feels to be alone again."

"It feels good, I'd say. Just the three of us, each in our own head, and nobody talking to us out of the sky. For however long it is until it starts up again."

"It will start up again, won't it?" said Sundira.

"I suppose," Lawler said. "And we'll have to fight it all over again. We can't allow ourselves to be swallowed up. Human beings have no business becoming part of an alien world. We weren't meant for that."

Delagard said in an odd tone, soft and wistful, "He sounded happy, didn't he?"

"You think so?" Lawler asked.

"Yes, I do. He was always so strange, so sad, so distant. Wondering where God was. Well, now he knows. He's with God at last."

Lawler gave him a curious look. "I didn't know that you believed in God, Nid. Now you think that the Face is God?"

"Quillan does. And Quillan's happy. For the first time in his life."

"Quillan's dead, Nid. Whatever was talking to us just now wasn't Quillan."

"It sounded like Quillan. Quillan and something else, but Quillan even so."

"If you like to think so."

"I do," said Delagard. Abruptly he stood up, swaying a little as though the effort made him dizzy. "I'm going to go over there and join up."

Lawler stared at him.

"You too?" he said in wonder.

"Me, yes. Don't try to stop me. I'll kill you if you try. Remember what Lis did to me when I tried to stop her. We can't be stopped, doc."

Lawler was still staring. He means it, he thought. He actually means it. He's really going to go. Could this really be Delagard? Yes. Yes. Delagard had always been one for doing what seemed best for Delagard, no matter what effect it might have on those around him.

To hell with him, then. Good riddance.

"Stop you?" Lawler said. "I wouldn't dream of it. Go ahead, Nid. If you think you'll be happy there, go. Go. Why should I stop you? What difference does anything make now?"

Delagard smiled. "No difference to you, maybe. But to me, plenty. I'm so fucking tired, doc. I was full of big dreams. I tried this scheme, I tried that one, and for a long time everything worked out, and then I came here and it all fell apart. *I* fell apart. Well, fuck it. I just want to rest now."

"To kill yourself, you mean?"

"You think that's what it means. But I'd never do that. I'm tired of being the captain of the ship. I'm tired of telling people what to do, especially when I see now that I don't really know what the fuck I'm doing myself. I've had it, doc. I'm going to go over." Delagard's eyes brightened with newfound energy. "Maybe this is what I came here to do all along, only I never realized it until this minute. Maybe the Face sent Jolly home to bring the rest of us to it—only it took forty years, and then only a few of us came." He looked almost jaunty now. "So long, doc. Sundira. It was nice knowing you. Come visit me sometime."

They watched him go.

"It's just you and me, kid," Lawler said to her. And they laughed. What else was there to do, but laugh?

NIGHT CAME: A BLAZING NIGHT OF COMETS AND WONDERS, OF FLARING lights of a hundred different coruscating colors. Lawler and Sundira remained on deck as darkness came, sitting quietly near the mainmast, saying little to each other. He felt numb, burned out by the things that had happened this day. She was silent, exhausted.

Great explosions of color burst overhead. A celebration of the newly conquered, Lawler thought. The auras of his former shipmates seemed to sparkle in the sky. That great slash of stormy blue: was that Delagard? And that warm amber glow: Quillan? Could that scarlet pillar be Kinverson, and the splash of molten gold near the horizon, Pilya Braun? And Felk—Tharp—Neyana—Lis—Gharkid—

It felt as though they were close at hand, every one of them. The sky boiled with radiant color. But when Lawler listened for their voices, he was unable to hear them. All he could make out was a warm harmony of undifferentiated sounds.

On the darkening horizon the frenzied fertility of the island across the strait went on unabated: things sprouted, writhed, quivered against the deep hue of the sky, sending up showers of luminous energy. Waves of streaming light rose toward the heavens. There was never any rest over there. Lawler and Sundira sat watching the show far into the night, until at last he rose and said, "Are you hungry at all?"

"Not a bit."

"Neither am I. Let's get some sleep, then."

"Yes. All right."

She stretched her hand toward him and he pulled her to her feet. For a moment they stood close together by the rail, staring at the island across the strait.

"Do you feel any sort of pull?" she asked.

"Yes. It's always there—biding its time, I think. Waiting for the moment when it catches us off guard."

"I feel it too. It isn't as strong as it was, but I know that that's only a trick. I have to hold my mind clenched against it all the time."

"I wonder why we were the only ones who were able to hold fast against the urge to go," Lawler said. "Are we stronger and saner than the others, better able to live within our own identities? Or just so accustomed to feeling alienated from the society around us that we can't possibly let ourselves go and plunge into a group mind."

"Did you really feel so alienated when you lived on Sorve, Val?"

He considered that. "Maybe 'alienated' is too strong a word. I was part of the Sorve community, and it was part of me. But I wasn't part of it the way most of the others were. I was always a little to one side."

"The same with me on Khamsilaine. I was never much of a belonger, I suppose."

"Nor I."

"Or even wanted to be. Some do, and can't manage it. Gabe Kinverson was just as much a loner as we are. More, even. But suddenly a time came when he didn't want to be, any more. And there he is, dwelling in the Face. But it gives me the shivers to think of yielding myself up and going over there to join some alien mind."

"I never understood that man," Lawler said.

"Neither did I. I tried to. But he was locked up in himself all the time. Even in bed."

"I don't need to know about that."

"Sorry."

"That's okay."

She pressed close against him.

"Just the two of us," she said. "Stranded at the ass end of nowhere, all alone on a castaway ship. Very romantic, for however long we last. What are we going to do, Val?"

"We'll go down below and make wild love. We can have the big bunk tonight in Delagard's cabin."

"And after that?"

"We'll worry about after that after that," said Lawler.

9

H E AWOKE JUST BEFORE DAWN. SUNDIRA WAS SLEEPING PEACE-fully, her face as smooth and unworried as a child's. He slipped from the cabin and went up on deck. The sun was rising; the dazzling show of colors that the Face constantly emitted seemed more subdued this morning than it had been yesterday, far less flamboyant. He could still feel the pull of the Face tickling at the corners of his mind, but that was all it was just now, a tickle.

The figures of Lawler's former companions were moving about on shore.

He watched them. Even at this distance he was able easily to identify them: towering Kinverson and little Tharp, stocky Delagard, bandy-legged Felk. Father Quillan, nothing but bones and sinew. Gharkid, darker-skinned than the others and light as a wraith. And the three women, heavy-breasted Lis and sturdy square-shouldered Neyana and lithe handsome Pilya. What were they doing? Wading along the edge of the water? No, no, they were walking out into the bay, they were coming this way, they were returning to the ship. All of them. Easily, calmly, they were paddling through the shallow water toward the *Queen of Hydros*.

Lawler felt a tremor of fear. It was like a procession of the dead coming through the water toward him.

He went below and woke Sundira.

"They're coming back," he told her.

"What? Who are? Oh. *Oh*."

"The whole bunch of them. Swimming out to the ship."

She nodded, as though it were no great chore for her to take in the concept that the physical shells of their former shipmates were returning from the inconceivable entity that had devoured their souls. Perhaps she wasn't quite awake yet, Lawler thought. But she rose from the bunk and went up on deck with him. There were figures bobbing all around the ship now, just below the rail. Lawler peered down at them.

"What do you want?" he called.

"Throw down the rope ladder," the Kinverson-figure replied, in what was recognizably Kinverson's voice. "We're coming on board."

"My God," Lawler said, under his breath. He shot a horrified look at Sundira.

"Do it," she told him.

"But once they're up here—"

"What does it matter? If the Face wanted to turn its full voltage on us we'd probably be helpless before it anyway. If they want to come aboard, let them come. We don't have very much left to lose, do we?"

Shrugging, Lawler tossed down the ropes. Kinverson was the first to scramble aboard, then Delagard, Pilya, Tharp. The others followed. They were all naked. They stood in a quiet little group. There was no vitality to them; they seemed like sleepwalkers, like ghosts. They *are* ghosts, Lawler told himself.

"Well?" he said, finally.

"We're here to help you sail the ship," said Delagard.

Lawler was baffled by that. "Sail it? Where?"

"Back where you came from. You can't stay here, you realize. We'll take you to Grayvard so that you can ask for refuge."

Delagard's voice was flat and calm and his eyes were steady and clear, with none of their old manic gleam. Whoever or whatever this creature was, it was something other than the Nid Delagard Lawler had known for so many years. His inner demons were at rest. He had undergone a deep change—a kind of redemption, even. All his scheming was at an end, his soul seemed tranquil. So, too, with the others. They were at peace. They had surrendered to the Face, they had yielded up their individual selves, a thing that Lawler found incomprehensible; but he could not deny to himself that the returnees appeared to have found a happiness of some sort.

In a voice light as air Quillan said, "Before we leave, one last chance. Would you like to go to the island, doc? Sundira?"

"You know that we don't," Lawler said.

"It's up to you. But once you're back in the Home Sea it won't be a simple thing to return here if you change your mind."

"I can live with that."

"Sundira?" Quillan said.

"Me too."

The priest smiled sadly. "It's your choice. But I wish I could make you see what a mistake it is. Do you understand why we were attacked so constantly all the time that we were at sea? Why the rammerhorns came, and the limpet, and the hagfish, and all the rest? Not because they're malevolent creatures. There aren't any malevolent creatures on Hydros. What they were trying to do was heal the world, that's all."

"Heal the world?" Lawler said.

"Cleanse it. Rid it of an impurity. To them—to every life-form of Hydros—the Earthmen who live here are invasive, extraneous beings, because they live outside the harmony that is the Face. They see us as viruses or bacteria that have invaded the body of a healthy organism. Attacking us was the equivalent of ridding the body of disease."

"Or cleaning grit out of a machine," Delagard said.

Lawler turned away, feeling anger and disgust rising in him.

Sundira said to him in a quiet voice, "How frightening they are. A bunch of ghosts. No, worse: zombies. We're lucky to have been strong enough to resist."

"Are we really?" Lawler asked.

Her eyes widened. "What do you mean by that?"

"I'm not sure. But they look so peaceful, Sundira. They may have changed into something alien, but at least they're at peace."

Her nostrils flared in contempt. "You want peace? Go on, then. It's only a short swim."

"No. No."

"Are you sure, Val?"

"Come here. Hold me."

"Val—Val—"

"I love you."

"I love you, Val." They embraced unself-consciously, ignoring the returnees around them. She said, close to his ear, "I won't go across if you don't."

"I'm not going, don't worry."

"But if you do, we'll go together."

"What?"

"You think I want to be the only one on this ship who's still real, sailing with ten zombies? It's a deal, Val. Either we don't go at all or we go together."

"We don't go."

"But if we do—"

"Then it'll be together," Lawler said. "But we don't go."

As though nothing whatever out of the ordinary had happened at the Face of the Waters, the crew of the *Queen of Hydros* set about making preparations for the voyage back. Kinverson cast nets, and fish swam obligingly into them. Gharkid moved placidly through hip-deep water, gathering useful algae. Neyana, Pilya, and Lis trekked back and forth between the island and the ship, carrying casks of fresh water that they filled from some spring on shore. Onyos Felk pondered his sea-charts. Dag Tharp tuned and tested his radio equipment. Delagard surveyed the rigging and sails, the rudder and the hull, and noted where repairs were needed, and he and Sundira and Lawler and even Father Quillan took care of what had to be done.

Very little was said. Everybody moved about their tasks as though part of some well-ordered machine. The returnees were gentle with the two who had not gone to the island, treating them almost like troubled children who needed great tenderness; but Lawler felt no real contact with them.

Often Lawler stared in wonder and perplexity at the Face. The display of lights and color coming from it was unending. Its constant berserk vigor fascinated him as much as it repelled him. He tried to imagine what it had been like for the others to be ashore, to move among those groves of live, sizzling strangenesses. But he knew that such speculations were dangerous. Now and again he felt a renewed pull, sometimes unexpectedly strong, from the island. In those moments the temptation was powerful. It would be so easy to slip over the side like the rest, swim quickly through the warm, welcoming waters of the bay, scramble up onto that alien shore—

But he was still able to resist. He had held the island off this long; he wasn't about to surrender to it now. The work of preparation went on, and he stayed on board, as did Sundira, while the others freely came and went. It was a weird time, though not an unpleasant one. Life seemed suspended. In an odd way Lawler felt almost happy: he had survived, he had withstood every sort of adversity, he had been tempered in the forge of Hydros and was emerging all the stronger for it. He had come to love Sundira; he felt her love for him. These were new experiences for him. In whatever new life awaited him when the voyage was ended, he would be better able to cope with the uncertainties of his soul than before.

It was almost time to leave now.

It was late afternoon. Delagard had announced that departure would be at sunset. That they would be leaving the vicinity of the Face in the dark didn't seem to trouble him. The light of the Face itself would guide the ship for a time; and after that they could sail by the stars. There was nothing to fear from the sea, not any longer. The sea would be friendly now. Everything on Hydros would be friendly.

Lawler realized that he was alone on deck. Most or perhaps all of the others had gone to the island: to make a farewell visit, he supposed. But where was Sundira?

He called her name.

No answer. For one wild moment he wondered if she had gone with them. Then he caught sight of her at the stern, up on the gantry bridge. Kinverson was with her. They seemed deep in conversation.

Quietly Lawler moved down the deck toward them.

He heard Kinverson telling her, "You can't possibly understand what it's like until you've gone over yourself. It's as different from being an ordinary human as being alive is from being dead."

"I feel alive enough now."

"You don't know. You can't imagine it. Come with me now, Sundira. It takes only a moment. And then everything opens up for you. I'm not the same man I was, am I?"

"Not remotely."

"But I am. Only I'm so much more, besides. Come with me."

"Please, Gabe."

"You want to go. I know you do. You're staying only because of Lawler."

"I'm staying because of me," Sundira said.

"It isn't so. I know. You feel sorry for the pitiful bastard. You don't want to leave him behind."

"No, Gabe."

"You'll thank me afterward."

"No."

"Come with me."

"Gabe—please—"

There was a sudden doubtful note in her voice, a tone of weakening resolve, that struck Lawler with sledgehammer force. He jumped up on the gantry bridge next to them. Sundira gasped in surprise and backed away. Kinverson stood where he was, regarding Lawler calmly.

The gaffs were in their rack. Lawler grabbed one and held it out, practically in Kinverson's face.

"Leave her alone."

The big man eyed the sharp tool with amusement, or perhaps disdain. "I'm not doing anything to her, doc."

"You're trying to seduce her."

Kinverson laughed. "She don't need much seducing, do she, now?"

There was a roaring sound of fury in Lawler's ears. It was all he could do to hold back from thrusting the gaff into Kinverson's throat.

Sundira said, "Val, please, we were only talking."

"I heard what you were talking about. He's trying to get you to go to the Face. Isn't that so?"

"I don't deny that," Kinverson said easily.

Lawler brandished the gaff, conscious of how comic his anger must seem to Kinverson, how petulant, how foolish. Kinverson hulked above him, still menacing for all his newfound gentleness, invulnerable, invincible.

But Lawler had to see this through. In a tight voice he said, "I don't want you talking to her again before we sail."

Kinverson smiled amiably. "I wasn't trying to hurt her any."

"I know what you were trying to do. I won't let you."

"Shouldn't that be up to her, doc?"

Lawler glanced at Sundira. She said softly, "It's all right, Val. I can look after myself."

"Yes. Yes, of course."

"Give me that gaff, doc," Kinverson said. "You might hurt yourself with it."

"Keep back!"

"It's my gaff, you know. You got no business waving it around."

"Watch it," Lawler said. "Get away. Get off the ship! Go on: back to the Face. Go on, Gabe. You don't belong here. None of you do. This ship is for humans."

"Val," Sundira said.

Lawler gripped the gaff tightly, holding it as he would a scalpel, and took a step or two toward Kinverson. The fisherman's lumbering form rose high. Lawler drew a deep breath. "Go on," he said again. "Back to the Face. Jump, Gabe. Right here, right over the side."

"Doc, doc, doc—"

Lawler brought the gaff upward and forward in a short, hard thrust at Kinverson's diaphragm. It should have speared right into the big man's heart; but Kinverson's arm moved with unbelievable swiftness. His hand caught the shaft of the gaff and twisted, and pain shot the length of Lawler's arm. A moment later the gaff was in Kinverson's hand.

Automatically Lawler crossed his arms over his middle to protect himself against the thrust that he knew must be coming.

Kinverson studied him as if measuring him for it. Get it over with, damn you, Lawler thought. Now. Quickly. He could almost feel it already, the fiery intrusion, the tissues parting, the sharp point going for the heart within the cage of ribs.

But there was no thrust. Calmly Kinverson leaned forward and dropped the gaff back in the rack.

"You shouldn't mess with the equipment, doc," he said gently. "Excuse me, now. I'll leave you and the lady alone."

He turned and went past Lawler, down the gantry ladder, to the main deck.

"DID I LOOK VERY STUPID JUST THEN?" LAWLER ASKED SUNDIRA.

She smiled, very faintly. "He's always seemed a threat to you, hasn't he?"

"He was trying to talk you into going over. Is that a threat or isn't it?"

"If he had picked me up bodily and carried me over the side, that would have been a threat, Val."

"All right. All right."

"But I understand why you were upset. Even to the point of going after him with that gaff like that."

"It was dumb. It was an adolescent thing to do."

"Yes," she said. "It was."

Lawler hadn't expected her to agree so readily. He looked at her, startled, and saw something in her eyes that surprised and dismayed him even more.

There had been a change. There was a distance now between the two of them that hadn't been there in a long while.

"What is it, Sundira? What's happening?"

"Oh, Val—Val—"

"Tell me."

"It wasn't anything Kinverson said. I can't be talked into something as easily as that. It's entirely my own decision."

"*What* is? For Christ's sake, what are you talking about?"

"The Face."

"What?"

"Come over with me, Val."

It was like being pierced with Kinverson's gaff.

"Jesus." He took a step or two back from her. "Jesus, Sundira. What are you saying?"

"That we should go."

He watched her, feeling as though he would turn to stone.

"This is wrong, trying to resist it," she said. "We should have let ourselves yield to it, the way the others did. They understood. We were blind."

"Sundira?"

"I saw it, everything in one flash, Val, while you were trying to protect me from Gabe. How foolish it is to try to maintain our individual selves, all our little fears and jealousies and petty games. How much better it would be to drop all that, and join ourselves into the one great harmony that exists here. With the others. With Hydros."

"No. No."

"This is our one chance to let all the shit that oppresses us fall away from us."

"I don't believe you're saying this, Sundira."

"But I am. I am."

"He hypnotized you, didn't he? He put a spell on you. *It* did."

"No," she said, smiling. She held out her hands to him. "You told me once that you had never felt at home on Hydros, even though you were born here. Do you remember that, Val?"

"Well—"

"Do you? You said divers and meatfish feel at home here, but you don't and never have. You do remember: I see that you do. All right. Here's your chance to make yourself at home here, finally. To become a part of Hydros.

Earth is gone. What we are is Hydrans, and Hydrans belong to the Face. You've held back long enough. So have I; but I'm giving in, now. Suddenly it all looks different to me, now. Will you come with me?"

"No! This is insanity, Sundira. What I'm going to do is take you belowdecks and tie you up until you come to your senses."

"Don't touch me," she said very quietly. "I tell you, Val, don't try to touch me." She looked toward the rack of gaffs.

"All right. I hear you."

"I'm going to go. What about you?"

"You know the answer to that."

"You promised that we'd go together, or not at all."

"Not at all, then, that's the deal."

"But I want to go, Val. I do."

Cold anger surged in him and congealed his spirit. He hadn't expected this final betrayal. Bitterly he said, "Then go, if you really mean it."

"Come with me?"

"No. No. No. No."

"You promised—"

"I'm going back on my promise, then," Lawler said. "I never meant to go. If I promised you that I'd go if you did, then I was lying to you. I'll never go."

"I'm sorry, Val."

"So am I."

He wanted again to seize her, to pull her belowdecks, to lash her down in his cabin until the ship was safely out to sea. But he knew that he could never do that. There was nothing he could do. Nothing.

"Go," he said. "Stop talking about it and do it. This is making me sick."

"Come with me?" she said yet again. "It'll be very quick."

"Never."

"All right, Val." She smiled sadly. "I love you, you know. Don't ever forget that. I'm asking you out of love, and if you won't do it, well, I'll still love you afterward. And I hope that you'll love me."

"How could I?"

"So long, Val. But I'll be seeing you later."

Lawler looked on, not believing it, as she clambered down the gantry ladder to the main deck, walked to the side, climbed over the rail, dived smoothly and expertly into the waiting sea. She began to swim toward shore, moving swiftly, vigorously, legs scissoring powerfully, arms cutting through the dark water. He watched her as he had watched her once before, a million years ago, swimming in the waters of Sorve Bay. But he turned away, unwilling to watch any longer, when she was still less than halfway to the shore. He went to his cabin and locked the door behind him and sat down on his bunk in the gathering darkness. This would be a good moment for some numbweed, a jug of it, a tub, drink it down in one great gulp, let it wash away all the pain. But of course none of it was left. So there was nothing he could do but sit quietly and wait for time to pass. What might have been hours went by, or years. After a while he heard Delagard's voice above, calling out the order to get the ship under way.

HE HAD RARELY SEEN THE SKY AS CLEAR, OR THE HYDROS CROSS AS brilliant, as it was this night. The air was utterly still. The sea was calm. How could the ship be moving, in such a glassy sea, on such a windless night? And yet it moved. As though by a magic spell, gliding smoothly through the darkness. They had been traveling for hours. The brightness of the Face had dwindled until it was only a purple glow on the horizon, and then less than that, and now it could hardly be seen at all. When morning came they would be far off in the Empty Sea.

Lawler lay by himself, on a pile of netting near the stern.

He had never felt so alone in his life.

The others moved about the deck in silence, doing things with the sails, the ropes, the backstays, the booms, the whole intricate rig of nautical paraphernalia that he had never really understood and now had banished from his mind. They had no need of him; and he wanted nothing to do with them. They were machines, part of a greater machine. Tick. Tick.

Sundira had come to him soon after they sailed. "It's all right," she said. "Nothing's changed."

He shivered and turned away when she approached him. He couldn't look at her.

"You're wrong," he said. "Everything's changed. You're part of the machine, now. And you want me to be in there with you. It ticks and you dance to it."

"It isn't like that, Val. You'd *be* the machine. You'd be the ticking, too. You'd be the dance."

"I don't understand."

"Of course not. How could you?" She touched him lovingly, and he pulled away as if she had the power to transform him with a touch. She looked at him in regret. "Okay," she said softly. "Whatever you want."

That had been hours ago. He hadn't gone to the galley to join the others for evening mess, but he felt no hunger. If he never ate again, that would be all right. The idea of sitting down at table with them was unthinkable. The one unchanged man, in this ship of zombies—the only one still real—

Alone, alone, all, all alone
Alone on a wide wide sea!
And never a saint took pity on
My soul in agony.

Words. Fragments of memory. A lost poem out of a lost ancient world.

The Sun's rim dips; the stars rush out:
At one stride comes the dark;
With far-heard whisper, o'er the sea
Off shot the spectre-bark.

Lawler looked up at the cold blaze of the distant stars. An unexpected calmness had come over him. He was surprised at how calm he felt, as though he had passed beyond any realm where storms might reach. Even in the days when he had had the numbweed to ease him he had hardly ever felt as peaceful as this.

Why? Had the Face worked some mystery on him even at long range, as it had on Sundira?

He doubted it. Nor could it be affecting him now. Surely he was outside its range. There was nothing here to work on his mind now but the dark vault of the sky, and the quietly surging sea, and the hard clear light of the stars. There was the Cross, spanning the southern sky, the great double arch of suns—billions of them, someone had once told him. Billions of suns! And tens of billions of worlds! His mind staggered under the image. Those teeming multitudes of worlds—cities, continents, creatures of a thousand thousand thousand kinds—

He stared upward at them all, and as he stared a new vision grew in him, slowly, formless at first, then clarifying itself with a mighty rush, until there was scarcely room in his mind for anything else. He saw the stars as one vast web, one single immense metaphysical construct, linked into a mysterious galactic unity in just the same way that all the separate particles of this water-world were bound in union.

Lines of force pulsed in the void, streaming through the firmament like rivers of blood, connecting everything to everything. An infinite connectivity throbbed between the worlds. He could feel the universe breathing, a living entity, aflame with unquenchable vitality.

Hydros belonged to the heavens; and the heavens were a single great fiery sensate thing. Enter Hydros and you were a part of the All. The offer was there. And only he, of all the universe, had chosen to refuse entry into that one great thing.

Only he. Only he.

Was that what he truly wanted? This solitude, this terrible independence of spirit?

The Face offered immortality—godhood, even—within one enormous united organism. And yet he had chosen to remain Valben Lawler and nothing but Valben Lawler. Proudly had he turned away from what had been extended to those who had made this voyage. Let poor troubled Quillan deliver himself up gladly to the god he had sought all his life; let little Dag Tharp find whatever comfort he could in the Face; let the mysterious Gharkid, who had searched for something greater than himself, go to the Face. Not me. I am not like them.

He thought of Kinverson. Even he, that rugged, solitary man, had opted ultimately for the Face. Delagard. Sundira.

Well, so be it, Lawler told himself. I am who I am. For better or for worse.

He lay back, staring at the stars, letting the fierce brightness of the Cross fill his mind. How peaceful it is here now, he thought. How quiet.

> *I woke, and we were sailing on*
> *As in a gentle weather:*
> *'Twas night, calm night, the Moon was high;*
> *The dead men stood together.*

"Val? It's me."

He looked up. A starlight-shadow crossed his face. He saw Sundira close by him.

"Can I sit with you?" she asked.

"If you want."

She dropped down beside him. "I looked for you at mess. You weren't there. You should have eaten."

"I wasn't hungry. You still eat, do you, now that you've been changed?"

"Of course we do. It's not that kind of change."

"I suppose. How would I know?"

"How would you, yes." She ran her hand lightly across his arm. This time he didn't flinch. "Not as much has changed as you'd think. I still love you, Val. I said I would, and it's true."

He nodded. There was nothing he could say.

Did he still love her? he wondered. Was it possible even to imagine that he did?

He slipped his arm around her shoulders. Her skin was smooth, cool, familiar. Pleasing. She nestled against him. They might have been the only two people in the world. She still seemed human to him. He bent forward and kissed her softly in the hollow between her chin and her shoulder, and she laughed.

"Val," she said. "Oh, Val."

That was all, just his name. What was she thinking, what had she left unsaid? That she wished he had gone to the Face with her? That she still hoped that he would? That she prayed that he would go to Delagard and beg to have the ship turned around, and taken back to the island so that he too could undergo the transformation?

Should I have gone with her?

Was it a mistake to have refused?

For a moment he saw himself inside the machine, part of it, part of the All—surrendering at last, dancing with all the rest.

No. No. No. No.

I am who I am. I have done what I have done because I am who I am.

He lay back, with Sundira curled against him, and looked upward at the stars again. And one more vision came to him: the Earth that once had been, the Earth that had been lost.

His great romantic fantasy of old vanished Earth, that blue and shining planet, the shattered mother-world of humanity, filled him once again: he saw it as he wanted it to have been, a peaceful and harmonious world teeming with loving human beings, a haven, a perfect entity. Had it ever really been like that? Probably not, he thought. Almost certainly not. It had been a place like any other, evil mixed with the good, flaws, failings.

And in any case that world was gone from the universe, swept away by malign fate.

And here we are. Here lie we. Rest in peace.

Lawler peered into the night, imagining that he was looking toward the place in the heavens where that world had been. But he knew that for Earth's surviving people scattered through the universe there was no hope of regaining the lost ancestral home. They must move on, they must discover some new place for themselves in this vast universe into which they had been flung as exiles. They must transform themselves.

They must transform themselves.

They must transform themselves.

He sat up as if jolted by a blast of burning light. It was all so wondrously clear to him, suddenly. The people he had known who lived their lives from day to day as though Earth had never existed had been right, and he, hopelessly dreaming of what once had been, long ago and far away, had been wrong. Earth would never return. For the Earthmen on Hydros there was only Hydros, now and forever more. To hold yourself apart, clinging desperately to your ancestral Earth identity amidst the native life-forms of your adopted world, was folly. On whatever world you might find yourself living, it is your task to make yourself fully a part of that world. Otherwise you will always be an outsider, alien and alienated.

And so it was. Here I am. More alone than I have ever been before.

And Hydros had offered to take him in, but he had said no and made the refusal stick, and now it was too late.

He closed his eyes and saw Earth bright and beautiful in the heavens once again. That vision of lost Earth that he had carried in his mind for so long was gleaming more vividly than he had ever seen it before. The blue Earth, lovely and strange, with its great golden-green landmasses shining by the light of a sun he had never seen. As he watched, the broad blue seas began to boil. Steam rose from them. The land was swept by flame. The golden-green immensities parched and blackened. Deep jagged fissures darker than night sprang up across their broad surfaces.

And after the flames: ice, death. Darkness.

A shower of small dead things, falling through space. A coin, a bit of statuary, a potsherd, a map, a rusted weapon, a chunk of stone. Tumbling helter-skelter, plummeting through the windless wastes of the galaxy. He followed them with his gaze, tracking them as they fell.

All gone, he thought. Let it all go. Forget it. Begin a new life.

The sudden thought astounded him.

What was that? he asked himself. *What are you saying?*

Surrender? Join? Was that what he had meant? Lawler began to tremble. Sweat broke out all over him. He sat up and looked out to sea, back in the direction of the Face.

It seemed to him that he could feel its force after all, reaching him even over this much distance, infiltrating his mind, wrapping its tentacles around his soul, pulling at him, drawing him in.

He fought it. Frantically, furiously, he struggled with it, hacking with desperate urgency at the strands of alien power that seemed to be invading him. For a long silent moment he worked at it, fiercely trying to cleanse himself of its intruding energies. The image came to him of Gospo Struvin, all the way back at the outset of the voyage, battling with that tangle of moist yellow fibers that had come up out of the sea to ensnare him. Struvin kicking in air, shaking his foot, attempting vainly to extricate himself from that sticky, persistent thing that enfolded him. It was like that now. Lawler knew he was fighting for his life, as Gospo had done; and Gospo had lost.

Get—away—from—me—

He summoned all his energies for one great cleansing thrust. And launched it.

Against nothing. There was nothing there. No nets held him. No mysterious force entwined him in its snare. Lawler understood that and had no doubt of it: he was struggling against shadows, he was fighting with himself, really, only with himself, no one but himself.

So you want to go to it? he asked himself numbly. *Despite everything, you actually do want to go? Even you? Is that what you want? What is it that you want, anyway?*

Once again he saw the blue Earth gleaming in his mind as it had been before, and then once again it began to boil and blacken, and he beheld once again the ice, the death, the darkness, and the tiny objects falling.

And the answer came: *I don't want to be alone any more. God help me, I don't want to be the last Earthman when there's no more Earth.*

Sundira stirred, warm against him. "What are you thinking, Val?"

"That I love you," he said.

"Do you? You love what I am now?"

He drew a deep breath, the deepest he had ever drawn, pulling the air of Hydros far down into his lungs.

"Yes," Lawler said.

Where Earth had been in his mind, there was only a flawless sphere of shimmering water. The scattering of tiny objects that had fallen from the dying world hovered for a moment above the surface of that great sea, dropped into it, vanished without a trace.

He felt a great easing, a sudden thawing. Something breaking within him like an ice-floe at the end of winter. Breaking up, streaming away, flowing. Flowing.

HE SAT UP AND TURNED TOWARD HER TO TELL HER WHAT HAD HAP-pened. But there was no need. She was smiling. She knew. And he could feel the ship moving in a big arc beneath him, already swinging about, heading back through the luminous sea toward the Face of the Waters.